Praise for Wen Spencer

Tainted

"Spencer continues to amaze, cranking up both suspense and wonder."—Julie E. Czerneda

"A fun read, definitely worth checking out."—*Locus*

"Spencer's skillful characterizations, vividly drawn settings, and comic exploitation of Ukiah's deceptively youthful, highly buff looks make the romp high light entertainment."—*Booklist*

"A unique and highly entertaining reading experience."—*Midwest Book Review*

Alien Taste

"Each and every character is fascinating, extraordinarily well-developed, and gets right under your skin. A terrific, memorable story."—Julie E. Czerneda

". . . revelations ranging from surprising to funny to wonderfully inventive. A delightful new SF mystery with a fun protagonist."
—*Locus*

"Spencer has written an intriguing contemporary science fiction tale. Her characters come alive on the page and their uniqueness will grab and hold you."—*Talebones*

"The characters are fully developed and understandable. This novel is keeper shelf material."—BookBrowser

"Spencer takes readers on a fast-paced journey into disbelief. [Her] timing is impeccable and the denouement stunning."
—*Romantic Times* (4-star review)

"A fabulous mix of science fiction, suspense, romance, and the nature of wolves, in a story like none you've ever seen."—*Science Fiction Romance*

ALSO BY WEN SPENCER

ALIEN TASTE
TAINTED TRAIL

BITTER WATERS

Wen Spencer

A ROC BOOK

ROC
Published by New American Library, a division of
Penguin Group (USA) Inc., 375 Hudson Street,
New York, New York 10014, U.S.A.
Penguin Books Ltd, 80 Strand,
London WC2R 0RL, England
Penguin Books Australia Ltd, 250 Camberwell Road,
Camberwell, Victoria 3124, Australia
Penguin Books Canada Ltd, 10 Alcorn Avenue,
Toronto, Ontario, Canada M4V 3B2
Penguin Books (N.Z.) Ltd, Cnr Rosedale and Airborne Roads,
Albany, Auckland 1310, New Zealand

Penguin Books Ltd, Registered Offices:
80 Strand, London WC2R 0RL, England

First published by Roc, an imprint of New American Library,
a division of Penguin Group (USA) Inc.

First Printing, May 2003
10 9 8 7 6 5 4 3 2 1

Cover art by Steve Stone

 REGISTERED TRADEMARK—MARCA REGISTRADA

Printed in the United States of America

PUBLISHER'S NOTE
This is a work of fiction. Names, characters, places, and incidents either are the product
of the author's imagination or are used fictitiously, and any resemblance to actual persons,
living or dead, business establishments, events, or locales is entirely coincidental.

To James Larkin,
who taught me not to waste daylight

Thanks to D. Eric Anderson, Barbara Carlson,
George Corcoran, Starr Corcoran aka Lady Jade,
Amy Finkbeiner, "Agent" Joan Fisher, Nancy Janda,
Kendall Jung, James and Carol Larkin, Heidi Pilewski,
Dr. Hope Erica Ring, June Drexler Robertson,
Lara Van Winkle, and all the Snippet Hounds of sff.net

And special thanks to Ann Cecil

CHAPTER ONE

Wilkinsburg, Pennsylvania
Sunday, September 12, 2004

Ukiah Oregon peered up the city street that climbed the steep hillside; normally so narrow that passing cars risked clipping side mirrors, it was now lined with television news trucks and police cars. Red and blue strobe lights were reflected in every raindrop. Nations of people gathered in the islands of light generated by the streetlamps: curious bystanders with umbrellas, tired cops in rain gear, and TV crews trying to ignore the drizzle as they prepared for the eleven o'clock news report.

"Well, this is certainly the right street." Ukiah scanned the row houses stepping up the hill on either side of the street. "2197 would put the house at the top of the hill."

"Ah, Christ, what a circus," Max Bennett, Ukiah's partner, muttered as he threaded the Cherokee up the slick paving bricks and found a parking space. "Are you really up to this?"

After two grueling weeks in Oregon solving a missing persons case, Ukiah and Max had flown out of the Pendleton Airport at dawn, West Coast time. Bruised, battered, and bone-weary, they had planned to go straight home once they landed at Pittsburgh International Airport. Ukiah had looked forward to seeing his fiancée, Special Agent Indigo Zheng, and his son, Kittanning. An urgent call about a missing boy, however, caught them at the layover in Houston, and reluctantly, they agreed to check out the case.

Ukiah eyed the confusion of people and vehicles. "Yeah, I should be fine—this is Pittsburgh."

There was a tap on Ukiah's window, and he lowered it to find Pittsburgh policeman Ari Johnson standing beside the Cherokee.

"Hey, Wolf Boy!" Ari grinned at him. "How's that kid of yours?"

"Kittanning?" How did Ari know about Kittanning? Considering the alien Hex created Kittanning out of Ukiah's blood without benefit of a woman or the normal nine months of waiting, they kept the baby a family secret.

"Ukiah. Kittanning. I get it. You named him after the town." Ari guessed correctly. "He's what? Like three months old now? Hopefully it's been a quiet three months, not like when he was born."

Ukiah's memory clicked in: Ari had been at the shoot-out the day Ukiah recovered Kittanning; the officer had provided them with diapers, clothing, and formula.

"Um, yeah, three months," Ukiah said.

"Is he sleeping through the night yet?" Ari asked.

Max scrubbed at his face. "Jeez, Ari, you sound like an old woman."

"Triplets do that to you," Ari said. "My life is all about babies and guns at the moment. You look like shit, Bennett!"

"Eight hours on a plane will do that." Max tilted his head in puzzlement, and then squinted at Ari. "You put them on to hiring us?" In "you," Max meant the cops, not Ari as a person.

"You've been out of town," Ari said. "We've had too many kids go missing lately."

"How many is too many?" Ukiah asked.

"Personally, one is too many, but the count is higher than that. This makes five."

"Within the last two weeks?" Max looked like he'd bitten into something sour.

"Yeah. It's been one every two days or so. Everyone's fairly jumpy."

"Shit." Max sighed, looking out his driver's window and seeing hidden danger in the night. They had learned the hard way that kidnappings usually meant people with guns and the will to use them. In the following moment of quiet, rain lightly tapped on the roof of the Cherokee. Max swore again, and turned to Ukiah. "Well?"

"We do it."

"Okay. I'll deal with the family, kid. Gear up the best you can."

As a result of two layovers, some of their checked luggage had gone astray: specifically the bag with their body armor and some of their more sophisticated electronics. Luckily their guns and basic communications gear hadn't.

Ukiah slid up the window and opened his door to step out into the rain. "Fill me in, Ari."

"The missing boy is Kyle Yonan." Ari took out his notepad and glanced at it. "He's white, approximately four-one, sixty pounds, brown on brown." Meaning the boy had brown hair and eyes. "Last seen wearing a red shirt, blue jeans, and tennis shoes. He turned four in July."

So, they were looking for a child of limited abilities except for finding trouble.

Ari tucked away his notepad. "The kid has a history of winding up in odd places. Locked himself in a car trunk once. Disappeared at Monroeville Mall and ended up in the mock-up of Santa's workshop. Weird shit like that all the time. We're hoping that it will be something like that again and not another grab and run."

"How long has he been missing?" Ukiah lifted the back hatch on the Cherokee.

"About ten hours. There's a small patch of yard in the back. Kyle was playing in it with an older brother this morning. The brother came into the house for a drink, and Kyle vanished. The family looked for three hours before they called us."

Us being the police.

"No ransom demand?" Ukiah asked.

"None of the missing kids had ransom demands." Ari went dead serious. "We're praying you can find this one."

And with four kids missing already, the police had the parents call Bennett Detective Agency to get the legendary Wolf Boy involved.

"How long has it been raining?" Ukiah found his rain gear—boots, pants, and coat—and pulled them on.

Ari glanced upward, as if noticing the fine rain for the first time. "Maybe about two hours. Off and on. It's the first time in weeks that it's rained, wouldn't you know. The family turned the house upside down, and we've combed the neighborhood. Not a sign of the kid."

"This rain is going to make it tough," Ukiah told him.

Ari shrugged with a rustle of rain gear. "They say you're the best at this."

Ukiah knew they said a lot more than just that. He found the bag with the GPS equipment and pulled it out of the pile of luggage. It felt odd threading the tracer into his belt without first putting on his body armor.

Max returned with a baby blanket as Ukiah pulled on his radio headset. "This is Kyle's blankie."

Ukiah brushed his fingertips over the worn blue cotton, finding genetic traces of a dark-haired boy with dark eyes and a tendency toward hyperactivity, who would someday be tall and intelligent if he survived his adventure. Ukiah pressed the blanket to his face, closing his eyes, and breathing in the boy's scent. No blood trace or sign of violence stained the cloth. He came up out of focusing on the blanket to find he missed most of what Max had said, but it was stored in his hearing memory, recorded despite his lack of attention to it.

"This is going to be nuts, kid," Max had said, checking on the tracer's signal. "This boy sounds like he has less sense than God gave a rabbit. They've got two locks on his bedroom door just to keep him in at night."

"He's not stupid," Ukiah told Max. "He's just got too much curiosity, too much energy, and no experience."

"That's just as bad."

Ukiah considered what he knew of the area. They were on the edge of Wilkinsburg, where it climbed up into the hills that separated it from Penn Hills. Like much of Pittsburgh, the houses dotted the steep hills wherever one could find a foothold to build. Pockets of scrub woods occupied the parts deemed too sheer. At the foot of the hill lay the rest of Wilkinsburg, with plenty of buildings standing empty and a reputation of being a rough neighborhood, and then the river. Fascinating danger lay in every direction.

"Yes, I suppose it is."

A flood lamp gleamed on the tiny, rain-bejeweled backyard, littered with toys. Barely ten feet by twenty feet, the fenced-in area of worn grass seemed a relatively safe and escape-proof area. Ukiah ignored the toys and grass to concentrate on the fence. As he expected, the rain-slick steel held traces of the boy's climb to freedom. Beyond the fence, the land fell away into a nearly sheer drop, its steepness disguised by wild cherry trees and banks of dying goldenrod. Animals had pushed paths through the tall brush, and the boy had followed.

The path came out on the parallel street, lower down the hillside. The cement of the sidewalk seemed washed clean by the rain. Ukiah crouched at the edge of the woods, sweeping hands over the wet stone, trying to find any clue. Max drove up in the Cherokee, turning off the headlights as he turned the corner so as not to blind Ukiah's now highly light-sensitive eyes.

Focused on the hunt, Ukiah was only dimly aware that Max had gotten out, and signaled Ari in his squad car to kill his lights. The policeman got out with the thud of a car door and the quiet squeak of rain gear rubbing against itself.

"How does he do it?" Ari asked quietly. "I can't even see."

"He was raised by wolves." Max misled Ari. It was true Ukiah spent years running with the wolves, but it had nothing to do with his abilities.

"I thought all that wolf boy stuff was bullshit."

"Not all," Max said. "By the way, Ari, thanks for the baby stuff in June. It was a lifesaver."

"No problem," Ari said. "You two really weaseled out of there fast; not that I blame you, the first of the media was already showing up. Hey, that reminds me though. There's a new federal agent in town asking questions about the shootout."

"Federal agent? What branch?"

Ari grunted and searched his pockets for a business card. "Grant Hutchinson. Homeland Security. He pulled me into questioning on Friday. He had photographs of you two."

"Us?" Max asked as Ukiah glanced up, startled out of his focus. Max flashed the business card so Ukiah could see it and then studied it himself. "What kind of photos?"

"Professional photographer's photos, really high-quality stuff. Most of the pictures were of you guys, but he had one of me. He wanted me to ID you two."

"Did he say why?" Max asked as Ukiah went back to tracking.

Ari made a rude noise. "No. Not a clue. He kept me in interrogations for an hour, asking everything from my religion down to if my belly button was an innie or an outie."

"What did you tell him about us?" Max asked.

"Your names," Ari said. "That the kid is a tracking wonder and that you two were out in Oregon, trying to find Kraynak's niece. I don't know any more than that, other than, as far as I've ever heard or seen, you're good people."

"Thanks," Max said. "Friday, eh?"

"Friday afternoon, just after I went on shift," Ari said.

As Max questioned Ari about the federal agent, Ukiah finally found the trace he had been searching for: the rich earth of the hillside stamped into the shape of a small shoe print. All but crawling, he followed the track down the street another hundred feet before it vanished. He crouched in the drumming rain, patiently sweeping the cement with his fingertips. The chill of the night vanished for him, as did the beat of the rain. The distant hiss of tires on wet pavement silenced. Even the light went as he focused in tight on the rough cement. He became aware of the sand versus gravel content. The faint feel of bird tracks left from a sparrow crossing the newly poured cement sometime in the far past.

Nothing of the boy.

He flicked through his other senses. Unless he found something here, the trail was gone. He could begin a spiral search pattern, hoping to stumble across a new start, but in the rain, every minute made the chance less likely.

Fine-tuned, he realized he was drawing in air ever so faintly tainted by blood. He stilled completely, aimed at the scent. It pressed against his skin, invaded his nose. Locked onto the smell, he sniffed, nostrils flaring, casting about dog-like. Slowly, he worked his way to a corrugated pipe set into the ground where a side alley joined the main road. Water ran in a tiny stream down the street and into the mouth of the pipe. No water, he noticed, poured out of the pipe on the other side of the alley.

"Kyle? Kyle?" he called into the pipe. His voice echoed back at him.

Under the sound of rain and rushing water and his own heartbeat, he thought he could hear the faint ragged breathing of something small.

"You found him?" Max came to crouch beside him. Ari trailed behind.

"I think he's in this pipe." Ukiah considered crawling into the drain. No, only a small child would fit. He examined the narrow darkness with his flashlight. "It's T-shape with a drain in the center. If he's in there, he's down the center pipe some-how. There's so much white noise with the rain that I can't be sure. I'm smelling blood."

He sniffed again, drawing in the coppery smell. Blood, but not enough information to tell the source.

Ari shifted restlessly behind them. "It could be a wounded raccoon or possum."

"You said he got into weird places," Ukiah countered.

Ari eyed the pipe as if it would bite him. "Yeah, but, shit, that's a creepy little hole in the ground."

Max stood and swept his flashlight back up the hill to the boy's yard. "His brother told me that they had been playing with a ball, throwing it back and forth. If the ball landed on this street, it would have funneled down into this pipe."

Lying in the water, Ukiah reached in as far as he could stretch, questing with his outstretched fingers. His fingertips found the ragged edge where the pipe turned down, water pouring over the lip, washing away any sign of the boy.

The rain started to come down harder, moving from a light patter to a quickening drum.

Max swore. "If he's down there, this is going to get ugly fast. This is part of Nine Mile Run." Sometime in the past, several creeks had been routed completely underground in concrete culverts that converged to form Nine Mile Run; it was a deadly labyrinth they had dealt with before. "Damn, if the airline hadn't lost our luggage, we could snake one of the minicams down the drain to be sure."

"I'll call for a rescue team and look for a manhole," Ari offered, seeming anxious to get away from the narrow pipe.

The rill of water coming down the hill was already deepening. Ukiah flashed to another child in the storm drains, a maze of swirling dark waters and an unhappy end, when Max was forced to pull him out half-drowned. "Max, I don't want to do that again—wander around lost while the kid drowns. We should see if we can find a map of the system."

"The rescue team can deal with the storm drain," Max said. "All we need to do is convince them that he's really down there. Are you sure?"

"No," Ukiah had to admit. How he could squeeze into the pipe and see if Kyle was actually stuck in the pipe? If he was younger, closer to Kyle's age, he could fit.

It occurred to him there was a way to *be* smaller.

Ukiah dug his Swiss army knife from his pocket and made a deep cut across his wrist.

Max swore in surprise and caught Ukiah's shoulder. "What the hell? Ukiah? What are you doing?"

"I'm going to make a mouse." Ukiah caught the flow of hot blood in his palm. "And I'm going to use it as an extra set of eyes."

Max released him. "Okay. Just keep it out of sight. I'll keep Ari distracted."

Ukiah clung to the memories of the boy as the rest of the day drained down into his hand. The blood stopped as the wound healed shut. He concentrated on the blood cupped in his hand, urging it to take form instead of seeping back into his body, merging with him again. It formed a quivering sack. Bones took form, a racing heart, and then finally the dark fur of a black mouse.

"Thank you," Ukiah breathed, and carefully placed the

mouse as far into the drain as he could go. "Go on, find the boy."

He leaned his body against the pipe, and thought only of the mouse as it skittered fearfully along water into the darkness.

. . . cold wet steel, undulating in frozen minihills, a rushing river of muddy water, a vast curving ceiling echoing back the white noise of water, something huge ahead, the growing smell of blood, the edge of a great hole, clinging to the edge, trembling with fear . . .

Ukiah tried to send comfort and encouragement over the fraying link. He could create the mouse because he was in truth a collection of independently intelligent cells acting as a whole. Whatever method his cells used to communicate, endowing him with telepathic abilities with his mice and those closely related to him, depended much on mass. The smaller the collection of cells, like the mouse, the shorter the distance he could communicate with it.

If he had been reduced down to hundreds of mice, none of them would venture down the terrifying drop. They would be too hard-wired by instinct to follow that course. They would flee to a safe dry place, and eat until they had energy to merge into a larger, stronger creature, hopefully human, hopefully with enough of his memories intact to return to being Ukiah. Thus, only with Ukiah's human mind directing the mouse remotely, did it overcome its fear and carefully pick its way down the rusty cliff.

. . . brown curly hair, a male human, a chilled cheek, closed eyes . . .

"It's him," Ukiah whispered.

"Unfortunately," Max's voice came over Ukiah's headset. "The nearest manhole is way down here, around the corner, and it's really started to pour. Damn, where's that rescue crew?"

Ukiah murmured an answer, trying to coax his mouse back out. It was on the edge of his influence, though, and frightened. It scurried back and forth on the imagined safety that the boy provided, hesitant to face the dark alone. Suddenly it slipped into the fast-moving water that chuted down over slick bare skin. Ukiah squeaked in surprise as the mouse was swept down through a hole between child and pipe and washed away.

"Ukiah!" Max called over the headset. "What's wrong?"

Ukiah leapt to his feet and bolted toward Max. "I've lost my mouse! I need to get it back."

Max exploded into curses.

The rain beat furiously down now, sheeting off the rest of the world so it seemed like Ukiah struggled within a pocket universe to save the boy. He rounded the corner and found his partner and Ari beside an opened manhole, shining lights into the hole.

Max looked up, obviously torn. "Kid, the water is already deep and fast, and it's raining harder now. We don't have ropes, and you're not even sure what direction to go. Just wait for the rescue crew."

"I've got to go," Ukiah said, wishing Ari wasn't there so he could argue with Max openly. Perhaps, it was better this way—he could never win arguments with Max. He hadn't considered losing his mouse when he sent it into the drain—a lost mouse was much too dangerous to the world. Hex had used a single stolen mouse to create Kittanning. With a second mouse, the Ontongard leader had nearly remade Max into a clone of Ukiah. Even without the evil intentions of the Ontongard, Ukiah could not ignore that somehow, some part of the dismembered child Magic Boy, perhaps just a lone mouse, had become the Wolf Boy, and eventually himself.

He had to get it back. He brushed past Max to the manhole, ignoring the look that spoke volumes.

The sound of water falling out the throats of countless feeder pipes, echoed by curving concrete, combined into an unending deafening roar. Ukiah climbed down the slick metal ladder into the ink blackness. The water grabbed his foot as he went to step off the ladder, trying to jerk him under. He braced himself against the current and found his footing. The water flowed up to his knees, numbingly cold, seeming nearly solid with the force it applied on him.

Ukiah stood a moment, waiting to adjust to the cave darkness pressing in on him. As his eyes adapted, the fist-sized disk of filthy concrete illuminated by his flashlight became a curving, grime-coated wall, a shimmer reflecting off the moving blackness that was water, and the thin paleness where the two met in a mud-tainted froth. Sound and pressure filled in what he could not see; he sensed the top of the pipe close to his head and the opposite wall just out of reach and out of sight.

Trying to ignore how little space was left between the flat plain of water and the top arch of the pipe, Ukiah concentrated on finding the boy and his mouse. Kyle had been west of the manhole, but this culvert ran north to south. Ukiah replayed the last moments of contact with his mouse. It had rushed away from him, heading south, not east toward this culvert. Nor could he sense his mouse now, or glean anything of the boy. Ukiah decided to follow the flow of water and see if there was a main junction pipe. Letting go of the ladder, he waded with the current, fighting to stay upright. The cement floor, unseen under the water, sloped with the steep hillside, which would make getting back hard. His flashlight danced through the cave darkness as he staggered forward.

Fifty feet down, the pipe ended, spilling its water down into a ten-foot-tall main junction pipe running east to west. The water was deeper, over his knees and creeping toward his hips. Much deeper and he'd lose his footing against the current completely. And he still wasn't sure if he was going the right direction. He played his flashlight down the left-hand wall of the pipe, looking for something that led back north to Kyle.

Max said something to him over the headset, the thunder of water drowning out his words.

"What?" He cupped his free hand over his ear, trying to keep the water's roar out.

"Which way are you going?"

"I went south. I'm going east now. First left!" Ukiah shouted and spotted a likely feeder, forty feet down. While only four feet in diameter, the pipe was still wide enough for him to travel without getting stuck. "I'm going to head north now. Hopefully it will take me back to Kyle!"

He overshot the feeder, shoved past the opening by the rushing water. Gripping the lip of the pipe, he hauled himself back and up into the pipe. He had to squat, duck-walking against the water, but luckily it only came to his shins. Fast-food drinking cups and empty pop bottles floated past him, washed out of gutters and into the storm drain. He came to a small dam made from a wedged tree branch and a Kentucky Fried Chicken box.

Perched on top was his mouse.

"Oh, thank God," he breathed. He picked up the tiny bundle of shivering wet fur and, unzipping his coat, tucked it into his shirt pocket. He broke up the tree branch, clearing it out of his way, letting the water float the debris away.

"Come on, Ukiah!" Max called over the headset. "It's turning into a downpour out here! You've got to get out!"

"I'm almost there!" He worked his way past the smaller pipes feeding into his, sniffing for the blood trace he picked up earlier. There!

His luck held. Kyle's pipe was little more than an elbow, doing an abrupt right angle into the drainpipe Ukiah crouched in. While only about a foot across, it should have been wide enough for the four-year-old to wriggle through. Ukiah worked his hands up between the boy and pipe. While Kyle's front was pressed tight to the pipe, there seemed plenty of room in the back. Why was the boy stuck?

Wedged tight against the center of the boy's back was a ball. Irregularities in the pipe kept the ball from descending, and the boy lacked any way to push the ball up, as his hands were trapped to his side.

"Ukiah!" Max was shouting.

"I almost have him, Max." Ukiah pushed the ball up and out of the pipe, and the boy slid down into his arms in a gush of water like a baby being born. Alive. Unconscious. Ice cold. "Got him!"

"What?" Max shouted.

Ukiah didn't bother to answer. He waddled awkwardly down the pipe, carrying the limp boy. At the mouth lip, he halted with a groan of despair. The water level had risen dramatically in the junction pipe; most likely the rushing water would come up to his chest now. Just dropping down into the flow would be like stepping out in front of a speeding car; he doubted he could keep his feet when it hit him. If he lost hold of the boy in this torrent, he wouldn't be able to get him back.

"Max! Where are the rescue crews?" He cupped his microphone to keep the water's roar out. "Max, I'm going to need someone on ropes."

"Hold on!"

He waited in the vast, dark wet roaring. Two lights appeared in the feeder upstream and picked him out. "I see them!"

The lights separated, one coming on while the other stayed, anchoring ropes. The first rescue worker came fast, carried on the rush of water like a piece of debris. Ukiah caught Max's scent as the first light slammed against his pipe, revealing that it belonged to his partner.

"What are you doing?" Ukiah shouted at him.

"Getting you out of here!" Max shouted back. "Come on!"

Max steadied him as he climbed down into the current. The water smashed into him, and then tried pulling him down and carrying him away. Together they worked their way back to Ari, standing anchor for the rope. The policeman was tied off with a second rope, leading back to the ladder.

Brilliant light and water streamed down through the open manhole. Hands reached down for the boy, and Ukiah blindly passed the small limp body upward.

"Go on," Max shouted.

Ukiah ducked his head, lost between cave black and brilliance. "I can't see!"

"Go on, Ari!" Max waved the cop ahead, and then guided Ukiah's hand to the ladder. "Can you make it alone?" Ukiah nodded. "I'll go first and act as your eyes."

Max climbed up, and was there, a steadying hand and voice, when Ukiah scrambled out of the manhole. Rescue No. 1, the heavy rescue truck from the Shadyside station, Engine No. 14 of the Oakland fire station, and another squad car had filled the street while Ukiah was in the storm drains. The night was full of flashing lights, blaring radios, moving bodies, shouting voices, and restraining hands.

Ukiah covered his eyes as they shifted painfully back to human normal, trying to block out some of the confusion around him. At least the earlier cloudburst had ended, and the rain had tapered down to a fine drizzle.

"He's fine." Max fended off an attempt to get him onto a gurney. "Just give him a moment."

A compromise of him sitting on the fire engine's bumper was reached, and a woman pushed away his hand, commanding, "Let me see. Do you have something in your eyes?"

"The light hurts." He blinked open his eyes, squinting against the glare. "I got used to the dark."

"Then you probably don't want me to do this." She shone a penlight into his eyes and watched them dilate. Behind her, the ambulance pulled away, whisking Kyle off to Children's Hospital. "You really should leave this stuff to us," she chided. "Good work, though. It's great to have finally found one of the missing kids."

A few minutes later she announced him completely fit. By then, word of the rescue had reached the media, and four TV news reporters from the local channels arrived, followed by cameramen and more bright lights.

"Mr. Oregon, how did you find the little boy?"

"We're told he's been taken to Children's Hospital. How badly was he hurt?"

"Were there any signs of the other four missing children?"

"No. He just went after a lost ball," Ukiah told them, following Max as his partner cleared a path to the Cherokee. "He climbed down into the storm drain and got stuck. This wasn't connected to the kidnappings."

"How did you find him? The police searched the neighborhood for hours. People here say you've only been on the case for less than an hour."

"Did you follow his scent, Wolf Boy?"

"No more questions." Max unlocked the Cherokee remotely, and opened the passenger door for Ukiah. "We've had a rough day and we're heading home now."

The reporters chased Max around the Cherokee as he threw the damp climbing ropes into the back and then got into the driver's seat, repeating the same questions while he shook his head and said, "No comment."

Max and Ukiah were silent until they turned the first corner, leaving the chaos behind them.

"Did you get your mouse?"

"Yeah." Ukiah took the mouse out of his pocket and found a power bar to feed to it. "Where did you get the ropes?"

"Bought them off a neighbor. Rock climber. I paid the little shit twice what they were worth."

"So you paid him all the money in the world?"

Max looked at him, surprised, and then grinned. "I suppose that is what they were worth to us."

Their offices were in Shadyside, a small, affluent neighborhood filled with boutiques and mansions. Max had bought the house when he was happily married, planning to fill it with antique furniture and spoiled children. His wife died in a car accident, changing those plans, and the mansion was now the office for Bennett Detective Agency. To Ukiah, it was a second home, complete with his own bedroom.

The mansion had a carriage house converted into a detached four-car garage. Max parked the Cherokee in the second bay, between Ukiah's motorcycle and Max's Hummer. "Go ahead and get cleaned up. We'll deal with the equipment tomorrow. Don't forget your mouse."

Ukiah had forgotten the sleeping mouse. It was annoying that perfect recall did not mean one always remembered important things. He picked up the tiny sleeping bundle of fur, waking it. A moment of concentration reverted it to blood, and then the cells merged with the skin of his palms, making his hands feel bloated and hot.

In the darkness between the garage and the back door, Ukiah stripped down to his boxers. After scrubbing off the storm drain stench upstairs, he dressed in jeans and a black T-shirt labeled PRIVATE DETECTIVE, BENNETT DETECTIVE AGENCY across the back and went downstairs to raid the fridge. What was in the refrigerator section, however, had sprouted mold while they were in Oregon. The smell when he opened the door was an assault on his sensitive senses. He

closed the door quickly and checked the freezer. Max had it
stocked with ice cream bars for Ukiah.

"All the leftovers in the fridge are really foul," he told
Max when he ducked into Max's library office to say good
night.

Max grunted, his attention on the answering machine. It
played a series of sharp clicks followed by a time stamp; late
Friday afternoon was measured off in half-hour increments.
"The same person called five times and hung up after the answering machine started to record."

The next message was from the Volvo car dealership,
complaining that the agency's custom-ordered car had gone
unclaimed for several weeks.

By the mysterious and archaic rules of depreciation, the
agency's Buick had reached the end of its usefulness despite
being in perfect working order. In early June, when Max ordered a Volvo to replace the Buick, Ukiah had only cared
about its color. At that time, he had been a childlike Wolf Boy.
He looked barely seventeen and could recall only eight lean
years of living with humans.

Since then his life had been massively altered. He had
learned that he was a half-breed alien who aged only when
wounded, had been given genetic memories of his father's
race stretching back eons, and, most recently, recovered memories of his hundred-year enforced childhood among his Native American family. He had been kidnapped, beaten, and
killed, only to heal back to life, aging him body and soul.
Some of the changes in him were easily seen in the mirror; in
months he had aged years. Most were subtler, surprising him.

He caught himself wondering how Max determined it was
time to trade in the Buick, why he chose a Volvo to replace it,
and what the agency would end up paying for the change in
cars. Surely this was what moths went through after emerging
from their cocoons and first considered the mysteries of
flight.

"I told Chino and Janey to call the dealership last week."
Max punched the delete button. David Chino and Moisha
Janey were two part-time private investigators that the agency
employed. While the two worked well closely supervised,

covering the agency while Max and Ukiah were in Oregon proved too much for them. "I'll pick the Volvo up tomorrow morning."

A message from their accountant followed, stating simply, "I wanted to talk to you about end of quarter."

Another mysterious business thing Ukiah had left to Max since being raised by wolves gave him a weak understanding of all things concerning money. It bothered Ukiah that he had no real idea what "end of quarter" might mean for the company. Neither the Ontongard nor the Native American child had experience with business accounting, but he gained some depth in personality, someplace, that wanted to know. As the term "partner" implied, the agency was half his.

The next message was from the airport, stating that they found the lost luggage after Max and Ukiah left, and would be forwarding them to the agency in the morning.

"That reminds me . . ." Max took out his PDA and jotted a note. "We need to order new body armor to replace the stuff that got shot up in Oregon, get it express-shipped."

The last message was from Samuel Anne Killington, the female private investigator they had worked with in Pendleton. They had hired her to drive Kraynak's Volkswagen van back from Oregon. Max had given her a wireless phone in case of emergencies.

"Hey there, it's me." Sam's voice was rough with exhaustion. Max had kissed her good-bye that morning at the Pendleton Airport. As their small airplane climbed and turned toward Portland, Ukiah saw her pulling out of the parking lot in Kraynak's van, starting her trip to Pittsburgh. When she arrived in a few days, Max planned on talking her into joining the agency.

"I made Cheyenne, Wyyyyyyoming." She drawled the state's name out and gave a tired laugh. "I probably could have put in another hour or two driving, but that would put me in the middle of nowhere." A pause, as if she hoped they'd pick up. "I thought you'd be in by now. Well, I'm calling it a night and getting up at some obscene hour tomorrow. I'll call you in the morning."

She hung up, and the machine voice added, "Sunday, nine-

thirty p.m. End of messages." Since Sam left Pendleton before six a.m., she'd driven over fifteen hours of the forty-hour
trip.

"We just missed her," Max said, tapping the caller ID button. "I don't recognize the area code on the hang-ups. Do you
remember the phone numbers on the business card Ari had
from the federal agent?"

Ukiah closed his eyes to sort back to that memory, the
small rectangle of white in the cone of light from Max's flashlight, the cold fingers of rain running down his back. "Office
or cell?"

"202-555-3524?" Max read a number from the answering
machine's caller ID.

"Cell phone," Ukiah identified the number.

"Damn." Max sighed.

Which meant Hutchinson had called them. "Did he leave
any message?"

"Nope, just hung up when we didn't pick up." Max held up
a hand to warn off any more questions. He dug a small electronic tool made to detect listening devices out of his desk and
flipped it on.

Ukiah waited, his stomach clenching into a knot. They had
been leery of any government interest in Ukiah since the para-
military biker gang known as the Pack kidnapped him in June.
The Pack revealed the truth of his half-alien parentage, their
own alien origins, and the fact that they were locked in a secret war against their genetic brethren, the Ontongard. In
movies, the government always tried to capture the alien to
"study" him.

Max walked the tool about his offices before indicating
Ukiah could speak again. "Whatever Homeland Security
wants, they haven't gotten around to bugging my office while
we were gone."

"Do you think they really would?"

"I don't know, kid." Max put the tool away. "After the last
two weeks, I'm seriously jumpy. I'm probably just being
overly paranoid."

"What do you think the deal with the photos is about?"

"The mind boggles." Max flicked on his computer. "I'm

going to see what I can dig up on this Hutchinson; I want to know whom we're dealing with. Go home to your moms."

"I can help." He didn't want to be sent away like a little boy.

Max shooed him off. "Go say good night to Kittanning. I'm sure he missed you."

Only for Kittanning's sake, Ukiah went home.

CHAPTER TWO

Evans City, Pennsylvania
Sunday, September 12, 2004

Mom Jo's wolf dogs were in full chorus as he made the last turn into his moms' driveway. The storm had rained itself out, and the night skies were clearing. Ukiah had the Hummer's windows down, letting in the chilly autumn air. He was home, and enjoying the familiar scents. The rain had dampened the cut fields of hay and corn. The road shone slick black in his headlights, the leaves drifting down in whirls of brilliant gold and crimson to vanish into the darkness beyond the twin pools of light.

Had the wolf dogs heard and recognized the Hummer's engines? It was unlikely—he rarely drove the big sports vehicle. Still he liked to imagine that they were singing him home. He went slow, savoring the small changes he noticed on the way. Mom Lara had pumpkins and cornstalks out already at the end of the drive by the mailbox. Yellow mums were planted at the bottom of the hill. When he topped the hill, his headlights cut through the kennel, and the wolf dogs showed as dark forms and glowing eyes, eight pairs in all.

As he stepped out of the Hummer, a dark form detached itself from the shadows and moved toward him. The wind changed, bringing him the scent of his Mom Jo just before she called to him. She smelled of herself, wolves, and an exotic blend of animals she worked with at the zoo.

"Did you find the little boy?" She was still just a shadow with a familiar voice.

"Yes." The gravel crunched under his feet as he moved to join his adopted mother in the darkness. She reached out a hand and touched his arm, and used it to guide herself to him.

She hugged him fiercely, typical of the rough affection with which she raised him. "Good boy." Mom Jo was a lean, dark-haired woman, a shade under average height. When she first trapped him in a humane wolf trap years earlier, he tucked under her chin. He had grown in odd fits and starts over the years, and she now had to cant her head back to look up into his eyes. "You've grown again. It must have been a rough trip." She meant the trip to Oregon, and it had been. "I wish Max wouldn't drag you into these things. One of these times—maybe we should find you something else to do."

"Mom!"

"You're good with animals. We could expand the kennels and board pets. It would give you lots of time with Kittanning, and you could even go to school, maybe get a degree."

"I like my work. I'm good at it."

"It got you killed in June." She hugged him tight. "And it got you killed again in Oregon. One of these times you're not going to come back to us."

"I'll always come back." He was glad now that he didn't mention the flooding storm drain. "Look, I'm tired. It's been a long day."

"I'm glad you're home in one piece, this time." Then, as if speaking of pieces, she said, "Kittanning has missed you horribly. He's been trying to talk; it sounds like 'Dada.' He says it over and over again, as if he's calling for you."

"Is he still awake?" He mentally reached for Kittanning. "Ah, no." He found only warm cottony thoughts. "He's sleeping."

"You should look in on him before you turn in." Her tone indicated that it was a command.

"I will."

"And you need to clean your room; it looks like a tornado hit it."

Oh, God, she went up to his room? He winced, flashing

over his last seconds of frantic packing. To him, it was obvious that Indigo slept over one night while his moms were at Kitty Hawk, but would his moms notice? Could they smell the sex? Had they changed his sheets? Did they find Indigo's forgotten socks and panties in his laundry basket? Had they emptied the waste can?

Not that Indigo and he planned the one night—they had fallen asleep after making love. Nor did his moms actually forbid her staying over, but during a frank conversation about birth control, they also let him know that they thought he was too young, emotionally, to handle a sexual relationship. Since then, they continued, in looks and silences, to express this belief, but not once had they tried to prohibit it either.

On the heels of his panic came a surprising flash of anger. Why had she gone up to his attic bedroom? His parents' bedroom had always been off-limits to him; after his first big jump in maturity, he'd asked for the same respect. Laundry proved to be a minor stumbling point, since Mom Lara still washed his sheets, towels, and dress shirts for him. He took over those responsibilities to gain privacy and independence. There should have been no reason for her to go into the attic.

"What were you doing in my room?"

"I'm sorry, but Cally was playing private investigator with your stuff," Mom Jo said. "I went up to get her out of your bedroom and was surprised at how messy it was."

"I was in a hurry. We only had a few hours to get ready before flying out to Oregon."

"It still needs to be cleaned." Mom Jo stopped them even with the Hummer. "Where's your bike?"

"I had too much luggage to bring home on the bike." He illustrated by taking said luggage out of the back. Actually, between the troubles of the Oregon trip and the federal agent checking into them, Max was jumpy and wanted Ukiah in something that afforded more protection than his motorcycle. If he told his mother that *Max* insisted on the heavier vehicle, though, she would worry.

"You should have taken the Cherokee or the Buick." Mom Jo picked up his carry-on. "You don't realize how expensive Hummers are to repair. You did ask before you took it?"

"Max said it was okay."

"I don't know what that man thinks of sometimes," she said, meaning Max. "Letting you drive off with a hundred-thousand-dollar vehicle. I hope you thanked him for letting you take it."

"Mom, it's a company car; insurance will cover any damage, and Max values me more than the Hummer." He slammed shut the hatch, pressed the lock button on the key fob, and picked up his other bag. "The Cherokee still had all of Max's luggage in it, and Max is trading in the Buick tomorrow morning."

She took a deep breath and sighed it out. "I'm sorry, honey. I shouldn't snap at you." She started for the kitchen door, and he followed. "Kittanning has been desperately unhappy since you left and he has stopped sleeping through the night. Cally started kindergarten and has gotten *very* clingy. It's been bitter cold and dry—between the two we lost all our late harvest crops. Oh, good news, Lara got a surprise part-time job at Pitt, but her Neon is dying, and we've got a depressing lack of money for everything. We shouldn't have gone to Kitty Hawk; even with staying at Aunt Kat's place, we spent too much money."

"Mom got a job?" He had heard about Kittanning, Cally, and the weather when he called home last week and talked with Mom Lara. The early onslaught of fall spelled a possibly hard winter for his moms with higher heating bills and less homegrown food stockpiled. The job was news—as was the Neon dying, but that was to be expected, considering its age.

"She's going to be teaching one class a week at Pitt starting Tuesday," Mom Jo said. "But her first paycheck won't be until October. We're going to have fun juggling things until then."

"Still, that's great!"

"I know." She sighed tiredly. "But the timing sucks; we're having a fund-raiser here on Saturday, the twenty-fifth, to mesh with the Octoberfest down in Evans City."

All of Mom Jo's wolf dogs had been rescued from humane shelters over the years. There was a small thriving group of breeders selling the mix-breed dogs, although almost none had access to purebred wolves. Large, frequently unpredictable, often destructive, rarely trainable, and very adept at escaping, the animals made poor pets. New owners were often unable or unwilling to deal with the difficulties of raising wolf dogs. Many humane societies and animal control agencies, however, had policies against placing any problem wolf dog up for adoption. Mom Jo took in animals from western Pennsylvania that couldn't be placed, saving them from being destroyed.

The big dogs needed room and lots of food. On the farm, they had the room. Dog food companies sometimes donated food as a tax write-off, requiring the shelter to pay only for the shipping. Even so, his moms were always short of money. Fund-raising was a common family activity, but it was Mom Lara who did the lion's share of the work.

"I'll take Kittanning in to work with me tomorrow." Ukiah set his bag down in the mudroom, and pulled out his wallet. Prior to leaving for Oregon, he had pulled out two hundred in cash, but Max had covered most of his expenses. He left himself a ten, and handed the rest of the bills to his mom. "Here, take this."

She eyed the money with dismay. "Honey, you pay rent already, and you're paying for Lara's health insurance."

"But there's Kittanning now." Ukiah pushed the money into her hands. "Between the formula and diapers, he's not cheap."

Things had to be bad for her to tuck the money away with no more protest; his mothers were still struggling with medical bills left over from Mom Lara's illness, several years ago.

"Maybe we should talk to Max," Ukiah suggested. "He's very good with money."

"No!" Jo snapped, and then gave a wry smile to soften the word. "Honey, I like Max, even though he occasionally drives me nuts, and I know you trust him, but I'm not about to turn my life over to a man."

"As I get older, am I going to increasingly become the enemy, one of *them*?"

"No!" She swatted him on the shoulder. "It's just—it would feel like an invasion of privacy. Like undressing in front of him. And then him telling me what I've done wrong and how to fix it." She shuddered a little. "I've got a PhD, for pity's sake."

Since financial counseling was out, he tried another route of helping. "I can go food shopping too, since I'll have a reliable car."

"Are you sure? You've never gone shopping by yourself before."

"Mom, I stop almost every night for milk, or bread, or diapers, or something."

Mom Jo swallowed whatever argument she was going to make, and messed his hair. "All right. Mom Lara can give you a list. What would really help would be for you to take Kittanning on Tuesday, so we don't need to pay a sitter."

"I'll take him tomorrow and Tuesday," he promised, though the agency was extremely behind in its cases; he'd make it work somehow. "It will give us time together. What about Cally?"

"My cousin Steve's little boy is in Cally's kindergarten class." Mom Jo's family had lived in Evans City for several generations, and she had a huge extended family in the area as a result. Each person had a different level of willingness to deal with Jo's "wife," wolf boy son, fatherless daughter, and wolf dog hobby. "We've worked it out so his wife takes Cally home on Tuesday and Lara takes both kids on Friday."

He remembered the woman to be laid-back and friendly so this news surprised him. "She won't take Kittanning?"

"She says that she's done changing diapers."

The kitchen smelled of lasagna and chocolate chip cookies, evidence that Mom Lara was already in pre-party cooking blitz mode. The kitchen timer started chiming as Ukiah and Mom Jo entered, and Mom Lara shouted from the back porch, "Can you get those?"

"Okay!" Mom Jo called back, opening the oven to a blast of chocolate heat. "Go see your mom."

The tiny changes to the house since he left struck him like spots of color on black and white photos, grabbing his attention. While the lighthouse beside the overflowing bills-to-be-paid bin was quite nice, the seashells scattered along his path through the dark house reeked of sea salt and dead shellfish.

Mom Lara sat on the railing of the back porch, staring at the northern night sky. A stiff wind was pushing the last of the rain clouds out, and stars gleamed brilliant in the moonless sky.

"Welcome home, honey." Mom Lara hugged him. "I was afraid it wouldn't stop raining in time! Look!"

"At what?" he asked.

She pushed him to sit on the railing and then stood behind him, pointing out the northern edge of the sky where ribbons of color waved. "It's the aurora borealis. They had some terrific sunspot activity a few days ago, and they were predicting we'd be able to see them this far south. Aren't they beautiful? The charged particles from the sun are spiraling down the Earth's magnetic field. That's why they look like blankets, they're actually falling in sheets."

It was so like her and Mom Jo, filling him with odd bits of scientific information. He had a patchwork education, stitched together with a perfect memory.

While in Oregon, Ukiah found memories of his childhood as Magic Boy. Dismembered with an ax early in the previous century, Magic Boy's various body parts fled his murder site. Some unknown amount went on to form Ukiah, a child running feral with the wolves. Magic Boy's hand or foot transformed into the turtle Little Slow Magic, who made his way back to his mother's people. A quirk in his alien genetics meant that the turtle retained much of the memories that the child had lost completely.

Absorbing Little Slow Magic and the memories the turtle held, Ukiah added to his quilt work of knowledge, a heritage only half-remembered. "My people believe they are ghosts dancing."

Mom Lara turned to look at him, the star shine pale on her blond hair. "That's so poetic. I'm so happy you finally managed to find yourself."

Yes, he had found parts of his ancient past, but only at the cost of contaminating his present self. Magic Boy lived for nearly two hundred years, several lifetimes of joy and sorrow, rewards and frustrations. Ukiah felt like a child that put on his father's clothing and stood before the mirror, lost in the skin he one day would grow into. Even though Ukiah had completely forgotten his childhood with his mother's people, much of Magic Boy's personality remained, seemingly a rock-solid base that could not be erased. In the overlarge memories, Ukiah could now see the roots of his own personality. Much of what he thought Mom Jo and Mom Lara taught him were only reinforcements of what his mother, Kicking Deer, laid down.

"But you really should have called instead of leaving Kittanning with Indigo," Mom Lara said, continuing blithely, unaware of his turmoil. "I could have flown home and been here before you left."

Unfortunately, all the similarities between Ukiah and Magic Boy only made judging the differences harder. Was it him or Magic Boy who bristled at Mom Lara's comment? "Indigo was happy to do it."

"It wasn't fair to her," Mom Lara said. "Letting her play mommy and then taking it all away from her."

Indigo was listed as Kittanning's mother on his birth certificate, and Ukiah had every intention of marrying her, making her Kitt's mother in truth. Why couldn't his mothers accept that he knew what he wanted? If he was man enough to drive, drink, and carry a gun, surely he could marry a woman as good and strong as Indigo. Were their objections to Indigo based on the fact that she was only six years younger than they were? Or that she was part Hawaiian-Chinese?

Ukiah snapped his mouth shut on words that would have just led to more trouble, and instantly wondered. Was it truly *him* that was angry—or Magic Boy—and which part of him had the wisdom to keep silent? Certainly before he left for Oregon, they'd fought over Indigo; but now he saw his moms' actions in a more hostile light. It never occurred to him before that they might be bigoted or saw Indigo as an age-equal to themselves.

"I'm sorry, Mom," he said instead of all the uncomfortable truths he could have spoken. "It's been a rough day. I'm going to pop into Kittanning's room, and then crash."

"All right, honey," Mom Lara accepted his tactical retreat. "I told Mom Jo that I'll go shopping for you tomorrow if you give me a list of what you need."

Even his moms didn't realize how well he saw in the dark once his eyes adjusted. She winced at his offer, but said brightly, "That will be a great help, honey. I'll work up a list and give it to you tomorrow morning. Good night, honey."

He climbed the stairs wondering. His perfect memory told him that nothing had changed between his mothers and him, except his own point of view—or more correctly—the addition of Magic Boy to his point of view. What had been comforting now seemed restrictive.

A memory fragment from Magic Boy rose in Ukiah's mind.

He stood on the cliff edge, overlooking the Umatilla River, the wind coming off the prairie roaring in his ears, stinging his eyes nearly as much as the burning tears. He raised his arms up, wondering, What if all I need is faith? Maybe if I leapt now, would I turn into something more than just a little boy?

He leaned against the wind, closing his eyes, trying to summon the courage to believe.

"Magic Boy," his mother, Kicking Deer, said behind him. "What are you doing?"

He didn't turn to face her, see how old she had grown while he stayed the same. All his younger half brothers were men now, with wives and children of their own. Only he stayed the same. "I'm thinking about flying."

"You have no wings, Magic Boy."

"Perhaps while my feet are firmly on the ground, I need no wings. Maybe I need to be in the air to have wings."

"Don't be foolish. You're too old for it."

"Tell that to the old men of the tribe! Tell them I am too old to still be considered a child. Tell them that the baby at your breast when I went out the last time for my manhood rite had a son of his own today."

"My son," Kicking Deer said softly. "Every full moon I take a string out and measure you as you sleep. Years I have measured you from the top of your head to the back of your heels, and always you are the same. There is no gray in your hair and no lines on your face. Like the stone Coyote gave me to swallow, you are unchanging."

"So I am unchanging! They made Five Crows a man yes-terday. He has only seen eleven summers to my thirty, and to-morrow he might die if a bear struck him or a snake bit him. Am I, who is unchanging, any less a man than Five Crows, who might die without changing? He is shorter, and slower, and weaker than I, but they made him a man."

Years of injustices fueled his anger, and he raged on bit-terly. *"And you know why? If I were a man, I would over-shadow them even as I am. I am faster and stronger than all of them. So they keep me a child and order me about when-ever they can."*

"Aiieee. My son. It is the spirits that keep you a child."

"I am sick of being a child. I am sick of babies swagger-ing about the dance grounds, thinking they can tell me what to do because . . ."

"Because the spirits chose a different path for you. A longer path. Five Crows's journey is already half over, and yours has barely begun. Do not be angry because you do not see the same things along the path that he does; you are bound for different places."

He sighed, turning away from the cliff. *"Why is it that you are always so much wiser than me? You are not really that much older than I am."*

She tweaked his nose. *"Because I'm always running to stay ahead of you."*

Magic Boy hadn't flung himself from that cliff face that day. Ironically, if he had, he would have aged. But his mother had been right, he had taken a long, twisting path before see-ing his totem animal and becoming a man. A small niggling part of Ukiah pointed out that he still lived as a child in his mothers' house, but he had, for the most part, all that Magic Boy desired: a position in society as an adult, a woman, and a child.

Kittanning lay in his crib bed, a mobile of Mickey Mouse dancing over his head, dreaming of the day's anxiety.

Although Kittanning started as a stolen blood mouse, and had been all of three days old when Ukiah finally won him back, Ukiah hadn't been able to take Kittanning back. Not in the physical sense—no, Ukiah probably could have forced the merger. But Kittanning was now a human infant. Whereas Ukiah's mice felt like lost pieces of the greater whole, always joyful at the prospect of returning, Kittanning had a sense of self, wholly separate of Ukiah. Perhaps Kittanning's individuality came from resisting Hex's will, perhaps it came automatic with the conscious mind of the human form, or maybe it was something more metaphysical, being gifted with a soul at the moment of his human transformation. Whatever it was, Ukiah had held the baby and known that Kittanning was no longer *his* as in the manner of fingers and toes, but *his* as in the manner of a son.

Prior to Ukiah's trip to Oregon, though, he had wondered at the truth of this, worried that he was mistaken. He had been ignorant of his mice nearly up to the day of Kittanning's "birth." What if the personality he felt in Kittanning was merely a projection of his own?

Now, knowing he wasn't the child born to his mother, but a blood animal transformed himself, Ukiah recognized that Kittanning was also a true individual. The knowledge, as he gazed down at the sleeping baby, banished all of Ukiah's worries and left him with only love for his son.

Lifting Kittanning out of his crib, Ukiah cuddled his son to him, waking him.

Daddy! Joy shimmered through Kittanning, and the tiny fists clutched tight at Ukiah. Between them, there was no need for words of love, it poured out unreserved. Tempered into the flow, though, was a sense of terrible sorrow as the weeks had passed with glacial slowness for the infant, and a faint terror that Kittanning would grow to forget his father.

"I'm home to stay," Ukiah promised and kissed the soft black hair.

Evans City, Pennsylvania
Monday, September 13, 2004

"It's just I feel funny not telling anyone," Mom Lara complained during the normal morning confusion, complicated by the addition of baby Kittanning to their family, and the recent start of school for Ukiah's sister, Cally. Lunch bags stood half-filled on the counter, morning coffee scented the kitchen, and a baby bottle shimmered on the cooktop. "I have a doctorate in astronomy. I've written papers on all of my tiny, almost insignificant discoveries. Now, I know everything about the most important discovery of mankind since—since the invention of written language, and I can't say anything!"

"I'm sorry, Mom." Ukiah rocked back and forth, patting Kittanning on the back. He still found it disorienting to cradle the infant to him. They were so identical that his senses could barely determine where his body stopped and his son's started. Ukiah could feel Kittanning's hunger as if it was his own.

"I'm hungry," Kittanning whimpered into his mind.

"I know, pumpkin." Ukiah yawned. Kittanning's hunger had woken them up in the middle of the night. With typical baby self-centeredness, Kittanning had shown very little patience with Ukiah's late-night fumbling and needed a great deal of rocking to settle back to bed. In all, an hour had been stolen out of the heart of Ukiah's sleep. Normally this wouldn't leave Ukiah yawning; that it did was proof he hadn't recovered fully from the battering he took in Oregon. "Your bottle is almost ready."

"Actually, it's not the scientific community that bothers me. Who would believe that ugly thing sat up there for two hundreds years or more, while a war between alien factions took place here on Earth, right under our noses? Only thirty-two percent of scientists polled believed that the ship posed a possible threat. Fourteen percent actually went so far as to say that interstellar conquest is an impossibility. No one is going to believe me if I try to claim that the alien ship was going to wipe out all life as we know it. I have no hard evidence."

"You have me and Kittanning," Ukiah murmured.

"Ukiah!" Mom Lara's hard look forbade him to even joke about the subject.

"Is his bottle ready?" Ukiah changed the subject.

"It should be." Mom Lara lifted the bottle out of the water, and tested it on her wrist. Satisfied with the temperature, she handed it to Ukiah. "What bothers me are the kids at Cally's school." Mom Lara did volunteer work at his five-year-old sister's elementary school, teaching astronomy and running science fairs. "They're scared silly that an alien fleet will be invading tomorrow. I could reassure them that there's no danger, that there was only that one damaged ship, and that the Pack forced it to self-destruct. But I can't. I can't even tell Cally, at least until she's older. It wouldn't be fair to ask her to keep a secret of that importance."

A clatter of little feet on the stairs announced the arrival of Cally, and they fell quiet. While born to Mom Lara, Cally had Mom Jo's dark curls and stormy nature, a result of in vitro fertilization. She paused at the doorway, frowning slightly at the feeding Kittanning. "Is he still here?"

"Honey." Mom Lara sighed, tugging on Cally's dark curls. "We've told you, Indigo only took him for a little while."

So things quickly turned to the second concern to the family: Cally was not taking well being suddenly supplanted as the baby. She pressed tight against Ukiah, frowning slightly at the feeding Kittanning.

"Why can't she keep him?"

"She might," Ukiah said carefully, getting a surprised look from Mom Lara. "If Indigo and I get married, Kittanning and I will go live with her."

"I don't want *you* to leave."

"He's not," Mom Lara said, setting out a cereal bowl for Cally. "He's too young to get married."

"You know that I'm not," Ukiah said.

Mom Lara pressed her mouth tight to keep from frowning. "You two barely know each other. Your Mom Jo and I dated all through college before deciding that we wanted to be together the rest of our lives."

"That's different," Ukiah protested. His mothers had been young when they first met, and by their own account, not even sure if they were homosexual or just horny. In the end, they decided that they were simply in love, and nothing else mattered.

"Not by much," Mom Lara said. "We had to decide whether to marry someone that our families might like, but would never fully approve of. We had to decide that we could take the pressure to find a 'more acceptable mate,' one that conformed to society's mores of what is proper. We had to come to terms with the possibility of being ostracized by friends, family, and neighbors. It takes courage to fly into the face of normal. You're asking a lot of Indigo. You're not the same race, age, or religion." With Cally listening intently, Mom Lara probably intentionally left out "species." "Give her time. There's no reason to rush."

"I'm afraid that if I give her time to think about all that, she'll say no."

Mom Lara came to wrap her arms around him, as if to shield him from harm. "If it's right, all the time in the world won't make her say no. But if it's wrong, it's better to figure it out before you get too deep and get hurt."

The problem was, Ukiah suspected that he was already too deep.

The wheeled garbage can sat empty at the curb when Ukiah pulled up to the office. He walked down the driveway and pushed it back to the garage. It took both hands and his teeth to carry Kittanning and his assorted baby accessories into the kitchen. Max stood washing dishes, by the smell, mostly containers of various refrigerated leftovers that had gone bad while they were gone. Max wore only his sweatpants, his lean muscled frame damp from his morning workout.

"Morning, kid," Max called without looking up. "I heard you bring up the can. Thanks. I was in the middle of my last set when I realized if I didn't get this stuff out this morning, it would sit here all week, driving you nuts with the stench."

"Thanks," Ukiah said, setting Kittanning's car seat on the table. "But I doubt if I could smell even that over someone's full diaper."

Max glanced up, saw Kittanning, and grinned. "Hey! How's my boy!"

"Stinky," Ukiah said.

Kittanning squealed with delight. *"Max!"*

"He's happy to see you," Ukiah translated, wincing slightly as the noise seemed to approach the supersonic range.

Which made Max smile wider. Max set the last dish into

the drying rack, let the soapy water out with a quiet sloshing noise, and dried his hands while Ukiah gathered supplies for a diaper-changing mission. Changing pad. Diaper wipes. Powder. Empty bread bag.

"Come here, big boy." Max lifted Kittanning out of the seat, and grimaced as the smell attacked him. "Oh, yeah, that's one stinky diaper! What're your moms feeding this baby? Curry and skunk weed?"

"It comes out deep green, whatever it is," Ukiah said, frowning as the search for a diaper was coming up empty.

"With your nose, how can you stand changing him?"

"I try not to breathe," Ukiah said, checking the next bag. He knew that by the end of the day, everything in the bags would prove invaluable, but it still mystified him as to how someone so small needed so much stuff. "I think I'm out of diapers. Oops, no, here's some." He pulled three diapers out of the bottom, and then searched a little more to verify that they were the only diapers left. "Looks like I'm going to have to run to the store in a few hours."

"While you're there, could you pick me up some stuff?" Max asked, and yawned deeply. Kittanning took the opportunity to stick a hand into Max's mouth.

The yawn served to remind Ukiah about Max's late-night search. "Did you find anything out about Hutchinson?"

"Not as much as I hoped." Max pretended to munch on Kittanning's fingers, making the baby laugh. "The government frowns on people investigating their agents. I ran the standard nonintrusive background check. Credit reports. Newspaper articles. Courtroom caseloads. I printed everything out so you can scan over it."

"What's the condensed version?" Ukiah laid out the changing pad.

"Born and raised in New England, he attended Boston University and moved to Washington, D.C., to join the NSA. He appears to be a serious bulldog; whatever he latches on to, he drags down and nails cold. He's paying on a Saturn, has two credit cards with modest balances, and rents an inexpensive town house in Maryland. I ran across an old engagement announcement, but no signs of a marriage. In 2002, after

Homeland Security formed, he ended up under their umbrella. I'm clueless, though, what he might want with us. The Pack, as a biker gang, falls into FBI jurisdiction."

"Ari said he had photographs of us." Ukiah positioned the rest of the diaper-changing accessories clockwise around the pad. "Professional quality. I'm ready for Kitt now."

"Every case you've been on usually has had at least one newspaper photographer covering it." Max handed Kittanning back to Ukiah, and then tugged on Ukiah's braid. "What's this?"

Ukiah grabbed hold of his braid and inspected the band holding the end. "A hair tie."

"It's purple."

"It's one of Cally's." Ukiah tossed his braid over his shoulder. "The other choice was pink."

"Time for you to get your hair cut."

"Indigo likes it long." Ukiah steeled himself and peeled the diaper tapes back. Amazingly, the smell could get worse. "Besides, Magic Boy always wore his hair long. It's the way of my people."

Max shook his head as the phone rang. He crossed the kitchen to pick up the phone. "Bennett Detective Agency." Ukiah couldn't hear the voice on the other side, but judging by the sudden full smile, it was Sam. "You're up and about early."

"I'm not up yet." Sam's voice was audible as Max glanced at the kitchen clock, visibly doing the math. In Wyoming, Sam was two hours behind them, meaning it was only six-thirty for her. "I'm just lolling around in bed, thinking about you."

"You are?" Max all but purred as he turned his back to Ukiah.

Ukiah couldn't hear Sam's response, but it made Max laugh. Ukiah concentrated on the messy diaper and not on the small prick of jealousy. After his wife was killed in 1998, Max fell into a near-suicidal depression; Sam was the first woman Max showed any interest in since then. For Max's sake, Ukiah was glad. Still, after three years of being partners, it was hard being on the outside.

Ukiah got a fresh diaper onto Kittanning, strapped him back into his car seat, and dropped the diaper into the bread bag, which he tied shut, effectively enclosing most of the foul odor.

"No, no, no," Max said to Sam. "You don't want to go that way. That puts you into Chicago. You should drop down to Route 70 at some point. Here, let me get a map."

The second line rang. Carrying Kittanning to his office, Ukiah picked up the phone. "Bennett Detective Agency."

"Is this Max Bennett?" a man's voice asked.

"No. He's not available at the moment. Can I help you?"

"Who am I talking to?"

"Ukiah Oregon." He identified himself reluctantly. "Who is this?"

"You're the boy raised by wolves?"

Ukiah looked at the caller ID display. It was Agent Hutchinson's cell phone number. "Yes. I *was* a feral child, Agent Hutchinson. Is there something the Homeland Security needs help with? A tracking case?"

"How do you know who I am?"

"We had a missing persons case last night. Officer Ari Johnson was there. You gave him a business card. You're calling from your cell phone."

"I see." A stylus tapped out notes on a PDA close to Hutchinson's receiver. "And Bennett lets you answer the phone?"

"Yes," Ukiah said simply—Max held that the less you gave out, the more you kept the upper hand. "Can you tell me why you're calling us?"

"I want to talk to you both." Hutchinson appeared to hold the same belief. "Face-to-face. Today."

"Max won't be available until later today."

"I'll be at your offices at four this afternoon. I'd advise both of you to be there."

CHAPTER THREE

Shadyside, Pennsylvania
Monday, September 13, 2004

"Why didn't you get me?" Max had gone straight from talking to Sam to the shower, so Ukiah caught him on the way out to tell him about Hutchinson's call and their afternoon appointment.

Ukiah shrugged. "I was handling it."

Max looked at him as if surprised. "Is that a little bit of Magic Boy surfacing?"

"Perhaps."

Max frowned at the news; he'd been against Ukiah taking in Magic Boy's memories at the risk of losing himself. Obviously he was still worried about the consequences.

Ukiah indicated the pile of luggage stacked in the foyer. "I see that the luggage made it home. Did you order the armor?"

"Yeah. It should be here in a day or two." The grandfather clock struck nine, reminding Max that he had someplace to go. "I've got to go pick up the Volvo. Since I'm going to be over in the South Hills, I'm stopping by Kraynak's to see if he and Alicia got home okay." He snapped his fingers, remembering something else that needed to be done. "And I need to stop in on Picray." Picray was Michael Picray, their accountant, not to be confused with Mike their mechanic, and Michael, Janey's sometimes boyfriend. "He left a message on Friday that he needed to talk to me. Quarterlies are due at the end of the month."

"What are quarterlies?"

Max startled at the question, and then seemed torn between being pleased at his interest and annoyed at his timing. "There are certain things, taxes and such, that we have to pay every quarter, which is every three months: unemployment, workmen's comp, social security. I also escrow everyone's wages for the next quarter, in case something happens to me, it gives you time to learn the ropes."

"I'd like to learn the ropes now."

Max sighed. "Today isn't the day to start, kid. Picray and me bickering will only mystify you. I'm not even sure how to teach you this stuff; we might have to back up to basic math before you can grasp it."

"I can add and subtract and everything."

"Oh, kid, double entry accounting is as simple and a hell of a lot more complicated than just adding and subtracting. Look, we'll talk about it later. Today, it's important for you to work with our open cases, get us back on track with them before we lose the bread and butter accounts."

"Okay."

"I'll be back at three then." Max handed Ukiah a shopping list on a Post-it note. "When you go to the store, could you pick up this stuff for me? I ordered everything else on-line and it should be delivered tomorrow morning early."

Max and Ukiah's partnership had started by chance; Mom Jo picking the Bennett Agency solely on the large yellow page ad that read SPECIALIZES IN MISSING PERSONS. In truth, Max had been playing at being a private investigator, turning away everything but missing persons cases. The agency had been little more than that ad, one room of office furniture, and Alicia Kraynak answering phone calls between her freshman college classes. The grandfather clock in the hall measured out time to a nearly empty house.

From the start, though, something between Max and Ukiah *worked.* Max had the ability to see through people's surfaces to see their true selves; he alone looked at the Wolf Boy and saw the potential man stagnating at his mothers' farm. Ukiah's open honesty moved Max out of his grief-stricken depression to the land of the living. It was a balanced mix of liking, trusting, appreciating, and plain needing each other.

Ukiah started by tracking for Max a few scattered days at a time, but his work schedule slowly evolved into almost daily commutes to Pittsburgh. Ukiah remained, though, a part-time employee until they ran into serial killer Joe Gary. During the short, vicious battle, something changed in their relationship, or more specifically in Max. In the weeks that followed, Max rearranged the business and Ukiah's future; giving half of the agency to the boy, Max started to train Ukiah as a full partner.

At first Ukiah hadn't been aware of the change. Later he thought gratitude had been Max's motivation, or perhaps guilt about nearly getting him killed. With the Pack's and Magic Boy's knowledge of humans, Ukiah could see the events with new eyes. Their brush with death had made Max realize that he loved Ukiah like a son. Max recognized too that Ukiah had neither the ability nor means to live alone in the world; a simple accident could reduce Ukiah to a savage adrift in a hostile world, this time without even wolves to protect him. All the changes Max made to the business had been acts of love.

With the new edge to the business, however, they had to take on two part-time employees, Chino and Janey. The two had their strengths—investigative work wasn't one of them. While Max and Ukiah were in Oregon, Max had directed the two through the open cases long distance. A quick glance at the files showed that they were floundering.

They truly needed Sam as a third full-time investigator.

Hampered by Kittanning, it took Ukiah most of the morning plugging holes to keep the cases afloat. He had just fed Kittanning, changed his diaper, and started to settle him for his morning nap when the front door opened and closed softly.

"Ukiah?" Indigo called.

"Stay here." Ukiah tucked a blanket around him. Kittanning fussed quietly as Ukiah walked away, wanting attention. *"I'll be right back."*

Indigo waited in the foyer, stylishly composed as always in a black wool pantsuit and white silk blouse. Her only jewelry was a strand of pearls, which gleamed with soft luster at her throat. With her raven-black hair combed, and her clothes still carefully pressed, only a slight smudging under her eyes indicated that she had been working for hours on a case.

Ukiah felt a smile take control of his face. He wrapped himself around her compact serenity, burying his face into the warm hollow of her neck. Throughout the long difficult case in Oregon, just her voice had acted as his wellspring of peace, soothing away troubles with unflappable reason. In this chaotic morning, it was a blessing to hold her tight.

"Welcome home," she breathed.

"I'm so glad to be home safe," Ukiah said.

Yet, there was a tension, a flaw, to Indigo's stillness. She hid it well as she hugged him tight, and then, responding to Kittanning's burble in the next room, went a shade too quickly to his office, saying, "Oh, you have Kittanning here!" with a micro-tremor in her voice that no one but Ukiah would have heard.

"What's wrong?" Ukiah asked, following her.

Indigo had draped a blanket over her shoulder and cradled Kittanning to her now. She glanced to Ukiah; lips pursed that melted slowly to a sad smile. "You're learning to read me too well."

He put his arms around her and she nestled against him, Kittanning in the protective center. Man, woman, and child. Ukiah felt complete. This was right. This was good.

"Tell me what's wrong."

"Something upset me, but I'm fine now." She tilted her head up to be kissed. Her mouth was wonderful because it was hers. He could feel her tension, though, in the tautness of her muscles.

"You're still upset. Please tell me what's wrong."

She sighed kisses along the line of his chin. "It's work." She was quiet for several minutes, breathing warmth against his neck. "Four children were kidnapped from foster homes in the last two weeks. A landfill worker found one of them early this morning. She was only a year old. The worker thought she was a very realistic doll at first, naked in the garbage."

What did one say to someone that witnessed such an awful

sight? He kissed her temple, only able to give her wordless comfort.

"I had to break the news to her parents. The autopsy is in a few hours and I'm—I'm sitting in on it."

"You'll find who did this and make them pay."

She turned in his arms and kissed with bruising desperation. He tried to pour comfort out to her. With a quiet whimper, she drank it in. Kittanning protested, sensing their distress. Ukiah took his son from Indigo, and put him into the car seat with a gentle command of *"sleep."* Slipping a thumb into his yawning mouth, Kittanning slept.

"Let's go upstairs," Indigo whispered, reaching for the handle of the car seat.

He hid a moment of unease. This was his second home. Before he had gone to Oregon, he had been comfortable being intimate here. He was suddenly aware of Max's ownership of the house; to make love here felt like marking another male's territory. Only he knew Max didn't care, and he certainly didn't have a place of his own, except his treehouse at his moms' farm.

So he locked the doors as Indigo carried Kittanning upstairs to the nursery and settled him into his crib. She met Ukiah in his bedroom, baby monitor in hand. Usually she locked his bedroom door; this time he did. She handed him her suit jacket, and as he hung it up, she stripped off her gun and shoulder holster.

"You've grown some more," she whispered as she ran hands over the hard muscles of his abdomen. Her fingernails were painted the same warm white of her necklace, each nail carefully rounded and neat, they gleamed like pearls on his dusky skin. Under her blouse was a silky camisole and white lace bra—delicate things that graced her body like pieces of jewelry. They went slow, rediscovering each other, savoring the reunion.

"It's ten after twelve," he said, gazing over her shoulder at the clock beside his bed. Max had said three, but he might be back earlier.

"Hmmm," she said without uncoiling from his embrace. "I

should start to get ready. I don't want to go, though. It's going to be heinous, cutting a baby up like that, and why? Mostly for evidence at the trial, where we play games at justice."

So he held her as she talked.

"She had these wounds all over her. The coroner said that they looked like electrical burns, like you get from a Taser. The thought of an adult using something like that, over and over again, on a child barely able to walk, a baby they stole away just to kill—I can't find any way to distance myself from my rage."

"Is it such a bad thing, to be angry?" he asked, because he could see no way to prevent such a natural thing. He had not seen the photos of the missing child, handled the abused body, spoken to the grieving parents, or faced the grim autopsy, and yet he still felt anger.

"I don't want to give such monsters that control over me, to *make* me angry, or scared, or anything. I will choose what I feel."

"Can't you choose to be angry?"

"If I let myself be angry, then when I find the people responsible and have my gun trained on them, it might be my anger that chooses to pull the trigger." She slid out of bed. "Fighting the Ontongard has loosened a demon in me. Killing came so easy, since they were nothing more than walking dead, to shoot without feeling."

There was fear now in her voice, fear of herself. He got up to wrap his arms around her and kiss her bare shoulder blade. "You know the difference, and you won't kill out of anger."

"How can you know, when I don't know for sure myself?"

"I have this long memory, now, of human nature. You're a very strong-willed person. People like you might fear how they react, but when the time comes, they do the right thing."

"You trust me so much."

"I trust you because I know you. Even the Pack recognizes your strength."

"I love you," she whispered. "And I'm going to be late if I don't start moving."

"Do you really have to go to the autopsy?"

"If I go, I'll be there to answer questions for the coroner, and not have to wait for his report. There are three other children still missing."

"All the same kidnapper?" he asked.

"We're reasonably sure. The MO is the same." She ticked through the points as she did a quick wash in his bathroom. "The kidnapper walks in and takes the child before anyone can react. We're looking for at least two people working as a team, maybe more. Witnesses have verified that the kidnappers are not family members or close friends. All the children were in the foster care system and there haven't been any ransom demands."

"They just take the child? No one tries to stop them?"

"The kidnappers seem to monitor the house and strike when the caretaker is distracted; in another room on the phone, doing laundry in the basement—" She rolled her hand to indicate that the other two kidnappings followed the same pattern. "Two have been in supermarkets, where the guardian was distracted for only a second. Very well timed. Very professional. The first one was so slick that we mistook it for an opportunist crime and focused on the neighbors. It wasn't until the second kidnapping that we realized that the kidnappings were extremely well planned."

"And all the children are in foster care?"

She nodded. "We thought that since the first two mothers were in Allegheny Women's Correctional for drug charges that connected the two kidnappings. Then they moved to a baby who had been found abandoned a few months ago. Now—now this." She pressed a hand to her mouth, keeping in whatever emotion that wanted to slip free. When she trusted her voice again, she dropped the hand away. "We're contacting other field offices to see if these are serial killers that moved hunting grounds."

"How did they find the foster children?"

"Hmm?" She had been focused on hooking her bra.

"It's not like foster children come with big signs."

"We're not sure." Camisole slid on over bra, and she reached for her silk blouse, carefully hung up to prevent wrinkles. "It might be someone employed by CYS, but it could be anyone from a caseworker down to a janitor. We've moved many of the high-risk children to new homes, and started doing background checks on everyone that came in contact with the placing information."

"If there's anything I can do to help find the missing kids, I'll be happy to do it," Ukiah said. "Max might talk about needing to get paid, but that's mostly trying not to set the precedent of working pro bono."

"Give a man a fish, feed him a day," Indigo said. "Your mothers probably would have rather he taught you something safer."

"I'm good at this."

"Yes, you are." She stepped into her skirt, pulled it up to her hips, and zipped it close. It was a good thing that they had just finished, or he'd be tempted to take it back off her. "Here." She slipped a small plastic self-sealing bag out of her skirt pocket and handed it to Ukiah. "They're using stolen cars during the kidnappings and abandoning them. This white powder was found in all four cars. The lab is working on it, but I was hoping you could tell me what it is."

The bag was roughly the size of his thumb. Ukiah pulled open the seal and slipped his forefinger into the gritty white material. He sniffed it and touched the coated finger to his tongue. "It's limestone that has been reduced down to lime by baking and grinding. There's sand in it. There's very old animal hair mixed into this; some of it's cow and the rest is horsehair." As he rubbed the last of the fine residue between thumb and forefinger, he found flecks of oil-based paint. "It's horsehair plaster. At least a hundred years old. Before they used drywall or gypsum plaster, they used horsehair plaster to do walls. The horsehair is to help hold the mix together. Any house older than seventy or eighty years old would have some or all of its walls made of this stuff."

"Three-quarters of Pittsburgh, then," Indigo said with utter disgust. She shrugged into her shoulder rig, making sure that the leather straps lay smooth over her white blouse, and the holster was snug under her left armpit. "I was hoping it would be much more unusual than that."

"Considering the age, you might be able to show it's all from one house."

From the nursery came noises of Kittanning waking up and not happy at finding himself alone.

"Good timing." Indigo slipped her pistol into its holster.

Kittanning had rolled over, crawled to the edge of the crib, and was trying to pull himself to stand when they came into the nursery. Mom Lara had mentioned Kittanning starting to crawl a few days before; remembering how long Cally had taken before crawling, Ukiah could only guess that Kittanning had grown impatient with his lack of mobility.

Kittanning grinned in toothless delight at the prospect of being picked up.

"He's probably wet," Ukiah warned.

"I know." She allowed Ukiah to pick Kittanning up, hovered close, stroking Kittanning's puppy-soft hair. "I need to go, but I'll be back after work. I want to hear everything about your trip that you couldn't tell me over the phone: like what the Ontongard scout ship was like, and what you remember now about growing up with the Kicking Deers."

While they had talked at length the entire time he was in Oregon, he'd edited what he said over the phone, just in case someone overheard. It reminded him of Hutchinson.

"There's a Homeland Security agent coming to the offices later today. He's been asking questions about me and Max and the shooting at the airport," Ukiah told her as he walked her to her car; Indigo carrying her suit jacket.

Worry flashed across her face. "Why?"

"I don't know. I'm worried someone might have linked it back to the Mars Rover."

"I've gone over all the reports by the police and the coroner's office: they read like two biker gangs went to war over a site for a rave. It should be strictly a local FBI case."

"A rave?"

"Dance parties held in abandoned buildings." Indigo used her key fob to unlock her car. "It's nearly textbook contamination of reports: one of the first people into the old terminal decided that the Ontongard equipment looked like the audio/video setup for a rave and influenced everyone else."

"Are you sure someone else didn't doctor the reports?"

"I'm fairly sure." Indigo slid on her suit jacket, covering

up her pistol now that they were out in public. "There's a history of the Hell's Angels and the Pagans fighting turf wars here in Pittsburgh. I heard more than one reference to the Hell's Angels supplying drugs to raves that afternoon."

Ukiah winced as the combination of "Ontongard" and "drugs" connected in his brain with lots of sharp edges.

"What is it?" Indigo asked, seeing the reaction.

"Maybe nothing." He stalled her as he backtracked through his memory of exploring the scout ship. His father, Prime, had sabotaged the scout ship so it crashed, and then used explosive charges to bury it under the Oregon Blue Mountains. By all evidence, Prime had smashed everything useful during a running fight, and Hex, wounded to the point of forgetting the ship's location, had never found his way back.

"Tell me." She covered his hand with hers.

"Every ship carries an arsenal of machines that create bioweapons. The machines are called the Ae."

"And they weren't on the scout ship," she guessed, eyes going wide.

He nodded unhappily. "The armory was empty. There were broken weapons scattered all over the ship, but I just realized that I didn't see the Ae among them." Kittanning squirmed, adding a wet diaper to the list of world-threatening problems. "If Hex took the Ae with him, though, he has had them for over two centuries with the Pack hounding him the whole time. It's possible a Pack dog, even Rennie himself, has already destroyed the Ae and Rennie was too wounded to remember."

"But you don't know where they are."

"I'm going to find out," he promised her.

After Indigo kissed them both good-bye, promising to call after the autopsy, Ukiah carried Kittanning back into the mansion to change his diaper.

"Last diaper," Ukiah told Kittanning as he arranged the diaper-changing supplies. "We'll have to go shopping now."

His mind, though, was on the Ae. Rennie had given Ukiah a blood mouse with genetic memories stretching back count-

less generations of Pack and Ontongard, to a time when Ontongard were nothing but pond scum. Ukiah sorted through
those memories now, trying to juggle through several lifetimes — Rennie, Coyote, Prime — to find the last memory of
the Ae.

While both Rennie and Coyote searched often for a sign of
the machines, neither had found any clue to their fate. Alarm-
ingly, Prime's only references to them was that he dare not
tamper with them while working on the destruction of the
mother ship and other assorted plans including Ukiah's conception; the mounting number of disasters made Hex obsessive
about all the weapons.

Linked through all the memories — naturally enough —
were references back to the Ae's creators, the Gah'h. The Ae
had been a last defense stolen out of their hands; as a race all
that was left of them were Ontongard memories.

Kittanning had been mouthing on his fingers. He held up
his hand to Ukiah's inspection now. *"My hand?"*

"Yes, that's your hand."

Kittanning stuck his hand into his mouth and gummed it
some more. *"Why is it like this? I can remember it as something else."*

Kittanning was made after Rennie had given Ukiah the
blood mouse, thus he was "born" with a full set of the ancient
memories. As he grew, though, those memories deteriorated,
leaving a confusing hodgepodge of earlier hosts with different body types, from wolf down to the octopilike Gah'h. Apparently Ukiah's thoughts had stirred up Kittanning's
memories too, leaving him disorientated as to which were
truly his.

"Those were the ones that came before us," Ukiah tried to
explain. "They're all gone now."

Kittanning took the tiny hand out of his mouth again and
held it out, concentrating on it. Ukiah felt the cells in the hand
readying themselves to change and shift, rearranging them to
the Gah'h ancient design — a long boneless tentacle with
suckers.

"No, no, no, no!" Ukiah cried, catching hold of Kittanning's tiny hand, forcing his own will onto it. "That was someone else's hand. We like our hands this way."

"We do?" Kittanning voiced doubts, comparing his limited abilities as opposed to remembered fluid grace.

"This is Daddy's hand." Ukiah held it up to show that it matched in shape the littler one, built on the identical blueprint. "Doesn't it feel nice?" He massaged Kittanning's feet. "It can touch, and tickle, and give you your bimpy." This was the family nickname for the pacifier. "And pick you up, and love you."

"Daddy." Kittanning gurgled in delight at being cuddled.

Kittanning's sense of self wasn't as strong as Ukiah expected. He would have to be careful to keep his thoughts on the here and now.

Ukiah loaded Kittanning back into the Hummer. Concentrating on the task of gathering Kittanning's things and the slight worry of Kittanning changing shapes at the supermarket, Ukiah shrugged into his shoulder holster out of sheer habit and locked the gun safe. He was arming the security system when he realized what he had done. Rather than taking the time to reopen the gun safe and lock his pistol up, he opened the back closet and pulled out a windbreaker. It covered up his pistol, but anyone that could read bumps under clothing would be able to tell he was carrying.

While Ukiah easily handled highway and country driving with the Hummer, city driving with the big, manual transmission SUV challenged his abilities. The narrow Murray Avenue was insanely busy as usual. He fought the clutch to keep the Hummer from stalling as he coaxed it into the Giant Eagle's small, crowded parking lot designed by Escher. The only true near accident was with a white Taurus following him down Murray, apparently startled by his turn into the supermarket. Luckily he found an end parking space since the slots were all slightly too narrow for the extra-wide car.

Max had desensitized Ukiah to the Giant Eagle's confusion years ago, when they first became partners. It was all new to Kittanning, who went wide-eyed and silent at the sudden bombardment of stimuli. Ukiah locked Kittanning's car seat into the basket of a shopping cart and started into the produce section.

Mom Lara had given him a detailed list with brand names, sizes, and little notes to check for dings in cans, broken seals on jars, and expiration dates on everything. It was Max's list, handed to him so casually, which was going to be a challenge: a ripe cantaloupe, a wedge of good Brie cheese, crackers, steak, potatoes, and "salad makings."

After picking his way through a myriad of possible lettuce, tomatoes, and potato choices, using his perfect memory to pick up what Max usually bought, Ukiah found himself in front of the cantaloupes. He eyed the unrevealing green webbed rind. How did you tell if a cantaloupe was ripe? He picked one up and turned it in his hand. Did one assume that all of the cantaloupes were ripe? What exactly was a cantaloupe, anyhow? He knew it was a melon, but were melons fruits or vegetables? Ukiah could recall seeing people shaking and sniffing them. He shook the melon, squeezed it experimentally, and then sniffed at it.

The woman on the other side of the pile saw his confusion and said, "There's two ends to a cantaloupe. One where the stem was, one where the blossom was." She showed him the difference. "To tell if a cantaloupe is ripe, versus not yet ripe, the spot where the stem was should be slightly squishy but still firm. The blossom side should smell of cantaloupe." She demonstrated a sniff. "To tell if a cantaloupe is overripe, shake it: if it rattles it's overripe."

She suddenly gasped, looking beyond him.

Ukiah turned, registered only that a tall man was lifting Kittanning out of his car seat, and snarled, about to fling the cantaloupe in hand as his opening attack. Recognition clicked in, and Ukiah checked his throw.

"Easy, Cub." Rennie Shaw finished the motion of laying Kittanning on his shoulder. It was easy to know why the woman shopper had reacted with alarm; from shaggy gristle hair down to steel-shod biker boots, the tall, muscular leader of the Dog Warriors radiated menace. "It's only me."

"Rennie." Ukiah could not stop growling, nonetheless. Apparently no amount of Magic Boy could erase the Wolf Boy instincts. Shrugging aside the confusion of the crowded supermarket, he could now sense other Pack members scattered around him. They prickled against his awareness like high-voltage electricity. "What are you doing here?"

"I'm just holding my grandson," Rennie said lightly. "No need to stir up the other customers."

Ukiah realized that the cantaloupe lady had frozen in place like a deer in headlights. "It's okay," he told her. "He's family. I just didn't expect to see him here."

She thawed out of her shock. "Oh, I see, yes, there is a family resemblance. It's just that for a minute there—" She gave a shaky laugh. "All the kidnappings have made me skittish; you can't turn on the television without hearing someone talk about the children being snatched right out from under their guardians' noses. Good luck with the cantaloupe!"

"What's wrong?" Ukiah demanded to know, telepathically.

"Nothing is wrong, Cub."

"You're here just to see Kittanning?" Ukiah asked, feeling like he was missing something.

"It's been nearly a hundred and fifty years since I gave up raising my son to fight the Ontongard," Rennie said. *"I'd rather not miss seeing my grandson grow up too."*

Over two hundred years ago, an Ontongard ship entered Sol's star system. If their invasion had gone as planned—following the same course as countless invasions prior—after a scout ship secured a landing site, the Ontongard would have landed en masse. Ukiah's father, Prime, though had been a mutated rebel among the Ontongard ranks, physically like them, but mentally an individual. Prime sabotaged the mother ship so it crashed on Mars, and then, as part of the crew of the scout ship, sabotaged it too. Only one Ontongard survived, Hex.

Hex, like all Ontongard, could grow himself by infecting humans with his alien genetics, spreading from the one body to countless others. Wounded and dying, Prime had no choice but to infect the first creatures he encountered, a wolf pack, and hope that one would survive to carry on his fight. Coyote was the only wolf that survived, and he went on to infect hu-

mans with his wolf-tainted alien DNA, and thus the Pack
came into being.

Rennie had been born human in 1834. He was the first
human to survive Coyote's attempts to make a Get. He had
abandoned his wife and infant son to carry on the war Prime
started; the decision was based partially on the desperation
level of their secret war, and partially on the desire to keep his
all-too-human loved ones out of the cross fire. When the Pack
found Ukiah, Prime's long-lost child, they decided to view
him as their son; they were, after all, extensions of Prime. The
same logic that made Kittanning Ukiah's son, also made the
infant grandson to all of the Pack.

Despite looking only in his late twenties, Rennie was full
of grandfatherly pride as he held Kittanning. "What a big boy!
Someone is impatient to grow up!"

"That makes two of us," Ukiah thought.

Catching Ukiah's thought, Rennie laughed. "Like father,
like son." Then, because it suddenly struck Ukiah that his own
impatience might be spurring Kittanning on, Rennie added,
"It's Pack blood, Cub. It doesn't like being helpless. He'll
slow down once he's up and running. Bear did."

As if summoned by his name, Rennie's lieutenant, Bear
Shadow, came around the corner pushing a cart. Unlike Rennie, who was in jeans and a muscle shirt, the Cheyenne warrior wore a full leather duster and smelled faintly of gunmetal.
He had a hawk feather tied into his black braid and necklace
of bear claws at his neck. "What did I do?"

"Grew up fast after the Ontongard reduced you back to in-
fancy with that bomb," Rennie told Bear. "We gathered what
we could find of him that wasn't burnt to a crisp," Rennie explained. "Getting the mice to merge wasn't difficult, but they
chose to form a bear cub. We had to work to get them to convert to Little Bear, and then he wasn't happy until he was running on two legs, so he grew like crazy."

Kittanning was staring at Rennie with fascination. Ukiah
wasn't sure if it was just the novelty of being able to read the
Pack leader's surface thoughts or if Kittanning was fastening
onto the idea of growing up quickly.

"Don't give Kitt any ideas." Ukiah shook the cantaloupe at

Rennie. "It's hard enough to explain my having a son, let alone why he's suddenly a toddler."

Rennie laughed. "People expect babies to grow fast."

"Not that fast," Ukiah growled at him and sniffed the cantaloupe. It seemed ripe enough. He added it to his cart. Bear, he noticed, had picked up yams, pineapples, sweet onions, red peppers, and was now looking at the mushrooms. "Are you actually buying food?"

Normally the Pack ate at a long list of bars where they could get a decent meal and yet blend in with the other customers. They rotated through the list so that their visits appeared random. It was a necessity dictated by the lack of time for food shopping and cooking, the desire to travel light, and the need to stay one step ahead of both the Ontongard and the law. Bear's careful study of the mushrooms, though, indicated that they planned to eat the food instead of abandoning the full cart later.

"We've decided to have a cookout," Rennie explained. "And do some howling at the moon."

They paused at the bakery counter.

"Desserts?" Bear asked.

"Cheesecake." Rennie patted Kittanning on the back as he eyed the selection. "Carrot cake. And Key lime pie."

"Key lime," Bear agreed happily.

They left Bear there, waiting his turn like a normal person. Hellena, alpha female for the Dog Warriors and Rennie's mate, stood in the next aisle, reading a can of baked beans' label. Like Rennie, she seemed devoid of weapons, leather pants too tight for anything concealed, her black lace camisole too skimpy to hide a weapon. Ukiah could smell gunmetal on her, an exotic perfume of forged steel, oil, and old powder. He wondered where she had it hidden.

There was something mind-boggling about the Dog Warriors food shopping. They were Pack. Protectors of the planet. FBI most wanted. Hardened killers. Elite soldiers. It didn't seem right for them to stand in the stark clean aisles of a supermarket and study nutrient guides on food packages. All much younger-looking than their sometimes hundred years of age, they looked like art students stocking up for a tailgate party.

"Natural flavor," Hellena said without looking up. "What do you suppose natural flavor is when it's an additive?"

"We can make beans from scratch." Rennie picked up a large bag of loose dried beans. "Your beans are better than anything we've had out of a can."

"I don't put chemicals into my beans and call it natural flavoring." Hellena took the bag and put it in the cart. "I'll need to get bacon, onions, brown sugar, and the rest of the makings."

She went off for the other ingredients.

Ukiah consulted his mother's list and added a bag of dried beans to his own cart. "Why are you having a cookout?"

"Because life is good," Rennie said. "We're home safe from Oregon. Hex is an urn full of ash and we've made a sizable dent in his Gets. For once, we're on top and we've got our teeth in their throat."

The cantaloupe woman wheeled past them as Rennie talked about teeth and throats with the baby on his shoulder. She gave Ukiah a look that indicated she thought he should retrieve his son from the scary man, family or not, and edged on by.

They moved on to the baby goods' aisle. The smell of baby powder perfumed the air from a thousand sources. They paused in the flood of baby sweetness.

"And this is what it's all about," Rennie said, tracing a chubby baby smile on a diaper package. "Life, fresh and new, individual as snowflakes, innocent of yesteryear as it is of yesterday, free to be as good and noble as it chooses to be." Rennie picked a bright rattle off the shelf, stripped it of its tag, and handed it to Kittanning, who crowed with delight. "And you're going to be a very good boy, aren't you?"

"Rennie!"

The Dog Warrior laughed. "We'll pay for it."

Ukiah picked up a package of diapers, made sure they were the right size, and dropped it into his cart. "So we're winning this war finally? It sounds like it."

"I'd like to think we are," Rennie said. "The problem of

cutting the head off the hydra is finding the body before it grows new heads. We've lost the trail and all the Gets left seem to have gone into deep cover."

"Where they can be making countless more."

Rennie shrugged. "The odds have always been in our favor. For every thousand people they infect trying to make a Get, only one survives, and the big spike in the death rate tells us where they are. If they weren't so bloody hard to kill, we would have wiped them out by now."

"But that's what they're most likely doing, isn't it? Infecting everyone they can get away with?"

"Perhaps." Rennie sobered. "The Ontongard is one vast creature spread across trillions of bodies scattered through the universe. Try as it might to keep to one pattern, its knowledge base is uneven. What one Get might know from its host, another won't know until the information is shared via a mouse, and only after the source Get has recalled the information in order to store the knowledge in genetic memory instead of whatever the host uses for a brain."

"Yeah." Ukiah wasn't sure where Rennie was going with this line of reasoning.

"Well, each host has a different knowledge base, sometimes overlapping, sometimes totally unique. Hex and Prime had similar memories and abilities, but not identical. At some point, they have a common origin point, where their knowledge base merges, but it's impossible to tell how many generations back that might be. They were the same host race, but the creature that infected the hosts could have been one of a hundred thousand of the invading force."

"So we don't know how Hex thinks."

"We've got a lot of experience figuring him out, but no, we don't. And we're not dealing with Hex anymore, but one of his Gets, or even several of them. Because of their host memories, the Gets might go where Hex wouldn't have led."

It was a sobering thought. Ukiah took hold of the cart to move on.

Kittanning squealed as they started out of the aisle, *"Beef and applesauce!"* And he whacked Rennie on the head with the rattle for emphasis.

"I think he wants us to get beef and applesauce," Rennie said mildly, getting whacked again.

"Kitt!" Ukiah scolded, scanning the small jars. "The baby books say he shouldn't be eating beef yet."

"He's a growing Pack baby," Rennie said. "He could eat road kill and thrive."

Father and infant both winced at that, and Ukiah said, "Let's just stick to beef and applesauce." He collected four jars of each and put them into his cart. "What about the Ae? They weren't on the scout ship. If the Ontongard are losing the war, would a Get use the Ae when Hex hasn't after all these years?"

Rennie stilled. "The Ae weren't in the Armory?"

"It was empty." He fell silent as a young mother came down the aisle, pushing an infant in her cart while trying to keep a toddler in line. *I thought only about the guns; they were scattered all through the ship from Prime's running fight.*

"Completely stripped?" Rennie growled, his thoughts running over the handful of more exotic weapons. Many simply rendered opponents helpless so they could be infected; once the battle moved to the cellular level, the Ontongard themselves were powerful weapons. *"By the time Coyote created me, as the first of the Pack, Hex had been reduced to knives and rifles."*

"You think if he had the Ae, he would have used them then?"

Rennie shook his head slowly. *"He knew about the ship on Mars; it had to be a powerful carrot. If he used the Ae, and killed off mankind, what would he use for Gets? Pigs? Squirrels? He needed intelligent tool users to save the rest of himself, between starting in Oregon and his reluctance to risk himself, it might have been a hundred years before he knew about monkeys."*

"Thank God," Ukiah murmured.

Hellena came up, carrying an armful of baked bean ingredients. She looked back and forth between scowling Rennie and tense Ukiah. "Can you come tonight and eat dinner with us?"

"We'll be at McConnell's Mill," Rennie said.

McConnell's Mill was an old gristmill complete with waterwheel turned into a state park north of Pittsburgh, located in a gorge cut through bedrock by glacial runoff. It was a place of craggy outcrops, giant boulders, hidden niches, and green moss. A favorite haunt of the Pack, they were cautious, however, not to use it often; their secret war with the Ontongard had made them enemies with the human government. The Pack had ancient ties with the family that owned land beside it so that their camp actually fell on private land. A barn provided shelter and the surrounding farmland privacy, and thus they had all they needed.

"If you're howling way out there, why are you shopping here?"

"To extend you the invitation."

"You could use the phone. Humans have had them for over a hundred years now."

Rennie made a rude noise. *"And have known how to tap them for over fifty years. They are clever monkeys, you know."* Annoyance mixed with pride in the statement. *"Besides, this way I get to see my grandson."*

Rennie didn't state it, but Ukiah sensed that Rennie didn't expect him to bring the infant out for a late night in the cold autumn air, Pack blood or not.

"I'll try to make it," Ukiah said. "I made plans with Indigo though."

"She can come. The howling might do her good," Rennie said. "Ease some of that tension she bottles up inside."

Ukiah shrugged. "I don't know if it would be wise for her career to hang out with wanted criminals."

"We won't tell."

Ukiah's mind was leaping onward. "Oh, shoot. And there's this federal agent coming to the office this afternoon. Can you keep out of sight for a while? I don't want him seeing you on his way in."

"What does he want?"

"I don't know," Ukiah admitted and told them what Ari Johnson had told him, and then went on to describe the morning phone call.

"Maybe we should keep a close eye on you," Rennie said. "In case he wants to arrest you, we'll take him out."

Ukiah shook his head. "If you get involved, I might lose everything."

It was a little after two-thirty; Ukiah had just put Kittanning down for his afternoon nap and changed for the upcoming meeting with Homeland Security. As he came down the front staircase, he heard someone on the front walk, heading for the doorbell. He bounded to the door and jerked it open, hoping to keep the eight-toned Westminster chime doorbell from going off.

A lean man in a black suit stood at the top stair, seeming to study the front porch before committing to it. He appeared young, but his black hair was shot full with silver, short and stiff as a wire brush. He turned sunglasses onto Ukiah while his face remained neutral.

"Can I help you?" Ukiah asked.

"Is this the office of Bennett Detective Agency?" The man asked as if he expected the answer to be "no."

Ukiah was tempted to lie and send him away. There was something about the man that made him uneasy, but there was a bronze plaque beside the front door stating BENNETT DETECTIVE AGENCY, 9–5 WEEKDAYS, OTHER HOURS BY APPOINTMENT in three neat lines. "Yes."

The man stepped onto the porch, folding away his sunglasses, exposing dark questioning eyes. They swept down over Ukiah's moss-green silk oxford shirt, Dockers slacks, and leather hiking boots. "You're the boy raised by the wolves?"

The voice, once Ukiah adjusted for it being unfiltered by a phone line, and the phrase clicked together. This was Agent Hutchinson, an hour and a half early.

"Yeah." Ukiah held out his hand to shake as politeness required. "Ukiah Oregon."

Hutchinson eyed the hand as if checking for weapons and then shook it. In that moment Ukiah realized it was the suspicion and a seed of hostility in the federal agent that he was reacting to.

The silver in his hair was premature; Hutchinson was only in his mid to late twenties. He smoked Winston cigarettes infrequently. He wore an expensive wool suit, neatly tailored, but under a coat of fresh polish, his shoes were only moderately expensive and worn, and all his personal hygiene products generic. Ukiah supposed it was wise of Hutchinson, to spend the most money on the most visible part of his wardrobe, but it gave Ukiah an onion layer impression of the federal agent, without a clue to what lay underneath.

"Agent Grant Hutchinson of Homeland Security." Hutchinson produced a government photo ID that confirmed his claim.

"Come in."

Hutchinson followed Ukiah into the mansion, his eyes busy taking in details. They took note of the rich chestnut burl paneling, the sweeping staircase, the crystal chandelier, and the grandfather clock. "The PI racket pays better than I thought it did."

"We do okay." Ukiah didn't feel the need to explain that Max was a millionaire, leftover from his life prior to becoming a private investigator. "You said four o'clock."

"I wasn't aware at that time that you had been on the television news last night and in the paper this morning."

"So? I'm in the news a lot."

"It might change things." Hutchinson started to explore beyond the foyer.

People didn't like to intrude on personal space, Max explained once, which was why people seemed to have trouble "encroaching" on the office. They saw it as a private home. When Max had been deeply depressed, people's reluctance to enter the building suited him well, but now it hampered business. They found that a sterile foyer, oddly enough, put people more at ease than pretty knickknacks. So they stripped both the foyer and the reception area down to the basics: the stately grandfather clock, a leather sofa, a pair of wingback chairs, heavy cherry end tables, and a single landscape painting over the fireplace. Beyond this area, where they didn't want visitors to roam freely, Max hung personal photos to act as an invisible barrier.

Hutchinson, however, ranged down the hallway without outward qualms. "Who took these pictures?"

"Max did."

"A man of multiple talents," Hutchinson murmured. "He's very good; he caught the wolf in you."

Ukiah shifted uneasily. Taken while he was tracking, focused on the trail, the photos did catch the inhuman side of him. Alien. Wolf. Feral. Whatever. The human eye took it as wild beauty, so it usually didn't bother Ukiah. But then, most people weren't federal agents. "What is that supposed to mean?"

Hutchinson ignored the question. "Tell me, how did you end up with Max Bennett?"

"Why?"

"I'm curious how he got his hands on a feral child." Hutchinson tapped the earliest of the photographs; Ukiah looked fourteen, which was neither his real age, nor the one they thought he was at the time of the picture. Hutchinson gave a microscopic sneer. "Did he buy you off a circus? Or is the Wolf Boy thing all a scam?"

"My adoptive parents hired him to find my real identity."

That startled Hutchinson out of his hostility. In a tone far easier to take, he said, "I thought Bennett was your legal guardian."

"No."

"But all your records list this address as your residence."

"That's to protect my family. Some of the cases Max and I work on turn into a media . . . circus."

"So he's not your adoptive father?" Hutchinson actually attempted diplomacy, and asked in a hesitant manner, "And it's just a business relationship?"

"Yes. We work well together."

Hutchinson moved to walk into the kitchen.

Ukiah put up his arm, blocking him. "That's a private area, let's go into the office."

The hostility came back to Hutchinson's face. "Do you have something to hide?"

"No."

"So what's your worry?"

"I find missing people. I'm very good at it. Often the people are dead when I find them. It wouldn't be hard for someone to construe that I had something to do with their deaths."

"Occupational hazard, I suppose." In a dry, slightly mocking tone, Hutchinson observed, "Construe; that's a big word for a wolf boy."

"I have a perfect memory, and parents with doctorates. They tell me what 'big words' mean when they use them, which is often, and I remember."

Hutchinson seemed to measure him up. Slightly over six feet tall, the federal agent had several inches height and reach on him. Thanks to his alien heritage, though, Ukiah carried a more compact build, hard muscles rippling under his dress clothes. They stared at each other as the grandfather clock measured out a minute.

Hutchinson broke the silence. "Okay, let's do the office thing."

Ukiah led the federal agent to his office and took the position of power, as Max called it, behind his desk.

Hutchinson inspected the two visitors' chairs and chose the one by the window. He sat with surprising grace. "Are you religious?"

"Pardon?"

"Do you belong to a church?"

"What does this have to do with anything?"

"Answer the question."

"Yes. Do you?"

"No, I'm agnostic, increasingly so every day." Hutchinson reached into his suit coat and pulled out a pack of Winston cigarettes. He tapped out a cigarette with a force that indicated a barely controlled anger. "Religion is just a tool that power-hungry men use to steal intelligent people of their common sense." He tucked away the pack, produced an elegant gold lighter, and lit his cigarette. "Most Christian doctrines are laughable in their claim of following the word of God; the King James Bible is translated from highly edited Hebrew text and then fudged to sound beautiful. How can it be the exact word of God if it keeps getting changed?"

"I'm not the person to ask."

"Because you were raised by wolves?"

"No, because I'm Unitarian."

Hutchinson laughed. The smile flashed onto his face, warm and easy, and then vanished completely, like water spilled in the desert. After seeing how full his eyes could be, it was easy to see their emptiness now. Max had been that way when Ukiah first met him; something had scoured the happiness out of Hutchinson's life. Ukiah felt sudden sympathy for him.

"Which church do you go to?" Hutchinson seemed unaware that his mask had slipped.

"We go to the Unitarian Universalist Church of the North Hills, on Ingomar Road."

"Do you like it there?"

Ukiah nodded, not sure if Hutchinson was asking out of politeness or this had something to do with his investigation. "They're very accepting of my family."

"Do you use the Internet?"

"Yes," he said without considering why Hutchinson might be asking. It wasn't the question that threw Ukiah, but the abrupt change in subject.

"Do you post on news groups and chat rooms?"

He considered the question this time; it seemed harmless enough. "No, I don't socialize on-line. I don't have enough time."

"Bennett keeps you busy?"

"It's an hour commute from my parents', and we're short-handed. We're hiring a new full-time employee this week."

"We? You have a say in hiring?"

"We're equal partners."

Hutchinson leaned back in his chair, taking a deep drag of his cigarette, thinking.

"Why are you here?" Ukiah asked. "What is it you want?"

"Tell me about June 24, 2004."

The date of the shoot-out. Ukiah moved an ashtray in front of Hutchinson to give himself a moment to think. That Wednesday had been a busy day, trying to pick up the pieces of his broken life. Hex had shot Ukiah dead late Saturday night, and while he healed back to life, the Ontongard had raided his moms' farm, killed half of the wolf dogs, created Kittanning, tossed the office, kidnapped Max, and tried to make his partner a Get by injecting Ukiah's stolen blood into Max. But he couldn't tell Hutchinson that.

Normally his lies lacked the complexity of his truth. Simply, given only a moment to think, he could not imagine as many details as the reality supplied. In this instance, however, he and Max had woven a rich cloth of truth and fiction, stored faithfully in his perfect memory. With slight dismay, Ukiah realized that they had focused only on his going to the abandoned airport terminal and retreating to Cranberry Township. What if Hutchinson wanted something prior to that?

Ukiah stalled with, "What part of that day?"

"The interesting parts," Hutchinson said, blowing smoke.

"You're investigating the shoot-out?"

"Is there something else to investigate?"

Ukiah spread his hands. "For all I know, you're looking into a minimarket robbery. June twenty-fourth, though, was the day of the shoot-out at the airport terminal, so I figured that's what you wanted to talk about."

"Yes, it is."

So Ukiah told his elaborate lie. Since his desperate search for Max was public, that part remained fairly intact. The change started with Ukiah discovering that the Pack, not the Ontongard, had seized Max, and continued with a highly edited version of what happened inside the old airport terminal. Since police reports showed Ukiah kidnapped by the Pack and released days prior to the shoot-out, a second kidnapping was believable, if not equally obscure. By changing from the Ontongard to the Pack, there was no need to explain the Ontongard's interest in them. Hutchinson could even question the Pack, if he had the desire, determination, and a great deal of luck; Rennie and the others knew the revised version of the day and would back Ukiah.

Hutchinson sat still while Ukiah talked, listening with his eyes as well as his ears. After Ukiah finished, Hutchinson took the moment of silence to gaze about the office. His dark eyes lingered on the private investigator license, the bookcase stuffed with research material, the current case files still filling in the in box.

"So, your parents hired Bennett to find your real parents. He discovered that you're highly intelligent, good at observation, mature for your age, have a real talent for tracking, and the perfect memory doesn't hurt. He took you on, taught you the trade, and made you a full partner."

Again, Ukiah was thrown by the direction that the conversation took. "Yeah."

"He did fairly well by you."

Ukiah decided to take it as a compliment. "Thank you."

"And when he went missing, you were willing to move heaven and earth to get him back." It wasn't a question. There was no doubt in Hutchinson's eyes. He believed Ukiah would risk everything.

"Yes."

"And what would he do to rescue you?"

"He'd do the same."

The clock struck three as Hutchinson gazed at Ukiah with something like sorrow in his eyes. In the silence afterward, he said, "I believe I envy you."

The back door opened and closed, and Ukiah realized with great relief that Max was back.

"Max?" he called.

"Hey, kid!" Max called back, coming through the kitchen to his office. Seeing Hutchinson in the visitor chair, Max checked at the door. "Who's this?"

"This is Agent Hutchinson," Ukiah said. "Agent Hutchinson, this is my partner, Max Bennett."

Max threw Ukiah a worried glance, saying to Hutchinson, "You weren't supposed to be here until four."

"Yes"—Hutchinson studied Max through his smoke— "your partner reminded me."

Max's eyes narrowed with anger. He jerked his head toward his office. "Let's move to my office."

Max settled behind his desk and indicated which chair he wanted Hutchinson in. "What are you doing here? What is it that you want with us?"

"I'm currently stumbling around in the dark, looking for

clues." Hutchinson flashed his smile, the mask slipping again. "You two have the dubious honor of being the current long-shot leads that I'm following. To be truthful, the more I know about you, the less I know why I'm here."

Max glanced to Ukiah to see if he understood Hutchinson. Ukiah shrugged.

Hutchinson reached into his suit pocket and pulled out an envelope. He sorted through its contents until he found what he was looking for and laid it on Max's desk. The grainy black and white photograph was most likely taken by a sur-veillance camera and then enhanced via a computer software package. A man stood in a bank lobby. While it was easy to see he was Caucasian with blond or light brown hair cut short, and had the beginnings of a beard growing out to hide a weak chin, it was difficult to see why Homeland Security might be interested in him. He was average build, wore a black running suit, and appeared unarmed. Hutchinson added two similar photos, the others slightly blurred as the man turned away from the camera, making them worse than the first for identi-fication. Other bank patrons came and went around him. "Do you know this man?"

The photo sparked no memory in Ukiah. "No."

"He goes by the name William Harris." Hutchinson looked to see if the name meant anything to them. Max was shaking his head. "That might be an alias—both first and last names are on the top twenty most common names in the United States. The only other name we have for him is Core. He's the founder of a cult known as the Temple of New Reason."

Ukiah shook his head. The only William Harris they had dealt with had been a very dark African-American; the other Harrises—Daniel, John, James, Carl—weren't this man ei-ther.

Max indicated that he didn't know the face or the name. "What does he have to do with us?"

"That's one of the questions I'm looking for an answer to." Hutchinson pointed to the other bank patrons. "These two we only have code names for: Ping." A young Asian woman in a black running suit, and then a blond man, partially hidden by a potted plant. "And Ice."

"Did they rob this bank?" Ukiah asked.

"Something more sinister than that." Hutchinson pulled a fourth photo and put it down with a slight reluctance. "They were at the bank with this woman, Christina Amelia Whillet of Dover, Massachusetts."

She was a woman caught between extremes. Small but muscular, a face free of baby fat but filled with wistful innocence, more striking than beautiful, she seemed too old to be a teenager, too young to be in her twenties. Bare of makeup, barefoot, in cutoff shorts and midriff T-shirt, she sat on the hood of a small blue convertible with wide racing stripes and Massachusetts plates.

"A Dodge Cobra. You don't see many of those." Max identified the car, then indicated the diamond tennis bracelet that the woman wore. "If those are real, she's worth money."

"About ten million dollars." Hutchinson grounded out his cigarette butt. "She inherited it from her grandfather in a trust fund that she can't touch until she's thirty, but started drawing a yearly allowance of a hundred thousand dollars when she turned eighteen. Until Harris got hold of her, she always donated a large portion of her allowance to charities, most of them dealing with terminally ill children and battered women."

"Is she dead?" Ukiah asked.

Hutchinson looked pained. "We don't know." He tapped out another cigarette, the want to do violence plain in his body language. "Along with donating money, Christa did fundraising, public awareness, and support work via Web sites, newsgroups, and chat rooms. She met members of Harris's cult over the Internet; it started as a seduction of words, then, somehow, it went deeper than that. She had been using the screen handle of Crowsong, because her initials were CAW; after interacting with the cult, she changed it to Socket. Finally she met with them. I—I've been told that she used safeguards: a public place that she knew well, people she trusted to escort her to and from her car. An hour into the meeting, though, she got up and left with them."

Why the fumble with words? Ukiah glanced to Max, who

indicated with a tick of his mouth that he'd heard it but didn't know what to make of it.

"She's been missing since then?" Max guessed.

"No, she came home the next day with Ping." Hutchinson paused to light his cigarette with the gold lighter. "She apologized for worrying her parents, wrote out good-bye notes to everyone who might miss her, and packed her things." He tapped the photographs. "She and Ping met Ice and Core at her bank and cashed out her allowance for the year. They moved on to nearby computer stores and charged her credit cards to the limit. Witnesses say she seemed happy, relaxed, and at ease. Last stop was at a pawnshop, where she pawned her jewelry. All in all, it was nearly three hundred thousand dollars in cash and electronics that Christa handed over to Harris at the end of the day."

"Okay, something definitely went hinky there," Max said. "We don't do it, but there are private investigators who will kidnap kids back off of cults and noncustodial parents. Her parents didn't try something like that?"

"They did." A fifth picture joined the others, a gorilla of a man. "They hired John Rizzo, a private investigator out of Boston. Not the wisest choice of men, but they were essentially paying him to break the law. They had a staff of expert deprogrammers on hand to break whatever hold the cult had on Christina." Hutchinson leaned back, taking out his cigarettes, as Max and Ukiah studied the photos. "Rizzo is, by all reports, a greedy son of a bitch. He would have earned a hundred thousand dollars; instead, he joined the cult. We believe he now goes by the name of Hash."

"Core, Ping, Socket, Hash," Max murmured. "They're all computer terms."

"Christina placed a lot of emphasis on the fact that they became her friends without knowing how much money she had."

Max snorted. "It wouldn't have been hard to hack her identity."

Hutchinson regarded Max for a moment of silence. "Do you know a lot about hacking computers?"

"Regardless of what I know about computer security, it

doesn't explain how all this relates to us. A Massachusetts high-society girl runs off to join a cult in New England. What the hell does it have to do with us?"

"I said you were a long shot. Bear with me. This is going to take some explaining." Hutchinson leaned back and organized his thoughts for a minute before starting to talk. "The cult maintained a commune on a farm in New Hampshire. In January, they sold the farm and moved with great secrecy."

"To Pittsburgh?" Max asked.

"No. Buffalo, New York." Hutchinson held up his hand. "I'm almost to you. They stayed in Buffalo for a few months, renting a lakefront house off-season. The lease ran out at the end of May, but they pushed it into July. We'd just located them when they vanished again."

"To Pittsburgh?"

"Maybe. Maybe not." Hutchinson pulled another photo out; it took Ukiah a moment to realize that the man in the photo was dead, lying on a metal gurney. "Last week the police stopped this man for speeding on the Pennsylvania Turnpike. He was driving a car with expired registry from New Hampshire with no proof of insurance or ownership. He had no driver's license or ID; he said his name was Zip and wouldn't give any other name."

"So how did he end up dead?" Max asked.

"The police impounded the car and took him in for questioning. He refused his one phone call and right to an attorney. They put him in holding and called the public defender, who couldn't get him to talk. Late the next day, he died of an aneurysm."

"I suppose that's a literal dead end there," Max said.

Hutchinson gave him a dark look. "We're working on an ID on him; it might give us a lead."

"And the car?"

"Registered to a John Pender of New Hampshire. His parents report that he joined the cult two years ago. But the John Doe isn't him."

"And this connects with us how?"

"Zip, the John Doe, had these." Hutchinson laid five photos out like a poker hand.

"Oh, fuck," Max muttered.

Ukiah recognized the first two photographs; a professional photographer by the name of Gunter Dettersen took them for a magazine article on the agency. Gunter had followed them in a punt boat through the freshwater marsh, taking roll after roll of pictures, as Ukiah tracked a lost little girl. Gunter had used mostly black and white film to capture the bleakness of the day: the vast marsh, the thick fog, and the lone tracker. Max and Ukiah had gone through all the photographs after the magazine article came out and bought the six that they liked best. The two photographs that Hutchinson held showed Ukiah at two extremes of the search. The first in profile caught him at the beginning of the track, clean, fresh, tense, and focused only on the girl. The second showed him at the successful end, filthy, exhausted, cold, and exuberant, smiling at the camera.

While he could place the first two pictures down to the click of the camera taking them, Ukiah didn't recognize the third. It was a color photograph of Ukiah and Max at the start of another search. They stood in front of bushes that were blurred beyond recognition. Ukiah ignored it to focus on the last two, obviously taken after the shoot-out at the airport terminal. They showed Ari Johnson and Max standing together behind Ari's patrol car, off center, as the subject of the photos were the Ontongard dead. In the first, Max's back was to the camera, but the second one caught him in profile.

Ukiah scanned through his memory of the shoot-out's aftermath. Gunter had been in the vanguard of media arriving as Ukiah and Max pried themselves free of the confusion.

Hutchinson pointed to the Pittsburgh Police badge — a round shield encircled with a belt and buckle — painted on the door of Ari's squad car. "From the emblem on the police car, we knew Officer Johnson was with the Pittsburgh Police. We had his captain identify him, and he identified the two of you."

That matched with what Ari told them. Gunter, though, had been extremely protective of his photographs; he wouldn't have given them out freely.

"Do you know where the cult got these pictures?" Ukiah asked.

"Gunter Dettersen, a free-lance photographer." Hutchinson turned the black and white photos over to reveal Gunter's copyright stamp. "He was attacked at his studio last week; he's currently in a coma. His attackers dissembled his filing cabinet and carried off all his negatives but left a fortune in photography equipment."

"I . . . don't get this." Max checked the other three photos for copyright stamps and found their backs blank, which probably meant the cult had developed the photos from negatives. "The cult attacked Dettersen to steal pictures of Ukiah? Why? What does a bunch of religious loonies want with us?"

"We don't know," Hutchinson said. "If nothing else, we hoped that you'd be able to shed some light on where they might be. They've gone completely underground. We're assuming that all of the members are still alive, but we might be tracking a mass grave at this point."

"What do you mean?" Ukiah asked.

"The problem with nutcases," Hutchinson said bleakly, "is that they tend to crack in spectacular fashion. Waco. Jonestown. Heaven's Gate. If the leader loses it, he generally takes the whole cult out with him."

CHAPTER FOUR

Shadyside, Pennsylvania
Monday, September 13, 2004

They talked with Hutchinson for another thirty minutes, but with no results. Simply, from what the federal agent told them, they could find no connection between themselves and the Temple of New Reason besides the photographs.

At the end of the meeting, Hutchinson gave them both a business card and asked to be called if the cult contacted them.

Max walked Hutchinson to the front door and firmly saw him out. Max went to the window then and scanned the street. "There are times I'd like to be able to read minds."

"Why?"

"None of this makes sense. Cults are FBI matters. Why is Homeland Security involved? What does this cult want with us? Why does Homeland care?"

Ukiah shrugged. "I don't know."

"Well, let's see what we can find out about them." Max turned from his study of the street.

Ukiah could do Web searches, but Max worked the Internet like a wizard, opening multiple windows, designing searches, and flipping through the results faster than Ukiah could read the text.

"Well, they're not registered with the National Database of Nonprofit Organizations." Max closed three of the windows. "If they're a church, they don't have to file an annual return with the IRS. I think. I'm not totally clear if they need to be registered or not to be tax exempt. I'll have to ask Picray."

The filtered search on "Temple of New Reason" pointed to one URL, but clicking on it took Max to an error message saying THE PAGE CANNOT BE FOUND.

"Looks like they took down their Web site." Ukiah pulled around one of the visitor chairs to get comfortable.

Undaunted, Max opened new windows. "What most people don't realize when they throw up a quick Web page is that nothing really disappears off the Internet. Too many places are cache sites.

"What's this?" Max muttered as his attempts continued to return PAGE CANNOT BE FOUND error. "Oh, I see. Tricky. Making the front page look like an error message."

"How can you tell it's a trick?"

"The site's really returning a 200 OK code but displaying the text that normally comes up when the page is missing." Max saw that he didn't understand and tried another explanation. "Web sites return a numeric code. '200' means the server returned the desired page. Anything in the 400s means there's an error."

"But it's still there."

"Yeah, they're doing security through obscurity." Max tried several guesses at URLs before discovering the true index page with professional-looking graphics reading Temple of New Reason. "Weird. Looks like they started with a Heaven's Gate mindset but then decided to go underground."

"What's Heaven's Gate?"

"A cult that ran a Web page design business. They had a very public Web site that basically spelled out that they were going to kill themselves; unfortunately no one seemed to notice until afterward. This was back in nineteen ninety"—Max thought a moment, doing math—"seven. They got some crazy idea that the Hale-Bopp comet signaled the end of the world or the second coming or something. They did a very neat and orderly mass suicide. Somewhere around forty of them, laid out on their beds covered with purple shrouds, with five dollars in their pockets, as if the cost of the ferryman had gone up with inflation. It was all very creepy."

Ukiah had started to work with Max in 1999. While well meaning, his moms had sheltered him from the world, and so the tragedy had gone unrecorded in his perfect memory. "Forty? At once?"

"No. The truly creepy thing is it was over a three-day period, in groups of thirteen or fourteen. I don't remember the exact number. Apparently, one group would kill themselves, and the remaining members would clean everything up, lay them out, and start the next round."

Ukiah stared at his partner, horrified. "They killed themselves? Are the police sure an outsider didn't kill them? Why would that many people all want to kill themselves?"

"Suicide is infectious." Max spoke with calm, personal knowledge of a survivor. "Once the idea of killing yourself gets in, it starts to grow, until it crowds out everything else. Death seems like a release, wiping clean all the darkness and pain."

"But all of them, together, like that?"

"Cults are like the Ontongard; they erase the individual. The leaders of these things do research into brainwashing and adapt the methods, all dressed in religious mumbo jumbo. For example, they might set up a ritual that deprives the new members of sleep; fatigue can really warp your judgment. 'Fasting' is just a way of controlling a person's food intake. You isolate a new member away, control everything down to his ability to use the toilet, work him until he drops, and so forth until his mind is putty, then you can mold him into a willing follower that believes everything you tell them."

"I don't understand why anyone would stay."

"Well, we're not talking about the strongest-willed people here. People who join cults are unhappy and searching for something better. They want to belong. And then the human mind is a funny thing. One of the simple brainwashing techniques requires a person to stand in one spot for hours. The person starts with a determination to stick it out. But as time goes by, and discomfort becomes pain, the person realizes that his own determination is the reason for being in pain. Basically the technique pits one's strength of will, your moral fortitude, against the limits of your body. One of them has to give out."

Max grunted as he clicked through the Web site. "These pages are from the 1990s, but already they've stripped the members of their real names and given them computer terms as a 'designation.' Parity. Gopher. Zip. Veronica."

"Veronica is a computer term?"

"Very Easy Rodent Oriented Net-wide something or other Application. It's a gopher, meaning it retrieves documents. This cults sounds like a bunch of deluded hackers. Eck."

"What is it?" Ukiah leaned forward to read the page Max had stopped on. It was titled *"A Ferruginous Comet Caused Plagues of Egypt."*

As the Earth moved through a tail of the comet, a fine red dust turned the Nile "into blood." Next, there was a rain of glowing debris from innumerable little meteors burning in the atmosphere, causing "boils on man and beast." When the Earth passed through the densest part of the tail, a hailstorm of large meteorites bombarded Egypt. The next plague was an impenetrable darkness, accompanied by a mysterious state of lethargy among men: "They did not see one another, and none of them got up from his own place in three days." Such a state of lethargy is a typical symptom of people who have been exposed to cyanogen, or "cyanide gas." Many comets are surrounded by a cloud or coma-containing poisonous cyanogen gas. Spectroscopic analyses indicate that Hale-Bopp does contain, among other things, large amounts of reddish dust and cyanogen gas! Cyanogen is easily soluble and gives a very bitter taste when dissolved in water . . .

It all sounded very plausible.

"Is it true that a comet caused the plagues?" Ukiah asked Max.

"Oh, who knows? I've heard similar arguments that it was a volcanic activity. Actually thinking about it, the volcano thing is more credible. The whole Red Sea thing can be explained as a tsunami wave triggered by an earthquake; the water level drops drastically and then returns as a massive wall. That's the problem with these cults; they start out with something that sounds halfway possible, but the deeper in you get, the crazier their logic is. It's not a good sign that they're mentioning Hale-Bopp."

"Do you think they might all be dead?"

"They might be." Max clicked through the Web site. "It depends on how crazed the leader is and plain stupid luck. If nothing happens to set off the leader, then everything runs fairly smoothly. But if federal agents start sticking their noses into things, or cult members start walking away because the second coming isn't appearing as prophesized, then we could be talking full meltdown."

Max had been clicking through the various pages, scrolling quickly over the information. "There's not a lot here except garbage. 'The Russian name for wormwood is *chernobyl.* In Norwegian it's *malurt,* not unlike Marduk.' Talk about covering all bases."

"Huh?"

"Wormwood is a star mentioned in the book of Revelation that falls to Earth and poisons the water." He scanned the text and made a rude noise. "They build an elaborate theory where the nuclear meltdown at Chernobyl was the foretold 'falling star,' thus we're currently living through the End Days. They go on, though, and add that 'wormwood' could also be translated as Marduk, which is the mythical twelfth planet that was supposed to crash into Earth last year, which was yet to happen when they wrote these pages."

"Anything on Wolf Boy Aliens?"

In a sudden flurry of typing, Max called up a dozen windows and jumped to the bottom of various pages. "Okay this is odd. No, nothing about Wolf Boy, but with the exception of the member testimonials, everything is copied off other people's Web sites." Max pointed out where the original authors were cited. "No wonder it's conflicting."

"So it doesn't really tell you what they believe."

"No. What it would do would suck in anyone that was a hard-core believer of quack theories already."

"Yeah, but they hid everything."

"Maybe they only want hackers as members." Max started to examine the source code for the pages. He made a noise of discovery and pulled up the crude home page of a teenage Asian girl named Lei Lu Lee. Under her smiling thumbnail photograph, the girl had written a greeting in broken English. "This is my page. My big brother tell me to do this. He is silly." Max read. "Cute."

"What's this?"

Max clicked on the girl's photo and a password box that popped up. "The first site apparently was just to suck in members. They've abandoned it; it hasn't been updated in years. This is their new site, totally covert." He grunted. "Shoot. It's a secure server. I'm not sure if I'll be able to hack it. Let's do a *whois* lookup. They probably lied on the Admin listing, but if they're using someone else's machines, then they won't be able to control that info."

A long listing scrolled up the screen. Max flicked downward and chuckled.

"What?"

"They used the boys in the bunker."

"Pittsburgh Data Haven?"

"Yup." Max smiled smugly.

When Max owned his Internet company, he had hired three brilliant young men of questionable morals to maintain his servers. They used his office space, equipment, and T1 line to start up a data haven business. When he discovered the budding company chewing up his resources, he'd given the men a week to move out instead of scrubbing all their data instantly. The men relocated to an old, low-slung, windowless, concrete cable utility building with the nickname of "the bunker."

"They owe me big time. I'll call them and see if they'll let me check the site out." Max glanced at his watch. "Sam shouldn't be in until late afternoon tomorrow; that should give me enough time to find out why the Temple is interested in us."

"I think a better question might be *when* did the cult develop their interest? If it was at the time of the shooting, then maybe they've been taken over by Ontongard. They could be Gets going after the only breeder."

Max grunted, indicating a doubtful agreement. After a moment of thinking, he countered with, "But Hutchinson said that Zip died of an aneurysm, not a mouse-riddled fever. 'Aneurysm' suggests that they did an autopsy and didn't have the problem of vanishing bodies, or dead coroners. Besides, an aneurysm would barely slow a Get down."

Ukiah had to admit all that was true.

"I hate to say this, but you should tell Rennie about these kooks. Just in case they turn out to be Ontongard."

"I don't know; they just sound like suicidal nutcases to me. I hate to get the Dogs involved—the Pack tends to overreact."

"If they're suicidal, then they're sure to welcome a visit by the Pack," Max said. "After what happened in Pendleton, I want to cover all bases. Let Indigo know too; see if she can find out if Hutchinson is giving us the straight shot here. I've got a bad feeling about this."

The last few times Max got a bad feeling, Ukiah ended up dead.

Kittanning stirred. Ukiah winced. He had hoped to get real work done while Kitt slept, but Hutchinson's visit and the search for information on the Temple of New Reason had chewed up all that time. The day was almost over, he had gotten little done, and he already had two commitments for the evening.

Ukiah called and made arrangements with Mom Jo to swing by the office and pick up Kittanning and his moms' groceries before heading home. There was slight disappointment in Mom Jo's voice that he tried to ignore. He promised to stay home on Tuesday night, knowing that Max would love the excuse to be alone with Sam. He stripped the guest bed and threw the sheets into the washer; it gave him time to think about what to say to Indigo.

She answered her phone with a terse, "Special Agent Zheng."

"It's me," Ukiah said. "Rennie asked that we come for dinner tonight. They're doing a cookout and a howling. My moms will watch Kittanning."

"Both of us? He wants me there? What's up?"

"Nothing. They want to see me. They'll like it if you come too."

There was silence from the other side of the phone.

"We do an early dinner, and I'll go on alone," he offered. "Or we can do breakfast tomorrow." When the silence continued, he said, "It's just a cookout; I can skip it."

"No!" It was a hard sharp denial. Indigo took a deep breath, and let it out. "I can't isolate you from your people. You told me how alone Magic Boy was, how unhappy he was, how desperate he was for someone like himself—it got him killed. I can't take the Dog Warriors away from you."

"You don't have to go with me. I can go alone."

"How can I slight your family and then ask you to spend time with my family later?"

"Well, your family isn't a collection of FBI most wanted."

"Granted, but I think this is important. It's a package deal. I get them when I take you."

"You didn't know that at the start."

"Life is full of surprises," she said. "Don't tell me where the Howling is, though, I might be tempted to raid it just to vent some frustrations."

"You would?"

She laughed lightly at the surprise in his voice. "No. Probably not. I'd rather not have to deal with the temptation though. Can you pick me up?"

Dusk gathered in the shadows of skyscrapers while Ukiah rode his big Kawasaki Ninja motorcycle through downtown. When afternoon's rush hour ended, evening usually found Pittsburgh a deserted town, everyone fled to suburb homes. The Kawasaki's gas gauge read low, he noticed, but there was enough to run up to McConnell's Mills and back. Ukiah pulled up in front of Indigo's athletic club; she had wanted to burn off frustration and change into street clothes before heading out to the Howling. She came out wearing leather pants so tight he wanted nothing more than to be alone with her to take them off. That he couldn't only made him more miserable than he already was.

"What's wrong?" she asked, reading his face.

"Kittanning wasn't happy about going home with Mom Jo." Worse, Kittanning had been able to reach mentally into Ukiah and project all his consuming fear, hurt, and anger. "He kicked up a fuss."

"He was fairly cranky the whole time you were gone." Indigo pulled on her helmet. "He missed you." She swung her leg over the back of the bike, and tucked up against his back, arms about his waist, her inner thighs pressed tight on his upper legs. Even through the two layers of leather, he could sense her living warmth. "I missed you."

He pulled out of the parking lot, made his way to the I-279 on-ramp, and headed north. Like one body, moving together, they leaned into the curves and wove through the light traffic.

It was like their lovemaking, purity without words. It seemed like an open communion of souls, but how much did it show him of Indigo's heart? And how could he expect to know her true desires when he didn't know his own.

It was full dark as they threaded their way through back roads, cutting down through the gorge and across the picturesque covered bridge beside the old gristmill. Ukiah only had Rennie's memories of the place: a hilltop farmhouse surrounded by ten to fifteen acres of level land, a set of well-kept outbuildings, and the rest of the farm's acreage rolling away in a series of steep hills. A large sycamore shaded the front yard, and a bonfire had been built up just beyond its spread, so that the flames shone on autumn-gold leaves and bone-white branches.

The fire made Ukiah slow while making the turn into the drive. The Pack never built fires as big as signal lights unless there were Ontongard to cremate. There were people moving around the fire, some of them turning at the sound of his engine, his headlights reflected in wolf eyes.

Rennie?

So, Cub, you did make it after all.

There was a knot of motorcycles parked together, too

many to be just the Dog Warriors. He paused beside them, wondering if one of the Pack clans was moving through the area and stopped for the Howling. Doubtful—the Pack never parked all of its vehicles in one area, out in the open where they could be seen by any passerby.

He continued on past the parked bikes and into the shadows of a wagon shed.

Something hung in the tree, and it took him a moment to realize it was a deer skeleton wired together, complete with antlered head, with huge leather wings attached. When he killed the deep rumble of his engine, he heard then the deep thumping bass of heavy metal music.

"What's going on?"

"The land has passed on to a younger generation, who's a twit." Rennie's presence grew stronger as the Pack leader moved unseen through the darkness toward Ukiah.

Ukiah scanned the yard. While the Pack kept to the shadows, he could sense their minds on him and caught the occasional gleam of their eyes. The strangers must have come doubled up on the bikes parked out front; they outnumbered the Pack nearly two to one.

"Who are all these people?" Ukiah asked aloud for Indigo's sake.

"Smack came out yesterday to see if the old alliance still held." Rennie drifted into the shifting light thrown by the bonfire. "The twit said all the right things, but then called his friends and invited them to the Howling. Pack wanna-bes. They've made it an early Halloween party."

Indigo startled slightly, her hand slipping into her jacket to touch her pistol grip before relaxing. "Shaw."

"She's wound tight," Rennie said. "Thank you for coming."

"It's the kidnappings," Ukiah told Rennie. *"The case is getting to her."*

"I'm surprised you haven't run them off." Indigo meant the wanna-bes.

"They're mostly harmless," Rennie said. "You might have to look the other way tonight, Ms. FBI. I don't think these brats would learn 'discretion' even if you carved it into a bat and beat them with it."

"I'm not going to pretend I'm blind just to protect your reputation as big, bad asses," Indigo said.

Rennie grinned, teeth flashing in the darkness. *"He's got a quarter acre of marijuana growing at the center of that cornfield, and there are others here dealing in harder drugs."*

"Can't you discourage them? Without doing permanent harm to them?"

"Oh, you want to make it tricky," Rennie said silently, and then said aloud, "We just finished putting out the food. We're set up in the barn. The kids have food in the house, but it's mostly pizza and chips. Go. Eat. Relax."

Rennie drifted off to go "scare off drug dealers." Ukiah took Indigo's hand and they strolled toward the barn.

"What got said that I didn't hear?" Indigo asked quietly.

"Things that would upset you if you heard."

"I wish you wouldn't do that," she said. "You might be silent, but your body continues to talk. I can see the conversation going on around me, and I'm left guessing."

"Your family speaks Chinese in front of me."

She winced slightly, nodded in acknowledgment that it was true, and changed the subject. "I'm surprised the Pack is letting outsiders stay."

It was his turn to wince. The Pack often encouraged wanna-bes trailing at their heels; it gave them a ready supply of bikes, guns, money, and Gets. He changed the subject again, telling her of his conversation with Mom Lara and Magic Boy's impatience with his mothers. "Before I left, I was happy to let things ride as they were. Now, though, I want to move forward, but I'm not sure how to take that step. Where do we even stand, you and I?"

"I—I don't know. I've been avoiding it because it's too hard to know what I should do."

Marry me!

His eyes must have shown his unspoken words, because her face softened and she pressed her hand to his cheek.

"Sometimes it seems like a cold swimming pool in early summer, so clear and perfect, but the only sane way in is to leap in all at once instead of trying to ease into it. Once you get to the waters, you don't know why you were so hesitant about swimming."

He wasn't sure what "it" was. Marriage? Their future together? Their love? "Is it that you're not sure you love me?"

"Oh, I know I love you." She took his hands in hers. "But is love enough? Having that time alone with Kittanning was so wonderful and awful. I loved him so dearly, and yet trying to take care of him and work was so hard. It was a relief to stop, to hand him over to your moms, and yet afterward, I was so desperate to have him back as mine again.

"I don't know what I want. No, I know what I want, but it's not real. I can't have all the good without the bad. And I'm not sure if I can take the bad. Nor am I sure what would even be selfish of me. Would it be selfish of me to say that I don't want to jeopardize my career and that I'm afraid that one day it could become horribly important for me to give birth to a child that is genetically *both* of ours, or is it more selfish to try to have it all, even though I wouldn't be the only one hurt if it all went to shit?"

He winced. There was a certain irony that as Earth's only breeder, he'd been mandated by the Pack not to sire children. In their war with the Ontongard, the Pack did not want him providing perfect hosts to their enemies. Luckily, since the first time he'd been with Indigo, she'd provided protection even his biology couldn't defeat; else the Pack wouldn't have been so lenient with him dating.

"We could make it work. Even Rennie says that if the Ontongard are dealt with, we can have kids together, someday."

"But what if I mess us all up? You mar people forever with divorces. I can't bear the thought of making you bitter and hard, of Kittanning being one of those kids being shuttled from house to house because his parents broke up, of what it would do to me."

"From what all I've seen, patience is the most important thing in a marriage. If you're willing to step back and give things time to work out, there's not much that you can't deal with. You and I, we're patient people."

She laughed. "Most people don't think so. We had sex before we dated. We had a baby almost before we had sex."

"Well." He struggled for something to say to that. "That just happened. We were a little busy at the time, saving the world and all."

With Hex dead, and a large number of his Gets destroyed, finding the Ontongard had become increasingly harder. The other Pack clans continued to hunt the continent. The Dog Warriors, however, kept close to Pittsburgh, watching over Ukiah and Kittanning, while they patrolled for new incursions of Ontongard. To stay ahead of the law, the Dogs moved their sleeping site daily, using mostly campgrounds and abandoned buildings, seemingly in random order. In truth, the Dog Warriors moved down a long list known to them all. They could scatter to the winds for an extended period of time and still know where to find each other at the end of any given day. The cookout deviated from the list, a sudden desire to celebrate—thus Rennie's personal invitation.

The great doors of the hay barn stood open to the crisp night air, lit by electric fixtures screwed to the massive hand-hewn beams. Ukiah paused just inside, marveling at the difference between the Ontongard's squalor and the Pack's comfortable cleanliness.

The Dogs had swept the rough wood planking clean, cleared the rafters of dust and cobwebs, and even scrubbed the high arched window the owners had installed in the back wall. Clothesline, strung at the seven-foot mark, divided up the empty haylofts into smaller, private sleep areas via quilts pinned to the line. While the Pack considered their belongings readily disposable, it hadn't stopped Hellena and others from quilting scraps of material into beautiful wall panels. Futon mattresses and other personal items had been tucked in the sleeping areas.

In the center of the barn, the Dogs had set up trestle tables and loaded them heavily with food. Starting with sizzling chili with a sour cream side, it worked its way down to the chilled watermelon cut into easy-to-manage wedges.

"Oh, good, no dog food," Indigo said cryptically, finding the plates and handing one to Ukiah.

"If you don't see anything you like, we can stop on the way home and get something," Ukiah murmured quietly to her, although the Dogs probably could hear every word.

"This is fine," Indigo stated, although the tension in her voice said otherwise. "It looks great, actually, and I'm starving. I didn't have anything for breakfast or lunch."

He supposed that it was just as well, with her having to stand through the autopsy. He nearly asked how the autopsy had gone, then realized now wouldn't be a good time to talk about it. "Is there anything I can do to help with your case?"

"No!" she snapped and then sighed, concentrating on heaping food onto her plate. "I'm sorry. Today was just bad. Good people destroyed for no reason. The little girl, Kimmie." Indigo shook her head at the senselessness of it. "Her folks are good people who got in a fight with their white trash neighbors over a parking space. The parents won, and the neighbors falsely accused them of child neglect. Child Youth Services did a Nazi raid, took Kimmie into custody, and put her into foster care for her own safety." She stilled, fighting rage, seeking her center. "I had to talk to the damn vindictive bastards today, and they didn't even have the decency to be ashamed of what they'd done."

"Which ones? The neighbors or CYS?"

"The neighbors. The employees at CYS are all apologetic; it's the organization as a whole that's a well-meaning giant trampling half of what it's trying to save. Although right now the right hand is trying to help while the left hand tries to cover its ass."

"And the other three missing children? Any chance they were false accusations too?"

"One's a biracial baby found abandoned in May. The other two have single mothers in prison. The children were rightfully in foster care—you can't fault CYS there."

So it looped back to inexplicable tragedy. No one's fault except the kidnappers', no one to punish but the unknown villain, and no words of comfort that he could give her.

So they settled among the Dogs to eat as if they were any

normal family. The conversation centered around Hellena's sewing projects with occasional detours into the stopping power of various handguns.

Afterward, as they drifted toward the bonfire, someone killed the heavy music and an expectant hush moved through the wanna-bes until they were a ring of excited faces at the fringe of the firelight.

"You're going to howl with us?" Rennie asked, pausing to rest a hand on Ukiah's chest. Through the contact, Ukiah could sense the memory of small body changes needed in order to howl.

Ukiah glanced to Indigo holding his hand. Did she mind such an obvious display of his nonhuman side? Judging by the tightness around her eyes and mouth, she'd seen the question pass between him and Rennie, and wasn't happy, but she gave his hand a squeeze and let it drop. *Be with your family,* she seemed to say without speaking. And the part of him that had been Magic Boy, isolated from his kind for hundreds of years, went nearly shivering with excitement.

Rennie smiled and backed away, leading him into the loose circle of Dog Warriors. The change moved through him, a painful burn of forced rearrangements, of cells grudgingly changing function and shifting to make his voice box capable of creating howls.

The watching wanna-bes stirred restlessly, and a man laughed drunkenly and gave a yell, a pale attempt of the real thing. Rennie loosed a long, low-pitched and coarse howl, more the confrontational howl of an alpha male warning off strangers than the start of a chorus. A low growl rose from the other Dogs, leery of being watched during their celebration of their wolf taint. Ukiah drew in a deep breath and tried for an answering howl; his body wasn't ready yet and the howl came out high-pitched and short, so like a puppy's that the rest of the Pack broke into laughter. He grinned with embarrassment, and then closed his eyes and focused deep inside of him. There, and there, and there, short bursts of white-hot pain as cells unwillingly complied.

Eyes closed, Ukiah could still recognize Rennie's deep alpha howl as it rose, simple now for the start of the chorus.

Hellena's howl joined in two heartbeats later, alpha female, and then Bear Shadow's nearly deep as Rennie's. The three voices rose and twined in independent songs, wordless and wild. With his memories, Rennie had given Ukiah the pack's wolf taint, and sound shimmered along ancient instinct, taking meaning as clear as words. *I am here!* Ukiah took a deep breath and tried again, and was pleased that his howl came out low and long. And now the rest of the Dogs, en masse, joined in.

The chorus became more and more modulated, changing pitch rapidly in what might seem as chaotic disorder. From his Mom Jo, though, Ukiah knew that the chorus howl was to protect the pack's territory from interlopers, and with the discord, their numbers were exaggerated. Two wolves could seem to be six, and six seem to be twenty. *Beware! We are here! This is ours!*

It was a sound meant to carry the length and breadth of a wolf pack's hunting range, and standing at the heart of it was nearly deafening. The wanna-bes wore expressions of amazement, delight, and envy despite the level of sound. After a minute, the chorus wound down and stopped. In the sudden quiet, one of the humans whispered, "Oh, wow!"

Rennie grinned at this, filled his lungs, and loosed another low howl. And as the howl echoed out over the cornfield, Rennie reached out with his Pack presence, speaking now with all his being. *"I am here!"* It was a shout of individuality and existence across all spectrums, to which the watching humans were mostly deaf to. As each pack member took voice, they stretched out their own presence. Each howl similar, and yet different. Each mind holding the same ancient base memories, and a fine layer of individual personalities. They joined together seamlessly at that deep, shared level, and yet stayed bright stars of separate selves, so close that one could feel the beating of the other's heart as if it was under one's own skin. *"We are here! This is ours!"*

They sang through one chorus after another, reveling in the completeness it gave them, nearly one but yet, just as important, still a collection of individuals. The wind, scented with the cinnamon spice of fall and night chilled, rose and washed over them, bringing them reports of everything hidden in the velvet dark. The bonfire roared up, a half-tamed beast, and gleaming embers trailed off into the darkness like a swarm of fireflies.

As the Pack fell quiet after the last chorus, the human reverently silent, and only the wind and the fire talked, Rennie lifted his head, nostrils flaring to catch a scent. "Whitetail buck," the Pack leader murmured, and then loped away, wolf silent, in pursuit of the deer.

Without thinking, Ukiah followed, as if Rennie's going had created a vacuum that sucked him in after Rennie.

The buck was in the cornfield. The cornstalks, spent of summer green, whispered dryly as they slipped in among the rows. The wind changed, taking their scent to the buck, and it bounded away, flashing its white tail. Beyond the corn lay a country road, and then a woodlot of hickory trees and maples, at first dark as a cave, and then as Ukiah's eyes adjusted to the shadowed black, full of dappled moonlight and vivid grays. The buck leapt a fallen tree, a six-foot jump, graceful as a bird taking wing. Rennie followed without breaking stride, Ukiah close on his heels.

Through a sudden clearing, deep in knee-high grass that bruised with their passing, a flash of deep green perfume against the rich earth scent of the woods. Why they were chasing the buck, Ukiah couldn't say, but he knew that he was grinning in wild delight. He could feel the others slipping through the darkness around him, sharing in the fierce joy. They fell into ancient patterns of a wolf pack on hunt.

The hunt moved out of a creek bottom, swinging east to run parallel to Slippery Rock Creek, heading north where the lay of the land narrowed into the gorge. Even as Ukiah realized that the gorge cliffs were close at hand, the buck swerved toward the rocky edge.

Rennie leapt forward and caught hold of the buck. "No, no, no. None of that."

Ukiah joined him at pulling the deer around, away from the cliff. The buck fought their hold, trying to bring its antlers into play. Ukiah controlled it, holding it fast so it could harm neither them nor itself. "Easy." He was suddenly stunned with the knowledge that no human hand had ever touched the buck before, nor would again while it was still living.

Rennie grinned, teeth flashing in the moonlight, well pleased in the deer, the night, and Ukiah. "Let's turn him around." Once facing safely inland, Rennie took his hands away, saying, "Go on! Go tell your brothers that you outran the wolves of hell tonight!"

Ukiah watched the buck bound away, and then glanced back toward the cliff. Beyond the land dropped down into the gorge bottom, and the opposite side rose only half the height of the side he stood on, giving him full view of the northeast sky. Mom Lara's aurora borealis was dancing in the sky, but his eyes were drawn to the big dipper. Ursa Major. The bear.

The constellation brought up his strange vision in Oregon's Blue Mountains.

A male grizzly bear towered over him. It roared, a sound that filled his ears and senses. He saw the huge mouth open, the yellowed canines, the deep cavern of its throat, the red rim of gum and the drool. The hot breath blasted over his upraised face. The carnivore smell of old meat. The spittle touched him with information on the huge beast before him, the ancient link with all bears and the twisting path down to this giant creature before him. The sound rippled over his skin, felt as well as heard.

It stood there, real in all his senses. But its eyes—its eyes were great pools of blackness filled with stars. And into his mind he felt the firm impression of something unreal, something huge and unknowable, something beyond anything he and any of his ancestral memories stretching back eons had ever experienced. The bear, he somehow knew, wasn't truly there. And so, where he should feel fear jazzing over his nerves like electricity, he felt only serene awe.

It was one of the few times his perfect memory was proving to be a handicap. Reliving the experience brought back the stunning grandeur and awe, and yet the memory underlined the profound difference in him. The careful detective that went to Oregon still struggled to understand *what* or *who* had appeared to him, and *why*. Magic Boy, though, accepted it without question; the bear was his totem animal. It appeared to him in his time of need and set him on his quest.

He had the memory of his mother, Kicking Deer, telling the story of his birth, of how the thunderbird crashed in the mountains, carrying a piece of the sun in its beak, of the crow people that killed his uncle and aunts, and of the trickster god Coyote saving his mother only to trick her into giving birth to Ukiah. He knew that the thunderbird had been the scout ship crashing, the Ontongard had been the crow people, but he couldn't explain Coyote's part in the story. Had the trickster god crouched in the briars with his mother, telling her to swallow a magic stone, or had his mother just made it up, a simple way to explain her perplexing survival and his birth?

Magic Boy believed his mother completely.

Looking into the star-filled eyes of the phantom bear, Ukiah could not be sure of anything.

"You've been holding out on us, Cub," Rennie whispered hoarsely. The Pack leader had tried for sarcastic and failed utterly.

Ukiah startled and turned. The Dog Warriors ranged around him, minds still linked with his, experiencing the bear through his senses. Even as his surprise broke off his recall, they replayed the memory, copied in detail, hoarding it. They seemed even more profoundly moved than he had been; tears shimmered in the moonlight.

"God has not turned His face from us," Hellena said. "We didn't lose our souls when we became Pack."

Ukiah understood then. Many of the Dog Warriors were deeply religious; born during a time when miracles were unquestioned, and the state of one's soul extremely important. They had suffered for centuries, thinking themselves damned, to find redemption possible.

"Did we leave Indigo alone at the farm?" Ukiah asked as he realized *all* of the Dog Warriors stood around him.

"Oops." Rennie looked almost fearfully back toward the farm, the bonfire a flickering light in the distance. "That wasn't smart of us."

Ukiah headed back at a run. *"I hope she's not mad."*

"I hope she didn't start arresting people."

                              *   *   *

They found Indigo sitting on a log bench in the dancing light of the bonfire. The wanna-bes were clustered on the far side of the bonfire, eyeing her silently, fearfully. Neither Indigo nor the wanna-bes were inclined to mention what had happened in their absence, except for one man who murmured to Rennie, "That's one creepy chick your kid is dating."

Ukiah knew he'd messed up big. Indigo didn't say it, but he suspected that she was thinking it. It was hard to go back to the normal interaction with humans after the wordless rapport with the Pack: needing to guess what someone was feeling and explaining his actions. He wondered if he would be any better at it if he'd grown up normally, from child to full adult in one heady rush, surrounded by family and strangers alike. Both the times he'd grown up, it had been slowly, shielded by his family or the forest from strangers.

They said their good-byes. During the return to Pittsburgh on his bike, they were pressed just as close, and yet, now, they seemed worlds apart. Her car was in the Kaufmanns' garage; he killed his engines when he pulled up beside it.

"You're angry at me," he said.

"I've got lots to think about," she said.

"I'm sorry I left you alone. I went without thinking."

"I'm not angry with you." Was that a hint of exasperation?

"Do you want me to come home with you?"

"No." He must have let the hurt on his face show, because she pressed her hand to his. "You said before that the best thing for us is to step back and give things time to work out. I need time. It's one thing to *know* you're one of them and that it's a package deal; it's something completely different to *see* it. Tonight gave me a lot to think about."

Mom Lara was up with Kittanning when Ukiah finally reached home. She met him on the front porch, Kittanning bundled against the night chill.

"What are you two doing up?" Ukiah asked.

"He heard the bike coming." Lara handed him Kittanning as the baby wriggled violently, trying to reach Ukiah. "Why did you bring the bike home?"

For the second time in one night, Ukiah realized that he had totally messed up. He had promised to take Kittanning to work with him, something he couldn't do on the motorcycle. Maybe he should think about getting a car.

"We'll ride into town with Mom Jo." Ukiah took Kittanning and soothed away the separation anxiety. "Don't worry, we'll work something out."

CHAPTER FIVE

Cranberry Township, Pennsylvania
Tuesday, September 14, 2004

Sam was waiting patiently for Ukiah at Jorden's Auto Repair Shop; leaning against Kraynak's dead Volkswagen van, tapping a booted foot in time to loud rock music. The pose accented her long legs and tomboy good looks, earning her stares from the mechanics that she was ignoring along with the cold wind blasting out of the clear autumn sky. As Ukiah pulled into the gas station, she turned her sunglasses his way, wind ruffling her short blond hair. She had her leather jacket half-unzipped, unintentionally showing off that she wore a black turtleneck shirt under a corded green sweater and her nine-millimeter Heckler and Hoch in a shoulder holster.

She recognized him through the windshield and came to his driver's window as he shifted the Grand Cherokee into park. He pulled into the only slot available on the lot, by a large sugar maple just starting to turn fall colors.

He toggled down the window, letting in a blast of cold and her scent of leather, gunmetal, female sweat, and traces of Obsession perfume. "Hey."

"I was starting to wonder if you were going to show." Sam leaned against the Cherokee. "It's cold out here." She indicated the waiting room. "And too hot in there with my jacket on."

And with her pistol on, she wouldn't want to take off her jacket. Guns spooked most people, rightly so.

"Sorry, I hit a snag." He glanced at Kraynak's van, smelling the overheated engine from where they stood. "So it melted down on you."

"They say I broke a coolant pipe, and apparently it's not easy to find replacements. They say it's going to be a day at minimum."

"Grab your things and I'll take you to the office."

She had two large sports bags. Ukiah hit the universal unlock and got out to open the back for her. He closed the back quietly as possible, and did the same with his door, wincing when Sam slammed shut her door.

She went to fasten her seat belt and checked, seeing the occupied child seat for the first time. "What the hell? Whose kid?"

Ukiah glanced over his shoulder and was pleased to see Kittanning was still asleep, thumb in mouth. "Mine. His name is Kittanning, but we call him Kitt sometimes. He's ten weeks old."

"Still counting in weeks." Sam reached back to move a blanket aside to get a better look at the black-haired infant. "What a sweetie, but that's no surprise considering his stud muffin for a father."

Ukiah blushed.

Sam had broken down on the turnpike, just inside the Pennsylvania state line. She called the office, getting Ukiah. He arranged a tow truck to get Sam and the van to Cranberry Township's Triple AAA repair shop. Getting Kittanning in the car required a bottle, a burping session, a change of diaper, and set of clean clothes for both of them.

Sam considered Ukiah silently as he pulled out onto busy Route 19, heading for I-79. "I thought it was a big no-no for you to have kids. The whole 'breeder' thing and all."

"Well, Kittanning isn't my son in the normal way." Ukiah explained, "Just as I'm a surviving piece of Magic Boy that became human, Kittanning is a piece of me."

Sam glanced again at the sleeping baby. "He's a blood mouse?"

"Yes. Hex stole one of my blood mice and made Kittanning."

"And you just didn't take him back after you got him back? Like you did with Little Slow Magic?"

"I couldn't do that!"

"Why not? It seems saner than trying to raise him."

He looked at her sharply, then paid attention to merging with the high-speed traffic of I-79. While he jockeyed the Cherokee into a safe slot, he tried to form a reply. "I'm what's left of Magic Boy, but I'm not him, I'm a totally new, separate person. And Kittanning is a new, separate person, and taking him back would be too much like murder."

"But you could take him back?"

Ukiah shifted uneasily. "He has his own identity. He *knows* he's Kittanning and not me. He has his own soul."

Sam startled in the seat beside him. "How do you know? Can you see souls?"

"I don't think so."

"You seem so sure he has one."

"If I have a soul, then he must have one too."

"And you know that you have one?"

"I think I do. How else could I tell right from wrong?"

"I have to say one thing, kid, conversations with you are never boring. So, where's tall, dark, and scary?"

"Rennie Shaw?"

"Yeah, your sort-of dad."

Ukiah reached out to feel for the faint prickle of Pack presence. He felt Bear Shadow ranging at the edge of his awareness. "The Pack has an eye on me most of the time, but nothing overt. I'm not sure where Rennie is, but we're being followed."

Sam turned in her seat and scanned the cars behind them as they took the exit onto I-279. Most of the midday traffic consisted of large trucks, and a handful of cars. "Which one? The bug, or one of the sedans?"

"I think he's on Route 19 still, paralleling. They keep only a loose watch over me—Pittsburgh's a fairly safe town."

"Pendleton was a very safe town, and look what happened there."

."That was different," Ukiah said.

They rounded the curve of I-279 and Pittsburgh did its

magic act, having been cunningly tucked away until this moment to appear, a sudden collection of towering skyscrapers.

"Where's Max?"

"We had some trouble crop up yesterday." Ukiah explained about Agent Hutchinson and the cult as he threaded his way through the odd Celtic knot that dropped them onto Bigelow Boulevard. They left the skyscrapers behind, skirting the Hill District, to cut through Oakland to Shadyside. "Max is at Pittsburgh Data Haven that owns the server the cult's Web site is on. He wanted to go last night, but they put him off until this morning."

"He's just going to walk in and toss a secure server?"

Toss? Ukiah glanced at her and realized she meant rifle through it. "Probably. The owners owe Max a favor and he dangled some bright electronic gear in front of them." Max had the money and connections to ride the bleeding edge of technology. His toys always outclassed anyone else's.

"Ah." Sam fell silent as the neighborhood changed from the low-income Oakland area to the mansions of Shadyside. "Are these single family homes?"

"Some are," Ukiah said. "Some have been renovated into condos."

She fell silent again, murmuring only, "I should put out a trail of bread crumbs," after they made a series of turns to shortcut through Shadyside's one-way streets.

He pulled up to the office's four-car garage and tapped the garage door opener. The middle door slid up. Sam took off her sunglasses as he slotted the Cherokee into the dark opening.

"Wow! Whose Hummer?"

"That's Max's."

Sam turned to look at him, eyes narrowing. She walked out of the dark garage to stare at the looming splendor of Max's mansion. The green of her eyes were like spring ice. "This is the office?"

The question was void of all emotion; still it set off alarms in Ukiah. "Ummm, yeah." He jiggled through his key ring to the back door key. "Come on, I'll take you to your room."

Ukiah unlocked the back door, disarmed the security system, and set Kittanning's car seat in the center of the kitchen table. Sam followed wordlessly with her two bags. He took her up the back steps to the second floor. "This is the laundry, if you want to do any wash while you're here. This is my room, when I spend the night, which isn't often. This is Max's room." Actually it was a full suite complete with working fireplace, sitting room, kitchenette, king-sized poster bed, and master bathroom. Friends teased that Max planned to bunker down in it if World War III broke out. "Guest bedroom."

Max talked about being torn between wanting to set a vase of a dozen roses in the guest bedroom, and knowing full well that he shouldn't. Sam's job offer had to be without strings attached, Max maintained, that would continue even if his romantic hopes crashed and burned.

Thus there wasn't really anything for Sam to stand in the doorway and scowl so. The queen-sized cherry sleigh bed matched Ukiah's, so he knew it was comfortable. He'd washed the linens so they were clean, and Max had made the bed to military neatness. Full bath, walk-in closet, towels, extra blankets and pillows: there was nothing missing.

"What's wrong?"

Sam slanted a look at him. She opened her mouth, considered, and closed it. Finally she said, "It probably wouldn't have occurred to *you* to mention that your partner is a fucking millionaire."

"What's wrong with that?"

"What's wrong?" She tossed her bags into the room, cursing softly. "It would have been nice that sometime in the last few weeks, along with 'the kid is an alien' and 'we're going to do a salvage run on an alien spaceship,' someone—no, no, not just anyone—Max—would have said, 'Oh, yes, I'm a millionaire.' "

"He had a lot to think about."

Sam snorted. "It's just that I spent the last three days, driving that damn manual transmission van across country, worrying that you guys wouldn't have dough to pay me when I got here, and bitching to myself for agreeing to sleep on a cot in the office back room in some bug-ridden, cold-water, third-story walk-up flat to save you money, and half-scared to death that I wouldn't be able to get home without hitchhiking."

"Third-story walk-up?"

"I've had a lot of time to think up worst-case scenarios!" Sam snapped, and then rubbed at her eyes. "I'm sorry, kid. You're not the one I should be yelling at."

"Max has had a lot on his mind lately. He makes most of the decisions for the agency, and then he's got his own personal investments—and he dropped all of that to go to Oregon to find Alicia."

"I know, I know. Between you being killed, and fighting with Degas, and all that *really weird* shit with the mice and the turtle and the spaceship and everything—" She took a deep breath. "How much is he worth?"

The pronoun threw Ukiah. Which "he" did Sam mean? "Max?" Earning a nod, Ukiah fumbled for an answer; he never asked Max about his personal finances, but his perfect memory had recorded bits and pieces of information. "I don't know exactly. He sold his Internet company for forty million dollars in 1998, but he's made a lot more since then. Bought low, sold high, and got out before the big high-tech crash." A firm number eluded him. "The agency's Dun and Bradstreet is two million, and we share it even."

Sam eyed Ukiah. "You're equal financial partners in the company?"

"Max gave me half of it, after I saved his life."

"Ahhh," Sam said with the note of sudden understanding. She looked off at a distance, staring at an oil painting hung across the room. "Well, all the little techno gadgets, and the multiple airplane tickets, and the expensive dinners, and the nice designer clothes, and the expensive cologne, and the—oh, shit."

"What?"

"Oh—just that everything just got so much more—complicated. Well, at least I can stop worrying about you paying me, and how I'm getting home. We'll deal with the rest when Max gets back. When does that happen?"

"He hoped to get back around five." He felt Kittanning stir in the kitchen. "Kitt is awake. I need to go downstairs."

Sam cocked her head to listen. "How can you tell?"

"Pack can sense Pack," Ukiah said.

"Ooooooookay." Sam scrubbed fingers through her hair. "I'm going to take a shower and catch a nap, and maybe throw some things into the washer. Does he have a pool in this mansion?"

"No. Your bathroom has a Jacuzzi and a steam shower."

"Decadence—got to love it."

"Max had the kitchen fully stocked today."

"Had?"

Ukiah assumed that she caught the implication that Max hadn't bought the food himself. "He ordered food over the Internet before we left Pendleton. It was delivered this morning. If you want something to eat, help yourself; anything in the kitchen is fair game. Max is kind of picky about the wine cellar, but what's upstairs in the game room's bar is okay to drink."

"Go on, deal with your kid. I need a long hot shower."

The office doorbell rang, a play of Westminster chimes in eight solemn tones.

"Bell," Kittanning thought.

"Somebody's here." Ukiah headed for the door, testing the bottle on his wrist. Upstairs, the water in the guest bathroom turned off.

"Bottle?" Kittanning added a cranky verbal complaint.

"It's too hot, honey," Ukiah said, opening the door.

Later he would remember the man in painful detail.

He was tall, broad in the shoulders, with a handsome face ravaged by acne in his youth. The hair was a dull color, once a mousy blond but grayed to muddy flatness. The eyes were gray and cold and looked at him with clinical dispassion. A jeans jacket hung over a plain white T-shirt. Jeans. A belt. Heavy steel-tipped shoes.

"Can I help you?" Ukiah gave the quick rote query, his attention on the indignant squawks coming from Kittanning.

The man glanced past him, toward the kitchen door.

"It's my son's feeding time," Ukiah said. "Could you hold on a moment while I give him his bottle?"

Ukiah had turned, and gone four steps back to the kitchen when he heard the man move—a rustle of clothing, and a slight click of a snap behind undone, and then the whisper of gunmetal over leather.

He spun, saw a gun in the man's hand as the man pulled the trigger.

It made so little noise for something that hit him so hard, again and again, tossing him down the hall.

"Daddy!" Kittanning's screams of terror filled him before the darkness washed in.

"Ukiah! Come on, son. Talk to me."

Ukiah opened his eyes. He sat propped up in the dim office hallway, nearly to the kitchen. The smell of blood and spilt milk bombarded him. Mice with formula-covered feet darted across his limp palm to hide in his blood-crusted clothing. Max held his face in a vise, fury clear on his face.

"Max?" He shuddered, room temperature to his core. He had been dead. "Max? What happened?"

"I need you to tell me!" Max said.

"I don't remember. Sam called needing a ride, so I got Kittanning ready and—" He stopped. At the thought of Kittanning, he had reached out with his senses to check on his son.

Kittanning wasn't in the house.

"Kittanning!" Ukiah cried. "Where is he?"

"Whoever killed you took him."

CHAPTER SIX

Shadyside, Pennsylvania
Tuesday, September 14, 2004

"What? Took him?" Ukiah cried. "Oh, no. No!"

As Ukiah flailed to get to his feet, realization hit Max. "Wait! You've already picked up Sam?"

There was a black hole punched through his memories. He could recall carrying Kittanning out the back door, anxious because he had already made Sam wait so long, and then nothing. "I don't remember."

Max bolted up the curving front stairs, shouting, "Sam! Sam!" His footsteps traveled the upstairs hall to the guest room. After a moment of silence, he came back at a run. "She was here and had a shower, but she's gone too!"

Ukiah hunted weakly through his clothes for mice as Max unlocked the gun safe and pulled on a shoulder holster.

"What happened?" he cried at the first mouse he grabbed. "Where's Sam? Who took Kittanning? What happened?"

Flashes of recall from the mouse's perspective. Sam standing over him, giant tall, still wet from the shower, her gun thundering. Sam paused at the door, looking back at his body.

"Sam shot at whoever took Kittanning. She ran out after them."

Max swore, "We need to find them."

Ukiah reached out and found Bear ranging at the edge of his awareness. *"Bear! I need you! Call the others!"* Bear acknowledged the summons as he muscled his bike into a tight circle. "Bear is coming. He can track Sam. The others are coming."

"Why the hell weren't they here before this? I thought they kept an eye on you and Kitt."

"I told them to keep their distance because of Hutchinson."

Max spat a swear word. Bear's motorcycle rumbled up outside. Ukiah swept a hand across the bloodstained wood floor and found a single hair from Sam.

"Here, give this to Bear. Go. I'll catch up with you."

"Shit!" Max wavered at the door, obviously torn.

"Go!" Ukiah shouted at him.

Max went.

"Take good care of him," Ukiah told Bear.

"I'll keep him safe," Bear promised.

Alone, he took inventory of himself. Caught in the narrow hallway, he'd been hit by three bullets. The first struck him high in the left collar bone, shattering the bone, which deflected the bullet back out of his body. The bone shards grated together when he tried to move his left arm, giving out jagged peaks of pain to accompany a continuous low throbbing agony. The bullet must have turned him with its force; the second bullet tore a path through his body, right to left. Entering just under his ribs, it missed his lungs, but clipped a major artery. It was the cause of his death as his body shut down, trying to keep from pumping out his lifeblood. A delicate web of protein now held together all the jagged edges, keeping his precious fluids in, but just barely. He had to move carefully or risk tearing the patches open.

The third bullet nearly missed him altogether, cutting a thin gouge across his back.

Wincing at the pain that the movement triggered, he pulled his phone out of his pocket and selected Indigo's number. As he lifted it to his ear, motes of blackness appeared on the edges of his vision and cascaded in, drowning him in darkness.

"Special Agent Zheng." Her voice came out of the darkness. She was in a crowded place, voices murmuring all around her.

"Indigo." He slid down the wall so his hand was level with

his heart, not above it. Slowly light filtered back in until he looked up at the ceiling. "Someone just kidnapped Kitt. They shot me and took him."

In the silence from Indigo that followed, he heard her friend and co-worker, Agent Joan Fisher, say, "Indigo, what's wrong?"

"How hurt are you?"

"Extremely. I've got mice everywhere." Safe code words for *I was dead, I don't remember what happened.* "Sam's on foot somewhere in Shadyside chasing after the kidnappers. Max and Bear just left to find her."

"I'll put out an APB indicating that's she's chasing kidnappers and should be assisted." She snapped her fingers, and Agent Fisher murmured something about a pen. "Female. Blond. Height? Weight?" Ukiah supplied them. "Any idea what she's wearing?"

Ukiah picked up the nearest mouse and checked the memories that it held. "A T-shirt and underwear. And a gun."

With a rustle of paper, Indigo handed off the description to Fisher, who said, "Well, that will make her easy to spot. I'm on it!"

There was a change in background noise as Indigo changed rooms or shut a door. "Where are you? Are you safe?"

"I'm at the office." He told her as Rennie's presence rolled into his awareness like a thunderstorm. "Rennie is almost here."

"I hate to admit how reassuring that sounded." Her revolver clicked distinctly as she checked it. "Call me when you remember anything about the kidnapper."

"Will do."

"I love you. Be safe," she commanded, and hung up.

After fumbling his phone back into his pocket, he concentrated on getting up without fainting. He actually had managed to stand, leaning against the wall, when Rennie stormed in the front door. The leader of the Dog Warriors wore his duster and a shotgun slung by his side like a sword, cloaked by long folds of black leather. In his left hand he held a Dog Warrior clan jacket. Rennie pressed a callused palm to

Ukiah's chilled face, rage and concern fighting for control of his features. "You were dead."

Ukiah tried to push away his hand, but Rennie only tightened his hold. "The bastard took Kittanning. Walked in, shot me, and took my son."

Rennie turned Ukiah's chin, exposing the mice hiding in his hair. "You remember anything?"

"No."

Releasing his chin, Rennie gingerly lifted Ukiah's T-shirt to eye his wounds. "These were made by a forty-five caliber. One. Two. Three." He counted the holes in Ukiah, and then scanned the hall. "Four. Five. Six. Seven. Eight. Nine." He fingered two of the shells lying on the ground. "He emptied his gun. Your partner's love, Sam, shot once." He went to the door, crouched, and lightly touched a spot of blood glistening bright red on the sill. "She hit him. White man, middle age, blond hair."

"Ontongard?"

"No."

"Why would a human take Kittanning?"

"I don't know, Cub." Rennie came back to Ukiah as more of the Pack arrived, their bikes growling their anger. "But I should get you away from here quickly, in case your neighbors have called the police. There are too many bullets and too much blood for them to overlook." Rennie held out the leather jacket. "Here, put this on. You've got an obvious entrance and exit wound. Anyone with the imagination of a doorknob can guess you shouldn't be up and walking."

"I'm not anywhere near walking," Ukiah growled, angry at his own helplessness.

Mom Jo laughingly called the Hummer Max's G.I. Joe car, but in truth, it was his war paint. It masked Max's fear, called up the spirits of those who fought beside him in the Gulf War, and announced his intention to the world: *I am a warrior seeking vengeance; get out of my way.* With Ukiah shot, Kittanning taken, and Sam missing, it came as no surprise to Ukiah that Max had taken the Hummer.

Rennie helped Ukiah out to the garage, pausing on their

way through the kitchen long enough to empty the emergency stash of power bars. Rennie got Ukiah into the passenger side of the Cherokee, and slid in behind the wheel. The car smelled of baby powder.

The Pack raced out in front of them, their minds linking together into one great hunting beast. Bear had tracked Sam on foot through a zigzag course; apparently the kidnappers had tried to lose her by turning at every possible corner, hampered by the rush-hour traffic. Abandoning that strategy, the kidnappers then turned down Morewood Avenue to Baum Boulevard.

"She's cut her left foot on a piece of metal," Bear reported at the distant intersection as Rennie hit Baum half a mile down. *"She's leaving a blood trail."*

Rennie slid down the windows, and under the smell of hot pavement and exhaust, they caught the scent of blood. *"We're on it."*

Thus they beat Max to Sam.

Baum Boulevard cut a rare straight line along well-to-do Shadyside and into the poor neighborhood of East Liberty. At the end, Baum collided with Penn Circle, changing names and continuing straight another block before ending, as Penn Avenue took traffic on a dogleg turn before shooting off toward Wilkinsburg. Sam's trail led down Penn as far as the busway, and then suddenly veered across the street and into a bar called Aces and Eights.

Rennie slammed the Cherokee to a stop in front of the bar, sprang out of the SUV, and went snarling through the door. Ukiah stumbled along in his wake. The bar was a narrow, dark, smoky cave of a room, inexplicably crowded, a shock to Ukiah's senses. A wall-size menu of beers explained the countless varieties of smells that hit him. Pirates baseball played on the TV screen, generating roars from the men packed around the bar and milling between the crammed tables. In the back corner was a doorway, leading to a dining room.

Sam's voice came from a back room, loud and hoarse. "If you haven't noticed, this is a fully loaded, semiautomatic nine-millimeter pistol and I'm very pissed off. Unless you want your balls blown into the next county, fuck off!"

Rennie had checked just inside the door, orienting himself. He exploded into movement now. Ukiah had never seen Pack fight normal men before. It was like watching a wolf tear through a display of rag dolls. Heavily muscled men swung at Rennie, only to strike at thin air. Rennie struck back, iron hard, lightning fast, and deadly accurate. Those that didn't get out of his way fast enough were flung through the air, landing behind the bar, through the window, behind tables. After Rennie mauled through the bar patrons, the rest of the Dog Warriors poured through the shattered windows and pinned the hapless prone men, making sure they stayed down.

The last man already had his hands up in the air, surrendering to an armed and pissed off Sam.

Rennie stalked forward, drawing his knife, murder on his mind.

"Rennie! No!"

Sam fired at Rennie's feet, the crack of her bullet making the Dog Warriors tuck themselves behind hard cover, pulling weapons out.

"I'm on the phone!" Sam snapped, her pistol still aimed at the Pack leader. "Keep the noise down!"

"Damn it, woman, that's a good way to get shot," Rennie growled.

Sam just glared at him and told the person on the phone, "Yes, that was gunfire! No, I'm not in danger. I told you to get on your fucking radio and call it in! They're getting away! They took the baby down a limited access road just across the street from where I'm standing. No! I don't know the name of the road!"

"It's the busway," Ukiah told her, pushing past Rennie. The Pack leader was already directing scouts out to scour the limited access road.

She made a surprised, choked sound and dropped the phone to reach out to Ukiah. "Kid! Oh, shit!" She pulled him into a painful hug. "I thought you were dead—again—oh, damn, I forgot about your weirdness."

"It's okay," Ukiah said. "I'm fine. They went down the busway? What kind of car was it?"

"Yeah. Where the buses were coming up." Sam freed Ukiah to slump against the bar's back wall, the fight draining out of her. "A Ford Taurus, white, fairly new. The license plate was CBC 3002. I put a bullet into the back window. I didn't see the kidnappers themselves, except for one guy's back."

And the Dog Warriors surged away en masse, relaying her information to the forerunners. Ukiah wavered in place, wanting to go, but reluctant to leave Sam hurt and alone. Max appeared, pushing his way into the bar against the sudden outflow of Dog Warriors.

"Max, can you take care of Sam?" Ukiah pointed at the bloody footprints on the bar's industrial tile floor. "She's hurt!"

"And you're not?" Sam snarled.

"How bad are you cut?" Max asked her.

"I don't know." Sam lifted her left foot and displayed a bloody, grit-filled wound. She swore at the sight.

"I'll take care of her," Max said. "Ukiah, get out of here before the police come or they'll be dragging you to the hospital too."

"I can take care of myself," Sam said.

"You're hurt. You're half-naked." Max put an arm around her, encouraging her to lean on him so he could get her out to the Hummer and its first-aid kit. "You've got a gun but no carry permit or ID. And there's the trashed bar complete with unconscious men. Even if you weren't hurt, I wouldn't walk away and leave you to deal with that alone."

Sam deflated. "Add totally lost and you've hit it pretty good."

"I'll call you if we find anything." Ukiah started for the Cherokee.

"Wait!" Max caught Ukiah by the arm, and tucked a tracer into his pants pocket. "Okay. Go. Find Kitt. And keep yourself safe."

"I'll keep him safe," Rennie promised. "Anyone trying for him will have to go through me first."

"Let's go," Ukiah said.

"The busway goes downtown or out to Wilkinsburg." Rennie half carried Ukiah back to the Cherokee. "Which way do we go?"

Downtown would have dropped the kidnappers beside I-279 or I-376, rushing away from Pittsburgh in two and three lanes of express traffic. Nearby Wilkinsburg was one of the poorer neighborhoods in Pittsburgh, providing countless nooks and crannies to dive into. The Pack had the advantage, though, that if they got close enough to Kittanning, they would sense his presence.

"Downtown," Ukiah decided. If the kidnappers had buried themselves in Wilkinsburg, then the Pack would dig them out. But if the kidnappers had headed downtown, every second made it less likely he would find Kittanning.

So he and Rennie followed the busway toward downtown, the walls of the road rising up, crowned with chain-linked fencing, guaranteeing that the kidnapper hadn't veered off it, nor abandoned his car.

Ukiah shared two of the power bars out to his hungry mice. He was too hurt to take the mice back; the lost blood cells had expended all their stored energy taking mouse form, and at the moment, the effort of merging the cells back into his body would kill him. He'd have to wait, building up both his own and the mice's strength before he could take them back and discover what he'd forgotten. The mice took their share of the food and scrambled to the dashboard to stare out the window shield, looking for their lost brother.

"Do you think that the Ontongard might have finally gotten smart enough to use a human to take Kittanning?" Ukiah asked.

"Hex would never trust a human."

Hex wouldn't, but Hex was dead.

Nine of the Pack roared through downtown, bullying their way through the heavy rush-hour traffic, looking for any sign of Kittanning or the Taurus. Their reports trickled in even as Rennie reached the end of the busway and nosed out into the stalled traffic.

"There's an accident in the Liberty Tunnels; no one's get-

ting out of the city that way." Hellena made a U-turn at the mouth of the tunnels to work her way back into town. *"The parkway looks like a parking lot."*

Confirmation came from Smack working his way through the parkway congestion, riding the centerline since there was no berm.

"Everything's crawling as far as Greentree on two-seventy-nine south," Heathyr reported, nearly a whisper, at the limits of the Pack's telepathic range. Unfortunately, that range depended on number of body cells; Kittanning's smaller size meant his reach was much shorter.

"North Side, South Side, West End," Rennie named the possible directions that the kidnapper could have gone as the Dog Warrior narrowed down possibilities. "Two-seventy-nine north."

"Two-seventy-nine," Ukiah decided after a moment. "A quick run as far as the turnpike in Cranberry. If we don't pick up Kitt's trail, we'll double back and start combing the suburbs."

The food kicked in and Ukiah slept without warning.

He had been scanning the cars they passed, and then he was asleep. The deep echoing horns of tugboats woke him. Ukiah opened his eyes to find himself reclined nearly flat in the bucket seat. Headlights from an oncoming car cut through the dark Cherokee's interior. For a minute he lay confused. Where was he? A faint scrabbling noise caught his attention, and he turned his head to look into five pairs of tiny anxious black eyes.

Kittanning.

He levered himself up, feeling guilty, herding his mice into his lap. "Any sign?"

"None," Rennie murmured.

They were running along one of the rivers on a desolate stretch of road that Ukiah didn't recognize. Ukiah glanced at the mileage counter and noted that they had put several hundred miles on the Cherokee, endlessly driving through the side roads and back alleys, working their way through the dozens of Pittsburgh's neighborhoods. "This random looking isn't working. We missed the chance while I was dead, and now we're running like a chicken with its head cut off."

Rennie growled softly. "What else is there? Hex has had since June to lay his plans, and the humans can sense neither his Gets nor Kittanning."

"There were several kidnappings in the area while you and I were in Oregon." Ukiah's stomach rumbled with hunger, emptied by his body's frantic healing of itself. "The MO on Kitt's kidnapping is nearly the same: two people working together grab a kid out of his home and run. Indigo is the agent assigned to the case. She can tell us details on the other cases and maybe that will give us a lead."

Grudgingly, Rennie considered possibilities other than the Ontongard. "What about that federal agent?"

"Hutchinson?" Ukiah thought about what the federal agent had said, and what he hadn't said. "He said this cult of religious lunatics called the Temple of New Reason had photographs of me, implying that they had some interest in me. The Temple's Web site was full of biblical verses about the second coming. Hutchinson is looking for the cult; they've gone into deep cover for some reason."

Reluctantly, Rennie conceded. "But you can't go back to your offices looking like that." Rennie turned the Cherokee in a tight U-turn. "With the bloody mess you left behind, any cops you run into will probably want to see what you look like under the jacket. You need to clean up first."

Neville Island was a few miles downriver of Pittsburgh, a long strip of land in the center of the Ohio River, home to numerous industrial sites. Storage tanks that dwarfed many Pittsburgh skyscrapers sat at the head of the island, and I-79 leapfrogged across the river at its center. The ethereal flame that burned over Neville Island licked the night sky.

The Pack had taken over the office area of an abandoned Dravo Barge dry docks, replacing a padlock on the chain-link gate with one of their own. Rennie had sent Smack on ahead, so the gate was open when they reached it.

"He needs to be bandaged," Rennie told Smack as the Dog

Warrior helped Ukiah out of the Cherokee. "The less notice-able his wounds, the better. I'll be back."

Whoever had pulled den duty had swept out the offices and pinned up the tapestry dividers, but the futons still sat stacked by the door. Ukiah wandered about the empty space, wanting to sit down before trying to take off his bloody clothes. Smack produced a folding chair, and then worked at setting up a washbasin with hot water. Ukiah carefully lowered himself onto the chair. Trembling, he plucked at his shirt; there didn't seem to be a method of getting it off that didn't involve flex-ing in some painful way, and parts of it were stuck to him.

"Here. That's past saving." Smack pulled out his boot knife and cut off the T-shirt in sections, leaving what was stuck to the healing wounds. The blade sliced through the blood-crusted fabric like tissue paper. "We'll have to soak the scabs to get the rest off. You don't have a knife or gun on you?" Smack slipped the blade back into its sheath and then pulled the sheath from his boot. "Take this one. I'll pick up another one tomorrow."

Ukiah didn't argue; if he had been armed, perhaps he could have stopped the kidnapper.

Rennie returned as they washed the last of the dead blood cells out of Ukiah's hair; all of Ukiah's clothes except his boots had been reduced down to strips of bloody cloth lying on the wet floor around him. The Pack leader growled at the damage done to Ukiah and held out a bag of McDonald's food. "Eat, and then take back your mice. See what they can tell you about the kidnapping. We'll find your little one," Rennie promised darkly. "And we'll make this man sorry he ever thought to lift a hand against either of you."

CHAPTER SEVEN

Dravo Barge Dry Docks, Neville Island, Pennsylvania
Tuesday, September 14, 2004

After Ukiah had eaten, absorbed his mice, and given both Rennie and Smack a full replay of the shooting, he climbed painfully into the Cherokee. Rennie slid behind the wheel to drive Ukiah back to the office, while Smack locked up the gate behind them.

Unsure of how things stood with Indigo, Max, and Sam, Ukiah checked the company's voice-mail system. Max had guessed that the Pack would feed Ukiah and let him sleep; instead of calling Ukiah directly, he'd left a series of messages in a tight, harassed-sounding voice.

Sam's wound proved to be deep enough for stitches. The police, though, had arrived, responding to Sam's 911 call, and needed to be dealt with first. Luckily there was no one conscious to connect the private investigators to the "untimely coincidence" of the Pack's trashing of the bar.

After giving statements on Kittanning's kidnapping, Max and Sam drove back to the office for Sam's clothes and ID. There, they ran into a second mess. Neighbors had reported Sam's single gunshot and police found an empty house with a foyer full of bullet holes and blood. With a lack of a gunshot victim, the questioning grew decidedly hostile. Then Indigo arrived with her FBI team, full of icy rage, and found a volunteer to focus her frustrations on.

"One of the cops made the mistake of asking if she was

'the F-B-I' and smirking." The police had used the initials to nickname Indigo "the Famous Bitch of Ice" in reference to her glacial calm. "You'd think by now the cops would know not to piss her off. It was like watching a surgeon work as she took him apart—very quiet and precise. Sam's impressed, and I think a little afraid of Indigo now." Max summed up the meeting of the two women.

Like the Pack, Indigo stayed only long enough to get the make and model of the car; she left to personally lead the search. Agent Joan Fisher remained behind to get a full statement and fight skirmishes over jurisdictions.

During everything, Max and Sam kept to the edited version of the truth; someone had shot "at" Ukiah and taken Kittanning. No, they didn't know how badly Ukiah had been hurt, but he had left in the Cherokee to find his missing son. Max neglected to mention that Ukiah had his phone on him; Max didn't want the police pestering Ukiah while he was sleeping. "At least that's what I'm hoping you're doing right now."

Finally, Max drove Sam to the hospital to be stitched up, given a tetanus shot, and released. At the hospital, Max had thought to call Ukiah's moms and had given them an edited version of what had happened. "I left out the part about you being shot. I figured it would only worry them."

"We're heading back to the office," Max said in the last message. "Give me a call soon. I'm getting worried about you. If I don't hear from you soon, I'm heading out to look for you. I've called Chino to hold down the offices while Sam is sleeping."

Ukiah glanced at the dashboard clock as the voice mail gave the timestamp of nine-thirty; he had been listening to the messages when Max recorded the last one. He and Rennie were already downtown, meaning they would hit the office just minutes after Max and Sam returned.

Of Indigo, though, there was no word, so he called her.

She answered with a curt "Special Agent Zheng."

"It's me."

"Any good news?"

"No."

"I can't talk now. Have you gotten your mice back?"

"Yes, but there's not much to tell. I answered the door and got shot."

"Where are you?"

"Passing through downtown. We've just swung onto the Tenth Street Bypass. We're heading to the office."

"I'll meet you there."

The Hummer, its engine still ticking, was in its place in the garage when Rennie pulled into the second bay.

Rennie cocked his head, catching the murmur of voices from the mansion. *"Your partner has company."*

"Stay here," Ukiah said, in case it was the police.

The back door of the mansion was unlocked and opened to the smell of old blood, gunpowder, and spilt milk. The kitchen was dark. Like a cave opening to daylight, the unlit hallway led to the brightly lit living room, which doubled as the office's reception area. Sam sat in the wing chair by the fireplace, her bandaged bare foot propped on the ottoman, talking to someone standing out of sight. Max paced the room, wrapped in anger. Ukiah paused in the dark kitchen, nostrils flaring to catch the stranger's scent.

"I've already told both the police and the FBI what happened," Sam was saying. "And I only saw the back of the kidnapper's head, so I don't know if he was one of these people or not."

The interloper was Hutchinson, sitting in the second wing chair. "Please, just tell me what happened."

He reported the visitor's identity to Rennie while stripping off the Dog Warrior jacket, glad now that Smack had cleaned the blood from him. He hung the incriminating jacket on a kitchen chair and moved quietly to the living room's door. Stealth came to him as natural as breathing. Hutchinson was focused on Sam, who glared angrily back at the federal agent. Only Max seemed aware that Ukiah had entered the offices, giving him a hopeful look, so that he had to shake his head, *no, no, they hadn't found Kittanning*. Max gathered his rage closer.

"The doorbell rang just as I turned off the water," Sam continued without noticing Ukiah's exchange with Max. "The baby started to scream, and I yanked on a T-shirt, some underwear, and found my gun."

"Just because the baby was crying?" Hutchinson asked.

"Screaming," Sam said. "I don't know why but it just hit me at gut level, and I reacted. The only reason I got any clothes on at all was I didn't want to flash Ukiah if it just turned out his son regularly screamed like someone was killing him."

"Go on."

"I heard a heavy thud, the kind you hear when heavy furniture tips over or a person falls, and someone running through the downstairs, and the baby screaming," Sam said. "When I say it, it seems so sane, but it was really creepy, like listening to a soundtrack for a horror film. I ran down the back steps and into the kitchen as someone ran out the front door with the baby."

"Why the back steps?" Hutchinson indicated the sweeping front stairs. "You might have been able to stop them if you had gone down the front staircase."

"I don't know the layout of the house. I just drove in from Oregon this morning. I wanted to go downstairs, and the back steps were right outside the bedroom door."

"You didn't hear shots?" Hutchinson asked.

"No. The shooter must have been using a silencer. When I got to the kitchen I could see Ukiah lying in the hall and someone running out the door, carrying the baby. I shot once at the kidnapper, and I think I hit him, but he kept on moving. There was a car waiting at the curb. He got in the car and it drove away. I chased after the car but I couldn't keep up with it."

"Where was the kidnapper when you hit him?"

"On the front porch."

"So all the blood in the hall, that's Ukiah's?"

"I suppose so," Sam said.

"If you came down the back steps and went to the front door, you had to step over Ukiah. Didn't you notice he was bleeding?"

"I noticed."

"Did he say anything? Tell you who shot him?"

"He wasn't conscious at the time," Sam said.

"Did you stop and check how badly he was hurt?"

"He was okay when I saw him later."

"He was unconscious and bleeding and you didn't check on him?"

"Leave her alone," Max snapped.

Hutchinson glanced up to retort, saw Ukiah standing beside Max, and straightened. "Where the hell have you been?"

Ukiah growled, glaring at Hutchinson through his dark bangs.

"I told you," Max said. "He was out looking for his son."

Hutchinson took out a pack of cigarettes, tapped one out, and lit it. His attention stayed on Ukiah, the gears in his mind spinning behind his watchful eyes. "Some of the bullets they took out of the wall had passed through a body first."

Ukiah lifted the bottom of his shirt to show the white of his bandages. "None of them hit anything important."

"Do you know who it was that shot you?"

"I saw him." He had taken back his mice before leaving Neville Island; while slightly fuzzy in quality, like viewing through a hazed window, his memories were complete. "I didn't recognize him."

The front door opened then. Ukiah had been focused on Hutchinson and had missed the person's approach. The swing of the door, however, brought him Indigo's scent. She checked at the door, hand still on the doorknob at the sight of Hutchinson.

"Who are you?" A half octave lower than normal, her voice sounded so hard and authoritarian that Ukiah barely recognized it as hers.

Hutchinson startled, looking to Max and Ukiah in surprise. "I'm wondering the same thing. Who are you?"

"This is Agent Hutchinson," Ukiah told her. "Homeland Security."

"Can I see some ID?" Indigo held out her hand.

"Who are you?" he said, handing her his ID.

Indigo inspected it a moment before returning it. "Special Agent Indigo Zheng, FBI." She showed him her ID. "This is an FBI case."

"The NSA believes that this kidnapping might be related to a case that we're investigating."

"The Temple of New Reason?" Indigo said. "From what I've been able to gather, there's no connection between the kidnapping and their interest in Mr. Oregon."

Surprise flashed over Hutchinson's face and he glanced to Max before smoothing his features back to neutral. Still, under the careful facade, he showed signs of being disturbed by Indigo's foreknowledge. "I see. Have you received cooperation files?"

"There hasn't been time," Indigo said.

Hutchinson turned back to Ukiah. "Counting the three bullets that went through you, and the six in the wall, the shooter emptied his gun at you. That's a little excessive. Are you sure you don't know him, Mr. Oregon?"

"I would remember. It's part of having a perfect memory."

"And yet two days after you've returned from an out-of-state trip, this stranger nails you and takes your kid." Hutchinson reached into his jacket and took out an envelope filled with photographs. He dealt the top four onto the coffee table. "Are these photos of you with your son?"

The photographs were taken the day of the shoot-out with the Ontongard. Kittanning, wrapped in Ukiah's black tracking T-shirt, was merely a dark shapeless bundle, identifiable as a baby only by Ukiah's body language. In the first picture, Ukiah had his son tucked in the crook of his arm. In the second photo, he started the careful transfer of Kittanning to his shoulder, still stunned and awkward by his sudden fatherhood. In the third and fourth photo, he settled Kittanning on his shoulder, carefully protecting the wobbly head and tiny body.

"Where did these come from?" Ukiah said.

"The five I showed you earlier was just a selection of those we found on the cult member. There are nearly three hundred in all showing either you or your partner. Is this your son?"

"Yes." Ukiah felt sick. The Ontongard in Pendleton hadn't known that Hex found him and made Kittanning. Did this mean another group knew that Ukiah and Kittanning existed but hadn't known where to find him? Why not take them both while Ukiah was helpless? Why use a human in the first place?

He realized that Hutchinson was speaking and ran back through his memory to catch up with the conversation. Hutchinson was pointing out that Ukiah's personal information all indicated that he lived here at the offices, not out at the farm with his moms. Someone looking for Kittanning would have had to wait until Ukiah returned from Oregon before knowing where to find the baby.

"That's a possibility," Indigo said. "Kittanning, though, is not the only child kidnapped. The kidnappers have taken four other children. The first was August twenty-fifth, the second was August twenty-ninth, the third was September second, and the fourth was September sixth. Two boys, two girls, all under the age of eighteen months."

Hutchinson took out his PDA and took notes as Indigo spoke. "And the MO is the same as this case?"

"Yes. The kidnappers steal a car. They change license plates with another car of the same model and color as the stolen car to muddy the waters. We think they spend a day or two stalking their next victim until an opportunity arrives to snatch the child. They then abandon the car at a parking garage, apparently after transferring the child to a new car or location. We've managed to lift several sets of fingerprints from all the cars, but so far they're not in the national database."

"The other children—weren't they in foster care? Kittanning doesn't fit the profile. This could be a copycat crime."

Indigo shook her head. "In all the previously recovered cars, forensics has found aged plaster in the floor mats, all from the same house. We've recovered the car used in Kittanning's kidnapping and found traces of the same plaster on the floor mats."

"You've recovered the car!" Ukiah cried.

"Yes." Indigo's sigh indicated that the find held no leads. "We assumed that they would follow normal MO and abandon the car in a parking lot. We contacted all lot owners, and it was reported in two hours ago."

"We have some fingerprints on file of suspected cult members; not all of them have been entered into the national database," Hutchinson offered. "We could cross-reference them."

"We will." Indigo turned to Ukiah. "You remember the shooter?"

Ukiah nodded. "White male. About six-two. Two hundred pounds. Graying mousy blond hair. Gray eyes. Lots of pockmarks on his face. Late twenties or early thirties." He dredged out the clothing information. "He had a shoulder holster, under the jacket. A forty-five with a silencer. He had a prison tattoo on his right arm. I saw it when he lifted his hand and his jacket rode up. It was a snake or a dragon done in blue, twining up his arm."

Indigo noted it down. "It matches the descriptions from the other cases, just a lot more detailed. Did you see the driver?"

Ukiah closed his eyes and carefully stepped through the memory. It was like flipping through photographs, only far more detailed. He opened the door and the man stood there, his nervous sweat now a glaring sign of things to come. Yes, and there was the scent of gunmetal, begging to be noticed. Ukiah changed the focus now, past the front porch to the street below. Mom Jo explained once that the human eye took in a room not in a single steady study, but a thousand seemingly random focus points that merged in the subconscious to make up a single impression. Most people couldn't separate out the individual points and sharpen in on those, but he could.

The white Taurus sat at the curb, presenting its flank, engines idling, the driver looking toward him. "The driver was a girl, white, blond, medium build. She's young, I would say she's only sixteen or seventeen, if that."

The car and the girl seemed familiar. Indigo said that the two kidnappers would stalk their victims, so he cast back through his recent memories for either one. He found the car in his memories of Monday— it had nearly back-ended him as he jockeyed through the Squirrel Hill traffic on Murray Avenue. Through glimpses in his mirror, and casual scans of the parking lot later, he watched as it pulled into the Giant Eagle's parking lot, found a space on the other side of the lot, and pulled facing him.

"They were following me yesterday. They parked, and he followed me into the Giant Eagle."

"I'm surprised they didn't try to take him there," Indigo noted. "Two of the kidnappings were in stores."

Ukiah remembered the cantaloupe woman, her fearful reaction to Rennie. She nearly had it right, only Rennie beat the real kidnappers to the punch. "I ran into some friends; they were buying food for a cookout. We shopped together. There was a lot of them, and some of them were armed."

Hutchinson looked surprised at this news. Indigo noted something down, presumably nothing that directly mentioned the Pack. Unease crept into her face.

"If they followed you to the store," she asked, "were they here earlier, say around noon, watching the office?"

When Indigo visited.

Ukiah scanned the street as they stood outside saying good-bye, Kittanning warm in his arms. "Yes."

"Were you armed when you went to Giant Eagle?"

"Yes."

"Here's a theory," Indigo said. "They stalk you and notice that you and your friends go armed. They deem it too dangerous to do their normal snatch and run, but decide to eliminate anyone armed prior to taking Kittanning."

Ukiah blanched, ticking through his mind all the possible people that might have answered the door instead of him. Max. Sam. Indigo. He started to growl in anger again.

"Are you up to coming downtown," Indigo asked, "to work with a police artist and look through the mug books?"

Ukiah nodded. "Let me get something warmer on. I'm still a little shocky from being shot."

Max and Indigo exchanged looks. Indigo asked *make sure he's okay* without speaking, and Max answered with a nod and a reassuring touch to her shoulder.

"I want to change too," Max said. "Give us a couple of minutes," he said to the federal agents, "and we'll follow you downtown."

As Ukiah started wearily up the steps, their part-time investigator, Chino, opened the door and came in. Max must have briefed him because Chino eyed Hutchinson with open suspicion. After a quick introduction to the federal agent, Chino helped Max get Sam upstairs to the guest bedroom. They got her settled while Ukiah peeled off his borrowed T-shirt and pulled on one of his black tracking T-shirts. It felt more comforting to have its familiar darkness press against his skin; the other shirt had been a constant reminder that a stranger had dealt him violent death and taken Kittanning.

Max came in as Ukiah pulled a sweatshirt out of his closet. "Hold on a sec." He pulled up Ukiah's T-shirt to check his bandages. He caught Ukiah's puzzled look and said, "I want to make sure all the holes are covered. I'm amazed those idiots even have bandages."

Idiots? Oh, the Dog Warriors. Ukiah was puzzled by Max's bitterness until he remembered the mess at the bar. "Were any of the men at the bar hurt?" And realizing that was a stupid question, he added, "Badly?"

"Some broken bones and mild concussions. Luckily nothing more serious, but it put us on the map again with the Pack. Right now we're considered businessmen in the same league as ambulance companies; we have a good reason to be at the scene of a crime without being considered responsible for it. This keeps up, and we're going to gain the reputation of troublemakers."

"I'm sorry, Max."

Max winced. "I shouldn't be chewing you out. We don't have time for it. I'm just generally pissed, that's all. We had to admit that you were at the bar, but you left alone. I've called and left messages on your phone. You've been out looking, no help from the Pack mentioned."

"Okay. We need to find out what we can on this cult. Hutchinson might be right. They had those photographs of me for some reason."

Max nodded. "Keep your mouth shut around him as much as you can, though, kid. If that cult is now Ontongard, and that's what Hutchinson is really poking his nose into, it's best you stay as far away from him as you can."

"If it is the Ontongard, we should warn him." Ukiah moved to pull on the gray sweatshirt. "Somehow."

"We'll figure that out if the need arises." Max plucked the

sweatshirt from his hands, adding, "No, not that one." Max flashed the PROPERTY OF THE FBI stenciled onto the front. "If Indigo is going to stay on this case, you can't be reminding people how personally involved she is." Max pulled out a white sweater. "This one. It's good for the innocent victim look."

Max went to change.

Ukiah's sensitive ears caught Hutchinson saying to Indigo downstairs, "I know it's not my place to say this, but you're setting yourself up to be hurt."

"What do you mean?" Indigo said after a shocked moment of silence.

"He might seem like any other man, but they're different from the rest of us. Nobody is going to look at the two of you and think that you're together for love. And in the end, that just tears you apart."

Did Hutchinson know that he wasn't human? Ukiah walked to the balcony to look down into the foyer.

Indigo stood with her arms crossed, the events of the day showing by the fact she was telegraphing her irritation. "I don't know what you're talking about."

"Cut me some slack." Hutchinson laughed, disbelieving, mockingly. "You walk in like you own the place, and you don't need to introduce yourself, or be introduced. It's obvious. And I'm just saying that it won't work, and you're just going to get hurt. Fed to fed; we take care of our own."

"Do you want to keep talking in code, or are you going to actually try to say something that makes sense?"

"Look, I've been there. I worked at a yacht club on weekends to help pay for college. And I made the mistake of falling in love with one of them. How can you resist? They're sleek, all defects surgically corrected, wearing stylish fashions and all so self-assured. The rest of the world is frumpy in comparison. The problem is that if you're not one of the breed, then you're a grasping social climber, just out to use them."

"You think I'm dating Max?" Indigo asked carefully.

It was nearly funny to see Hutchinson realize that he misstepped. "You're not?" He noticed Ukiah coming slowly

down the steps. "Oh!" And then the realization of her connection to Kittanning tripped in. "Oh! I'm sorry."

With the proverbial cat out of the bag, Ukiah put out his
hand to Indigo. She clasped it tightly.

"I'd rather not talk about this," Indigo said quietly.

Hutchinson nodded, his eyes narrowing. Whatever he
thought, he kept to himself. "I'll meet you downtown."

"Thank you," Indigo said.

Ukiah and Indigo held each other, offering comfort, seeking comfort, but there was no real peace to be had, not with
Kittanning gone.

Max came trotting down the steps, slowing as he saw them
together and Hutchinson missing from the foyer. "Did I miss
something?"

"Nothing," Ukiah growled.

"Hutchinson thought I was dating you." Indigo smiled
slightly. "He was warning me off; apparently a rich girl
dumped him, so he didn't want me hurt the same way."

"Dating me? What made him . . . ?" Max trailed off, snap-
ping his fingers. "Rich girl!" Max ducked into his office,
sorted through folders, opened one, and flipped through the
paper within until he found what he was looking for. He
scanned the paper, swearing softly. "Oh, kid, sometimes I
wish I had your memory." He handed a single sheet of paper
to Ukiah, saying, "I can't believe I didn't make the connection
until now. All I remembered was Hutchinson was going to
marry someone rich. This explains a lot."

It was a print off of a *New York Times* on-line article.
"Boston Debutante to Wed," it stated. "John Adams and Car-
oline Woods Whillet (of Dover, MA) announced the engagement of their daughter, Christina Amelia Whillet, to Grant
Charles Hutchinson (of Boston), son of Steven and Mary
Helen Hutchinson of Glouster. Christina is a graduate of Harvard and the honorary chairperson of the Make-a-Wish Foundation. Grant is a graduate of Boston University, cum laude,
and works in Washington, D.C. The couple plans a June wed-
ding next year at Martha's Vineyard and a honeymoon on the
Whillets' yacht."

The accompanying photograph was of Hutchinson and

Christina, formally dressed and rigidly posed. Knowing Hutchinson's height, the picture put the earlier photograph of Christina into scale; she was a very small woman, which made her look younger than her twenty-two years of age.

Ukiah checked the date. "They would have been married two months ago if she hadn't joined the cult."

"I wonder if he's gone rogue," Indigo said. "He could be on vacation and using his federal ID to carry on his investigation. If so, he could make a complete mess of this kidnapping."

"Well, at least you don't have to worry about him reporting that you have a possible conflict of interest."

At the police station, Ukiah gave his statement on his shooting and Kittanning's kidnapping. After he sat through an artist sketch session to produce pictures of both the male shooter and the female driver, they set him up with a computer running mug shots. He scanned them quickly, checking each face against those locked in to his memory. Females first, since there were fewer, and then the males. Neither face appeared in the computer files, or the old hardbound books.

Having exhausted what was open to the public, he quietly begged Indigo for information normally kept out of public hands. Her lips thinned as he talked.

"I can't have the Pack smashing their way through this case in a mad frenzy to find Kittanning," she said. "I want him found as much as you, but not at the cost of human life. Look at what they did today at that bar. A dozen men hospitalized because they happened to be between Sam and the Pack."

And it could have been worse if Sam hadn't stopped Rennie.

"I think I can control them if I have something to give them, focus their efforts. I'm not sure what they'll do if left to their own devices."

Anger flashed over her face. "Is that a threat?"

"No. It's just the truth, Indigo. The Pack is going to believe that Hex used a human to take Kittanning until proved otherwise. They'll do anything to get him back, kill anyone, and level this entire city to rubble, if that is what it takes. And it's not going to be just the Dog Warriors. If we don't find him quickly, Rennie will contact the other clans."

She sighed. "Fine. I'll make you a copy of the files. Try to keep the Pack away from the families of the other kidnapped children; they've suffered enough already."

"I will," he promised. "Can I examine the car?"

Indigo shook her head. "Forensics is still combing it."

"The plaster is distinctive enough that if you show me where the kidnappers left the car, I could track them."

"Most likely they drove to the parking lot in the stolen car, abandoned it, and got into a pickup car."

"They wouldn't want the pickup car to be seen close to the stolen car. It's possible that they left other evidence."

Indigo considered and slowly nodded. "Okay. Let's see what we can find."

The kidnappers had chosen their parking garage well. The sprawling warren under Gateway Center had multiple vehicle entrances and pedestrian exits. The automatic gate that let Indigo's car into the garage was unmonitored.

Max had followed them to the garage with the Hummer but didn't attempt to slot the extra-wide vehicle through the narrow, twisting passages. Instead, he stayed at street level, waiting for the hunt to work its way aboveground.

Indigo drove down the spiraling ramp to the third level, and then, ignoring multiple signs pointing out exits and lower levels, drove to an empty corner of the garage. Bits of yellow police tape marked where the car had been abandoned.

Indigo stopped the car. "Do you need more light? I can swing the car and put my headlights on the area."

"No. I see mostly with my hands."

She parked then in the opposite row, and they got out. The slamming of their car doors echoed through the heavy shadows.

Whereas Max usually either sat quietly, or did his own separate search for details his more experienced eye might pick up, Indigo watched him intently as he crept over the oil-stained cement, searching for the plaster dust. After five minutes, she started to pace.

"You can't find anything?" She broke her silence after ten minutes.

"Things have been muddied by the police." By walking over the kidnapper's footprints, the police created a swathe of dust-covered prints around the car. "Ah, here we go."

Some ten feet from the confusion around the car, Ukiah found a clear track finally. The plaster-dusted footprints headed off in a meandering trail across the parking garage. Now and again, he found microdots of kidnapper's blood, confirming that he was following the right man. On the far other side was a steel door protecting a stairwell.

"He went up the stairs."

Indigo eyed the stainless-steel doorknob. "We could dust the knob, but there's no way of knowing which of the countless people who used this last might have been the kidnapper."

Ukiah breathed deep, catching a faint familiar scent. He closed his eyes and focused on it. The metallic bite of blood drew him down, crouching, until he found the blood. "He touched this wall with a bloody hand. He must have opened the door with his right hand, and braced himself without thinking with his left."

"Perfect!"

The stairwell was lit with a harsh orange light and reeked of urine. The trail went upward three flights. He went slowly, ignoring everything to focus on the plaster and blood. Halfway up the second flight, the wounded kidnapper touched the wall again with the bloody hand. Ukiah pointed it out to Indigo and continued up the stairs. At the top of the steps, the kidnapper hadn't repeated his mistake with the heavy steel door.

The clear night air was a relief. Ukiah breathed deep to clear out the stench of urine and followed the ghost trail of the plaster to the curb.

A car must have been waiting for the kidnapper, for the trail ended there abruptly. Ukiah crouched there, on the edge of the sidewalk, scanning the buildings all around them. From cameras set up in ATMs to those hooked to the Internet, any city street had a chance of being under surveillance. Either the kidnappers had chosen the corner because of the lack of cameras, or they had just gotten lucky; there were none in sight.

Indigo called for a forensic team to lift the fingerprints they'd found so far.

Max had been slowly circling the block, waiting. He parked illegally and got out of the Hummer as Ukiah sifted through the grit lining the curb. "End of trail?"

"Yeah."

Max came and laid a hand on Ukiah's shoulder. "We'll find him."

Indigo exuded new energy when she returned from supervising the forensic team. "The kidnapper smudged up the print on the lowest level once he realized what he did, and he wiped down the doorknobs, but the print on the second flight is perfect. With the prison tattoo, and this much care in cleaning up the fingerprints, he has to be on file."

"One hopes," Max said. "Ukiah won't admit it, but he's about to crash." Ukiah gave Max a disgusted look. "Sleep, and tomorrow we'll nail this guy."

Ukiah opened his arms to Indigo and she stepped into his hug. "Call me as soon as you know anything."

"I will," she promised. "It will be a couple of hours to lift the print, get it processed, and pull files on this bastard. Go to the office and get some rest."

CHAPTER EIGHT

Bennett Detective Agency, Shadyside, Pennsylvania
Wednesday, September 15, 2004

The Dog Warriors invaded the office the next morning. Rennie found Ukiah asleep in his bed and shook him awake. Rennie and the Dog's presence conflicted with the familiarity of the office; Ukiah blinked at the Pack leader for a moment in confusion.

"What are you doing here?" Ukiah sat up and rubbed salt-laden sleep out of his eyes. His nightmares had been replays of Kittanning's kidnapping, and in his dreams, as he lay helpless on the floor, he wept.

"We need to talk." Rennie pushed a mug of hot cocoa into Ukiah's hands. "And you need to eat more before you're fully healed."

"I'm fine." Ukiah drank the cocoa. It had been made by heating whole milk to nearly scalding and stirring in as much sugar as the liquid would hold—a protein and carbohydrate shotgun.

Max appeared in the bedroom door, dressed only in sweatpants and shoulder holster, pistol in hand. He holstered his pistol, seeing Rennie. "What's up?"

"We need to pool resources," Rennie said. "We've scoured the area and found nothing so far."

Hellena was in the kitchen, the obvious source of the hot cocoa and the scent of fresh coffee; she studied maps of Pittsburgh and southwestern Pennsylvania spread out on the kitchen table. Smack and Heathyr guarded the back door; Ukiah could sense Bear and two others in the front foyer. The rest of the Dog Warriors orbited the mansion at a distance.

Max pulled the first-aid kit out of the front closet and set it on the counter. "Let's see how you're doing under the bandages."

Pulling up the bandage tapes was nearly as painful as getting shot, and longer in duration. Max frowned at the gaping exit wound. "You're not healed as much as I hoped."

"I just haven't eaten enough." Ukiah sorted through the box to pull out the largest pad. "I took a lot of soft tissue damage."

"He's pushed himself too hard to heal," Rennie stated, refilling Ukiah's cocoa. "He needs protein, and lots of sleep."

"I'm fine," Ukiah snapped. "Finding Kittanning is what matters."

"Yeah," Max said in a tone that meant that he agreed with Ukiah to a point, that being probably where Ukiah's own existence was in danger. Max squeezed out a half ounce of antibiotic to smear over the bruised raw wound. "Hold still. This is going to hurt."

It did, but not nearly as much as taking the tape off. Ukiah winced, and focused on shuffling through the maps. The problem was no one map would show all the areas involved in detail. He unfolded the Allegheny County map and placed it center on the table, and then arranged the maps from the counties surrounding it.

"What did your love tell you?" Rennie asked as Max finished bandaging the groove across Ukiah's back.

"General details," Ukiah admitted. "If this was an Ontongard case, Indigo would cooperate fully, but she doesn't want you rampaging over the case if it's just humans involved. She seems to think you'll hospitalize everyone remotely connected with the case."

"Perhaps," Rennie said. "They'll get better. Finding Kittanning is what is important."

Sam limped down the back steps. "Are we talking more of the guys as in Oregon?"

"It was a human that you winged yesterday," Rennie said. "Nor would it be likely that a Get would leave the cub."

Ukiah nodded. "He was still bleeding when they ditched the car downtown." He found the bag of plaster dust and handed it to Rennie. "This is the common link to all the kidnappings. It was on the kidnapper's shoes, heavy, like he'd walked through a lot of it."

Rennie opened the bag, and sampled the plaster dust. "I don't know the house." He scraped his finger clean and handed the bag to Hellena to pass among the others. "What do you know about the other children?"

"Indigo let me glance over the files. She'll make copies and get them to me later." Ukiah rooted through the drawer under the phone and found a multipack of colored self-stick flags. "There were four children kidnapped before Kittanning. Two boys and two girls, all under the age of one year old. All of the other children were in foster care, which, besides their age, was the only common denominator."

"First baby was Jonah, male, white, nine months old. His mother was found growing marijuana in her backyard in Penn Hills." He marked the approximate street address of the boy's home with a red flag. The FBI had already screened the neighbors; it was unlikely the Pack would find anything new but trouble. He scanned the map until he found Jonah's kidnapping site. "He was in a foster home in Monroeville, a ranch house. He was taken from a bedroom while the foster mother did laundry in the basement. The car was stolen from Robinson Town Center Mall parking lot." This required a second map of Fayette County, west of Allegheny County. "It was a silver Ford Escort, and probably where they swapped the license plates of the stolen car with the plates of a second silver Escort; that went unnoticed until after the kidnapping. The car was abandoned in Oakland, at the underground Soldiers and Sailors parking garage. That was August twenty-fifth.

"The second baby was Isaiah, male, black, ten months old." He used yellow flags for the second kidnapping. "His mother was busted for crack possession in East Liberty. He was fostered in Homestead, and was kidnapped while his foster mother was shopping at the local supermarket on August twenty-ninth. They used a white Chevy Neon from Cranberry Plaza parking lot." A flag in Butler County, north of Allegheny County. "And abandoned at the USX building.

"The third child was Kimmie, female, two weeks shy of a year old. Parents lost custody after false accusations of child abuse; she was supposed to be returned home the day after she was kidnapped." He put down a blue flag in Bloomfield for Kimmie's parents, and then Bellevue for the foster home. "She was taken from a screened-in back porch while the foster father answered the phone, September second. A red Escort stolen from Westmoreland Mall parking lot." A flag in Westmoreland County, east of Allegheny. "And abandoned Mellon Square parking lot. Her body was found at this landfill the day before yesterday. She'd been tortured."

That raised a growl of anger from the Dogs. Quite frankly he felt like growling too.

"The fourth child was Shiralle, female, appears to be biracial, who was found abandoned at the approximate age of one day old, and is currently five months old." Ukiah started to mark orange flags on the map. There was no "family home" marker. "She was fostered in Beechview. She was kidnapped September sixth. A white Cambray taken from Clearview Mall in Butler, abandoned at the Gateway Center parking garage."

Silently he added on Kittanning's flags in blue. "They're not sure where the Taurus was stolen from yet. The owners haven't been reached."

They stood looking at the flags.

"All the cars were stolen outside of Allegheny County," Max commented. "They're using the communications barrier between police departments, added with the confusion of the plates."

"They're using the most common color and models of cars to attract as little attention as possible," Sam said. "The cars are taken from large open lots where the thieves can easily troll for the type of car they want without attracting notice. They abandoned the cars in enclosed lots, where the line of sight is so restricted that the possible witnesses are limited, and in a step or two, it's possible to completely disassociate yourself from the car."

Rennie waved a dismissive hand at the maps. "All that's important is who they are. Does your lady of steel have any leads to whom? Someone they're watching, waiting for more evidence before confronting?"

"I don't think so," Ukiah said after some thought. "Indigo didn't mention anyone Monday, before I got personally involved. Last night we found a set of fingerprints that might identify the kidnapper. Indigo treated it as the first strong lead they've had."

"What about Homeland Security? Does this have something to do with why he came to talk to you?"

"Maybe," Ukiah admitted, and told them about the photographs. "Indigo is checking out to see what he's told us is the truth."

"What do you know about the Temple of New Reason?" Hellena asked.

Ukiah looked to Max to see if his partner had discovered anything he wanted to discuss openly with the Pack.

"Their public Web site had every crackpot religious theory out there." Max went to the kitchen desk and opened the middle drawer. "We found their private servers."

"They had more than one?"

Max nodded. "Two. Private and seriously private."

"Isn't the point of being a data haven is they protect their customers?" Sam asked.

"From the law." Max spread out the paperwork. "I had to promise not to show any of this stuff to Indigo—and consider investing a couple million dollars in their company. The first server seems to be where the Temple does their on-line chats, news groups and such with people who have passed their screening process. These are the possible converts. The server is very squeaky clean, although serious kooky; a convert can hack it and not find anything dubious. This is the cult's FAQ."

"Fact?" Rennie picked up the paper. Most of the Dog Warriors had been born before the invention of the telephone; they coped well with technology but the Internet was a foreign world to them.

"Frequently Asked Questions. The document is set up in a question/answer format." Max read off some of the questions. "How do you pick a true name? What is the armor of God?"

"Ephesians, chapter six," Hellena murmured. "Therefore, take up the full armor of God, that you may be able to resist in the evil day, and having done everything, to stand firm."

"Yeah," Max said uneasily. "The other server has the damning information, like full background searches on possible converts." He held up a stack of papers. "This is the dossier on Socket, aka Hutchinson's rich girlfriend. How much she was worth, what sites she visited, her spending habits, the works. Some of the information on the site, though, doesn't make a whole lot of sense." He shuffled through the paper. "I printed off some of the weirder things. Here, this is a geological map of upstate New York. According to the map key, these are fault lines." Max knew Ukiah well enough to add in without him asking, "Basically cracks in the earth where earthquakes are most likely to occur. The Appalachians are some of the most stable areas in the world, but we still get minor quakes. There was one in 2002 near Lake Placid."

"Nothing like the West Coast," Sam commented. "We have active volcanoes."

"I don't know what this is." Max pulled out another map, marked heavily with numbers and lines. He laid it down next to the map of the fault lines. "This is the same location, but I can't tell what they're mapping here."

"It's the power grid for that area," Rennie said. "These are electrical poles and what power loads they're carrying them from, and such like."

"Heaven knows, the Lord needs power." Max pulled out a CD from the drawer. "I sucked a couple hundred files down from the server, but a search for the words 'Ukiah, Oregon, Maxwell, Bennett, and Kittanning' on the entire server pulls up nothing. Nor could I find any hint to where the cult could be hiding now."

It sounded like a dead end.

Dismay suddenly rippled through the Pack like shock waves on a pond, starting with Bear in the hall, transmitted through Hellena, Rennie, and finally to Ukiah, as Bear's scent impression brushed against his mind.

Alicia had opened the front door and walked in unannounced, as she had done for years.

"It's okay," Ukiah said to the others, and then called, "we're in the kitchen."

Alicia came cautiously down the hall. Outwardly she looked very much like herself, in a black lace top over an iridescent cobalt-blue halter top, a tiny black leather miniskirt, and fishnet stockings above cobalt-blue high heel boots. Her hair, which had been of normal length and natural color in Oregon, had been cut short, dyed deep blue, and spiked in a thistle top with the exception of a rattail down the back. It wasn't her normal half-jaunty, half-sexual saunter, though, down the hall. She had lost her bravado in Oregon, along with part of her identity, and almost her life. Her clothes seemed almost too brazen, as if she was desperately trying to reclaim herself.

"I'm sorry," she said, edging around the room to keep at maximum distance from Rennie, whom she obviously recognized. "I know I should have rung the doorbell, but, you know, habit."

"It's okay," Ukiah said and went and hugged her.

She clung to him tightly. She reeked of perfume, not her normal brand, but Indigo's. Had she doused herself trying to reach the same level of sensitivity the Ontongard had? Did she realize it was Indigo's perfume? "I heard about the kidnapping. I want to help. I know how much you must love him. I know how important it is to the world to get Kittanning back."

"What do you remember of the Ontongard's memories?" Rennie asked.

"They're like dreams I had. Very vivid dreams." She paused, and then shook her head. "I suppose they're more than that. Sharp and clear, and yet so vague. I'm not explaining it very well. They're like music videos of a dream. All these surreal images impressed into your mind, vibrant and yet nonsensical."

"Was there a plan to kidnap the little one?" Rennie asked.

"Or plans to expand to using humans to do Hex's dirty work?"

"Humans? Never!" Alicia said. "One betrayal and billions would turn to hunt him down."

"Now there's an idea," Sam muttered.

"That's a two-edged sword to grasp for," Rennie said. "When Prime and Hex first arrived, witch hunts had just fallen out of practice. Between ignorance and superstition, the Pack would be lumped along with the Ontongard as demons. Even now, men might decide that being rid of all aliens would be best. By numbers and morals, however, the end result would be the Pack destroyed and the Ontongard just driven under deeper cover."

"What about plans for Kittanning?"

"I remember being surprised when I nailed Ukiah to the wall—when Quinn nailed Ukiah." Alicia faltered and looked distressed at having memories of acts she never committed. "T-t-then flying with only thoughts of escape."

She lapsed into silence. As she said, Quinn had been the one that drove a post digger through Ukiah, pinning him to a wall, and discovered that Ukiah wasn't a Pack Get but the lone born breeder. The battle ended with Quinn rendered down to a flock of crows, which flew away. Alicia must have received Quinn's memories at some point after that.

"The Oregon Gets didn't know about me," Ukiah said. "So they couldn't have known of any plans to kidnap Kittanning."

Despite the lack of useful information now, Ukiah could feel the Pack regard Alicia with interest. Never before could they peer into the mind of their enemy. There were assumptions they could make, based on Prime's memories of a sprawling intergalactic life-form with billions of individual bodies acting like cells of a single organism. Prime, though, had splintered away from the Ontongard long ago; Alicia had been part of the Ontongard just the week before.

"How does the Ontongard stay organized when separated?" Rennie asked.

Alicia rocked her head back and forth in a habit that was wholly hers; Ukiah was pleased to see it. After two minutes of thinking, she said, "He uses the phone. In Pendleton, he called any of him that was out of mental range."

"Hex or Gets?" Hellena asked.

"All of them are Hex," Alicia said.

"We know," Rennie rumbled. "We individualize Hex from his Get. He led and the others followed."

Alicia narrowed her eyes as she considered it from the Ontongard viewpoint. "He was the origin of the will, like the headwaters of a river, but he no more led than ran along with, all agreeing. One mouth speaks, but all form the word."

"Were the Pendleton Gets in communication with any others?"

"There was a sudden silence from Pittsburgh, and it was decided that it was too dangerous to communicate via phone long distances," Alicia said.

"Do you remember the phone numbers used to contact the Gets in other areas?" Rennie pressed.

Alicia closed her eyes and pressed fingers to her skull. She thought in silence for several minutes and then shook her head. "It's like reading in a dream. I can remember picking up the phone and hitting the buttons, but the numbers—I can't remember them."

"Indigo might be able to get phone records from everyone in Pendleton that became Gets," Ukiah said. "Most of them are dead, so protection of privacy won't be an issue. It will take some work to winnow out false leads, since we don't know when they were infected, but it might give us leads."

"This is not getting Kittanning back," Max said.

"I thought I could help," Alicia said. "I can man the phones, coordinate things a bit, cook, anything."

"Well," Max said, "you could make breakfast."

The ransom note came at breakfast.

None of the other children had been ransomed, so they had not expected it. They were gathered in the kitchen, the table covered with maps of the city and plates of hastily scrambled eggs.

The Winchester doorbell sounded and someone answered the door.

There was a startled yelp and suddenly a body came flying into the kitchen. A scruffy man scrambled on the polished wood floor.

"What the hell?" Max shouted.

Ukiah leapt across the table to check Bear who had pulled a knife. "Bear! Wait! What is it?"

Bear shoved a small package into Ukiah's hands with a wordless snarl.

Ukiah started to open the package, and then his breath got stuck in his chest as awareness hit him.

"I just delivered it!" The man on the floor whimpered, trying to squirm his way under the table. "I don't even know what it is! I'm just paid to deliver it! Please, don't hurt me."

"Ukiah?" Max asked. "What is it?"

"It's a mouse." Ukiah had to force the breath out of his chest to talk. "Kittanning's mouse."

There was a moment of stillness, as if grief and fear and rage coalesced into something solid and held them motionless.

"You shouldn't open it then. You'll confuse it." Max held out his hand for it, and reluctantly Ukiah gave it up.

Such a tiny box, like something you put a pair of earrings into. Max sat the box on the table, and opened it cautiously, as if afraid that the mouse would escape from all of them.

The body part had been too small to form a mouse. It took the shape of a miniature wooly bear caterpillar. It lifted its head up as if sniffing the air. Ukiah felt its tiny shiver of hunger. It sat on a folded piece of paper, stained with blood cells that died instead of transforming.

"What was it?" Max asked.

Bear came and carefully coaxed the caterpillar into his hand. "A finger. The left pinkie."

A soft rumble of rage underscored the stillness.

Ukiah picked up the paper and unfolded it, his hands shaking with the anger that wanted to explode out of him, pound against something yielding, preferably someone responsible for this but not even that seemed necessary. Anyone guilty of anything would do.

The note was inspired by too many movies, a collection of

cutout letters pasted to a sheet of paper. The kidnapper had used a ruled notebook, the edges still trailing the confetti of being torn from the notebook. "We want $200,000 in small bills unmarked DON'T we send you other pieces in small boxes we WILL call 3:00 p.m. NO COPS!!!"

"Two hundred thousand?" Max shook his head. "Small-time idiots."

"You have it?" Sam asked.

"Hell, I've got a good chunk of it in the office safe," Max said. "I can get the rest as soon as the bank opens."

They looked then at the delivery boy and he shrank under their collective gaze.

"I just—I don't—I don't know anything about it."

Ukiah crouched down to stare into his eyes. "You're going to tell everything you do know."

"I picked it up at the Oliver Building. The front desk. I got a call from the dispatcher saying that there was an Oakland run. I even tried to talk her into giving it to someone else. I hate biking up the hill on Fifth Avenue. She bitched me out and I went and got it. It was just sitting there waiting for me!"

"Who sent it?" Ukiah asked. The messenger held out a clipboard and Ukiah read the name. "Dewey, Cheetum, and Howe, attorneys at law. Third floor, Oliver Building."

Rennie took the clipboard and growled.

Ukiah saw the disgust on the others' faces. "What is it?"

"It's an old Three Stooges routine," Max said.

"Who?" Ukiah asked.

"Comedians," Max explained. "The firm's name is 'Do we cheat them, and how.'"

Ukiah snarled his frustration.

The messenger flinched away. "I had nothing to do with this. I make dozens of runs a day. I just pick them up and drop them off where they tell me to."

"Is there a security guard for the building?"

"Yeah. Some old fart."

They had suddenly gone from no leads to too many. "Bear, take the messenger downtown to visit his dispatcher. Find out what they know about this Dewey, Cheetum, and Howe. Call me with the info."

Max opened his mouth and then thought better of whatever he was going to say.

Bear carefully returned Kittanning's caterpillar to the white jewelry box, put the box down on the table, and then waggled fingers at the messenger. "Come, come, we don't have all day."

"I want to talk to the doorman." The box holding the caterpillar looked too fragile sitting there, alone; Ukiah picked it up. "I want to see what he recalls."

"The kidnappers have been fairly slick so far," Sam said quietly. "It's unlikely the doorman saw anything."

"Are there any security monitors in that lobby?" Max asked.

Over the years, their cases had taken them into a wide range of downtown office buildings, the Oliver Building being one of them. Ukiah called up memories of the lobby. "No."

Max swore and went to the hall closet to collect his leather briefcase.

"We should call Indigo," Ukiah said. "Tell her about the ransom demand."

"Wait," Rennie said. "Let us go to this Dewey Cheatum first, in case it's an Ontongard trap."

Ukiah knew that Indigo wouldn't want a possible crime scene compromised, but he didn't want her walking into a possible trap. "Okay. I'll give you a half hour start. Don't hurt anyone human."

"Only if they deserve it," Rennie compromised and stalked from the offices.

"Before we deliver the full ransom you should look over the serial numbers on the bills." Max headed to his office for the money from his safe. Ukiah followed, gingerly carrying the small white box.

Sam had followed too, but she checked at the door as Max moved the dictionary stand to one side and peeled up the carpet, exposing the office floor safe. "Do you really want me to see this? I haven't told you that I was staying yet."

"If I didn't trust you, I wouldn't have asked you to come to

Pittsburgh," Max said, making no effort to hide the combination.

Sam, though, studied the room instead; it had originally been a library, built-in bookcases filled with books, a ladder riding a brass bar to give access to the top shelves. She pushed at the ladder, sending it down its track.

"Do you really think we should pay?" Ukiah eyed the caterpillar in its box. He sensed its loneliness and desire to merge with a larger, less helpless being. "In all the books, they say it's a bad idea. The kidnappers rarely deliver even when the ransom is paid."

"I've got the money," Max said, opening the safe door. "I've more than enough money to pay it a hundred times over. I'm not going to risk Kittanning's life or existence by not paying, especially for what's just pocket change for me." He took stacks of bills out of the safe. Packs of twenties, still taped together with a purple band by the bank. He tossed them into the briefcase.

"Two hundred thousand. Pocket change." Sam snorted and came to riffle the stacks of twenty. "I've never seen this much cash at once. How much is each pack?"

"Purples are two thousand," Max said, closing the safe and locking it. "The one yellow pack is a thousand, and the red band is five hundred."

"Forty-one thousand five hundred," Sam whispered.

"Forty thousand." Max handed the two smaller bundles to Sam. "This is yours, for driving the van."

Sam stared at the money in her hands as Max closed up the briefcase. "Why didn't you tell me that you're loaded?"

Max looked surprisingly shamed. "I know. I should have told you."

"You say you trust me, and then you keep lying to me. Isn't me trusting you part of this? Or is it what I have to lose is just so damn insignificant? Just a place to live that I don't even own, some rented office space, and a beat-up ten-year-old car?"

"I didn't lie to you." Max held up his hand to ward off that claim. "If I put you up in some cheap hotel and set up a fake grungy office downtown, that would have been lying. What degree of truth do you want? I flashed plenty of money in Pendleton, from the airplane tickets to the fancy restaurants. I was fairly upfront that I had money to burn. Wasn't that plain truth enough? This fancy house, is that enough? This forty thousand in cash, is that enough? Or are you going to be mad later and say, 'You didn't tell me about that!' I don't have some easy number that I can give you and say, 'That's what I'm worth.'"

Sam clenched her teeth and shifted her jaw, like she was locking down on sharp retorts. Finally, she said, "Just get it into the ballpark. The kid told me a number, and it might be right, but you don't know that I know. Let's get it settled between us, a nice solid foundation."

"Fine." Max said. He looked up at the ceiling.

"Well?"

"I'm counting." Max said. "I told you that I don't have easy numbers to hand out.

"Rough estimate, I'd say a hundred million dollars—"

"Shit!" Sam said. "Why do you even work?"

"What would I do otherwise? Sit at home and listen to the clock?" Max asked.

They listened to the grandfather clock tick out ten seconds before Sam said, "Then travel around the world. Go snorkeling in Hawaii. Visit Russia."

"Go to a place where I don't know a single soul for thousands of miles? Where I won't even understand what the people around me are saying?"

"It just seems insane that you do something so dangerous for work."

"By risking my life, I'm reminded that I still have it." Max swept the briefcase off the desk. "Besides, I get to help people that desperately need it."

CHAPTER NINE

It was the end of Rennie's half an hour, so Ukiah called Indigo and told her that the kidnappers had sent a ransom note by messenger.

"Ransom?" she repeated as if stunned.

He told her the amount. "Max is going to pay it. I've got the ransom note here, but we're heading out to the bank to collect the rest of the money. Bear went off with the messenger to talk to his dispatcher . . ."

"What?" It was more an exclamation than a question. "You called the Pack first?"

"They were here when the package arrived. Kittanning's finger was included in the ransom note."

Indigo made a hurt noise, like someone had struck her. "The lab will want it to test—oh, oh!" Realization had hit her. "What is it now?"

"A wooly bear caterpillar. I've got to figure out what it will eat. It's hungry."

"They eat weeds: grasses and broadleaf plants and wildflowers. The plants are called herbaceous. I did a paper on wooly bears in a college biology class. When I was taking care of Kitt, I—I found one and let it crawl on his fingers and told him all about them!"

He managed to swallow down the comment of "Thankfully you hadn't shown him a house fly." The thought was far too macabre to deal with. "The ransom note says they'll call at three."

"I'll meet you to get the ransom note and then arrange to have a trace set up on the office line. Tell the Pack to stay off the phones. I really wish you hadn't gotten them involved. Hmmm?" The sound muted for a moment as she covered the receiver. "We've got a match on the fingerprints! The perp is Adam Rudolph Goodman. He did time in San Quentin Prison for convictions of sex with minors. The last known address for him is California though."

"Do you have a social security number for him?"

She read it off. "I'll make a copy of the file. We're putting an APB on him."

Ukiah told her which bank to meet them at, and hung up. He was writing down the info on Goodman when Max came to his door.

"Ready?"

"Indigo has a name and soc on the perp." He held out the note to Max. "They don't know where to find him, though."

"We can run a background check on him, see what we can pull up," Max said.

"How about I do it while you're gone," Sam said. "It still hurts to walk and two is already an overkill."

"Okay." Max took out his PDA, noted the information into it, and then passed the note on to Sam. "Alicia is good with this type of search, and she knows how to get hold of Chino and Janey. They follow orders well, but they need to be shoved in the right direction occasionally."

Max did a quick pocket pat and came up with his key ring. "Here's keys to the Volvo if you need to go someplace. Alicia knows where we keep the spare office keys, and she can show you how to work the security system."

"Okay, okay, okay. Go!"

While most of the mansion's grounds were kept immaculate by a landscaping firm, a narrow strip of land behind the garage fell into a no-man's-land. Since the weeds stayed low from lack of sun and rain, no one cared. As Max maneuvered the Hummer out of the narrow parking bay, Ukiah plucked a handful of various leaves, making sure that none had been treated with poison.

At the first red light, Max watched Ukiah offer up the leaves to Kittanning's wooly bear. "If we had to, can we grow Kittanning back with just that? We can just feed it like crazy, and demand that it grows."

Ukiah winced; more than once he had shared Kittanning's memories of being tortured until he changed from a mouse into a baby. Hex had simply supplied food, a desired goal, and lots of pain. Sealed in a box, there had been no escape except through compliance. Perhaps if Kittanning had been more than a fistful of cells, he could have resisted. In the end, Kittanning refocused the same mechanics of their extraordinary healing abilities into increasing body mass just to escape the agony.

"Even if it was that simple," Ukiah said, "I'm not sure I could stand hurting Kittanning like that."

Max shifted uncomfortably at that thought, but pressed on. "But can we? Or did the Pack destroy the machine that Hex used?"

"I'm not sure what happened to Hex's machine," Ukiah admitted. "But it wouldn't be hard to duplicate the effects. We could grow a baby from the caterpillar, inducing it to change to a larger life-form when the current form reached its limit, and probably in as few as three steps: caterpillar, octopus, baby."

"Octopus?"

"Bones slow growth down. Soft tissue is less structured, and thus faster growing."

"Ahhh." Max made a sound of enlightenment, and then confusion clouded his features again. "So why isn't it simple?"

"We'd never really get *Kittanning* back," Ukiah warned. "Even if we broke this caterpillar down to two smaller creatures, say two ladybugs, and used one as a memory holder while we pushed the other to grow and change. Even then, it would be like Little Slow Magic and I. We were Magic Boy together; but now that we're combined, I'm still Ukiah with Little Slow Magic's saved memories from Magic Boy."

"Because of Prime's mutation?"

What set Prime apart from all the rest of the Ontongard was that Prime remained an individual after being infected by the Ontongard viral code. It wasn't clear if the mutation had been a result of the host's biology, or the Ontongard that infected him, but the resulting being seemed unique in the long history of the Ontongard. As far as the Pack could determine, the individuality was an expression of how Prime's cells stored genetic memories. While the Ontongard basically suffixed all memories directly to their sole memory base, unable to determine where they began and someone else ended, the Pack stored "borrowed" memories separately from those they experienced firsthand. Because he and Little Slow Magic had once been one creature, Ukiah needed to stop and think which memories were his, but he could tell. With Rennie's memories, the difference was much more distinct.

"Yes. What we would have is a baby with memories from Kittanning, but wasn't him."

"Would it matter that much?" Max asked. "I can see it being different with you and Little Slow Magic. Both of you had ninety years of memories built up, separate from one another. Kittanning was only three months old."

"The mouse that Hex used to make Kittanning had my hyper-condensed memories and the fresh Pack memories Rennie gave me. Even though Kittanning has forgotten much of those memory sets in the last three months, he still had his personality formed by it. He's so headstrong that Hex probably couldn't have used him for breeding, even after he'd forgotten everything about me and the Pack."

Max followed the logic. "So the new baby wouldn't have the same scope to build on."

"Scope." Ukiah nodded. "Kittanning knew Hex had made him and more importantly, because of those condensed memories, why. Nor did he forget any of that; by snarling in Hex's face the day we found him, he changed those borrowed memories to his own. The new Kittanning would lose those memories as we forced him through shapes, and only know that we tormented him until he was the shape we wanted him to be."

"We'd be his torturers, not his rescuers."

"Yes," Ukiah said bleakly.

They arrived at the main office of Citizens Bank downtown minutes after it opened. Max asked for the manager and after his name had been passed on, the manager Fred Gross came out to greet them warmly.

"What can I do for you, Max?"

"My godson has been kidnapped."

"Oh, dear God, I'm so sorry."

"The ransom is two hundred thousand. I've got forty thousand here." He tapped his briefcase. "I need a hundred and sixty thousand in twenties."

"Good thing you came here and early," Fred said. "Most of our branches have a currency limit of two hundred and fifty thousand, and that includes coins, ones, fives, tens, and so forth."

"We only have a few hours to get this together."

"Well, luckily, we have four ATMs. Normally our currency limit isn't much higher than the branches, but the ATMs are allocated up to eighty thousand each, half of which is twenties. We can raid those."

Max took out his laptop, sat it on Fred's desk, and pulled up a spreadsheet. "The next question is, where am I going to pull it from?"

"Let me get a Currency Transaction Report form." Fred stood up. "And have Susie start pulling together the money. A hundred and sixty thousand, right?"

Fred left them alone, Max working through his spreadsheets. Ukiah took out Kittanning's memory and made sure it was getting enough air.

"The trick is going to be liquidating things that Citizens will let me tap today," Max murmured. "I could write a check from any number of places, but they'll want a couple days to let something that big clear through."

"Do you think the reason the ransom was two hundred thousand was because the kidnappers knew that was about the limit we'll be able to get, currency-wise, from a bank in a day?"

"Maybe." Max leaned back and looked out the open door, where Fred recruited a second teller to help gather the ransom. "This always makes me feel like Jed Clampett."

"Who?"

"A character on a TV show about rich hillbillies. It was supposed to be funny, as if somehow someone not born to wealth couldn't learn to adapt. It's not hard at all—people come out of the woodwork to show you how to spend your money."

Indigo met them in the bank lobby, the lack of sleep showing on her face.

Ukiah folded her into a hug. "You okay?"

Indigo nodded her head. "But if Rennie Shaw messes up this investigation, I'm going to nail him to the nearest wall."

"I'm sorry," Ukiah said because he couldn't promise that Rennie wouldn't. "The Dogs thought it might be a trap to lure us to the Oliver Building."

"What?"

"Well, it seemed sensible at the moment. The more I've thought about it, the more it doesn't make sense. I was so angry this morning that I could barely think."

Her annoyance drained away, and she whispered, "Where is Kittanning's memory?"

He took the small box out of his breast pocket and lifted off the lid. She pressed a trembling hand to her mouth and held it there as she blinked away a shimmer of tears.

"I suppose it could be worse," she finally whispered. "At least he'll grow that finger back."

He agreed to that, but, privately, he worried that it would get worse. Certainly, if Kittanning grew the finger back too quickly, he was bound to weird out his kidnappers. Unless, of course, they had maimed him knowing that he'd recover. That in itself led to horrific thoughts.

He made sure that the memory was healthy, if not totally happy, and slipped it back into his pocket.

"I've copied the files." Indigo forced herself back to being just business. She handed him a thick folder. He gave her the ransom note, tucked in a Ziploc bag. She held it up to the light. "This is going to have fingerprints all over it, but if Goodman's sidekick doesn't have a record, we're not going to have her prints on file."

"I'm the only one that handled it on our end. My gun permit has my prints."

She nodded and tucked away the bag. "I did some digging into Hutchinson, to see if he was telling you the truth." She hesitated, obviously torn between loyalties. "The Temple of New Reason is a classic for why Homeland Security was created in the first place. The central files have reports from nearly every intelligence agency. The FBI is investigating them because of the possible kidnapping and brainwashing of their wealthier members. The ATF has files on their known weapons purchases, which are substantial. From the purchase of certain equipment, the NSA suspects that they're carrying on wiretapping. The DEA is looking for them in cases linked to the sale of a new designer drug. There are files flagged NEED TO KNOW ONLY which seems to indicate that they've hacked into classified military systems."

"But there's something he's lying about?"

"The most recent file is the John Doe, alias Zip, stopped on the turnpike. Hutchinson isn't the agent on the report, a Glenn Chambers is. Chambers obviously saw the case as a dead end: a man dead of natural causes in a car obviously borrowed from another cult member."

"What about the photographs?"

"He notes them, but states that there's no way to identify the subjects. Apparently the photograph with Ari Johnson was the key to establishing your identity, but there's no report on Hutchinson talking to Johnson or you. I honestly think he's gone rogue; I've got a query in to his superiors to see if they know what he's doing up here."

There was no sign of the Dewey Cheatum and Howe law firm at the Oliver Building. The suite listed was empty. Amazingly, the Dog Warriors had scouted the offices without unduly manhandling anyone. They had verified that the Ontongard were nowhere to be found and left the actual questioning to the FBI.

The guard at the receptionist desk reported that a bin on the front desk saw a constant traffic of packages left for bike messengers, UPS, and Federal Express. He merely made sure no one walked off with the wrong one. He remembered the package being left, puzzled by the return address. He had been trying to find out if the suite had been rented without security being notified when the messenger arrived to take the package away.

Indigo showed the guard the two artist sketches. "Did you see either of these people?"

The guard studied the artist sketches. "Oh, yes, it was the girl. I guess they played me for a sucker. If this creep had left the package, I probably would have called the bomb squad. I let it ride so long because she was young and sweet. She was dressed like a temp, you know, a dress cut a little too high and a little too low for a regular secretary. I cut her slack, thinking she got the address wrong."

Max and Ukiah were back at the office before noon.

Sam had set up in the keeping room office just off the kitchen. She was on the phone when they came through the back door. She nodded a greeting but stayed focused on the voice on the other end of the line.

Whatever the voice was saying to her wasn't good. She sighed and shook her head. "No, it was a long shot. Hang loose. I'll get back to you. Thanks, Chino."

"How's it going?" Max kept the tension off his face, but not out of his voice.

"Not well." Sam hung up the phone. "This is what we've got so far."

Sam kept careful notes on a flip tablet, something that probably would change if she joined the agency. "Adam Rudolph Goodman, born 1970. Father dead. Mother dead. I just put Chino on trying to find distant relations. Graduated from high school in California in 1987 and held down security guard positions into the nineties."

"Ouch," Ukiah said. Security training was never good in a felon.

Sam acknowledged that by nodding her head. "Yeah, basic

knowledge of how cops catch thieves, and thus how to be
avoid being caught." Sam flipped over the sheet on her notebook. "The first job was at Disneyland, then next at an amusement park, and then a mall. I called them on the guise of
needing job references. They all indicated that he quit before
they could fire him, but wouldn't say why."

"Worried about civil suits from both sides," Max commented.

"Basically." Sam flipped to the next page. "He then got a
job as a janitor at a high school."

"Wait," Max said. "Didn't Indigo say this guy was in jail
for sex with minors? Amusement parks, mall, high school;
work hell, they're all hunting grounds."

"It's possible," Sam said. "In 1994 he was arrested and
convicted for multiple counts of sex with a minor, sentenced
to 10 years in San Quentin. He served out the sentence and
was released six months ago. That's where he disappears; he
just drops off the face of the earth."

"Drops off?" Max echoed, sounding leery. It wasn't the
kind of comment that sat well with Max, especially in his
present mood. From Janey or Chino, it would mean they
hadn't known where to take the search after the obvious
failed. The madness in Oregon aside, Sam was an unknown
quantity. Had they credited her with more ability than she actually had?

Sam sighed, scrubbing her fingers through her short blond
hair. "Goodman was released April second. No one picked
him up. He took the transit bus into San Francisco and
checked into the YMCA. He started up a bank account, applied for welfare, and began looking for a job. He even got a
library card. Two weeks later, he checked out, wrote out
checks that took his bank balance down to zero, and disappeared. He could have stolen a car, but he didn't buy one or
rent one, nor did he fly out of California anytime in April."

Sam obviously had covered a lot of ground while they had
been at the bank; it was not her fault that she lost the trail.

Max relaxed, settling on the edge of Sam's desk. "There's
the girl. She might have supplied the car."

Sam bobbed her head as if she was considering the girl. "She wasn't there to meet him at the prison. He was in the dorms at the YMCA, not a private room." She squinted, crinkling up her nose. "It's—it's the Pittsburgh thing that gets me. He laid out all the foundations of settling into San Francisco and then pulled up roots to come here."

"You don't like Pittsburgh?" Ukiah beat Max to the question.

"It's not that. It's just to leave *San Francisco*—for Pittsburgh? Or anyplace else in the Midwest. Cincinnati. Cleveland." She dismissed the steel cities with a wave of her hand. "You've got to have a good reason to go to that extreme, but I can't find any connection between Goodman and here. All his family was from the West Coast."

"He's been here for six months," Ukiah said. "Unless he's staying with the girl, he got someplace to live."

"Working on the assumption that he's here in Pittsburgh, I had Chino go to the"—she paused to search her memory— "Northside with the sketch of Goodman to see if he checked into the YMCA there under an assumed name." Northside was a seedier neighborhood across the rivers from downtown. "No luck there or in the Hill District."

That was the call Ukiah and Max had walked in on.

"When he opened his bank account"—Sam checked a number written on her desk pad—"he only had like seven hundred dollars. I picked up the info on the YMCA in California via his MasterCard. He used it extensively in the two weeks before he vanished, running up about five hundred dollars. The last check of his bank account that cleared paid off its balance. He hasn't used it since."

"If he's not using his credit card, and he used up all his cash, what's he living on?" Ukiah asked.

Sam shrugged. "It's not showing up on normal credit reports, whatever it is."

The grandfather clock struck noon.

Max sighed, standing up. "You're right—he dropped off the face of the earth. We've got three hours before the ransom call. I want to hit the gun shop before then. I know that you keep saying that this Goodman is human." This was to Ukiah.

"But this all feels wrong. I want to pick up some heavy ar-
tillery if we end up going against the Ontongard again."

Sam made a sound of disgust at the thought of fighting the
Ontongard. "I'll go back to digging, but I'm a little hampered.
I have tons of West Coast contacts, but nothing here in Pitts-
burgh."

"I can check to see if Goodman applied for welfare here,"
Ukiah volunteered. "I'll also see if he's contacted the DMV,
or any of the utilities."

"Eat something first," Max told him. "We need you in top
condition. I'll be back in an hour."

Ukiah ate at his desk as he made his calls. At first Sam's
voice was a constant background murmur, and then she fell
silent for so long that it drew his attention. He hung up on his
fruitless call and focused on Sam.

She was pacing quietly in the keeping room. While he listened, she picked up the third line and punched in a long-distance call. She continued to pace, murmuring softly, "Come
on, come on, answer the phone, you old fart."

A moment later she said, "Dad?" in a tone that was leery
and hard. "It's me, Sam. I need a favor. What? No, that has
nothing to do with it. How do you know about that anyhow?
Shit! I should have known Peter would call you." Peter was
Sam's ex-husband, and one of the main reasons she left
Pendleton. "Yes, I'm in Pittsburgh, but it's not like that; I
drove the hiker's car back to Pittsburgh. Look, I need a favor."
Sam let out a long exasperated sigh. "You'd sell Grandma if
you thought you'd get a good price for her! That's a crock of
bullshit! She didn't sell you to the circus, and we both know
that. Okay, okay, I need information; if what you give me is
good enough, I'll send you money. There's a guy who was in
San Quentin the same time as you, his name is Adam Goodman." Sam started to describe Goodman, but came to a halt
partway through. "Yeah, that sounds like the man. I need to
find him."

Sam listened for several minutes, scratching notes down
with a pencil. "But where is he now? Hell, no, I'm not sleeping with the Indian kid." She paused. "If I was sleeping with

his partner, do you think that's something I'd talk to you about? *Dad, I'm not going to answer that question."*

The last was a snarl worthy of a Pack member. There was a moment of silence, and then Sam continued in a quiet, but angry tone. "He's not older than you; he's forty. Dad, I'm nearly thirty, okay? No, Kendall Jane is twenty-two. 1976, Dad, I'm the bicentennial baby. Okay, twenty-eight and a half. He's thirty-nine. He's just over ten years—*why am I having this discussion with you? You of all people should know that Peter lies!"*

She stood and started to pace. "It's not like that at all. Max could have anyone and he wants me; do you know how special that makes me—*yes, anyone.* That's because Peter thinks with his dick. Max's handsome, intelligent, witty, mature, responsible, reliable—what the fuck do you want from me, Dad? To go back to that asshole? Because if that's what you want, that's not going to happen! Just tell me where the hell Goodman is and I'll mail you fifty dollars.

"He snatched a friend's kid." She paced for several minutes, listening with an occasional "yes." Finally all movement and sound stopped. "Is there anyone that you can check with that might know?" The silence continued. "Okay, thanks. No. I haven't decided what I want. I just don't want—I just want to be sure it's right, totally right, and just not the opposite of Peter." She listened to a question, and laughed. "I'm not going to tell you that! Because! You'll be always trying to borrow money from me if I told you! Yes, he'll pay for me to move. Give me more credit than that, Dad. He has the money.

"I know. I know. Well, thanks for the info. I've got to go." She said her good-bye with a stilted "I love you" as if the words came unnaturally for her, even for her father.

Ukiah got up and walked to the keeping room.

She was sitting with her head in her hands. She sensed him at the door and looked up. "I suppose you heard all of that."

"Yes."

She gave a soundless laugh. "I'd ask you not to tell Max about this, but if we're going to work together, I don't want to start things like that—taking sides and keeping secrets."

"Not a good idea," Ukiah agreed.

Max stepped through the back door at that moment. "What isn't a good idea? What?"

"Sam has some information on Goodman."

"Great! It is good, isn't it?"

"Not really." Sam scrubbed hands through hair, and then stood up. "There's not much, but it might give us an angle to work with." She took a defiant stance next to the window. "My father was in San Quentin same time as Goodman. One of the few redeeming qualities that my father has is that he's a fairly good judge of character, when he wants to be, which is usually when he's trying to con someone out of something," Sam paused. "Well?"

"I'm not going to say anything," Max said.

"But you're thinking it."

"I'm not sure what you think I'm thinking, but I'm not— I think." Max paused, trying to keep a vaguely puzzled look off his face. "I'm not a man that judges a person by the sins of their fathers."

"What did he say about Goodman?" Ukiah tried to distract them from whatever fight was forming on the horizon.

"Basically that if Goodman had true criminal tendencies, he'd be a master thief. He's got great skills at working out a simple plan, and executing it with precision. Apparently while he was in San Quentin, if you wanted something from outside and didn't mind dealing with a dangerous loon, you went to him."

"Loon?"

"My father's words." Sam showed her notes, where she had written "loon" and then branched it out to: Mental disorder? Doctor? Drug controlled? Prescription?

"Rumor mill has it that his family were right-wing, fundamental survivalists. The thing is, Goodman's sexual hang-ups usually cancel out any criminal ambitions he has. Apparently all his energy goes toward creating his perfect sexual fantasy."

"This is where the sex with minors comes in?"

"My father says it's some kind of survivalist wet dream, basically a stockpile of guns, a bomb shelter, and a doe-eyed teenager that can't say no."

"So he's a gun bunny, pedophile schizophrenic."

"Something like that."

"And this makes it easier to find him?"

"It makes him dangerous to find," Sam said. "It's nearly a sure thing he'll have guns coming out his whazoo."

Max nodded. "Nothing else?"

"Two things. Dad suggested that we check reported runaways in the area. Apparently even in prison, he hooked on to some naive virgin, and did this weird whammy that the two of them were God's gift to mankind, the virgin being one step behind him, of course. The fact that the girls were crazy in love with him were the only reasons he wasn't slapped with kidnapping and rape whenever the girl's parents caught up with them."

"That's one thing."

"I'm getting to it," Sam snapped. "The second is the kid he hooked up with in prison. Dad remembers he had some hick name like Billy Bob and was a serious Steelers fan. Word is that when Goodman got out of prison, he couldn't get a job because of the child molesting conviction. Billy Bob, though, had gotten out of prison a couple of years ago, gone back East, and nailed down something with money; he wired money for Goodman to join him. It was like a thousand dollars. Goodman flashed the money around and ended up taking the bus, nearly broke."

Max swore because an airplane ticket would have Goodman's name on it, making it easy to track him. A car with state registration, insurance, and inspection would have made finding Goodman simple. "Indigo can check with Western Union on the wire transfer. When was this?"

"Six months ago, when Goodman dropped off the face of the earth." Sam flipped through her notepad, tapping various notes with red checks beside them. "There haven't been hits on his credit reports. None of his past employers or old landlords have had reference checks. I got hold of a temporary secretary at his most recent employer, so I managed to talk a fax of his employment application off of her." She hunted through loose paper on her desk and showed it to them. Goodman had surprisingly neat handwriting, all the slots were filled in, and spelled correctly. It was the type of application that Max would have tapped for an interview just based on the attention to detail it showed. "I've tried all his emergency contacts, and if they're telling the truth, haven't heard from him since he came East."

"He hooked into something shifty," Max guessed.

"If I didn't know better, I'd say he was dead," Sam said.

If Sam hadn't winged Goodman, Ukiah would say that he might have been made a Get. Ukiah walked back through the conversation. The girl was key. If she was a local runaway, then she might have talked to friends or family after meeting Goodman.

"I think I should go see Vic."

"Vic?" Sam asked as Max said it was a good idea.

"Victor Danforth is head of missing persons for Allegheny County. We've worked with him a couple of times, a good guy."

Max wanted to stay by the phone, in case the kidnappers called early. He urged Sam to go with Ukiah to see Vic. "If you're going to stay, you should get to know your way around."

"Wolf Boy!" Vic clasped Ukiah's hand in a surprisingly warm greeting. "I heard about your kid. I'm really sorry. If there's anything I can do?"

"Thanks, Vic." Ukiah indicated Sam beside him. "This is Sam Killington. She helped us out in finding Alicia in Oregon. She might be working with us." Sam and Vic shook hands. Ukiah took out the artist sketch of the girl and explained about Goodman and his young female partner. "Sam's . . . source . . . in California suggested we check local runaways."

Vic studied the paper. "She looks familiar. Maybe." He handed back the sketch and walked to a filing cabinet. "You're talking the proverbial needle in a haystack, you know. We get a couple thousand runaways reported every year, and that's just us, not counting Butler or Westmoreland County. We don't have fingerprints for these kids. Heck, we often don't have recent photographs, and you know how much kids can change in appearance in a year. And the hell of it, most of them aren't runaways."

"What are they? Kidnappings?"

"They're walkaways. Driftaways." Vic shuffled through the files. "We call them couch kids; they sleep on the couches of friends and relatives—anywhere but home. These kids hit twelve or thirteen, and they think they've got the whole world figured out."

"I thought that was a definition of a teenager," Sam said.

"Some of them have good cause; they've been abused. A lot of them, though, just don't want to go to school, clean their rooms, or eat their peas. They're selfish little brats."

"Are they so bad for just wanting control of their own lives?" Sam asked.

"If we lived in a perfect world, no. But the problem is that they willfully jump into the cracks and never come back out. Sooner or later, they move out of my files and into someone else's. Burglary. Vice. Homicide." He pulled out a thick file and held it out. "This year's missing children. If she's one of ours, she's in here. You're welcome to look through it."

Vic gave them use of a desk. They split the file between them and started to flip through them. Ukiah studied the pictures, growing dismayed at the number and ages of the missing children. He thought of Pittsburgh as a safe place; he and Max were part of a system that kept kids from disappearing. Apparently for every child that triggered a massive manhunt, dozens quietly vanished. Couch kids. Runaways. Children snatched by noncustodial parents. Just plain missing.

And Kittanning was now one of them.

While in Oregon, Max had chanted, "You're nearly indestructible." Ukiah understood now how much comfort it provided.

Keeping in mind that the pictures might not be recent ones, and that children sometimes changed dramatically, he moved carefully through his pile. Sam occasionally handed him sheets on blond, teenage girls, saying, "What about her?" The last one, he stared at several minutes, before nodding. "Yeah, that's her."

The girl in the picture verged on heavyset, and looked

sullen and angry. Life with Goodman had thinned her down. Made her scared. Made her nearly unrecognizable.

"Eve Linden," Vic read the name. "Yeah, she moved from a mild annoyance to a real concern. She's been drifting for like two years, but her aunt gave her a cell phone and paid the bill to keep it connected, so the family kept tabs on her until last month. She hit her aunt up for money, saying she wanted to buy school clothes, promising that she was going to buckle down this year. No one has heard from her since then. Her phone was discovered in a Dumpster near the mall a day later and that's when her family reported her missing."

Ukiah flipped through the file, taking in names and addresses in a glance. "We were hoping that someone had talked to her, give us a lead on Goodman."

"If she's gotten in touch with anyone, they haven't let us know that she's alive," Vic said. "I'll fax this over to the FBI and let them know you've IDed the girl."

"Assuming you've got that all memorized, do we start calling her little friends? See if any of them have heard from her and not told the police."

Ukiah shook his head. "I think Goodman tossed the phone to cut her connection with her family and friends."

"Can't hurt to check though."

"Goodman's from California," Ukiah said. "He's been in Pittsburgh six months or less. He might be using her as a native guide. What we should ask her friends about is any secret hangouts that she might know about."

They got back to the offices by two. Max shook his head as they came in, saying, "No call."

Indigo arrived minutes after them and settled beside Ukiah on the living-room couch, leaning against his strength. As if they had been following her, the Pack gathered close to the house, waiting patiently for news.

They watched the hands of the grandfather clock creep around to three, then onto four, with only the clock chimes breaking the silence.

Max checked his wristwatch for the hundredth time. "He's not going to call."

Indigo's phone rang and she answered it with a tense, "Special Agent Zheng." As she listened, she reached out and caught Ukiah's hand, crushing it tight. "Yes. Yes. Yes. I'll be right there."

He swallowed hard against his fear. "What is it?"

"They found another baby dead," she whispered.

CHAPTER TEN

Bennett Detective Agency, Shadyside, Pennsylvania
Wednesday, September 15, 2004

The dead baby was Isaiah, the black boy infant taken from the Homestead supermarket. His body was found in a Dumpster behind a South Hills restaurant, thrown away like so much trash. Indigo excused herself to the bathroom, where she apparently meditated, coming out calm and focused. Under the composed surface, though, was a mountain of icy rage.

"If you come with me," Indigo said, "I'm not going to be able to let you disturb the crime scene."

"I'm going to take in Kittanning's memory and try to use it to find him. I'm not sure it will work; it depends on what memories it's holding."

She clasped his hand briefly as if touching him more would break her carefully built control. "Keep me up-to-date."

They readied for war, donning their new body armor that had just arrived and loading their guns with care: pistols for humans, shotguns for Ontongard. Max and Sam packed the Hummer with everything short of C4, and the Pack brought that.

Ukiah spilled the caterpillar into his hand, stroked the prickly bristles, feeling its shimmer of joy at being so close to its progenitor. He hated the idea of absorbing it, taking in what might be the only thing left of Kittanning, of obliterating his son from the world. He tried to keep forefront in his mind that it would be more merciful to welcome back these few cells instead of leaving them alone and afraid. Surely if he found Kittanning intact, his son would be better without these horrific memories.

"Come to me," he whispered, still feeling as if he were betraying Kittanning. "Give me your secrets."

It vanished into his hand, a tiny pool of blood quickly gone.

. . . light played on the ceiling of Kittanning's bedroom. It was at once both wonderful and irritating. Grammy had strung crystals in the window and they broke the light into dancing colors. Still, the room was so small when compared to the universe he knew existed beyond the ceiling, represented by the rarely glimpsed night sky. Those memories of brilliant stars, harsh blue whites and deep bloodreds, were winking out, disappearing before he had a chance to call them up and lock them away. His world, with all its joyful assault upon his senses of things, distracted him constantly. A sudden stirring in the bedroom above his reminded him that his daddy was home, and all else was forgotten. Impatient now for Daddy, he squawked, demanding attention.

"Good morning, dumpling." Grammy eclipsed the dancing lights.

Normally he'd be pleased to see her, but Daddy was just upstairs, stretching in bed and gazing at slants of sunlight across his own ceiling . . .

Ukiah pressed on through the fragments of memory, trying not to think about how in doing so he might be erasing the last living traces of his son. He immersed himself in the recall, and thus noticed that while Kittanning had an integrated personality, just like he did, the thousand-fold chorus of his individual cells lay close to the surface, busily relocating fuel reserves at a maddening pace. The cells fretted at Kittanning's limitations, and with alien-borne efficiency, pushed him toward mobility and the ability to protect himself. Normally Ukiah would have found this distressing, but now he found comfort in it—Kittanning's body could protect him through dangers that would kill any normal child.

Because the caterpillar had been more bone than blood, the back memories extended to Kittanning's birth. They had lucked out that the kidnapper had waited so many hours before wounding Kittanning. The memories of the kidnapping itself had been encoded into genetic memories, and fully accessible. He found the beginning of the kidnapping.

. . . shock slammed through Daddy's body as a bullet struck him down. Kittanning wailed, feeling the pain as if it were his own flesh being torn. Daddy's warm comforting thoughts vanished as he dropped dead onto the floor. The gunman came down the dark hallway, footsteps loud, his stride breaking where he stepped over Daddy's body. He cast a shadow over Kittanning's car seat moments before he loomed over the baby, gun still in hand, wreathed in gunsmoke. The smell of blood flooded the kitchen. Daddy's blood. Kittanning screamed in helpless terror and anger . . .

There, the true start, as Kittanning's car seat was roughly jerked upward.

Ukiah got up from his desk and walked through the kitchen, picking up his shotgun as he passed. There was the soft rumble like a gathering storm as the Pack started their motorcycles. Max cut short his conversation with Sam and climbed into the Hummer. Ukiah tucked the shotgun into the Hummer's gun safe and swung into the passenger seat.

"Start on the front street, heading south." He rubbed the spot where Kittanning's memory had absorbed into his skin. *"Hold on, Kitt, Daddy's coming."*

Goodman had carried Kittanning out to the waiting car; Eve opened the back door as Goodman approached the sedan. The kidnapper slid into the backseat, slammed the door shut, and sat bleeding and swearing. Eve drove hesitantly with lots of startled cries of dismay while Goodman shouted instructions.

Ukiah leaned back so his field of vision matched Kittanning's limited range, and guided Max through remembered turns and stops. The Dog Warriors followed, close at hand, on their motorcycles. Ironically, as their current time of day matched that of the kidnapping, they fought the same heavy rush-hour traffic. They crawled through the random turns that the kidnappers took trying to lose Sam, and then risked tangling with the police to follow the busway down to Grant Street rather than lose the thread of Kittanning's memories.

. . . the car cut down to the dusty, sun-baked parking lots of the strip district. There the girl, Eve, slithered into the backseat, and plucked a still crying Kittanning from his car seat.

Goodman got out, slammed the back door shut, and opened the driver's door. "Just like we practiced, remember? Piece of cake."

"What if I can't find you?"

"Just keep going around the block." Goodman slid in behind the wheel. "Now get out, hurry."

Eve threw open the back passenger door, stepped out of the car holding Kittanning, and swung the door shut. As Goodman pulled away, she shouldered Kittanning with an irritated, "Oh, be quiet, I'm not happy about this either."

Three steps and they were at another car, a dark blue Honda, just beyond the parking lot's barrier. She must have had a key fob; there was the solid "thunk" of doors unlocking. A car seat was already in place.

Her parking space was too good to be just luck. Goodman must have parked it late at night, when the lot was empty. From the parking lot, Eve doglegged to Fort Duquesne Boulevard, and then turned left onto Stanwix to stop at the curb where Ukiah had lost Goodman the night before. It was a short easy drive, even in rush hour, for an inexperienced driver.

"So far, so good," Max murmured.

Goodman took over driving, rounding the corner to jump on I-279. Ukiah and Rennie had guessed right—with the other routes deadlocked, the kidnappers had taken the only route with freely moving traffic out of the city—but they were too far behind to catch up.

"We drive straight for a long time," Ukiah said. "I think they're heading for the turnpike."

"Did Kitt see the outside of the car they're in?" Max asked.

"It's a dark blue Honda. He didn't see the plates. They're

going someplace very rural. After they arrive, his memory starts to fragment."

"Hopefully they didn't move him."

"At the end they start to talk about going to the bathroom, making something to eat, and going to bed. It sounds like they stopped wherever they've been living. Eve put a blanket over Kittanning as they got out, so I don't have any visual memories of the place." And after that, the gaps of blackness started.

They fell silent, neither wanting to speak about what happened to Kittanning the next morning.

"When we get there," Ukiah said finally, "you hang back and the Pack and I will go in."

"Like hell," Max snapped.

"If this is Ontongard, you're the only one that can be killed," Ukiah said. "Even if they're only human, you don't want to get between them and the Pack." Max glowered at the road until Ukiah added, "I won't be taking point either."

Goodman took the turnpike out to Irwin, a small town on the very fringe of Pittsburgh's sprawl. Housing plans gathered around the turnpike exit, still congested with commuters arriving home. They continued east, away from Pittsburgh, and houses dropped away to farms and woods. The road grew narrow and windy.

"Slow down," Ukiah said finally, watching the steep woodlot of wild cherry and maples alongside the road. "We make a right-hand turn soon. Slower. Slower. Here."

Here was a little more than a tractor path through the woodlot, climbing a short, steep hill as it curved to the left so its far end vanished behind the trees. Tall grass grew up the center of two hard-packed ruts, bent over by passing cars, indicating that the road had seen little travel all summer and only recently been put to use. A rusted-through mailbox leaned at a drunken angle beside the turn, the only indication that the dirt driveway led back to a house.

Max pulled into the drive far enough to get his back bumper off the road and killed the engine. Ukiah checked his clip and stepped out of the Hummer, closing the door quietly behind him.

The Pack settled around him, silencing their engines.

"We're close," Ukiah said, keeping his voice low, speaking aloud for Max's sake. "The car stops in a couple of minutes and Kittanning's taken out of the car."

Rennie flared his nostrils, sniffing the wind. "I don't sense Hex or Kittanning."

Fresh tire tracks pressed into the ruts, coming and going, several different makes of cars. The Pack walked their bikes up until they were out of sight of the main road and tucked them in among the trees, and then fanned out around Ukiah, armed to the teeth and pissed off.

Max handed Ukiah a headset. "Be careful."

Rennie and Bear took point, loping off on the hunt. Ukiah followed, gun in hand, keeping to the dappled shadows.

After the drive reached the top of the short hill, the scrub trees gave way to an old apple orchard, a layer of Macintoshes rotting on the ground under gnarled trees. The farm perched on a ridge wrapped around a steep hollow, shaped like a thumb pressed against a forefinger. The forefinger was a shorn field of wheat; the thumb was the orchard, the farmhouse, and its outbuildings, with a deep, narrow crease in the land between field and buildings. They had just climbed the base of the thumb. There, where the valley started its pleat, sat the stone foundation of a roofless springhouse. Water gushed out of a short pipe onto the ancient flagstone floor and out the doorless entry. A well-beaten path indicated that the kidnappers were using the spring as a water source. The path joined the road and headed toward the house with a barn beyond it, resting on the far knuckle of land.

A little farther down the driveway, a crude outhouse had been set up, basically a bench straddling a narrow pit. Diapers mixed with urine and feces in the open, reeking hole. Opposite the outhouse, a handful of worn gravestones marked a family graveyard. It would have been lost under knee-high wildflowers except someone had trampled down the flowers, and pried up one or two of the stones, leaving pits to mark the theft.

The house had been built sometime in the last century, a two-story clapboard farmhouse. Weather had long worn off

the paint, leaving bare gray wood. All the windows facing the
driveway were broken, leaving jagged dark mouths. The front
porch looking out over the valley had collapsed into a jumble
of rotten wood and slate roofing tiles. Some attempt had been
made recently to make the collapsing back porch safe—new
two-by-fours propped up the sagging porch roof and the
stolen gravestones were arranged to replace broken steps. A
massive oak shaded the backyard with autumn leaves that had
run to bloodred. Rennie moved ghost silent to the oak and
crouched behind its wide trunk to eye the back porch. Ukiah
dropped down behind him, and went still as only a Pack dog
could.

"Bad juju there," Rennie murmured into Ukiah's mind, indicating the gravestones.

Ukiah reached out, searching for Kittanning's Pack presence. He could sense the Dog Warriors ranging invisibly
through the trees and grass around him, but of his son, there
was nothing. Nor did there seem to be anything moving in the
house. *"Kittanning's not here."*

Rennie's lip curled back in a soundless snarl.

They moved as one to the back porch. Plaster dust coated
the worn wood, a fine grit underfoot as they crept to the back
door and peered through.

Built before modern utilities, the house had never been updated, thus the kitchen had no electric outlets or lights and
only a rusted hand pump for plumbing. Built-in wood cabi-
nets lined the walls, except where a wood stove once sat, its
access to the brick chimney still an open black sore, scenting
the kitchen with ancient soot.

Temporary adaptations had been made. A trestle table,
made of old lumber and sawhorses, held a propane camping
stove, various pots and pans and cooking utensils. Tucked
under the table, a large ice chest took the place of a refrigerator. A plastic dishpan and gallon milk jugs filled with spring
water stood in for a sink. A paper shopping bag served as a
waste container, a line of ants crawling down its side. Ukiah
lightly touched one of the ants, making it scurry off in a panic;
it wasn't Kittanning's. Two empty formula cans sat in the bag,
the source of the ants' interest. He caught the slight scent of

old blood and pushed the cans aside. A plastic bag from Borders bookstore held a folded newspaper, stained with Kittanning's blood, which had been sucked up by the paper and killed.

Ukiah pulled the bag free, smothering a growl. The newspaper was the Sunday Real Estate section of the *Miami Herald* with properties circled in red. The prices ranged between a hundred fifty thousand and two hundred thousand. They stole Kittanning for beachfront property?

Rennie had been focusing on the house. He shifted out of his stillness. *"There's no one in the house."*

"They parked their cars here," Bear stated from outside, indicating a patch of crushed, oil-stained grass, now innocent of cars.

Rennie opened the ice chest beside him, releasing the smell of raw meat. *"This is full of food. Ice is melted, but the water is still chilled."*

As Ukiah handed Rennie the paper, he spotted pruning shears among the cooking utensils. He touched the blades and found them coated with Kittanning's blood. This time there was no holding the growl in. Only Eve had handled the shears, and he felt an instant deep hate for her.

"You okay?" Max whispered in his ear.

"It will be hard not to kill this bitch that hurt my child," Ukiah growled through his clenched teeth.

"I'm coming in," Max said, and far off came the start of the Hummer.

By design, the adjoining room would have been a dining room, but it was bare of any furniture. Sun streamed through smashed-out windows to shine on an ancient linoleum carpet, cracked and buckling, and a mural freshly painted on the nearest wall. The front door out to the porch was missing, as were the steps leading up to the second floor. Heavy plastic covered the door beyond the cavernous hole that had been the staircase. Ukiah pushed his way through the overlapping sheets of clear plastic. It seemed to be the only room whose windows retained their glass. The fireplace had been used recently. An air mattress and sleeping bags made an adult nest in one corner. The smell of sex clung to the sheets. In the opposite corner, a clothes basket made a bed for Kittanning. Goodman and Eve had been using cardboard boxes as dressers; only someone had scattered the clean clothes onto the floor and overturned the boxes in a hasty search.

Another plastic-covered doorway opened to a spiraling back staircase. The ceiling of the second floor was slowly collapsing, damp from years of rainfall, and plaster littered the floor. All the windows were missing, and the wind breezed through openings, bringing Ukiah the scent of blood. He followed the smell through the empty rooms, the fine rubble crunching underfoot.

In the far bedroom, the edge of the broken glass remained in the only window, held in by ancient points, paint, and putty. Blood tainted the glass where Eve had gripped the window frame and cut her hand. Below the window, a story and a half down, Bear crouched in the trampled weeds. He glanced up at Ukiah.

"She jumped from there. Looks like she broke a leg and crawled away." Bear stood, and indicated a wavering trail pushed through the tall grass.

Ukiah filled his lungs, sniffing for the scent of blood. "Do you smell that? Somewhere a lot of blood has been spilled."

From the barn the sudden bristling of minds.

"The others found something."

They had found Goodman, only someone had found him first.

He had been stripped down to nude and nailed to the floor of the barn with ten-inch spikes driven through his outstretched palms and bare feet. His capturers silenced him with a wormy apple, wedged into his mouth to the point of choking. Judging by the blood, they had taken off the right arm, and then the left leg above the kneecap, leaving him still pinned, until the amputation of the right leg freed him. Then, bleeding to death, they let him struggle, thrashing on the floor, trying to unpin the remaining limb.

Had they promised him salvation if he managed to free himself, or had it been sheer determination to live that kept him fighting to the end?

One man walked through the blood then to crouch beside the dying Goodman. To hear some whispered confession? To check to see if he was alive? It was impossible to say. After several minutes of leaning over the hapless man, the killer stood, casually pinned Goodman with one foot to the chest, and beheaded him. It had taken several swings to hack through the muscular neck. Afterward, the axe man had sat on a wooden crate, blood dripping from his clothes and weapon, and studied his work for several minutes. The corpse finished gushing out its blood. The axe man returned to the body, prodded it with the axe, and then walked away, trailing the axe as if he forgot he carried it.

And after all that inhumane brutality, the killer threw up into the weeds beyond the barn doors. Smack found the axe in the deep grass a dozen feet away, flung as far as the man could throw it.

Eve was hidden in a blackberry patch, the ancient sweetness coming from the fruit dried onto the thorny stems. A bloody broken mess. The sight of her put a shiver of fear through Ukiah, and when he realized why, he started to growl with anger. He had Kittanning's memory of her holding his tiny finger between fingers and maneuvering pruning sheers into place.

"What have you done with the baby?" Rennie demanded.

She managed to shake her head, shivering from exposure and shock. "I know my rights. Right to remain silent. That's what they say on all the cop shows."

"Do we look like the police to you?" Ukiah growled. Her eyes widened. "I'm the father of the baby whose finger you cut off."

"Adam made me do it!" she whimpered. "He said if I really loved him, that I prove it."

"What did you do with my son?"

"They took him. They came and killed Adam and took your baby boy."

"Who are they?"

"I think it was Billy and his friends. Adam said that they were dangerous, all crazies, and never took me with him

when they went for the other babies. He said we were court-
ing trouble by keeping your baby to ourselves, that Billy
wouldn't like it. When Adam heard the car coming, he told
me to run upstairs and hide. Hide?" She gave a hysterical
laugh. "Where was I to hide? When I heard them coming up
the stairs, I jumped out the window. I think I broke my leg,
but I knew if they found me, they'd kill me. I crawled away,
quiet as I could, and never laid eyes on them."

"What's Billy's full name?"

"I don't know. There was just one Billy. He was Adam's
bitch in prison, but then he started talking back to Adam, acting like he was better than Adam. It was all the fault of his
new friends, who thought he was such hot shit, filling his
head up with maggoty ideas. That's what Adam said. That in
prison, Billy had crazy ideas, but they were small as fly eggs.
It wasn't until these new friends of his filled him up with so
much shit that the eggs became full maggots."

"This just gets worse and worse," Max said.

"Why did they want my son?" Ukiah asked.

"Adam said it was another maggoty idea. He said I was
better off not knowing all the crazy things that Billy wanted
for the world. He thought we'd be safe here; none of Billy's
friends knew about this place."

"How did they find you then?"

"I don't know. The farm's been in my family forever; we
lease the land but no one ever wanted to put money into fix-
ing the house, especially after it started to fall down. When I
told Adam about this place, he thought it was perfect, even
falling down like it is. He said it was best not to get dependent on outside luxuries, so we wouldn't miss them when they
go. But then it started to get bitter cold, and nothing we did to
stay warm helped. That's why we kept your baby. The other
kids, their folks were all just scraping by. You could tell just
by looking that your dad had money. Adam said we could ransom your baby, and once your dad paid, give your baby on to
Billy, because it would be dangerous to do otherwise. Then
we'd move to Florida and buy a new paradise."

"Your weren't going to give him back?" Ukiah growled,
wanting to hurt her.

"I told Adam that it didn't seem fair. He said if we gave him back to your dad, Billy would just kill us and steal him again."

"Why not just steal another?" Rennie asked.

"Because he's the one that Billy was looking for all along." The girl looked at Rennie as if surprised at such a question. "He's the one."

And all anger bled away. "What do you mean? Why is he the one?"

"That's just what Billy told Adam." Fear crept into the girl's face as she realized whom she was talking to. "He's the one."

The girl had been falling into shock when they found her. Fear now combined with shock to make her silent and trembling uncontrollably; they could get nothing else out of her.

Max took out his wireless phone and started to key in 911.

Rennie, however, caught hold of his hand. "If we get the police involved, we'll lose all control over her."

"She's going into shock," Max snapped.

Rennie shrugged, apparently not caring after what she'd done to Kittanning. "She's our only lead. The police will handle her with kid gloves."

"She's a child that's been warped and used by a man old enough to be her father," Max stated.

"She's old enough to know right from wrong," Ukiah snapped.

"There is no telling what she knows about the cub and Kittanning," Rennie said, "but at the very least she knows that it was a finger that they mailed to us, and if they fed him well, Kittanning grew it back. And then there's us, here, now."

"We don't have the right to let her die because someone else screwed her over first," Max said. "Doing anything but calling an ambulance is gambling with her life, and we don't have that right."

Rennie glared anger at Max, but then turned a carefully neutral face to Ukiah, indicating that it was his choice. The Pack's way or Max's? Ukiah sighed. If Rennie had charged down the road of mass destruction, he would have gladly followed, but being asked to pick the path, he couldn't knowingly endanger the girl's life. After what she had done to Ukiah and Kittanning, the Pack might kill her when her usefulness was over.

"Call nine-one-one," Ukiah told Max. "The house is practically empty; we can search it before the police come."

Rennie went off to lead the search, guarding what he thought of the choice. Did he think Ukiah weak, or had he wanted Ukiah to choose the right path, prove he was a good person despite the situation? Perhaps the latter, why else leave the choice to him? He wished that Rennie wasn't being so purposely obscure.

As Max called the police and reported Goodman's murder, Ukiah snugly wrapped the girl in a blanket fetched from the house. He was furious at her and yet at the same time alarmed at her faint racing heartbeat and cold skin. She was younger than he thought earlier, maybe only fourteen, and light as a bundle of sticks. His sturdy baby sister, Cally, weighed nearly the same amount. Her jump from the second-story window had broken her right leg, and it was now swollen and bruised to near black. She made no sound when he picked her up and carried her back to the Hummer. Max followed behind, patiently giving out directions to the emergency operator.

Bear was crouched in the area used as a parking area, examining the various tracks coming and going. *"There had been five people in the barn: four men and one woman. They came in one vehicle, something big, a SUV or a pickup truck, and drove off in two. They took whatever vehicle that Goodman and the girl were using; a compact car by the tracks. The woman was carrying a weight she shifted often, shoulder to shoulder."*

"Kittanning," Ukiah growled softly.

Bear handed a cigarette butt to Ukiah without comment.

The smoker had been the axe murderer, holding the butt with fingers tainted with Goodman's blood, blister discharge, apple juice, and vomit. The saliva on the tip revealed him to be a young white man, mousy blond and brown-eyed. Ground into grass and earth, there would be no possibility of lifting fingerprints off it.

"The killer, at least, wasn't Ontongard."

They scoured the farm, racing against the arrival of the police.

It was Hellena who noted the lack of baby items. While there were soiled diapers, used diaper wipes, and empty formula cans in profusion, there were no unused supplies. Whoever killed Adam and took Kittanning seemed to intend to keep him alive for some time. Heartening news indeed.

On the disheartening side, there was a profound lack of personal items in the house. If there had been anything in the house with a clue to Billy Bob and his friends' identities, Adam's killers had already taken it. Ukiah stopped in the ruined dining room and studied the mural. As a whole, the work was disturbing. There had been smudges of paint on Adam's hands, while the girl's had been clean, so Adam had been the artist. Loon was what Sam's father called Adam, and gazing at the picture, Ukiah felt he was seeing inside the man's twisted mind.

Most of the room had been given a base coat of white latex with something mixed in so the background glittered in the sunlight. Something that might have been a tree framed the majority of the images; it started at the floor as a black, thick trunk resting two feet off center of the hall doorway and grew upward to the ceiling in a thinning line that gradually shifted from the mat black to a deep blue. At knee height, the spindly tree threw out one twisted branch then ran its wavering way to the far side of the wall, done all in the dark blue.

On the left side of the tree, Goodman had painted a spiky sun up high, an arch of blue that might have been the rim of the sky, and a line of dark green fernlike leaves to the tree. Otherwise the area was blank.

On the other side of the tree, however, the images were penciled in so tightly together that only the color scheme allowed one to pick out individual figures. Goodman seemed to be fixated on one mythical creature: a half-snake, half-woman creature. Goodman had painted half a dozen on the wall. While its overfull breasts and female genitals were prominently displayed, the writhing gray snakes that made up the creature's hair always obscured its facial features. Throughout the room, the snake woman performed acts of sexual torture on slight blond figures. Dominating the mural, though, was a large copy of the creature masturbating beside an apple tree, snaky tail wrapped about the trunk; the tree's large red fruit making a mockery of the wormy apple stuffed into Goodman's mouth.

Goodman had done a self-portrait of himself naked and sexually rampant. Yet another slight blond figure knelt at his feet, back to the viewer in order to show hands elaborately bound tight, mouth exaggerated open in profile to show the person about to pleasure the man, eyes gazing up in a manner that suggested worshiping. One of the man's hands rested on the blonde's head, and the other was raised so that a bolt of lightning struck his pointer finger.

"Something about this really gets my hackles up," Ukiah said to Max as his partner came in from searching the kitchen.

Max followed Ukiah's gaze and shook his head. "He was one sick puppy."

"A lot of these are copies of his prison tattoos." Ukiah pointed at the snake woman around the tree. "That's the one he has on his right arm. It was her tail that I could see when he shot me."

Max studied the snake woman and then looked around the room, eyes narrowing in thought. "I'll go out on a limb and say his need to dominate his relationships is because his first sexual partner was a seriously twisted older woman. Maybe his mother."

"What?"

"The gray hair always obscuring the face, as if Adam didn't want to show her face. These blonds here are all male." Max pointed to the blonds being tortured. "The male being much smaller than the female could indicate that he was a young child. They say most men who prey on children were abused as a child themselves."

Ukiah studied the mural, growing aware that the hair on the back of his neck *was* raised. Why did he find it so disturbing? Just because his son had been at the mercy of this man, and would keep perfect memories of whatever had been done to him?

No, it was something deeper, more basic. Ukiah reached out and touched the apple tree, the most pleasant thing on the wall. Adam used acrylic paint, sienna brown with streaks of black for the tree bark. The tips of his fingers, though, tingled slightly, as if pressed against the ends of a flashlight battery. He slid his hand up the trunk and through the ruffled green leaves and swirls of red fruit. Why did it feel this oddly? He came to the end of the tree and slid over the expanse of white.

There, on the pure white, he found the source of his uneasiness. With no acrylic to cover the latex, he felt what was mixed in with the paint. It jangled through his senses like an erotic buzz, chiming softly in his ears as the nerve endings translated the energy to sound. Now that he was within arm's reach of the wall, the faint glitter intensified to a bright shimmer. He was completely aroused and suddenly panting.

Around him, the Pack went still, focusing on him.

"My God, where did he get it?" Ukiah whispered. "And why would he put it on the walls?"

"Get what?" Max asked.

"Invisible Red." Rennie stalked into the room. "And if Invisible Red is here, Cub, then you shouldn't be."

"I know I'm not going to like the answer," Max said, "but what's Invisible Red?"

"It's an Ontongard biological weapon," Rennie growled, catching hold of Ukiah's collar and dragging him back from the wall. "It's to encourage unions between hosts and breeders."

"It's an aphrodisiac?" Max said.

"To some," Rennie said as he half carried Ukiah out of the room, through the kitchen, and out of the house. "But to most, it's just a very pleasant death."

The spring water proved to be ice cold and pure. Ukiah's hands turned red and then pale white as he washed them until the chimes finally stopped tinkling in his ears. Even then the girl—young and firm and already plucked—loomed deep and powerful as a black hole on his awareness. That desire he could control, probably. What threatened to slip his grasp were an extreme irritation and a strange giddiness ricocheting through him at bullet velocity.

"Did you find anything?" Ukiah snapped when Rennie came to check on him.

"The Invisible Red wasn't enough?" Rennie said lightly although Ukiah could feel his unease. "We assumed, since Hex never used the Ae, they had been destroyed with the ship. Why would he start using them now?"

The number of inaccuracies the comments held forced a bark of laughter out of Ukiah. Once released, the laughter swelled up and tried to consume him. His eyes were tearing before he got it checked. "Hex is dead. The ship isn't destroyed. A Get wouldn't have given Invisible Red out to be used as wall paint."

"Yes, that's too imaginative for the normal Get to think of," Rennie agreed. "I hate to think of a mall painted with this stuff. This house needs to suffer a catastrophic fire."

The wind gusted, bringing Ukiah the girl's scent. She was still wet from a morning encounter with Goodman. He remembered that she wore only drawstring shorts, tied loosely over her flat belly.

"Not now." Ukiah moved upwind of Eve, determined to ignore the sudden desire to pull the string and unwrap her like a present. "Later, and bring the whole house down quick. Use a gasoline tanker if you have to. Don't give firefighters a chance to respond."

"I'll pretend I didn't hear that." Max joined them.

"Good." Rennie glanced toward the Hummer, eyes narrowing as he realized the source of Ukiah's problems. "It needs to be done. The house is a biohazard as it stands."

"It's like the walls are painted with poison!" Ukiah growled and then gasped as he realized that, of them all, Max was in the most danger. "Did you touch the walls, Max? You can absorb it through your skin."

"No," Max said. "I was being careful because of fingerprints. It's not that deadly, is it? Goodman had to have spent hours touching it."

"Invisible Red is like the black ops of biological

weapons," Ukiah explained as Rennie walked back to the house to fetch a cooking pot and carry it to the springhouse. "It seems completely safe. It's massively pleasurable to take, but it's nonaddictive, and there don't seem to be any lasting side effects. But in truth, it's an extremely complex, nearly nondetectable, nano device. It varies the speed and method that it kills so that it isn't linked back to the drug."

"I'm surprised that the Ontongard are that subtle."

"The original design is Gah'h, who realized that if the drug was recognized immediately as dangerous it wouldn't be distributed throughout the Ontongard. Even rats will avoid poisoned bait if there's another rat lying dead beside it."

Rennie carried the pot of fresh water upwind of the girl and set it in front of Ukiah. "Take off your clothes. Wash all of your exposed skin. And rinse out your mouth." To Max, he said, "Don't go back into the house. If it's in the air, it can affect you too."

Max eyed Ukiah worriedly. "Are you going to be okay?"

Ukiah nodded, kicking off his boots. "I'm fine! I'm fine!"

"It would never kill a breeder," Rennie explained to Max as Ukiah stripped off his pants. "But the cub is more susceptible to its manipulations. It cuts through any inherited instincts, lack of intelligence, or lack of interest a breeder might have to make him want to breed."

A fact made obvious when Ukiah peeled off his boxers. Max turned away with a wince.

"You're not bothered by the drug?" Max asked as Rennie searched Ukiah's jeans for wallet and keys to be saved when the Pack burned his clothes.

"It's inert in Gets." Rennie rinsed the keys and tossed them to Max. "We can't breed, so it doesn't try to manipulate us, and it's keyed to kill only nonuseful humans."

Max pocketed the key ring. "So why didn't it kill Goodman?"

"This has a complex logic tree of when to kill and when to wait. Anyone that repeatedly takes the drug might be either a supplier or a highly visible user, neither one the drug wants to suddenly drop dead."

"Goodman's constant exposure to the Invisible Red was

what probably saved him from it," Rennie said. "The drug would wait for a decrease of certain markers in his system."

"So a drug pusher could deal in this stuff for months," Max asked, "but it would kill someone exposed to it only once?"

"Like you?" Naked now, Ukiah rinsed his mouth and spat out the water with disgust. "Yes!"

"What about the girl?" Max jerked a thumb back toward the Hummer.

"It won't hurt her; she's viable breeding stock."

While Ukiah washed his face and neck, Max fetched the pack of clean clothes that they kept in the Hummer.

"What kind of name is Invisible Red?" Max asked when he got back. "Is it normally red, or invisible? How will I recognize it?"

"It's nearly invisible to a human." Ukiah pretended to be rubbing it between his fingers. "It would feel like dry oil, frictionless, so clear you probably can't see it. We call it red because we can see it, hear it, and smell it. It smells like red."

"Smells like red?" Max said.

Ukiah frowned, pulling on underwear and pants, trying to put the sensation into plainer English.

But from a border guard came a warning *"Incoming!"*

"No siren?" Rennie cocked his head, listening. *"Take cover."*

"Shit!" Ukiah tugged on a pair of boxer shorts. He motioned Max toward the trees. "We've got company."

They faded back into the apple trees and waited, guns ready. Seconds later Hutchinson's white rental sedan crested the hill, hesitated in the shadows, and then moved down the driveway toward the Hummer.

"Damn it," Ukiah swore and headed out to intercept Hutchinson. With the Dog Warriors so jumpy, there was a risk they'd take out the federal agent in the name of tying up loose ends. "What the hell are you doing here?"

Hutchinson ignored him, and zeroed in on Eve lying on the Hummer's tailgate, wrapped in the blanket so only the top of her head showed. He pulled aside the blanket, looked at her face, and sagged slightly. "I'm Agent Hutchinson of Homeland Security," he said once he pulled himself back together.

"What's your name? Are you hurt? What happened to you? Do you live here?"

Eve gazed at him in the mute shivering fear and shock.

Hutchinson glanced to Ukiah for help. "Who is she?"

"Eve Linden." Max joined them at the Hummer, carrying the change of clothes that Ukiah had left behind. "She's one of the two people that kidnapped Kittanning. Her partner's dead in the barn."

Hutchinson did a slow scan of the rolling hills of pasture, the woods, and the isolated farmhouse. "How the hell did you find them?"

Ukiah told him about finding the fingerprints and Indigo matching them to Goodman. He stopped there, leaving it to Max to come up with a better bridge than what truly happened.

"An informant who was in prison with Goodman suggested that we look for local runaways. Young. Desperate." Max indicated Eve. "We got a lead on the girl. This farm belongs to her family. It's all simple connect the dots."

As he listened, Hutchinson uncovered Eve in sections, examining her gently, and clicked his tongue at the broken leg. "You do this?"

"Hell no," Ukiah snapped and shifted downwind of her.

"She and her partner had a falling out with the people that hired them; they tried a double-cross by ransoming Kittanning." Max handed Ukiah his clothes. "She jumped out the second-story window. He didn't get away."

Covering Eve back up, Hutchinson eyed Ukiah's bandages, stark white on his ruddy skin. "Why are you half-naked?"

"He got into some poison ivy," Max lied smoothly. "It will stay on any clothes until you wash them, and you need to wash all exposed skin off immediately or get a nasty rash; it's an occupational hazard of tracking."

"Like nosy federal agents?" Hutchinson tapped out a cigarette. "Have you called the police?"

"Yeah," Max said. "They'll be here shortly. How did you get here before them?"

Hutchinson considered them, weighing his options, and

decided to confide in them. "I'm not sure if it's the farm I found, or just you. A little while ago, someone hacked into a top-secret spy satellite system and followed a car across country to this farm."

Max glanced at the Hummer with its distinct profile. "My Hummer? Or the blue Honda that Goodman was driving?"

"Yes, that is an important question, isn't it?" Hutchinson gave Max a dry smile and lit his cigarette. "The answer is, I don't know. I'll call my source and see if they have an idea of *when* the satellite was looking and *what at* as well as *where*." He took a long drag on his cigarette; his hand trembled with micro-spasms from adrenaline.

It hit Ukiah then the stupidity of Hutchinson rushing to this isolated spot without backup, chasing after a cult of religious loons, with no idea what he might find. It was an insane risk. Then Hutchinson's reaction to Eve connected with what Indigo had told Ukiah and he understood what Hutchinson hoped to find. "You came looking for Christina."

Hutchinson flashed him an annoyed look. "Yes. I want her back as much as you want your son back."

"What if she doesn't want to come back?" Ukiah asked. "Kittanning was taken. Christina walked away from you of her own free will."

"No, she didn't," Hutchinson snapped. "I don't know what they told her, but they lied to her, played on her weakness somehow." He took a deep drag on his cigarette. "Christa hated being the spoiled rich kid almost as much as she hated being short, but she knew that there wasn't much she could do about either one."

"There are high heels and charities," Max pointed out.

Hutchinson shook his head. "At four-ten, she was too short to be a cop or firefighter or any of the people she saw as making a direct difference in the world. And until she was thirty, she couldn't touch her trust fund's principal. Every year, she did give away most of her allowance. It drove her parents nuts." Hutchinson stabbed the air with his cigarette. "She handpicked all her charities, and she did volunteer work with them. Make a Wish. Children with AIDS. And then Harris got hold of her. He took her money.

He made her vanish. And I don't know how. I've asked my-self for two years—what did he do to her to make her give it all up?"

Ukiah shook his head, not able to even guess.

"If the cult didn't follow you to the farm, then they knew Goodman." Hutchinson waved his cigarette toward Eve. "Did she say anything about the cult?"

"Nada," Max said.

"What have you found besides the girl?"

"Goodman." Max pointed toward the barn, and cut Ukiah's warning off by saying, "Why don't you finish getting dressed, kid."

Ukiah pulled on clothes as Hutchinson walked down to the barn. "That wasn't nice."

"I'm not feeling nice at the moment."

Ukiah watched Hutchinson react. He expected mild sur-prise from the agent. Even from where they stood, Hutchin-son's stunned dismay was clear. "He's not taking that well."

They watched a moment longer, and then Max said, "Oh, hell!" and started for the barn.

Hutchinson retreated from the barn and was sitting on a fallen tree, trying to light a cigarette when they joined him.

"You okay?" Max took the heavy gold lighter from Hutchinson's shaking hand and lit it.

Hutchinson cupped shaking hands around the flame to light his cigarette. "No one has seen Christa for nearly a year. Hell, no one has seen any of them for months." He took back his lighter and sat rubbing it with his thumb like a rosary bead. "But it's one thing to know that the cult are complete nutcases, it's another that they've been killing people."

It's one thing to know . . . Ukiah winced as Hutchinson echoed Indigo's recent words.

"That is if they were following Goodman and beat us here," Max said. "Goodman, though, was in California until six months ago, and he came East to join his lover, who was a Pittsburgh Steelers football fan. That doesn't connect him up with the cult."

Hutchinson stared bleakly at the barn. "It's not who he is,

but how he died that connects him," he said, and then went as
stubbornly mute as Eve as a wailing chorus of sirens announced that the ambulance and police were arriving en
masse.

CHAPTER ELEVEN

Linden Farm, Sleepy Hollow Road, Jeannette, Pennsylvania
Wednesday, September 15, 2004

It was hours before Ukiah and Max could leave the farm. Ukiah could sense Rennie, near at hand, while they answered questions and made statements. The Pack ranged farther out, scouring the neighboring area for any clue to Kittanning's location. He became acutely aware too that he hadn't eaten since breakfast, and that he had been shot dead the day before. Like a windup toy, he slowed down, and finally stopped, sitting on the Hummer's bumper. Dusk lay on the shorn wheat fields like a blanket, hazing the air slowly into deeper shades of velvet blue, and filling his brain with cotton.

Despite everything, or maybe because of it, the Invisible Red still jangled in his system. It ate up his attention with sensual input, eliminating his normal ability to sense people approaching him. He found himself startling again and again as people took him by surprise.

"You okay?" Max seemed to appear out of the gathering darkness.

"I need to eat." If for no other reason than eating would help his system shrug off the effects of the Invisible Red.

Max pressed a hand to Ukiah's forehead. "Yeah, you're getting shocky. Come on. Let's go."

Pittsburgh possessed a surprising number of all-night restaurants, ranging from quiet family diners to noisy fa-

vorites of college students. The nearest proved to be the Park
on Route 30. Max called Sam and let them know where they
were headed. Max parked the extra wide Hummer in two slots
by the front door. With a low rumble that pressed against the
skin, Rennie pulled into the parking lot on his Harley David-
son.

It was a mark of how rattled Max was when he didn't comment on Rennie's presence, only stood by the door, waiting.
Rennie slowly prowled the entire parking lot, checking for
unmarked police cars and Ontongard. Finding the parking lot
innocent of danger, Rennie pulled in beside the Hummer.

A young, sassy redhead waitress with a pierced tongue
made Ukiah painfully aware that the Invisible Red hadn't
completely worn off. "Hey!" she said, coming up to seat
them. Her eyes widened as she swept him a head-to-crotch
look. "Smoking or nonsmoking?"

"Nonsmoking," Rennie said.

She gathered up three menus, led them to the back corner,
and managed to press full-body up against Ukiah as she
stepped back to let Max into the booth. For a moment, he
thought she had done it by mistake, and he put his hands out
to steady her. She relaxed slightly more against him, turning
her head to breathe, "Oops."

Under the sheath of her cotton dress, she was warm, lithe,
and firm. He knew without having to imagine what she would
look like naked.

"That's okay." He managed to set her away from him, and
slide into the safety of the booth.

"Our special of the day is meat loaf and hot, creamy
mashed potatoes." She handed them each a menu, and then
rested her right hand on the back of the booth, nearly touching Ukiah's shoulder. "Or a stack of buttermilk pancakes,
smothered with sweet, sticky maple syrup, bacon and eggs.
Soup of the day is chicken tortilla. Can I get you something"—she flashed Ukiah a heated glance—"to drink while
you look over the menu?"

Ukiah stared at the menu, only aware of her body canted
toward his. Rennie ordered something, a rumble of voice
from across the table. Max asked a question, and the waitress

leaned across Ukiah to point at something on Max's menu, pressing her full breast against Ukiah's cheek. He couldn't resist. He nuzzled into the wonderful softness and breathed in her clean healthy female scent. She wore anklet socks, so he found only warm bare skin under her skirt.

"You don't take your time running the bases, do you?" she purred, her voice going husky.

"Down, Cub." Rennie gave him a hard look.

"I'm trying." Ukiah controlled his hands back onto the table. *"She's not making it easy."*

"No, she's making it too easy."

"The fully loaded baked potato," Max finished ordering. "He'll have the same. A coffee with cream for me, please, and chocolate milk shake with no contact sport for him."

"Ah, you're no fun." She winked and went off to put their order in.

"How long is this stuff going to stay active in you?" Max murmured.

"It would help if she had any clue on personal space." Ukiah found himself focused on the waitress even as she sashayed away, trailing the scent of her arousal behind her.

"Oh, I'd say she knows exactly where her personal space intersects yours," Max said.

"Sixty million years of spotting genetically superior stock is hard to override." Sam's voice behind Ukiah surprised him. He turned, mentally backtracking, and realized that she had parked the Volvo next to the Hummer and limped into the restaurant while his attention was on the redheaded waitress. "If you want the girls to leave him alone," Sam continued, plucking at the mesh muscle shirt that Ukiah was wearing. "You shouldn't let him wear things to show off his buff body."

"What are you doing here?" Max asked.

Sam waggled her wireless phone at him. "You didn't ask where I was when you called. That navigation system on the Volvo is slick." Rennie stood up, and indicated that she was to slide in on Max's other side.

The waitress returned, their drinks on a tray. She brought a coffeepot, a creamer, and extra sugar. Rennie had gotten a root beer. Ukiah's milk shake threatened to overflow. She eyed the new seating arrangement—Sam tucked between Rennie and Max—and smiled brightly at Sam. "Hey! I'll get you a menu. What would you like to drink?"

"Coffee is fine," Sam said.

The waitress poured out a coffee for Sam and said, "I'll be right back with a menu."

Sam eyed Rennie's root beer. "What's wrong with caffeine? Ukiah never drinks Coke, and this morning, all of you had cocoa instead of coffee."

"Caffeine inhibits cell division," Rennie said. "The cells it effects complain about it. We can drink it, but it's just easier to drink something without caffeine."

"Ah," Sam said, and fell quiet as the waitress returned with a menu.

The waitress repeated the specials for Sam's sake, once again resting her hand behind Ukiah. As she progressed through the specials, her hand slipped down to rest on his shoulder, her thumb making lazy circles on the exposed skin of his neck.

What divine torture. A goodly part of him wanted to sweep her onto the table and drink her down like honey wine. Could he have resisted her without Rennie's brooding presence? He thought he could have, but was glad he didn't have to.

"I'll just take a cup of the soup," Sam decided, and thus released Ukiah from the torture. "She's really hot for you, kid." Then seeing the various reactions from the men, asked, "What am I missing?"

"The cub's been hit with an Ontongard drug called Invisible Red; it's a powerful aphrodisiac to encourage breeding. He's ready to jump graveyard angels."

"Oh," she said, and then enlightenment hit her. "Oh, that's why I'm over here and he's over there."

"Yes," Max said.

They brought her up to speed on Goodman's murder and the new twists to the case.

"Goodman painted the walls with it?" Sam said when they hit the Invisible Red. "Why did he do that?"

"Because he was a loon," Max said.

"One hopes that is all there is to it," Rennie muttered.

"Well, he must have had access to massive amounts of it," Sam said.

Ukiah and Rennie flinched at the thought.

"Yes," Ukiah said, unhappily. "Which makes it likely that he knows the person with the machine well."

The waitress returned with salad for Max and soup for everyone else. Ukiah's hand had been on his lap when she arrived; it wanted so dearly to return to her warm thigh.

"If you don't watch it, that hand is going to jump off the arm to get to her," Rennie murmured.

Ukiah snorted ice cream up his nose. "Rennie!"

Rennie gave him a smug smile that didn't reach his eyes; despite his teasing, the Pack leader was annoyed and ill at ease with the situation.

"Soooo, what's the shelf life of this stuff?" Sam asked after looking puzzled between Ukiah and Rennie. "Could Goodman just have found a stockpile?"

Rennie and Ukiah shook their heads.

"Invisible Red for one host species doesn't work on the next." Ukiah wiped his nose with the paper napkin. "It's specifically keyed to subtle differences in DNA and chemical balances in the hosts. You want it inert in everything but the desired targets, and then you don't want it killing off breeders or fertile females of the species."

"It's keyed to the cub," Rennie explained more succinctly. "It's standard procedure when creating a breeder; prior to insertion of the first fertilized egg into the mother, its genetic code is transmitted from the ovipositor to the Ae. While most breeders are basically watered down Ontongard, they're only as intelligent as their mother's species. By getting the genetic code early, you have insurance that if the breeder is tyrannosaurus rex in build, temperament, and intelligence, you've still got the means to control them."

"Hex couldn't have changed the key on that Ae without the ovipositor," Ukiah said. "Which we know was still on the scout ship."

"Once Hex realized Prime swapped in his own DNA," Rennie said, "Hex would have waited for the main ship, its ovipositor, and a chance to restart fresh."

"Even though it remains a good way to control humans and Ukiah?" Max asked.

Ukiah glanced to Rennie, who shrugged. "Since we're now dealing with Gets and not Hex, anything is possible. It's unlikely though."

"The danger is that there were three Ae that created much more deadly bio weapons stored with the Ae that makes Invisible Red," Rennie said. "If one Ae is in production, the others might be too. It's possible we've finally pushed Hex's Gets to a wall, and they've decided to eliminate the human race and use monkeys as hosts."

The waitress returned and put food in front of Max, who ignored it. "Can I get you anything more? More coffee? Maybe some dessert?" the waitress asked Sam.

"No. I'm not hungry," Sam whispered.

After the waitress left, Max asked, "I'm assuming that these bio weapons work on the viral level."

Rennie nodded. "The worst is an airborne virus with indefinite lifespan. Once it's released, there's no stopping it. The others are more contained, either by duration or spawn rate, or how it's spread."

"We *need* to find these machines," Ukiah said.

"Does the girl know where Goodman got the Invisible Red?" Sam asked.

"Indigo was going to the hospital to question her," Ukiah said. "We're guessing that the source was Goodman's killer, this Billy."

"Did you get anything more on him?" Max asked.

Sam shook her head. "I've tried getting hold of my dad again, but he's not at home. I've left a trail of messages for him to call me; I've put an offer of money for the information, so he should get back to me."

"Indigo has requested a list of Goodman's cell mates," Ukiah said. "She says it might be a few days until the paperwork goes through."

"If the girl doesn't know where Goodman got the Invisible Red," Max said, "and this Billy wasn't Goodman's source, we're screwed."

"The problem is that we have thousands of slim possibilities and nothing concrete." A plan took form in Ukiah's mind and he fumbled with it, trying to understand its shape. "We could waste lots of time and energy chasing wild geese. Hex took the machine off the scout ship. He wouldn't have created a stockpile of the Invisible Red while he knew the mother ship was on Mars; once the mother ship arrived at Earth, he'd start the breeding program over, using his DNA instead of Prime's."

Max understood enough to now follow his logic. "And any old Invisible Red would be worthless because its protocols are based on you."

"Yes." The plan was suddenly crystalline to Ukiah. "Obviously, Hex stored the Ae someplace. If we found that location, then we could probably find out where it went from there. And Hex knew where he kept it."

Rennie caught sight of the plan in Ukiah's mind. "Alicia Kraynak? She will only have the memories that Hex accessed while she was infected. Those machines have been in storage for nearly two hundred years."

"Yeah, but since the mother ship blew up, I'm going to be the only breeder Hex will ever get his hands on." Just saying it raised Ukiah's hackles. "When Alicia—when Hex shot me in Oregon, don't you think he was planning to connect me with Invisible Red sooner or later?"

Rennie nodded slowly. "Yes, you're right."

"But Alicia said she couldn't recall the memories," Max pointed out.

"She might remember something. Maybe not phone numbers, but maybe a warehouse that the Ontongard used."

"We could try hypnotism," Sam said. "Regress her mentally back to being one of those creepy guys, and see if she can remember it better."

Max glanced at his watch. "We're not going to find a hypnotist at this time of night. It's almost midnight. Besides, Ukiah's about to go facedown into the dishes." Ukiah made a rude noise, but he knew it was true. "We'll call Alicia first thing in the morning and set up something."

CHAPTER TWELVE

"Personally, I hate this plan," Max said while shoving scrambled eggs about in a frying pan. Sam, who was helping Ukiah rebandage his gunshot wounds, made a sound of agreement, followed with a murmured, "This is going to hurt."

"Yes." Ukiah hissed in pain as Sam yanked off the bandage across his back. "I know. It's unlikely to work and it's going to put lots of pressure on Alicia."

A good night's sleep, however, hadn't produced any other suggestions, Alicia had already been called, and Rennie was impatiently pacing the kitchen.

"Hell, that's not it." Max spooned half of the scrambled eggs smothered with cheddar cheese onto Ukiah's plate. He split the remainder between himself and Sam; Rennie had announced that he had eaten already when Max started to cook. "Alicia is a grown woman; she can say 'no' if she can't handle the pressure."

Ukiah tried not to attack the eggs and failed. Max made heavenly eggs to start; wounded as Ukiah was, the eggs were fluffy protein bliss. "If it does work," he mumbled around a mouthful, "we'll want to pump her for everything she might know, down to the smallest detail."

Sam turned the bandaging over to Rennie in order to eat her eggs while they were warm. "Considering the guilt Alicia's carrying around from what went down in Oregon, I think it will be good for her."

The men looked at her in surprise.

"What?" Sam said. "Don't tell me that you didn't know?"

"No," Ukiah said unhappily. "Poor Alicia."

"What I'm worried about is the hypnotist," Max explained after finishing his eggs. "If this works, he's going to hear everything. Think about it. Alicia is going to be giving out details on bio weapons and alien invasion plans while guys who look like they eat kittens for breakfast take notes." Max waved his hands as if trying to contain the scope of the breach in their secrecy. "Insane as what Alicia might say, the Dog Warriors will give her a level of creditability you're not going to be able to explain away."

"Exactly," Sam said. "If she's under, it's assumed that she's telling the truth. If she was mentally deranged, why are the Dog Warriors paying attention to what she's saying?"

Ukiah winced; he hadn't considered someone other than them would hear everything Alicia had to say.

"None of the Pack can hypnotize someone?" Max asked Rennie.

"We know how to steal, destroy, torture, kill, and evade capture," Rennie said.

"I figured that this was a little too subtle for your normal MO." Max glanced to Sam. "You?"

"My dad tried to teach me. I've seen him do it as part of a stage act he does when he's not scamming people out of money. I know it does work. I'm just too impatient or something. I've never been able to put anyone under, not even the easy ones."

Max considered the tidbit of personal information. "Okay." He turned to Ukiah. "I don't suppose your moms have a hidden elf talent."

"Well, I—I don't think so." He searched his memory. "When Mom Lara first started to have migraines from the brain tumor, and the painkillers left her so groggy, she tried hypnosis to deal with the headaches. It helped. But it wasn't Mom Jo that hypnotized her; it was Bridget. We could probably get her to put Alicia under."

"Bridget?" Max made a slight face. "I don't think we should use someone that knows your family. In fact, going to Ohio to have it done is a strong possibility. Hell, if we had the time, running up to Canada would have been the preferred option."

Ukiah thought about Bridget. She always struck the Wolf Boy as a solid, honest person. Even with Magic Boy's wisdom, he could see no flaw to her character, despite her unorthodox lifestyle. "I say we use her." When Max started to protest, Ukiah put a hand to his partner's shoulder. "Trust me, if not her."

Max gave a grudging nod. "Okay. We'll use her."

The phone rang and Sam, who had been sitting closest to it, picked it up with a well-practiced, "Bennett Detective Agency. Killington here." Which was really weird to hear. "Hey, Chino, what do you have? Yeah, I've got a pen." She copied something out, growing a deep frown. "My God, you made that up! Is that a real name? I would too. Anything else? Oh, great!" She made more notes. "Thanks. Are we going to see you later? Okay. Tonight then."

"What's up?" Max asked as she hung up.

"Chino got a lead on Zip, the dead cult member stopped on the turnpike. His name was D-D-mit-D-mi . . ."

Max leaned over to look at the note. "Dmitriy Zlotnikov." Then seeing Sam's stare at him. "I grew up Pittsburgh. We've got lots of Polish people here."

"Do the middle name." Sam tapped the paper.

"Yevgenyevitch," Max said. "Vitch means son, so his dad was probably Yevgenye. Eugene."

Sam gave Max an unreadable look and went on. "He went by Dan, so I'm obviously not the only one that has trouble with his name. And apparently he grew up in the area too. A next of kin claimed the body from the morgue after the autopsy. This is her address. Could be a wild-goose chase."

"Right now," Max said, "all we have is wild geese."

Alicia wore a scarlet camisole-styled shirt, black leggings, and sandals that showed off her tanned toes. She had toned down the false bravado of the day before but it was still there, from thistle-top blue hair to red-painted toe nails. It reminded Ukiah of how fragile she was after all she had gone through.

"You sure you want to do this?" Ukiah asked her. "I don't want to put too much pressure on you."

She laughed. "After what I've been through, this is going to be easy. A little talking in my sleep. I've been hypnotized before."

"Really?"

"After my parents died. It was part of my grief therapy," she said. "Actually this probably will be good for me. I've experienced the complete drowning of my self by an alien force, and now I've got to pretend it never happened."

"I didn't realize you . . . remained aware of Alicia when you were Hex."

"Oh, yes," she said quietly. "It was like falling down from a great height into a monster mosh pit. For a while the crowd fills your ears and you ride the sea of hands and it doesn't seem that awful. There's that sense of oneness—of hundreds of others holding you up, supporting you, passing you on. But then you fall down between the bodies and then they're all standing *on* you, pressing you to the floor, so you can't move, and can't be heard, and the whole time the monster roar of the crowd beats on your skin." He reached out and took her hand, and she clung to it, whispering, "But the worst was you could sense your body walking around killing—killing the people you loved the most."

He gathered her into a hug and rocked her. "It's okay. It's over."

"I tried so hard to stop my body, but I wasn't strong enough."

"You know it's not your fault. You were lucky to survive."

"I know. I know. I know." She let out a deep shuddering breath, and then said in an annoyed tone, "And the real pisser is that I used to so love mosh pits."

A surprise laugh slipped out of him, and he hugged her tighter. In a flash she had shown him that Alicia was still there, fully intact, and maybe stronger than he gave her credit for.

She patted him twice on the back and released him. "Let's go, daylight's burning."

She was right—barely. The sunlight was still a brilliant white of early morning. If Mom Lara hadn't been adamant about Bridget's household being early risers, Ukiah would never start out this early to someone's house.

They had planned to go to Bridget's alone, just the two of them, but Rennie appeared around the corner of the house and walked out to the Hummer with them.

"You're coming with us?" Ukiah asked.

"Yes."

"Why?"

"We don't have enough time," Rennie said, "to count all the reasons. I'm coming with you, and that's it."

Bridget's home was a low-slung contemporary house in Fox Chapel, an exclusive area of Pittsburgh with multimillion-dollar homes on rolling wooded estates. It presented the public road with a quiet, solid stonework facade.

Starr, Bridget's tall lean blond partner, answered the door. "Ukiah? My gosh, you've shot up in the last few months!" She stepped back to let them into the bluestone foyer. Beyond the entrance hall, the house branched out into private, public, and kitchen areas, with a sunken great room straight ahead. With a cathedral ceiling of rough-hewed barn beams, the great room was filled with houseplants and backed with a wall of glass viewing the wooded backyard. The effect was like stepping back outside. After the house's tame facade, the wildness was unexpected and magical.

A massive fireplace of uncut river rock dominated the east wall of the great room. Its blackened fire pit breathed out ghosts of ancient fires. An oil painting hung over the mantel; an antlered man stood in a mist-filled woods, lifting up a bone horn to sound, turned so his face was in shadows. There was a sense of quiet power in the painting.

If you could see into his eyes, Ukiah wondered, *would they be filled with stars?*

"Bridget's in the garden," Starr said, distracting Ukiah from the painting.

Starr led them out the back door to the far corner of the yard, a clearing in the woods with flowers intermixed with herbs and vegetable plants. Most of the vegetables had ripened and been picked, with the exception of pumpkins in a nest of vines. Cornstalks had been bundled into teepee sheaves. An apple tree lent sun-warm sweetness to the crisp autumn smell coming from the woods.

Bridget was kneeling in the riot of green, her auburn hair braided into a thick cord and pinned on top of her hair like a crown. She looked up with slight amusement. "What have you brought me?"

"A bear, a wolf, and a cock robin," Starr said.

"That sounds like the start of a fairy tale," Ukiah said.

"Or a dirty joke," Rennie said.

"At least you get to be a wolf. I think I'm the cock robin," Alicia said. "And if that's the case, I'm offended."

"Cock robins are good jolly brave birds," Bridget consoled her.

"This is Alicia Kraynak." Ukiah scrambled to handle the introductions. "She's a good friend of mine."

Alicia offered her hand and a nervous smile.

"And this is Rennie Shaw . . . " Ukiah wasn't sure what to add to that, nor did Rennie offer to finish the introduction. The Pack leader stood with a hard guarded look on his face.

"You look like a serial killer," Ukiah complained silently.

"I am a serial killer."

"Alicia?" Bridget offered a distraction. "Aren't you the girl that disappeared in Oregon?"

"Yes." Alicia smiled shyly and laid a hand on Ukiah's shoulder. "Ukiah found me and brought me safely home."

"Merry meet, merry part, and merry ye meet again." Bridget smiled warmly. "Lara called, saying you needed help, Ukiah. How can I help you three unlikely fellows?"

"We . . ." Ukiah fumbled for a simple explanation. "We need Alicia hypnotized to learn something she might know but can't recall."

"Sounds easy enough." Bridget rose and brushed the dirt from her knees. "Let's get comfy and give it a go."

Ukiah held out a hand to halt her. "The only thing is this

involves—well—something you are better off knowing
nothing about. Is it possible for you to hypnotize Alicia and
then let us question her alone?"

"Oh, goodness, no. I will have no part in lowering someone's mental defenses and then let two untrained strangers
muck around in her brain."

Ukiah had expected that as her answer. "We need you to at
least promise not to tell anyone what we talk about."

"Not to worry." Bridget led them back into the house to a
flagstone sunroom with white wicker furniture. "A hypnotist
is like a doctor in regards to patient confidentiality. Perhaps
even more so, since the patients aren't aware of what they've
said."

Rennie looked pointedly at Starr.

"My spouses know that they're not my secrets to tell and
keep their curiosity to themselves." Bridget waved Alicia into
a lounge chair. "Settle in and get comfortable."

"Spouses?" Rennie yipped aloud.

"I have a wife." Bridget motioned to Starr, who smiled
smugly at Rennie's surprise. "And a husband. He's at work
right now."

Rennie said nothing, Ukiah sensed Rennie's regard of her
shift slightly, unconsciously acknowledging her as an alpha
female.

"Why don't you give me a few minutes alone with Alicia
to put her under." Bridget made shooing motions, as if they
were schoolchildren. "People listening to the process sometimes go under inadvertently, and I'd rather only have one patient at a time. I'll warn you now, though, some people can't
be hypnotized."

Alicia started to say something, perhaps to mention that
she'd been hypnotized before, and then fell quiet, looking
troubled. Who knew what the infection and converting her
back to human had done to the structures of her mind?

Ukiah took Alicia's hand, squeezed it tight, and left her to
Bridget's care.

Starr led them back into the house to a kitchen filled with
drying herbs and spices. Rennie eyed the abundance of straw
brooms, the blue hollow glass witch's ball in the window, and

the locked hutch containing mistletoe, skullcap, and dragon's blood root, as Starr put the teapot on to heat and started to prepare tea.

"She's a witch," Rennie noted with surprise and uneasiness.

"She's Wiccan."

"I thought you said she goes to your church."

"She does. I'm Unitarian."

"And to think that other Christians kill each other over saying mass in Latin or not," Rennie said lightly, but nevertheless paid closer attention to the tea making.

Ukiah pointed out the poisonous herbs were all locked into the hutch. In focusing Rennie's attention on it, Ukiah noticed something he missed earlier. "Starr, what is this? These dark leaves."

Starr came to see what he was looking at. "That's wormwood. Artemisia absintium. It can be dangerous, so we lock it up."

"Why do you have it?" Ukiah asked.

"We use it in various ways. When smoldered as incense, we use it to summon spirits. It's good for expelling worms, especially roundworm and threadworm."

"Some carry it as protection against bewitchment and hexes," Rennie added, his brogue suddenly thick, as if he had stepped back a hundred years.

Starr grinned at Rennie, as if amused by his discomfort. "Why do you ask, Ukiah?"

"I think I saw it in a painting recently." Goodman's mural to be exact. "It's hard to tell. The leaves were small and not done with a lot of detail—more of an impression of the leaves than an accurate drawing."

The teapot started to whistle, drawing Starr back to the range. "Wormwood has lots of colorful history behind it. Its nicknames are 'Old Woman' and 'Crown of the King.' The Greeks thought it a cure against the poison of sea dragons, and it's in the Bible."

Sometimes the trick to being a private investigator, Ukiah decided, wasn't finding clues but ignoring all but the right one. Even if he was sure that Goodman had painted wormwood into his mural, Ukiah now had a wide range of reasons why. Had Goodman been trying to poison his monstrous mother? Had he believed he needed protection from witches?

"She's most likely done." Starr added a tin of powdered hot cocoa mix to the loaded tea tray and handed the tray to Ukiah. "Take this out to Bridget. I'll stay in here, sketching."

"Please picture a staircase in your mind," Bridget was saying when the men returned to the patio. Alicia sat with her eyes closed, her body relaxed. Bridget indicated to Ukiah to set the tea tray down on a nearby table with an absent wave of her hand. "It can be a staircase wholly in your imagination, or one you know very well. Perhaps it's the staircase in your house, or one at your school, or maybe it's somewhere outdoors, old and worn. When you see the staircase, please see yourself standing on the bottom step, looking up. When you can clearly see yourself and the stairs please nod your head."

Alicia nodded ever so slightly as Ukiah settled quietly in one of the chairs beside Bridget. Alicia's breathing slowed and her face started to sag in total relaxation.

"Please see yourself walking up the staircase. With each step you take you will go deeper and deeper into the hypnotic state. When you reach the top of the stairs you will be deeply hypnotized and ready to respond to the questions asked to you. Please take your time and walk slowly up the stairs. Just nod your head when you reach the top. Walk up the steps and be more . . . and . . . more . . . hypnotized . . . more . . . and more . . . hypnotized."

Alicia nodded once more.

Bridget glanced now to Ukiah. "She'll answer questions now."

"Alicia . . ." Ukiah realized he should have given more thought to what questions to ask. "Alicia, do you remember Hex taking the Ae from the ship? They were in the armory. It's empty now. Do you remember him taking them?"

"The Ae?" Alicia's face twisted into one of Hex's frowns. She continued in Hex's flat voice. "Prime planned an ambush for me while I was out collecting specimens for the creation of the breeder. I had taken heavier weapons with me than he expected. He waited; thinking I'd lay them aside, but I could sense his uneasiness, try as he might to hide it: like sandpaper against my nerves."

Ukiah stared at Alicia in dismay; he hadn't expected Hex to answer. Behind him, Rennie growled so deep and low that Ukiah felt it more than heard it.

"It was — disquieting." Alicia/Hex continued. "I think back to the mother ship but I do not remember him, nor does any *I* that shared memories with I prior to leaving the mother ship. He was a loner always, but *I* did not see that, surrounded by myself as *I* had been, but now that I was alone with him, I see that I was truly alone, and he was another, and not myself. He pressed me to set aside the weapons and I saw the truth and he saw with me, and in that moment . . ." Alicia/Hex paused, mouth working, trying to shape the confusion of the alien who had always been one, finding itself suddenly two. "We drew our weapons, I and he, and we fired, he and I, and wounded . . . both . . . ourselves."

"A simple yes would have worked," Rennie bristled, aware of how much information was spilling out to Bridget. *"Who would have guessed Hex was a talker?"*

Ukiah thought of all his brushes with the Ontongard. *"I've always found Hex to be amazingly chatty."*

Rennie grunted. *"Perhaps it's like talking with a deaf man; he doesn't know how loud he has to shout to be heard."*

"Or how much he has to say to be understood," Ukiah followed the analogy.

"What happened with the Ae?" Rennie growled, pushing Alicia/Hex back to the question.

Alicia/Hex lay quiet, drifting back through time. "I retreated, as did Prime. I had wounded him worse, but he got to the armory first. He chose to flee, and I gathered everything that he had left and put them on a sled. I could not see the shape of his plan; the utter foreignness of his rebellion blinded me. I reacted instead of acting. I took all that the sled could carry and gave chase. I should have stayed and found his bombs, but I chased after and the scout ship was destroyed behind me. Prime wounded me, and I lost even the memory of where its ruins lay."

"What did you do with the machines?"

Alicia considered the question and shook her head slowly.
"I—he—we." She paused, struggling, then as solely Alicia
said, "That's all from that time."

Despite his disappointment, Ukiah felt relief to hear *her*
voice, confirmation that Alicia still remained.

"Where are the Ae now?" Ukiah tried a different approach.
"Surely, when you—Hex discovered that the breeder survived, Hex thought about the Ae."

"Prime's breeder," Alicia/Hex growled. "I was disappointed at the loss of the breeder until I reviewed those
memories and realized what Prime must have done. Swapped
the DNA. Used his own. Poisoned the breeder. But it survived, so it might still be of use, but used carefully."

Ukiah shuddered. "You would need the Ae."

"Yes. The Ae are in storage. They were still safe when *I*
took the remote key out for reactivating the mother ship, untouched for nearly fifty years."

"Where are they stored?"

Long silence and then Alicia alone answered, "They're in
a mine."

Hex's personality had been so strong that it was almost
wrenching to suddenly hear Alicia as wholly herself, free of
the Ontongard taint.

"A mine? What type of mine? A coal mine? A gold mine in
the Rockies?"

"Um." Alicia swung her head, as if looking around. "It
looks like limestone. It's been converted to a storage facility.
Room-sized vaults. There's a gate and guards. Very high security."

"They're all standing on you," Alicia had told Ukiah.
"Pressing you to the floor, so you can't move, and can't be
heard . . . " Thus two personalities lay recorded in her mind,
Hex's thoughts and her own awareness as Hex used her neu-
rons to play his genetic-coded memories and make plans. Apparently with Hex exorcised from her, not only could they tap
the ghost impression of Hex, but Alicia could also peer into
those memories and reinterpret them.

"Where is the mine located?"

"Near a working limestone strip mine." Alicia traveled out

of the mine. "Everything is coated with fine limestone dust. There are farms along the road. There's a sign for the Pennsylvania turnpike, and it's pointing south."

"It shouldn't be hard to find," Ukiah said.

"What will be difficult," Rennie said, *"is getting in and finding the Ae. We'll need the name of the dummy company that Hex used, and how he got through security."*

Ukiah realized suddenly that once they had the three pieces of information, it should be fairly simple to gain access to the Ae. While Hex had been humanoid in shape and size, from his irisless eyes to boar-bristle hair, he could not pass as human. Ironically, because of Prime, Hex was very egocentric for an Ontongard and would not expose his original form to risk. And because of the Pack's relentless slaughter of Hex's Gets, Hex could not count on any one Get to be alive in order to retrieve the Ae. Thus Hex would have set it up so that any Get, current or future, would be able to access the storage facility. "How did you get through security to get the key?"

Alicia/Hex harrumphed, agitated. "Snow filled the city. I hate the winter. The air so cold it freezes the inside *I* lining my lungs; each breath is a murder of myself. There are six of me, I and five Gets. I am comfortable at this number. I am thinking—we are thinking—I am thinking about . . . a mansion of brownstone. I had been there, but I hadn't, another *I* had been there and I see through"—a pause as Alicia struggled with pronouns—*"my* eyes. The house is where it is warm, I will go there after *I* get the key, but there are humans there that will have to be dealt with, and it is annoying because they will probably die. I am angry at the snow, and the humans that die so easily, taking parts of me with them. Stupid, stupid planet."

"Where is the house?" Rennie asked, leaning forward. "Describe it."

But Hex's recall had run its course, leaving Alicia to puzzle it out alone. "The street is called Royal. It's narrow and straight, and the houses look like European, something old that's been updated, but not really changed for hundreds of years. I—he can remember it when only horses moved through the streets, and there was no taint of cars in the air." She considered for a minute and added, "The house number

is seventeen, with tall windows and tall ceilings, and it smells
of slow-cooked spaghetti sauce. Someone's practicing a
piano. They're playing 'Moonlight Sonata,' too slow, over
and over again, missing the same keys."

"Which town?"

"I don't recognize it." Alicia meant herself this time. She
examined alien memories of things she had never seen herself, shaking her head, as she found nothing familiar, and finally said, "The cars have Louisiana license plates. I can
smell a river."

"New Orleans," Rennie guessed. "How long ago was
this?"

Alicia thought for a while. At one point, driven to paranoia
by Prime's rebellion, only Hex made Gets. After the Pack
killed Hex, his Gets began making their own. Alicia counted
back, thus, the life of the Get that made her Ontongard, to the
point it had been created by Hex, and then the memories back
more. "Ten years ago."

So the piano player had been dead or changed into a Get
for a decade now.

Bridget whispered, "I'm confused, and somewhat
alarmed."

Ukiah winced at the flare of annoyance from Rennie. "Alicia was — taken over by an alien being called Hex. She's fine
now, but it's left its mark on her."

"What are these Ae?" Bridget asked.

"They're very dangerous machines that we need to find
and destroy," Ukiah said. "Alicia's the key. They — the other
aliens — don't realize we've rescued her and can tap her
memories, so they have no reason to move the machines."

"Why have you kept this secret?"

Rennie sprang toward Bridget and Ukiah leapt between
them. He caught Rennie inches from Bridget, but Rennie
didn't struggle, seeming content with the bolt of fear he sent
through Bridget. "Could you tell I was an alien? Do you know
how to tell a good alien from a bad alien? Can you tell an
alien from a human? *You* can't."

Unless you cut them to pieces, Ukiah thought, and suddenly flashed to Adam Goodman, carefully sectioned up, and

then watched. Someone knew how to separate humans from aliens—only what was annoying inconvenience to an alien proved extremely deadly to humans.

Rennie caught Ukiah's chain of thought. *"You're right. That's why they sat and waited after killing him. They were waiting to see if his pieces became mice."*

"It would be a witch hunt of the worse kind," Bridget said.

"Yes, it would." Ukiah attempted to drag the conversation back on track. "Alicia, in the mine, where exactly are the Ae stored? What's the company name they're stored under?"

"They're behind a red door." Alicia started as only herself. "The letters E-44 are on the door. The guards took us to it and unlocked it." She slid into Hex's recall. *"I dislike that they have the keys, but they have needs that can't be circumvented. It is a worrisome thing, this moving through the herds of hosts, needing to trust that they stay within their algorithms, especially knowing that often they don't. I touch the madness, over and over again; the disease that took Prime and twisted him so, but there is no understanding it. Salmon will all swim upriver to spawn. Sheep will blindly follow goats and do nothing more than eat and reproduce. Why is man so erratic?"*

"What name is it stored under?" Rennie pressed. "What name did you give to the guards?"

It was the second question that produced, "Omega Pharmaceuticals."

"Damn unimaginative bastards," Rennie muttered. "Do you use passwords to get in? What do you say to the guards to pass? Or did you have IDs from the dummy company?"

"I used a password. I wanted no trail leading back, no key to be stolen, no paperwork to block me."

"What's the password?"

"I am Hex."

They could not get the name of the storage facility. Alicia became agitated at her own inability to produce it, but Hex hadn't thought of the name, nor glanced at anything bearing the name on the one set of memories Alicia had access to. Bridget thought it best to stop there, despite the fact that Rennie ached to ask a thousand questions, ranging over a hundred years or more. Ukiah delayed, verifying first that the Ontongard had laid no traps, or split the Ae up at some earlier date. Everything Hex had taken off the scout ship was stored deep within the mountainside, guarded only by unknowing humans.

Rennie bullied Ukiah into taking a cup of cocoa and eating two of the scones as Bridget brought Alicia up out of the hypnosis. The Pack leader also poured out tea for Bridget and Alicia without taking anything for himself. Alicia took the cup from Rennie with a thin, tight smile.

"Do your mothers know all this?" Bridget asked Ukiah.

"Yes. We found out most of it in June."

"What does this have to do with your son?"

"I don't know."

"We're going to find out," Rennie promised. "Let's go, Cub."

Ukiah set down his empty cup and thanked Bridget. Starr met them at the back door, a sheet of paper in hand. "Here. I drew this while you talked. I thought your moms might like to have it."

Starr had drawn him in profile, surrounded by the trees. A bear rose out of the shadows, looming over him.

"Why the bear?" Ukiah asked, trying to be casual.

"There are spirits that guide and protect us," Starr said. "I get a feeling that yours is a bear."

CHAPTER THIRTEEN

Bennett Detective Agency, Shadyside, Pennsylvania
Thursday, September 16, 2004

Rennie drove back to the offices while Ukiah sat in the front passenger seat, using the Cherokee's deck to search the Internet for storage companies. While he pulled up a daunting number of hits, he quickly discovered his query was picking up self-storage businesses located aboveground, and geological information on Pennsylvanian mines.

"I'm not sure how close to Pittsburgh the mine was." In the backseat, Alicia had her eyes closed as she searched her memories. "It might have been Philadelphia area or Johnstown, but it felt like southwestern Pennsylvania."

"It's going to take a while to weed through this." Ukiah checked the next hit. "I'm assuming that it has a Web site; anything that secure is going to be a fairly large operation."

"I'll hit the library," Alicia volunteered, glancing at her wristwatch. "It should be open by now. I'll go through their yellow page collection and pull storage facilities for all of Pennsylvania, just to cover all bases."

Rennie glanced into the rearview mirror at Alicia, eyes still closed, looking inward. Whatever the Pack leader was thinking, he carefully buried it out of Ukiah's reach.

Max had left him a note to check his voice-mail messages—operating on mid-range paranoia level. Sam and Max had questioned Zlotnikov's next of kin, but Max went on to say that on the surface, at least, none of it was useful. Zlotnikov had spent a childhood on Polish Hill and moved late in his teens to Butler. The move had changed a boy on the social fringe to a total outcast, but he had lucked into a friendship with a popular son of a local minister. It was, his mother said, the start of his religious interest. After high school, the group splintered, the members scattering into different colleges. Zlotnikov himself had tried college, and failed out. He returned to live in her basement, being fired from a series of jobs. "This kid was on a downward spiral. What's left in his bedroom makes him look like the Unabomber. I'd hate to see what he took with him."

After high school, as his friendships became solely Internet-based, his mother lost track of who he talked to. Over time, he became more secretive, and then he disappeared altogether. She had been stunned to discover he was in the area when he died as she hadn't heard from him for several years.

"She gave me the names of his high school friends," Max added. "We're going to do an early lunch and then see if any of them know anything."

Speaking of lunch, Ukiah raided the refrigerator to fortify his wounded body, put the teakettle on the cooktop, and settled at his desk. He struggled to refine his search. After several false starts, he stumbled across a newspaper story on the national archive of photographs. It stated the archive had been moved to an old limestone mine in western Pennsylvania, in a high-tech, high-security, state-of-the-art environmental storage facility used by libraries, national companies, banks, and the film industry. The writer didn't give the facility's name, as he had been asked to stay discreet in the matters of location, actual clients, and security measures. Ukiah redefined his search and found the company name, and then their Web site. Out of habit of working with Max, he wrote out the contact information.

As the teakettle started to whistle, the doorbell chimed. He switched directions to cautiously answer the door.

Indigo waited at the door with all the icy stillness of a glacier.

"What's wrong?"

"It's just as well that Goodman's dead," she said in a completely neutral voice that sucked the warmth out of the air. "Otherwise I might have killed him myself."

Ukiah blinked at the statement. He had never seen her so furiously cold before; he wasn't sure what to do about it. There was a tension to her that suggested that hugging her was a bad idea; she was too angry to be cuddled. Yet, that she was here, at the door, indicated that she needed something from him. The teakettle continued its long whistle, so he said, "Come in. I was just going to make hot cocoa. You can make a cup of tea, and we'll talk."

Silently they made their drinks. He made an expensive instant hot cocoa that Max stocked the offices with, while she selected Earl Grey tea, pouring the hot water over the tea bag. Ukiah got out the honey, added it to his cocoa for a calorie kick, and set it beside her. She pulled the tea bag out of her cup when the water was dark, added a dollop of honey, stirred, and took her first sip before breaking the silence.

"Eve met Goodman at Monroeville Mall," Indigo said. "She had gone alone and he started to stalk her, touching her. She thought he was creepy at first, and was going to report him to the guards, but then he started to look 'kind of hot' to her. Later, he told her that he used the breeding drug on her, stroking it onto her bare skin until she was desperately aroused. By the end of the evening, she went out to his car and let him molest her. He told her everything a love-starved child wants to hear, while dousing her with more of the drug. She'd done heavy petting with boys her age, but the drug made it glorious."

Indigo took a sip of her tea, her eyes growing colder with controlled rage. "She bragged to me how clever it was of him to drug her like that, to pervert her will until she begged him for intercourse, let him do anything he wanted to her. Eve went on and on about how wonderful Goodman had been, while the doctors found evidence of his abuse, everything from using sharp objects to sodomizing her to branding his name on her.

"He twisted her until she thinks pain is love. Every relationship she'll seek out will be like this one, trying to recapture it."

Ukiah struggled to see Indigo's view of this. Yes, Eve was pitiful, but he knew with horrible clarity what she had done to Kittanning. That she acted not out of fear for her life, but simply to show her love of Goodman merely made both of the kidnappers contemptible to Ukiah. No. He couldn't forgive her. "She'll be going to prison, won't she?"

Indigo glanced at him, but whatever she thought of his lack of feeling was masked by the icy calm she held herself in. "With two babies dead and the others still missing, the district attorney is pushing to have her tried as an adult. Her fingerprints were found in all five stolen cars, so that alone will get her convicted of grand theft and kidnapping. She claims that she and Goodman handed the babies over to Billy alive, and so far there's no evidence linking her or Goodman to the murders, so she might not be charged with homicide."

Ukiah could only think that this Billy Bob now had Kittanning. "Any info on Billy Bob?"

"No," Indigo said. "The prison hasn't been able to establish an identity for him yet." She sipped her tea, staring into nothing. "Seeing what Goodman has done with this girl makes me question my own actions."

"What do you mean?"

"Aren't I guilty of the same thing, of seducing a child? You only had eight years of living with people, and I knew it. I should never have seduced you."

"It's not the same."

"Because I'm not a man? I've seen the walls of the farmhouse. A woman tortured Goodman when he was a child."

"You don't torture me," Ukiah said, and picked her up. "And in case you haven't noticed lately, I'm fully capable of defending myself."

"Ukiah!" She yipped and squirmed in his hold. "Hey. You can't deny that you were a virgin."

"And I was supposed to stay a virgin the rest of my life?"

"I just jumped you. I didn't even ask if you liked me."

"If I remember correctly, and generally I do, I had bought you a present and gave it to you before you jumped me."

"The wolf fetish."

"Yes." He kissed her. "Trust me, I was raised by wolves; I knew what males did with females. I wanted to kiss you. I wanted to take off all your clothes and explore all your nooks and crannies."

She giggled, a surprising sound out of her. "Okay, okay, I was being overly sensitive about the issue. Hey, what are you doing?"

Ukiah had started across the room, kissing her as he carried her toward the back steps. "Oh, I think I should give you a full demonstration of my physical prowess."

"Ukiah, I don't have time for this!"

"We'll just have to be quick, then!" He raced up the steps with her giggling and slapping his chest.

While there was nothing fragile about Indigo—under the silk suit was all muscle—she was still a small woman. Their sex was usually a dance between equals. This time he put his strength to use, supporting her in gymnastic positions. They ended, however, with her sitting on his chest, pinning him lightly, slick with sweat and glowing.

"Okay, Wolf Boy, you've made your point." She smiled down at him. "And I'm going to be sooo late, and I haven't told you everything I found out."

"Oops." He winced, only slightly repentant. For the first time since touching Goodman's poisoned wall mural, he felt at his normal sharpness. "Did Eve tell you where Goodman got the Invisible Red?"

"She didn't call it Invisible Red." Indigo gave him one last kiss before letting him up. "She called it Blissfire, and said it made the sex so good that you felt like you were going to go up in flames. Goodman got it off of Billy, last name still unknown."

"Are we sure it was Billy that killed Goodman and took Kittanning?"

"Yes." Indigo ran warm water into the sink to wash up. "Goodman told her to hide, so she went upstairs. She could hear them talking. Goodman seemed to be making excuses as to why he hadn't turned Kittanning over. She gave us an impressive list of guns that Goodman had, but apparently he went out to talk to Billy with only Kittanning in hand."

"There were no guns in the house."

"When we find Billy, he's going to be well armed." Indigo rinsed out the washcloth that she had been using and handed it to him. "She heard someone yell, 'What are you hiding in the house?' and a fight start. That's when she jumped out the window and crawled away."

"He protected her?"

"It seems like it." Indigo started to dress. "She wants to believe he did. She heard them kill him, but she doesn't seem to realize what she heard yet. To her, it was the sound of men hitting pumpkins with baseball bats."

He wondered about screams, and then remembered that Goodman had been gagged with an apple. "She told us that Billy was Goodman's prison bitch. I wonder if the relationship was as abusive as the one he had with Eve."

Indigo stilled, and he regretted bringing the conversation back to that point. "No," she finally said quietly. "Eve was quite proud of the fact that she was a better bitch for Goodman. In prison, he definitely topped Billy, but Billy grew claws and a backbone after being released. The relationship flipped, so Billy was the user, and Goodman was the used, and he didn't like that. Eve, Kittanning, and the ransom were all part of Goodman's plan to ditch Billy and buy a place in Florida."

"So Billy went through a radical personality change?" Ukiah rinsed out the washcloth and hung it up to dry.

"As far as Goodman was concerned, yes," Indigo said. "I tried to sound out if Billy had been infected by the Ontongard. Since Goodman kept Eve hidden from Billy, it's very difficult to judge, but I don't think he has been. You say that Invisible Red is inert in Gets, and apparently Billy and his friends use it to engage in orgies."

"Ontongard don't have sex, with or without Invisible Red."

"Exactly."

Ukiah frowned as he dressed. She came to stand in front of

him until he realized she was there. He wrapped his arms around her and nuzzled into her.

"What are you thinking?" She ran her fingers through his long black hair.

"These machines are not so much complex as obscure. The Ontongard never have anything like an instruction manual; they only have machines that they all know how to operate."

"And?"

"As Rennie says, humans are clever little monkeys. I wonder—did some humans find these machines and figure them out?"

If Rennie had returned prior to Indigo's departure, he stayed out of sight and out of mind until she drove away. Moments later, though, Rennie rumbled down the street and into the driveway; seemingly too well timed to be coincidence.

"I think this is the one." Ukiah showed Rennie the name of the storage facility: Iron Mountain. "It seems the closest match to the level of security that Alicia talked about."

"If she was telling the truth."

"You think she lied while under hypnosis?"

"It does not sit well that two days after Hex's reclaimed Get returns to Pittsburgh that a breeder is kidnapped."

"Alicia's human," Ukiah said. "She's back to the person I know, and that person wouldn't have helped steal Kittanning away."

"How can we know what permanent mark being a Get left on her? What if we've made some accidental hybrid with a human's ability to act and lie but with a Get's morals?"

It was a terrifying thought, but he rejected the possibility. "No, she's not acting. I've known her too long. She's herself—a good deal bruised, but not corrupted."

Ukiah and Rennie arrived at Iron Mountain shortly after noon. There was no signage at the entrance beyond the stylized company logo landscaped into a hillside. The employee parking lot was tucked back away from the road, and the drive leading down into the mines curved sharply beyond a guard shack and barricade. If they hadn't known what to look for, it would have been simple to drive on by.

Ukiah stopped at the guard shack and tried for an unconcerned smile. They decided he would drive and talk, as he looked the more harmless of the two. He was in office casual of white oxford shirt and slacks. "Hi! This is Iron Mountain, isn't it?"

"What are you here for?" the female guard asked.

"We're with Omega Pharmaceuticals. Apparently they've been looking for some records down in the main office, and they think they might be in storage out here. We were sent out to pick up the things."

"We have a service for that," the guard said.

Ukiah managed to keep the wince off his face.

Rennie leaned over and said, "We don't have an agreement for your employees to handle our records." Casual office clothes and a haircut did nothing to disguise the menace in Rennie; it was like engine grease, stained too deep into the skin to wash out.

"Hold on a minute." She called on a radio and a few minutes later a SUV pulled up and a man got out.

"You two with Omega Pharmaceuticals?" He ignored the fact that Ukiah was driving and addressed Rennie as the obvious senior in age.

"For now," Rennie said. "We're undergoing a merger at the end of the year with a Swiss company and undergoing a name change. We've done a lot of restructuring and layoffs, so no one knows what we have up here."

"Normally our staff pulls whatever materials are needed and ships them directly to the office."

"So we've been told." Rennie lied as smoothly as Max could, building on what they could assume Hex would set up. "But according to our records, and our procedures, we don't allow nonemployees to handle our records and so we didn't sign any agreement with your company to allow access to what's in storage other than to maintain the space itself."

"Let us check the vehicle and then meet me inside and we'll check you through." He said it to mean *we'll check to see if you're bullshitting.*

The inspection was thorough, checking through the back of the Cherokee, under seats, in glove boxes, and under the car. Afterward, Ukiah drove down a steep curving ramp into the monster maw of the mine entrance. Massive steel gates guarded over an opening approximately twenty feet high. To the right was a high-tech monitoring system. To the left, employees dropped off photo IDs as they passed through metal detectors on their way out.

Ukiah glanced at the metal detectors. *"Good call that they check for guns."*

Rennie grunted unhappily. They had hidden weapons in the Cherokee in hopes that they'd be able to drive it to the vault. It was a compromise that left them unarmed if they had to leave the SUV behind. Rennie only consented because of Alicia/Hex's rant on being surrounded by humans, and reluctantly since he didn't completely believe her. If the Ontongard had since taken over the complex, or Alicia had lied in the first place, they could be easily overwhelmed.

"We've done some digging into our records, and you're right. We don't write contracts like this but we inherited a few when Iron Mountain bought the facility. Omega Pharmaceuticals allow limited access only to their items in storage. You know, they've only been here three times in nearly fifty years."

Ukiah nodded. "That's what we've been told."

"We need photo IDs and to have you sign in. First, what's the password?"

It felt so wrong to say it. "I am Hex."

They signed in, and needed to argue over the right to drive back to the vault. In the end, they followed a guard in a golf cart through a maze of two-lane roads, several intersections cryptically marked. The miners in the previous centuries had left massive pillars of stone, twenty or thirty feet in diameter, to hold up the twenty-foot ceiling. They passed where they were pouring a cement floor for a new vault and the great cement truck fit easily under the high ceiling. Floodlights dotted the roads like streetlights, and the columns had been spray-painted silver to reflect the light, but even then darkness gathered in every corner. The air was chilled, sluggish, and dry. Most of the doors were marked only with letters and numbers. Some, though, had logos of large corporations and government branches. The guard stopped finally beside a red door, marked as Alicia said it would be, E-44.

Ukiah pulled into a small niche twenty feet farther down, trying to tuck the Cherokee out of the way. The guard stood jingling his key ring as Ukiah and Rennie got out and walked back to him. Just beyond the Cherokee, the tunnels reverted to something rougher and untouched from the mining days. A ventilation fan, painted red and two feet in circumference, roared as it fed fresh air into the tunnels. Even over the blast of surface air, Ukiah could smell water, which meant it had to be in vast amounts.

"I smell water," he said to the guard, and Rennie nodded in agreement.

The guard looked startled and pointed back into darkness where the pavement gave way to rough floor. Dimly Ukiah made out a wall of clear plastic stapled to a freestanding door frame. "There's a five-acre lake over there where the miners broke into the aquifer level. Basically it's the level of rock you'd tap into if you drilled a well. We use it for our drinking water and the toilets. We got a certified water treatment plant behind that door there." He pointed to a door nearest to the darkness. "And we go through like ten thousand gallons of water a day."

Rennie glanced upward at the mountain over their head. "How do you get rid of the waste water this far down?"

"Pumper trucks come in daily." The guard jingled his keys, now an obvious nervous habit. "I'm Mark Stewart."

Ukiah shook his head and introduced himself. Rennie merely glared, too on edge to do so.

"This door is legendary," Stewart said. "Omega was one of the first clients and yet no one entered the vault for half a century. Then one day, like five years ago, someone came."

Ukiah turned to him sharply as it jarred wrongly. "Five?"

"Yeah, I had just started working here. In 1999. We made end of the world jokes about it."

Ukiah glanced at Rennie. *"Alicia said ten years ago was the last time Hex was in."*

"We might be too late already."

"Did they take things out of storage?" Ukiah asked the guard.

"Well, they came with a U-Haul truck. Said they wanted stuff from storage. I locked up, though, and everything looked the same as when I unlocked the vault. I'm not sure what they did."

Stewart slotted the key into the door and turned it, opening the heavy steel door. The air was stale and cool. The room was basically ten by twenty feet deep and twenty feet high. The guard leaned in to turn on the lights, and fluorescent lights flickered on. There was nothing cavelike to the room, squared off, drywalled, and painted white, it seemed like any aboveground chamber except for the dry chill. In the far back corner sat four wooden crates of equal sizes, almost surreal in contrast, aged battered wood in the otherwise empty, stark room.

They were antique shipping crates, Ukiah recognized, from Wells Fargo when freight was moved by railroads and horse wagons. The wood still had traces of shipping labels from a hundred years ago. The four were now strung together via yellow plastic DO NOT TOUCH ribbon.

"No one has been in here since 1999?" Rennie asked.

"Well, we get in to check safety equipment." Stewart pointed up at the sprinkler system that ran the length of the room. "And check the lighting and such. We don't touch items in storage."

Ukiah and Rennie stalked across the room to the crates. They were larger than Ukiah expected — most likely the crates had layers of packing material protecting the equipment.

"If they're still inside," Rennie murmured.

"Is something wrong?" Stewart asked.

"Perhaps," Ukiah examined the box without touching it. At one time the lids had been nailed into place with old-fashioned rectangular-headed nails. These had been mostly pried up, leaving behind gaping rust-coated holes. It appeared that the lids now rested lightly on top of the crates instead of being attached. "I would think they would have nailed the lids back on if they just opened to check on them."

"Or taken the box," Rennie said and stilled as he focused on the box.

"What do you remember about the people that were here five years ago?" Ukiah asked.

"What? You think they weren't Omega employees?" Stewart walked over to join them. "They wore Omega uniforms."

"Uniforms?" Ukiah asked. The Ontongard wouldn't have bothered with that deep a deception.

"Hmmm, you're right!" Stewart said. "The lids are just lying on." He reached out to lift the nearest one up.

Ukiah felt Rennie start to move, accompanied with a wordless roar of protest, his motion intending to check Stewart. Ukiah was in Rennie's way, and the Pack leader changed his intent even as Ukiah turned, trying to carry out Rennie's plan. The smell of C4, released by the opening of the lid, hit him along with the awareness that this was Rennie's darkest fear, a trap. Later he would be able to step through the memory, finding the click of the trigger released even before Rennie's shout. At that moment, he was aware of only Rennie jerking him off his feet and dragging him backward even as he reached for the unsuspecting guard.

Then there was noise: a massive, bone-deep sound.

It struck him microseconds before the flame and shards of wood and a hard hand of displaced air.

Rennie's initial movement took them halfway to the door. The slapping hand smashed them the rest of the way. They hit the ground hard, Rennie on top of him, shielding him from the worst of the damage. Their clothes were burning and their flesh writhed, trying to escape the agony. Ukiah rolled to his knees, realized that Rennie was unconscious or dead, and picked him up. There was another deep bellow as the second crate exploded, set off by the first. He raced the oncoming wall of flame out into the tunnel. A hundred running steps, and he flung himself at the wooden door guarding the lake.

The door shattered, spilling him and Rennie into the shockingly cold water. The third bomb went off while they

were submerged. The shock wave slammed through the
water, a stunning roar. Ukiah floundered on the brink of unconsciousness.

What an irony, to drown in the middle of fire.

He hit bottom, though, and pushed off and found the surface in the cave darkness. Sirens wailed from somewhere in
the tunnel system. Flames and black smoke shot through the
open door, and Rennie stayed an unmoving weight in Ukiah's
arms.

CHAPTER FOURTEEN

Iron Mountain
Thursday, September 16, 2004

Ukiah's full panic dropped to only partial terror when Rennie groaned softly in pain. The fact that he didn't have to smuggle a dead body out of the high-security facility helped relieve some of his fear. Ukiah slogged ashore as the Iron Mountain's fire team dealt with the fire with surprising efficiency. Black smoke coiled around the ceiling, and the great roaring fan beside the lake had reversed, sucking out the smoke.

An employee spotted him and shouted, "We've got wounded here!"

"I'm fine, but my friend is hurt." Ukiah dodged the man's effort to stop him and carried Rennie to the Cherokee. "I need to take him to the hospital."

"We'll call for an ambulance," the employee said.

Ukiah juggled Rennie's limp body to get the Cherokee's passenger door open. "No, no, it will be faster if I take him. I think he's dying."

The head of security came out of the smoke, coughing. "You! What the hell happened?"

"I'm not sure. Someone swapped our stuff out and left bombs behind," Ukiah said. "I don't know who. I don't know why. Rennie is hurt bad; I need to get him to a hospital."

"Where's Stewart?"

Ukiah squinted at him in confusion until he remembered that the guard with them had introduced himself as "Mark

Stewart." Ukiah looked back at the flames licking out of the chamber. "Oh, shit! He's still in there!" He flashed back to the moment before the bomb went off. "He opened the crate and triggered the bomb. He took the blast full on."

Most likely the poor man had died instantly.

"How did you get out?"

"My friend carried me out. He shielded me from the worst of it." Ukiah motioned to Rennie. "I've got to get him to the hospital. I think he's dying."

The head of security looked at the heinously burned Rennie and swore.

"Let me take him to the hospital. I can get him there in the time it will take an ambulance just to get here."

"Fine, fine, let me get you through the front gate."

His mothers' home was the nearest safe harbor. The house was empty and still. Ukiah carried Rennie up to his bathroom, put him into the empty tub, and then raided the kitchen. Judging by the food crowding the refrigerator in strange dishes, and the many human scents lingering in the house, Mom Jo's large extended family had rallied to her side. On the kitchen table was last night's *Butler Eagle,* the headline reading "Second Baby Found Dead: Local Baby Taken." Pinned to the refrigerator by magnets was a MISSING flyer with Kittanning's photograph. Beside it was a crayon drawing by Cally of an empty crib labeled in crudely copied letters "taken."

He took the food upstairs and used it to coax Rennie back to consciousness.

"Where are we?" Rennie felt like a supernova of pain against Ukiah's awareness, the burnt skin cells peeling off in sheets.

Ukiah tried to mentally distance himself from Rennie's pain. "My parents'. Drink this." "This" being a quart of orange juice, eight raw eggs, and a bottle of chocolate syrup mixed together. "Where are the Dogs?"

"What day is it? What the hell happened?" Rennie gulped the drink down hungrily.

"We found a nasty surprise at Iron Mountain."

"Where?"

"I'll explain later." Ukiah gave up on trying to get information from Rennie. "We're safe now."

Rennie grunted and dropped the empty bottle over the edge of the tub. "More."

They split Uncle Johnny's homemade deer jerky, Aunt Kat's egg salad, a package of kielbasa, and an apricot Jell-O and cream cheese salad donated by one cousin or other following the family's traditional recipe. The last was solely a comfort food for Ukiah. Afterward, Ukiah cut away the wet burned clothes from Rennie, peeling off burned dead flesh with the cloth. Rennie's back was a blistering, bleeding mass thick with splinters of ancient wood. Ukiah used tweezers to pick out the largest pieces of wood—Rennie's body would eject the smaller pieces. When Ukiah had been healed back from being shot by Hex, he woke covered with the shotgun pellets.

When Ukiah had done all he could, he fed a jar of peanut butter to Rennie, exhausting his mom's ready supply of protein. "That's it. Go to sleep."

"Are you safe?" Rennie's thoughts were already clouded with sleep.

"Yes. Go to sleep."

Ukiah sat on the tiled floor beside the bathtub, hurt and heartsick, watching Rennie sleep, ashen and deadly still. His mind, though, was locked on those last few moments, the guard alive and unharmed beside him, smelling of Old Spice cologne, standing near enough that Ukiah could sense the heat of his body.

And now he was dead.

They had been so focused on Kittanning that they blinded themselves to the danger. He should have called Max and Sam. He should have told Indigo about the trip to Iron Mountain. Maybe one of them could have guessed that the trap left wouldn't ensnare, like he and Rennie thought it would, but simply kill.

"The 'what ifs' will drive you insane if you let them," Max had always said, and Ukiah knew that it was never so very true as now. But an innocent man was dead, blasted away.

There was nothing he could do, and Kittanning was still missing.

He got up to change.

He stripped out of his damp clothes, pulled on a pair of sweatpants, and rescued what was in the pockets of his wet slacks. His wallet was a soggy mass that he dropped onto his nightstand. His phone was dead, killed sometime between the bomb blast and the swim in the underground lake. He called Max on the house line.

Max answered, apparently reading the phone number on his display and leaping to a conclusion. "Is something wrong, Lara?"

"It's me. I've got a mess," Ukiah said and recounted what had happened at Iron Mountain.

"Iron Mountain?" Max swore. "Zlotnikov worked there. It was one of the first jobs he held down after dropping out of college." He read dates off to Ukiah.

"That's ten years ago, right?"

"Yeah."

"Damn, he was there when Hex's Get picked up the remote key. Hex set up password codes instead of the photo IDs and such that they normally use out there. Zlotnikov could have heard the code ten years ago, and then five years later, given it to cult members dressed as Omega Pharmaceuticals employees to steal the machines and leave bombs."

"If the cult is making Invisible Red, then it's the cult that has Kittanning," Max said. "And vice versa."

"But where?"

"Damned if I know. If they're from the area, though, they know it well. We've talked to half a dozen classmates already . . . oh, damn!"

"What?"

"William Harris. Billy!" Max snapped. "What's Harris's middle name? Robert?"

"Robert." Sam's voice was audible through the phone.

Max swore. "Hutchinson is somewhere in front of us on this. He's talked to the same people we interviewed today. If the cult has the machines, we're going to have fun getting to them before the federal government gets them."

"Only if Hutchinson can find the cult before we do."

"I'll put Alicia, Chino, and Janey on this," Max said. "One of his classmates might know where he is."

Ukiah frowned, missing a link. "Zlotnikov? He's dead."

"Billy Bob!" Max said. "William *Robert* Harris—Billy Bob Harris—was the popular minister's son that befriended Zlotnikov! According to the yearbook, his nickname in school was 'Will,' or 'Iron Will,' or 'God's Will.' He was in a half-dozen clubs: war games, ROTC, first responders, computer club, and a prayer group. We made a quick stab at tracking him down earlier, but let it drop when we hit pay dirt on others that graduated with Zlotnikov."

"Hutchinson knew Harris's name when he came to the office."

Max thought a moment and said, "That's right. I forgot that."

"Why did he miss the connection?"

"He might not have," Max said. "He might not be sharing everything he knows."

Ukiah heard his mom Lara's Neon pull up, the slam of doors, and Cally's high voice. "My mom just got home. I need to catch her before she finds Rennie."

"Okay. Call me back when things are settled there. We'll start looking for Harris."

"Be careful," Ukiah said. "If he's Adam's Billy Bob, he's deadly."

Cally was first through the kitchen door, slamming it open and squealing at the sight of him. She glanced quickly around the room and then rushed for the living room. Ukiah snagged her first, wincing as it pulled tight on the burned flesh of his back.

"Hey, hey, hey!" he said as she wriggled violently in his grasp.

Mom Lara came from the door, eyes hopeful. "Did you find him?"

"No," he said. "Rennie's been hurt and I needed to take him someplace safe."

Cally went still in his hold. "Kittanning isn't here?"

"No, pumpkin, we haven't been able to get him back yet," Ukiah said. "One of my friends is upstairs in my bathtub. He's hurt and needs you to be quiet. Can you do that?" He put her down. "Why don't you go out and play? I need to talk to Mommy."

Lara stood motionless as he approached her, arms wrapped tight around her.

"Are you okay?" he asked, rubbing a hand along her shoulder and back. When she nodded, he told her, in as few as possible sentences, about how the questioning of Alicia had led to the storage site, and the bombs left as a trap. Then, because she still seemed so distant, he said, "I'm sorry about bringing Rennie here. I don't know if the offices are being watched, and he's hurt too much to defend himself. He should be fine in a few hours, and we'll leave then."

Lara sobbed then and caught hold of him. "I wasn't going to cry. I wasn't. I could have been the strong mother, if you'd just be the little lost boy."

"I've got my own little lost boy to be strong for," he told her, which only made her cry more.

When Lara had calmed down enough to start lasagna for dinner, Ukiah returned to the attic to check on Rennie and changed into a dry T-shirt, underwear, and riding leathers. Sooner or later, Iron Mountain would check with Butler Memorial Hospital; once they learned Ukiah never arrived with Rennie, they'd probably report both men and the Cherokee to the police. Now was not the time Ukiah wanted to be answering difficult questions; he was going to switch vehicles to his motorcycle.

He was pleased to see that Rennie was recovering swiftly; the Pack leader would be back on his feet in a few hours. Unfortunately it left him without a backup. Picking up his jacket, he trotted back downstairs.

Max called him back just as he hit the last step. "Have you turned on the television?"

"No." Ukiah carried the phone into his moms' living room and turned on their modest set. It showed a helicopter view of smoke pouring out of the hillside of Iron Mountain. "The mine explosion on Channel Eleven?"

"It's on all the local channels. They're trying to decide if it's a terrorist strike. Apparently there are lots of government and banking records stored in the mine."

Ukiah flipped through the local stations, wincing at what he found. As Max claimed, reporters from the four or five major stations were speculating on which terrorist group could be responsible and why. He muted the sound and let the images continue to play. "Have you gotten a lead on Will Harris/Billy Bob, yet?"

"No one was at the manse, but one of the neighbors was home and we talked with her," Max said. "She had the television on and that's where we spotted the reports on Iron Mountain. Apparently, Billy was a middle-aged surprise for his parents; his father, the preacher, retired right after Billy graduated from high school, and his folks didn't have the money to send him to college. He had some EMT training, so he joined an ambulance crew."

"Did he work with anyone we know?"

"I'm not sure at the moment. The neighbor used little town connections: girlfriend's second cousin's in-laws. You know how it is—lots of interconnected relationships but rarely a full name. It sounds like Billy didn't fit in well though, the rest of the crew seemed to think he was an arrogant little son of a bitch whose sloppiness was going to get him fired or thrown in prison. Then he suffered a mental breakdown and started to talk about seeing demons and angels. His parents were trying to get him diagnosed when he vanished and showed up in California, arrested for assault and battery."

"Which is how he met Adam Goodman."

"So it seems," Max said. "The neighbor only knew that he came back to Pennsylvania, gathered up his old friends, and they moved to New England."

"What's in New England?"

"Who knows?" Max said. "But Hutchinson said they scrapped everything there and moved to Buffalo."

Ukiah recalled the Buffalo power grid they found on the cult's Web site. "Actually, that makes sense. The Ae need power. Usually you hook one of the portable generators up, like the ones we used in Oregon."

"If they have the Ae and they have the power, why are they in Pittsburgh kidnapping kids?"

"Maybe they thought they needed to key the Ae to a breeder."

"But Rennie said the one that makes Invisible Red is keyed already," Max pointed out. "Besides, how would they know Kittanning is a breeder? If they knew that, wouldn't they also know about you? Hell, how do they know about any of this stuff? I've seen Ontongard technology—how did Zlotnikov, a security guard with a high school diploma, figure out that they're alien doomsday devices? We're not talking honor roll student here."

"I don't think he did realize that the Ae are doomsday devices," Ukiah said. "Otherwise he wouldn't have been killed by it."

"Oh, shit, that's right. The Invisible Red wouldn't hurt him until it cleaned out of his system. When the police jailed him, it set him up to be knocked off." Max was silent for a moment, and then said, half to himself, "Zlotnikov knew enough to get one Ae to work, but how?"

Ukiah hoped that it was only one. "I don't know."

"Unless there're instruction manuals you haven't mentioned, this goes back to the Ontongard. We've used their machines only by wit of Pack memory."

"But if Zlotnikov is dead, he wasn't Ontongard."

"So we keep saying," Max said. "I hate to say this, but we might need to make sure that Zlotnikov was actually buried and not running around perfectly alive at the moment."

"Good point," Ukiah said. "Goodman is definitely dead, though."

"And how," Max agreed and sighed. "That's all we've managed so far. We're going to see if we can track down who all went to New England and if any of their families have heard from them, or know anything enlightening."

"Okay."

"Be careful," Max said sternly and hung up.

Ukiah sat massaging his temples, trying to make sense out

of the mess. He reviewed what he knew about the cult, from Hutchinson's first mention to the Web site tied with what Max just reported.

Was Zlotnikov human or a Get? The dead security guard at Iron Mountain had said that someone accessed the machines, counter to what Alicia/Hex remembered. Also the thieves made an elaborate production out of moving the Ae, using Omega Pharmaceuticals "uniforms." The Ontongard wouldn't have bothered with such props. So it seemed likely Zlotnikov was solely human and at least partially responsible for the Ae's theft.

Why the bombs though? Zlotnikov would have known that the Ae sat unchecked for fifty years. Why endanger so many human lives on a trap that might not be triggered for another fifty years?

Ukiah gazed at the muted television, still showing the smoke billowing out of the entrance of Iron Mountain. He picked up the remote and flipped through the local stations again: slices of the same disaster, seen from different angles.

The bombs weren't a trap. They were a warning signal to the cult: their theft had been discovered.

Whatever the cult had planned surely now would change. With this, they knew they were being closed in on. They would move. They would dig in deeper, someplace new.

One thing he learned from running with the wolves, one had to kill a snake before it went underground.

Cally had been sitting on the front porch steps when he walked out of the house. He patted her on the head as he passed, deep in his own thinking. Mom Jo's extended family might actually prove to be a good resource in finding William Harris, alias Billy Bob, alias Core, and his cult, the Temple of New Reason. Whereas he, Max, Indigo, and the Pack would all be outsiders stumbling over unfamiliar ground, Mom Jo's family had a vast, old, and trusted network throughout the entire Butler County region. There might even be members of the cult related to Mom Jo that he didn't know about, although he doubted it; otherwise Goodman's attack probably would have come at the farm.

But he knew Mom Jo's family well enough that they would respond best if Mom Jo organized the search rather than he or Mom Lara.

It was another twenty minutes before Mom Jo got home from the zoo, and his bike was nearly out of gas, so the best use of his time would to be to hit a local gas station.

As he backed his bike out of the wagon shed that served as the farm's garage, he noticed that Cally had followed him, and watched him with big sad eyes.

"What's wrong, Cally?"

"Kittanning *is* coming back. Right?"

"I hope so, honey."

She burst into tears. "This is all my fault."

"Pumpkin." He leaned down to hug her. "How could it possibly be your fault?"

"I asked God to take Kittanning away, and he did!"

"What?"

"I'm the baby!" Cally wailed. "I thought we could go back to the way it used to be, but everyone just cries when they think I'm not listening. And I didn't want him hurt, I just wanted him to go away, but those mean men have him, the ones that are killing all the babies, and it's all my fault!"

"Hey, hey, God wouldn't make Kittanning go away because you asked him to."

"He wouldn't?"

"Would Mom Lara or Mom Jo ever hurt someone just because you asked them to hurt them?"

"No."

"If God is wise and powerful, why would he do something Mama or Mommy wouldn't do because it was silly."

She frowned, trying to fit the two worldviews together.

"God wouldn't do it," Ukiah said firmly. "This isn't your fault."

He rode to town with Cally on his mind. Guilt had taken root in her beyond what simple logic could pluck out. He supposed it was the nature of being raised within a faith. All Cally's life she had been told that God would answer an earnest prayer, and now, beyond all reason, she thought he'd granted her selfish wish. She had heard Ukiah, understood, and yet, even as she acknowledged the wisdom of his words, she still believed in her too-generous God. Ukiah supposed it was the problem of all religions, that God was defined and thus limited by the worshiper; Cally had not foreseen the harm Kittanning's disappearance would cause, and thus neither, she believed, could "her" God.

There were two gas stations in Evans City. The first sat across from the bank on Main Street. To get to the gas station with slightly lower prices, he would need to take Main Street across the railroad tracks, past the elementary school, and out of town proper. He decided on the cheaper gas, but as he sat waiting for the red light on Main Street to change, his thoughts went then to his own beliefs. Not long ago, his view had been as simplistic as Cally's. The addition of Rennie and Magic Boy had done much to grow his view of God. From the Ontongard, he understood now the size of the universe, or at least the local galaxy, and from Magic Boy came a crowd of ancestral and animal spirits. Creation was huge, but they were not alone.

And so, when the light changed to green, it somehow felt right to detour away from Main Street, and swing up to the graveyard that overlooked Evans City.

The Evans City Cemetery was old and crowded with familiar names, testament that many of the town's families had been there for generations. Mom Jo's parents, grandparents, great-grandparents, great-aunts and -uncles, distant and some not so distant cousins, and so on all lay under worn headstones, lilacs, and yew trees. Parking his motorcycle, Ukiah walked the windswept hilltop, visiting the graves of the people he had actually known. Uncle Ollie. Great-aunt Minnie. Scotty. Grandma Pfiefer.

Ukiah crouched at Grandma Pfiefer's grave, hand on the warm stone, the cold wind cutting through him. "Grandma, have you been watching? Have you seen what's happened? Evil people have taken my little boy, and I can't find him. Can you help me? God, in heaven, please, please help me. He's so small and helpless, and I love him with all of my heart."

The wind had been blowing straight east, as it was wont to do in Pennsylvania. The wind shifted suddenly hard to the southwest, blasting through the cemetery with a roar of fury. It scoured over the graves, snatching up dead leaves like fragments of prayers, and flung them heavenward.

Ukiah stood, his hackles rising as a shiver of cold went up his spine. As he watched the leaves rise up, he noticed a great grizzly bear-shaped cumulus cloud lumbering across the sky, heading south.

It did not occur to him to question it.

He ran to his bike and went.

It was a quick whip down to 68 and up the twisting 528. Trees screened the sky from sight on the right as he climbed the reservoir hill, but the bear raced across the reflection on the water, leaving him behind. When he reached the on-ramp to I-79, it was nearly to Cranberry already, and on the exposed hilltop, the wind roared around him.

He opened the big bike up and flew down the highway, chasing the bear. Late evening, and both the northbound and southbound lanes contained only scattered traffic. On either side of the road, the wind rushed through the trees wrapped in fall colors and blasted the dead leaves off in a bright colored blizzard.

He caught up to the great shadow racing under the cloud just as the highway divided and wove around a hill, below an exit ramp and above other roads.

" . . . Daddy? . . . "

Ukiah felt Kittanning's presence speed past him, as if brushing across his back with outstretched fingers, and disappear. He braked hard, fighting to keep from flipping nose first, leaving a trail of smoking rubber behind him. "Kitt!"

The touch had come, east to west, in front, under and behind as he crossed over the Pennsylvania turnpike. The kidnappers had Kittanning in a car, going west on the turnpike, heading out of state. While the highways crossed here, both roads were heavily fenced to keep deer off them. He had already passed the on-ramp for the turnpike connector road, but he'd have to go back to it.

Ukiah dodged a tractor-trailer, its horn blaring, to U-turn

and head back against traffic. With his phone dead and left behind, Ukiah would have to find a phone and stop moving to make the call. And what would he say, his son was in *some* vehicle, type and color unknown?

He had to catch up with Kittanning before the kidnappers could leave the turnpike.

The connector cut from I-79, over State Route 19 and to the turnpike with a tangle of ramps connecting all three together in the name of lessening congestion. He flashed up the I-79 on-ramp, ignoring the blare of protesting horns, and darted across the oncoming traffic to the lanes entering the turnpike. There was a line of cars taking turnpike tickets. The center lane was blocked off with a red light and an orange cone. He ducked through the closed aisle, cut off a blue minivan pulling away from the far ticket machine, and barely made the turn onto the westbound lane. Once onto the level pavement of the turnpike, he nailed the throttle to open.

The speed limit was sixty-five, but most people traveled at seventy or seventy-five. The speeders cruised around eighty. Ukiah raced past them all, already at a hundred and climbing, darting through them as if they were standing still. Luckily the road curved constantly, so he rushed up and past vehicles before drivers could react.

Ideally he would follow the kidnappers at a discreet distance until he found a chance to call for help. He had to close the distance between them first; otherwise he'd be running blind. He risked a glance skyward, but the wind had shredded away any sign of the bear, if it hadn't been all his imagination. He quested with his mind instead, reaching for Kittanning.

"Kitt? Kittanning?"

A faint mental wail of hope and fear, growing quickly stronger. *"Daddy?"*

As the contact became stronger, Ukiah slowed, trying to judge which of the cars ahead Kittanning was in. A knot of vehicles traveled westbound. The first was a U-Haul rental truck pulling a trailer. The second was a red, extended cab pickup truck with a large dog carrier in the back. A gold minivan fidgeted in the back, and as Ukiah approached, pulled out into the passing lane.

The minivan? Ukiah reached mentally for Kittanning.

In the back of the pickup, a small dog leapt to its feet in the dog carrier to stare intently at him. It bounced excitedly as their eyes made contact. *"Daddy! Daddy!"*

And Ukiah realized the scent from the dog was that of wolf cub. "Oh, Kittanning, what have you done to yourself?"

Kittanning cringed at the rebuke. Memories of pain and confusion flashed through their mental link. When Hex created Kittanning, he had locked Ukiah's mouse in a sealed box, from which there was no escape from the pain except compliance to Hex's will. As Ukiah was telepathic with the Ontongard, Hex's mentally conveyed demands had been clear: take human shape. Somehow the cult had Hex's torture box. Inexplicably they had locked Kittanning into it and turned it on. They failed, however, to give Kittanning any clue to what shape they wanted him. In pain, Kittanning had chosen a form that was more mobile. Unfortunately he'd chosen one less intelligent too; the simple lock on the carrier confounded the puppy.

Ukiah slowed down and pulled behind the pickup truck as the minivan passed it and then the U-Haul truck.

There were three men in the pickup's cab. As Ukiah watched, the front passenger turned and Ukiah recognized him. It was Hash. The large man eyed the dog crate with a worried frown, leaving Ukiah to wonder how well they had the crate secured. Was Hash worried that the crate would fly out of the back? Or had Kittanning's transformation unnerved him?

Whatever the cause of Hash's unease, he turned back facing front, satisfied for now. He said something to the driver, who turned at the comment, giving Ukiah a chance to see his profile. He was the blond Ice, lean and ripcord to Hash's bulk, but still something in the look he gave Hash, and the fact that he was driving, suggested that he was the alpha male of the two.

Ukiah would have to follow them, waiting for a chance to call for backup or grab Kittanning. Much as he wanted to get Kittanning to safety, he had to think of the machines; he couldn't lose track of the cult.

A sudden bolt of fear went through him as his perfect memory flashed the recall of his gas gauge, the red needle hovering over the red line. He didn't need to look to know he was riding on fumes. He probably wouldn't even make the next exit.

He had to stop them, here and now.

He'd left his gun hidden in the Cherokee. He had the bike and his body, neither one he wanted to use. He glanced up the road, beyond the pickup, trying to estimate how close they were to an exit and civilization.

The Pennsylvania turnpike seemed to have been built with the minimum of waste in mind. Between the left lane and a cement center barrier, there was only a foot clearance. The breakdown lane on the right was only wide enough for a single car, and lined by walls to keep the crumbling hillsides from sliding down and blocking the road. The rental truck up ahead was traveling too fast for its trailer, and it had picked up a dangerous shimmy, suggesting a timely accident.

Ukiah glanced back. The road behind them was clear of other cars. If he acted now, before he ran out of gas . . .

But could he live with himself if he killed an innocent driver?

He swung out to the white dashed divider line and looked ahead to the U-Haul's side mirror to see the driver's face. Almost as if she felt his gaze, Hutchinson's Christa, alias Socket, glanced into her mirror to look back at him.

"They came with a U-Haul truck," the guard at Iron Mountain said shortly before he was killed. *"Said they wanted stuff from storage."*

Ukiah growled, and gunned his motorcycle. He shot around the pickup truck, and wove back to the far right until he threaded the yellow line of the berm. If given warning, Socket could probably take him out without danger to her truck. But if he could get her to overreact, pure surprise might do what a game of chicken couldn't. He judged the wild swing of the trailer and then nailed his throttle to over a hundred. Ten seconds he raced along the trailer, and then the huge truck body that could flatten him without noticing. He needed to get clear fast, before the pickup could warn her.

Back axle. Passenger door. And then he was at the right bumper. He glanced back to make sure his back wheel was clear of her bumper and cut straight across the front of the truck.

It was almost perfect.

With a scream of brakes, Socket jerked the truck to the left, trying to avoid him as he suddenly appeared in front of her. The already fishtailing trailer jumped to the breakdown lane, dragging the back of the truck enough so the whole truck now slid sideways at him. The movement was a graceful slide until the trailer's edge kissed the retaining wall. Instantly it ricocheted off, twisting on its hitch. With a sound like a gunshot, the tire blew under the stress, and when the bare rim touched pavement, the pavement caught hold of the trailer, yanked it hard from the back of the truck, and set it hurling through stunning somersaults of obliteration. It was like watching a tornado focused on only one object, quickly becoming many objects as the trailer burst open and its contents shattered into pieces, all with their own trajectories.

The pickup's brake joined the scream of protest, suddenly silenced by a deep thud of metal against cement. Later, he would remember the plastic dog cage vaulting from the bed of the pickup and smashing open, freeing a wobbly Kittanning.

Truly almost perfect. Only at that moment, the last fumes of gas spent, his bike died under him. He could feel the heavy front end of the rental truck bearing down on him, and there was nothing he could do. The truck was too wide to avoid. It smashed him to the ground, and he tumbled, a series of bone-breaking body-meets-unyielding-pavement impacts. His collarbone that had healed only the day before snapped along the still fragile knit.

Then there was silence and stillness. Then the click of toenails on pavement, and Kittanning was there, nosing into him, whimpering in distress.

"Oh, fuck!" a male voice said, a passenger in the rental truck he hadn't noticed.

"You okay, Parity?" Socket asked.

"Daddy?" Kittanning licked at his fingers, whining in distress.

The pickup truck's passenger door opened, and Hash spilled out. The two cultists in the rental truck got out.

"Run, Kitt! Get away."

Kittanning licked anxiously at his face. *"Daddy!"*

Ukiah pushed at him, gasping as the move shot pain through him. "Run!"

Yipping, Kittanning darted away, stubby tail tucked between his legs.

Hash started after the puppy, but Ukiah lurched to his feet, and blocked the large man, growling.

"You! You're the Wolf Boy!" Hash shifted into a fighting stance.

Ukiah snarled at the man, willing Kittanning to keep running.

Hash tried to feint left and then go right, ducking around Ukiah after Kittanning. Even wounded Ukiah managed to shift back and punch him. Hash rolled with the blow so that Ukiah barely tagged him, but he still felt his skin break and blood smatter his knuckles. With a roar, Hash tackled him to the ground. They tumbled, and Ukiah gained the top, only to be smashed aside by the pickup's driver, Ice. Seconds later he was pinned and Socket shoved a revolver tight to his forehead.

"Hold still!" The revolver seemed huge in her small hands. "Or I'll splatter your brains all over the pavement."

"Just pop him, Socket!" Hash shouted.

"He's the Wolf Boy!" Socket cried. "He's not one of them."

"Who gives a flying fuck?"

The gun barrel pressed hard against Ukiah's temple, rocking with Socket's agitation. "Give it up, damn it!"

Ukiah couldn't get the leverage he needed to wriggle himself free, the broken shoulder only cracking more under the stress. If he let them kill him, he'd be completely helpless. He forced himself to relax. "Okay. Okay. You win." Like it was a child's game.

"We should just shoot him anyway," Parity muttered.

"Ice?" Hash turned to the pickup driver.

"Bind him, get him into the truck," Ice said. "We'll let Core decide what to do with him. Dongle, get the cell phone and the GPS out of the Jimmy and go after the puppy. Someone will be back to fetch you in an hour or so. Stay out of sight of cops, but get the puppy back."

The third cultist from the pickup truck scrambled over the guardrail and after Kittanning. Hash forced Ukiah to roll onto his stomach, face to the hot pavement, and then knelt on the center of Ukiah's back. He quickly bound Ukiah's arms with a thin strong wire, wrapping it tightly from wrist to nearly forearms in a web of steel. Ukiah's shoulder became an endless wave of blinding pain. With Ukiah secure, Socket moved off, tucking away her pistol.

"We're going back?" Hash hauled Ukiah to his feet and pushed him to the rental truck.

"Core needs to know what happened." Ice unlocked the padlock on the gate, and he pushed it up to reveal that it was stacked haphazardly with boxes. "Clean out of the Jimmy," he ordered the rest. "We're leaving it here."

Hash and Socket moved quickly at the orders, well trained. Parity drifted, as if in a haze.

"Oh, shit!" Parity picked up something from the road. "One of the founts was on the trailer!" He turned the item in his hand and Ukiah recognized it as an Ae's shattered induction board.

"What?" Ice nearly shouted.

Socket brushed past them to climb into the back of the truck. "All of them were supposed to be on the truck!"

"Which one was it?" Ice asked.

"I don't know." Parity eyed the shard.

Socket scrambled over the boxes, peering into the dark corners, swearing. After a moment she came to stand in the doorway. "There's only one in here."

"Which one?" Ice asked.

"Huey," Socket said.

A distant siren wailed at the edge of hearing range.

"What do we do? What do we do?" Parity asked again and again like a mantra. "What do we do?"

"Parity, shut up," Ice said.

"But what do we do? We've lost the puppy. The Jimmy is screwed to hell. We've got . . ."

"Shut up!" Ice roared. "We take him and go! Before the cops come." Ice pushed Ukiah in among the boxes. "Parity, you ride in the back."

"Me?" the boy yelped.

"There's only room in the front for three."

Parity didn't reply, nor did he move.

"I'll ride in back," Socket said.

"Fine," Ice snapped. "Stay out of range of his legs."

Ice waited until Socket climbed in beside Ukiah, and then pulled down the gate, saying, "We're heading back to Eden."

CHAPTER FIFTEEN

"That was a damn stupid move," Socket said as the truck started up, jostling them roughly. With the gate closed, the back of the truck was dark as a cave. "You could have gotten us all killed."

When Ukiah remained silent, Socket nudged Ukiah with a foot. "Wolf Boy? Wolf Boy!" She nudged Ukiah harder. "You've whacked your head a good one. You probably have a serious concussion. Going to sleep would be bad."

Socket was worried about him.

"How do you know who I am?"

"Core showed me this newspaper article on Monday, about you saving the little boy in the sewer system," Socket said. " 'Find him for me, Socket.' So I did. 'Ukiah Oregon' pulls up hits on this little town in Oregon and a flood of stories about you finding missing hikers and lost children. It's wicked cool what you do. I had to filter the search like crazy to get the number of hits down to something manageable." Had she weeded out all the stories about his death in June? He had made the front page of all the local newspapers, with headlines of "FBI Agent Saved, Rescuer Killed." Did she know about the Pack? When the Dog Warriors kidnapped him, the story hadn't made the newspapers, but he had given the police a full report. "In an hour, I had verified your home address in Shadyside with a hack into the DMV."

"So you sent a killer there to shoot me and take my baby boy?"

"Adam wasn't supposed to hurt you," she snapped with anger. "He handled the others perfectly, just like Core said he would. He got greedy and that made him frightened and sloppy. Open the door to one vice and the rest will follow." She trailed off to a whisper. "Core was so upset that Adam disobeyed him in so many ways; he was sure Adam had fallen."

"So you chopped him up into pieces." Flicking back over the evidence left at the farm, Ukiah realized that the cultists must have driven the extended cab pickup to the farm. Socket had been there; she had been the woman that carried Kittanning. Ukiah found Hash's footprint pressed in the plaster dust of the farmhouse, and Ice's scent lingering in the second floor. Ukiah guessed that Core would have made the third man, the possible wielder of the axe. Who had been the fourth? Parity? Dongle, who even now chased after Kittanning?

"We thought he'd fallen, but we were wrong. We did absolution and cleansed ourselves afterward."

The pain made it hard to think. Fallen — as in made a Get? Sudden suspicion sent Ukiah searching back through his memories. Had he touched them all? Yes, he had made skin-to-skin contact with all of them during the brief tussle. No, none of them were Ontongard.

"Is that supposed to make me feel better? Bad Adam was only supposed to take Kittanning, not try his best to kill me? And you killed him for it. Trust me, if Goodman had tried taking my son without taking me down first, I would have ripped his throat out."

"We don't know how the baby ended up with you, and it's a shame that you got so attached to him, but he's not your son, and he was never meant for you."

"He's my son," Ukiah stated firmly.

"Just because your father found you and adopted you as his son, it doesn't mean finding a child makes him yours."

It hurt Ukiah's head to work through that statement. With only his public records to work with, the cult must have decided that Max was his adopted parent. They were equating his finding of Kittanning at the airport to Mom Jo finding Ukiah in the woods, not realizing there was a blood relationship between Kittanning and himself.

The truck turned sharply and climbed, spilling Ukiah sideways onto his side. He groaned with pain, and for a moment wavered in and out of unconsciousness. The truck stopped and started up again, and as Ukiah struggled to stay aware, he realized they had exited the turnpike.

"You okay, Wolf Boy?" Socket asked.

"My name is Ukiah!" He wanted to sit up, but moving hurt too much.

"I'm Socket."

"Socket isn't your real name."

"Yes it is. The name our parents give us are just names they make up, usually before we're even born. But that's not who we are. Core says that when we choose screen names for ourselves, we're reaching in and finding an echo of our true names. Just like people didn't have words for computer stuff until the computers were created, we don't have the words for our true names, so we just use the echoes. Socket might not be what my parents called me, and what the government thinks my name is, but it's the closest to my real name that I've gotten."

Ukiah grunted. Magic Boy could see the reasoning, but Ukiah didn't want to understand these madmen.

"Me using my birth name would be like you using Ukiah Oregon," Socket added. "Ukiah Oregon is a town, not a boy raised by wolves."

He snarled, furious at this woman, calmly denying him his own name.

"See, the wolf is your true nature."

Ukiah tried shifting to take the stress on his shoulder, and hissed as a bolt of pain flared out of the shattered bone. "At least I don't chop my 'friends' up in cold blood. I don't steal babies, torture them to death, and then throw them out in the trash."

Socket had started to sputter out a defense, and then fell into shocked silence. Finally in a quiet, hurt tone, she said, "We didn't hurt the babies." Did she even believe her own words? "We only needed a little bit of blood to test them; a simple finger prick."

"I've seen the FBI photos. Kimmie and Isaiah were tortured with burns all over their bodies and dropped in Dumpsters like so much garbage. Are they all dead, and we just haven't found all the bodies, or are the other two still alive?"

"They're dead? No! No, they can't be! They were supposed to go back home none the worse." She seemed very rattled by the news. "God damn his soul to hell. Adam must have killed them. Core gave them to Adam to return, but he must have killed them for his own sick fun. He was a monster, even if he wasn't fallen. Core said God had brought them together and he would not lightly turn away God's tool."

"Goodman wouldn't join the cult, would he? That's why he's Adam and not some silly computer name."

"We're not a cult," Socket snapped. "The word cult has lots of negative connotations to it. We're warriors of a religious order, like the Knights Templar; the ancient ones, not the modern ones—they're just a bunch of Shriners."

"He wouldn't join."

Socket was silent for several minutes, and then said quietly, "Adam had an attitude problem. He refused to attend Ice's kendo lessons, saying he learned whoop-ass in prison. Ice tried to get him to spar, and Adam waited until Ice turned away and hit him with a cue stick. Ice beat the shit out of him then, and Core nearly threw Adam out then for hurting Ice."

"Why did Adam stay?"

"Adam stayed for the sex. He liked the Blissfire, and he liked hurting . . . " She fell abruptly silent.

"He forced you," Ukiah guessed. Socket was, after all, exactly the fair hair, doe-eyed type that Goodman preferred. "Did he hurt you?"

There was a sound like a sob from Socket, and then a soft, hoarse, "No." She cleared his throat and said, "Core wouldn't let him do everything he . . . Blissfire makes it all . . . feel . . . great . . . Core stopped him."

As with Eve, Ukiah wasn't sure whether to pity Socket or be angry with her for staying in the situation.

"Adam wouldn't do the mental training either." Socket

continued in a ragged voice. "We're God's warriors; our minds are our greatest weapon, and must be honed. Adam refused to do the purification ritual in the waterfall, or keep night vigils, or do the fasting."

Ukiah was partially tempted to ridicule the training; Max had told him that cults used such tactics to brainwash their members. When Max talked about it, it seemed so clinically cruel. Yet now, Ukiah could remember times in his life that Magic Boy sought the spirits, fasting and keep vigils in the same manner. The difference was that when he stripped away all his defenses and opened himself, it was in solitude to receive God's touch; the cult used that time of defenselessness to their own ends, molding the person to their own needs, supplanting God.

A growl rose in his chest. "Why do you stay with them? They're just using you, keeping you ignorant. Is it sex? As long as Adam keeps away from you that is."

"I'm making the world a safer place," Socket said.

"By killing babies."

"We didn't kill any babies!" Socket shouted. "Adam did! He was a monster only interested in serving his sexual appetite. We're saving the world. We put our lives on the line to fight the spawn of the devil! We're like Buffy the vampire slayer and the Scoobie gang. Evil walks among us in the guise of humans, and we're the only ones that know, that can stop them."

"You've been killing vampires?"

"In a way. They're demons." Whatever anger had been carrying her fled, and she mumbled, "You don't believe me. I didn't believe until Core took me to a slaying. I was horrified at first, but then I saw that Core was right, that the thing wasn't human, that all its pieces would come alive and try to escape."

"If the demons look human, how can you tell you're not attacking a human by mistake?"

"Usually you can tell just by watching them walk, how they hold themselves, how they talk, that someone is a demon. Once you get good at spotting them, you can scan a crowd and see them; they stand out like someone with a physical handicap."

Full of memories of other bodies, the Gets moved with machine precision, lacking the fluid grace of the Pack who embraced their humanity.

Socket had paused, and now she continued, slower. "Actually, it's like a TV show where some magical device swaps everyone's body around, and the actors mimic how the other people play their characters, so Dick is now Jane, and Jane is Baby, and Baby is Dick. The first time it happens, someone has to explain it, but after that, you don't need explanations to see who is in which body.

"Once someone tells you to watch closely, you can see the demon inside. It's like there's only one demon, and we keep killing him again and again. They always react the same way and once you find a trap that works, it will keep on working until you're out of demons."

They could recognize Hex no matter what body he infested! Ukiah suddenly realized that the cult would have many advantages over the Pack in fighting the Ontongard. Hidden by the masses, human hunters could approach the Gets without being noticed, pick their attack point and never mentally signal their intent to their victim.

"How many humans have you killed by mistake?"

"Adam was the only one," Socket said. "And I'm not sure that was a mistake. He was evil still in human form."

"Are you sure? Core didn't make any mistakes before he could recognize them in a crowd?"

"Core's been touched by God," she said with full conviction. "God opened his eyes and made him to see, choosing him as His holy warrior."

"How do you know that these are demons?" Ukiah pressed, hoping that they were only killing Ontongard; that the Pack had slipped their notice, and that innocent humans weren't dying in scores.

"In Luke twenty, Jesus says, 'But those who are counted worthy to attain that age, and the resurrection from the dead, neither marry nor are given in marriage; nor can they die anymore, for they are equal to the angels and are sons of God.' "

"What does that mean?"

"It means that angels and demons and nephilim can return from the dead."

"So you kill them like Adam, cut them up?"

"Yes, and burn them quickly, before they can re-form and come back."

"How do you know you're not killing angels along with the demons?"

She laughed. "If you could see how ugly these things are, you would know. It's like all sense of God's beauty is blasted out of them."

Yes, that was an apt description of Ontongard. "And no one has noticed scores of dead bodies lying around?"

"One of our burn sites had been found. That's why we left New England. Between Ice and Hash, though, it will never be linked back to us."

Hutchinson had recognized Adam's death as similar to other murders; he had linked the Temple to the burn sites. Had he worried that Socket had been one of the dead, or one of the killers?

Thinking of the agent's reaction, Ukiah remembered how Hutchinson found the farm, and Indigo's discovery that other surveillance systems had been compromised. "You spy on the demons?"

"How else can we know where and when to get them alone? They're stronger and faster than humans. You need to set an ambush and take them out in one shot, and then box them before the separate parts can escape."

The truck had been pausing at random points, red lights and stop signs, but this time it stopped and the engine went quiet. Outside the truck, a man called out a surprised but pleased welcome of "That was fast! We haven't even started a second load."

"Get Core, Io. We had problems." Ice got out of the driver's door, slammed the door shut. "And they haven't gone away."

Ukiah heard Io move off, calling "Core!" The passenger door opened and the truck shifted as the others got out. A host of other voices gathered around the truck, asking questions of the returning three and getting no answers.

Silence moved suddenly through the cultists, and then a deep rich voice said, "What happened?"

"We were almost to Ohio when the Wolf Boy showed up on a motorcycle." Ice spoke, but it wasn't the same bullying Ice. This Ice was quiet and respectful. He jangled keys, hunting for the one for the padlock. "The Jimmy is toast, so is the trailer, and everything on the trailer is now roadkill, including at least one of the founts."

"Which one?"

"Huey is the only one on the truck," Ice murmured. "We loaded in such a rush; I don't know which fount was on the trailer or if there was more than one."

"Io," Core called out. "Go check on the founts. See which ones are missing."

"What if we lost Dewey?" Ice pulled free the padlock with a rattle of metal on metal.

"There is still Louie and Chewie," Core said.

"We didn't know what to do, Core," Parity whined.

"You did the right thing," Core said. "You returned for guidance."

The gate rattled up and the interior light went on. William Robert Harris—Billy Bob—Core stood framed in the doorway, the rich velvet of night backdropping him. Deep gold hair down to his shoulders, and his beard trimmed into a goatee, Core obviously had cultivated a Christ-like appearance since Hutchinson's photo had been taken. His gaze was at once warm and compelling in a way that no picture could convey. The others watched him with a mixture of respect and love. He wore black like the others, but with slacks and a silk dress shirt and a black silk duster standing in for robes.

Ukiah growled at him.

"Ah, the famous Wolf Boy."

"Ah, the famous killer of babies."

"Who killed what babies?" Parity asked.

Ice grabbed for Ukiah. Ukiah snarled, trying to twist away, but there was no room to turn. Ice caught him by the arm, and yanked Ukiah out of the truck, dropping him hard on the ground, broken shoulder first. Blackness washed over Ukiah, a moment of oblivion as his consciousness drowned in pain and resurfaced.

He lay on a driveway of cobbled stone in the square of light coming from the back of the truck. The stones were overhung by elm trees, a peaceful garden full of spent roses and daylilies just beyond, with the sound of running water playing nearby. The place had serenity at odds to the violence acting out in the driveway.

" . . . will be explained," Core was saying, examining Parity's bruised cheek while finger painting the invisible glitter of Blissfire onto the boy's face. "You've been hurt. This needs to be cleaned. Go see Ping."

The boy's eyes dilated wide, and he breathed out, "Ping." He managed to drag his attention back to Ukiah. "B-b-but . . ."

Core dipped his right fingers into his pocket and drew them out coated with Blissfire. "There's no need for you to concern yourself with all this. Go on." He pressed the drug-coated fingers to Parity's lips, silencing a protest. "Go to Ping for nursing."

Parity wet his lips, inadvertently ingesting the drug, and whispered hoarsely. "Nursing?" The boy lost to the drug's and Core's persuasion and stumbled away.

Core, though, seemed unaffected by handling the Blissfire; apparently he'd built up a resistance to the sexual stimulation.

"He needs more conditioning," Ice murmured, so quietly only Core and Ukiah caught the words. "You should have sent him to the waterfall for purification."

"All in good time," Core promised.

"You're going to kill him with that poison," Ukiah growled. In fact, it was probably too late for Parity, for all of the male cultists.

Core reached out and caught his chin, purring, "My savage little Wolf Boy . . . " The cult leader trailed off, staring into Ukiah's eyes. While Core might have been resistant to Invisible Red's normal level of persuasion, the direct skin contact triggered the drug's defensive protocols designed to keep breeders safe from territorial males. As the chiming in

Ukiah's ears grew louder, and his breathing grew ragged, Core's gaze shifted from hostility to dreamy sexual interest.

Ukiah jerked away from Core.

"Should I take him out and lose him in the backyard?" Hash took out a pistol; it was Goodman's gun, complete with silencer.

"No!" Socket cried, her scent suddenly alluring as the drug raced through Ukiah's system. "There's no reason to hurt him. He just wants his son back. His reasons are good and just."

"No," Core murmured softly, but it was his word that made Hash put the gun away. "He might prove to be useful. Waste not, want not."

"Where are the babies?" Socket's presence, as the only woman in the driveway, sucked in Ukiah's attention. In his drugged state, he was suddenly painfully aware that Socket wore black leggings like a layer of paint to her athletic legs, a black sweater dress belted with a wide leather belt, and no bra for her small firm breasts. "If we showed him that his son is fine, then maybe he'd join us. He's a good man."

"His son?" Core blinked as if coming out of a daydream. He looked around at the open truck and the cultists gathered around him. "Where's the puppy?"

"The crate broke open in the accident," Ice said. "I left Dongle to chase after it. We'll have to send someone to pick him and the puppy up."

Ukiah had to drag his attention away from Socket. "What do you want with Kittanning?"

"We know what he is, which is not your son, nor the son of any man of this world. Book of Enoch, chapter six. 'And it came to pass when the children of men had multiplied that in those days were born unto them beautiful and comely daughters. And the angels, the children of the heaven, saw and lusted after them, and said to one another: "Come, let us choose us wives from among the children of men and beget us children."' Their children were known as nephilim!"

"You think Kittanning's a nephilim?" Ukiah supposed it was worthless to argue that Kittanning was human, as he currently was a puppy.

"The Book of Enoch, chapter eight, says that the angel

Azazel taught men to make swords, and shields, and breast-plates, and made known to them the metals of the earth and the art of working them. Baraqijal taught astrology, Kokabel the constellations, Ezeqeel the knowledge of the clouds, Araqiel the signs of the earth, Shamsiel the signs of the sun, and Sariel the course of the moon."

"What does that have to do with taking Kittanning?"

"It has everything to do with the nephilim. The Book of Jasher tells us: when the angels spawn on the daughters of men, and the sons of men taught the mixture of animals of one species with other . . . God saw the whole earth and it was corrupt . . . and the Lord said, I will blot out man that I created from the face of the earth, yea from man to the birds of the air, together with cattle and beasts that are in the field."

Core caught Ukiah's chin again. "The fallen angels walk the earth, teaching technology to men, and men splice genes of men into animals. God is looking down, and he's seeing corruption. If we do not cut out this evil, he will blot out all living things from the planet."

Core's madness was being drowned under the desire to nuzzle into Socket.

"Core," Ice said softly. "We don't have time for this."

Socket laid a hand gently on Core's arm, coming maddeningly near. "Core, is he right? Are the babies all dead? What happened?"

Core flicked his eyes to Ukiah, and then riveted his gaze on Socket. His thumb, though, continued to lazily stroke Ukiah's cheek. "Adam sinned greatly. I entrusted him with the care of two of the children in good faith, and he betrayed us all. I'm sorry, Socket. I knew how hurt you would be by the news, and at this time when we cannot afford distractions, I kept it from you."

Socket flinched as if Core had struck her. "They're dead?" She struggled for control of herself. "We—we're giving the other two back. Right?"

"Yes, God willing."

Ukiah sensed that Core was lying to her. Were the children already dead, or did Core have something planned for them that Socket wouldn't cooperate with? What would Core do to her if she refused?

Core, though, found a simple way around her. "Socket, love, take the van and fetch Dongle and the puppy. Take two warriors with you, in case you need help catching the beast."

Ice shifted nervously before pointing out, "We need everyone focused on packing and putting as much distance between us and Iron Mountain as we can."

"We will be gone shortly," Core murmured. "Everything rests on having the puppy: we must get it back."

"You're not going to hurt the Wolf Boy?" Socket asked.

Core smoothed Ukiah's bangs out of his eyes. "I think we have him well in hand." And then, because Socket continued to waver, "He'll be here safe when you get back. Go on. We need the puppy."

"Yes, Core."

She gathered others like a good little trooper and went, only a hand wiping her eyes to show her distress.

Core ran his hand down the line of Ukiah's body and found him rock hard. "I'm glad to see the Blissfire works on you since it doesn't on the Fallen." Core nibbled lightly on the column of Ukiah's neck. "It saves us from doing messy and painful tests on you. You're far too beautiful to destroy lightly, but I will, if I have to. I'll cut you into pieces and burn you just like a Fallen if you don't stop fighting us."

Ukiah swallowed down a growl. If he was going to be any help to Kittanning and the other children, he had to give the cult no reason to kill him. Since they were used to destroying Gets, his healing abilities wouldn't save him.

"That's good." Core rubbed his hand back and forth, and murmured, "Show me that you can be trusted, and I'll share you with Socket. Under that dress, those leggings are so snug that you can see every crease and fold of her. There's not an ounce of fat on our Socket, and when you plug in, she's hot and tight."

The image drew shudders from Ukiah. He wanted her. If she had still been close, he wouldn't have been able to resist her.

"Core." Ice pulled the cult leader's attention back from

Ukiah. "What should I do about the rental truck? The police are going to find pieces of the trailer, and from there they'll know which rental truck to look for."

"Depends." Core left Ukiah reluctantly. "What did you find, Io?"

"Dewey and Louie are here," Io said. "I couldn't find Chewie or Huey."

This time it clicked for Ukiah. He had been hearing the names and not understanding. Du-ae, Chu-ae, Loo-ae, Hu-ae. The four deaths.

"Huey is on the truck." Ice indicated the rental truck beside him. Hu-ae. Little Death: the source of Invisible Red.

"Make room for Louie and load it onto the truck," Core ordered Io, pointing to the crowded back of the rental truck. "We'll put Dewey in the van. Everything else we can abandon if we have to. Ice, take the founts to the rendezvous, unload the truck, and then lose it someplace. See if you can locate another truck to replace it. We need to be gone from here, and soon."

"And afterward?" Ice asked. "Are we still going through with the Cleansing?"

Core nodded. "That's why I'm keeping Dewey close at hand."

Cleansing? Fear bolted through Ukiah. What were they planning? If they had figured out Hu-ae, then it was fully possible for them to get Du-ae, Water Death, functioning too. Hex had primed Hu-ae at Ukiah's conception, using a sacrificed part of himself along with Ukiah and Kicking Deer's genetic samples to key the machine so that the drug could tell human from breeder from Get. Had Hex primed Du-ae too? No, with the mother ship on Mars he needed the human race to build the Mars Rover, and after the ship's destruction, the Temple had the Ae . . .

. . . and they had kidnapped Kittanning to use with the Ae.

Ukiah felt a sickening sense of dread.

If the cult had figured out Hu-ae, they might also realize that it took three genetic samples to key Du-ae. Like Invisible Red, one slot made the waterborne pathogen from the Du-ae inert in Gets. The second slot specified a native life-form to be protected from the virus in order to become the future hosts. The third slot targeted the life-form deemed too dangerous to be a host. The variance between the second and third slot determined the virulence of the virus. Somehow, perhaps by spying on Hex and misunderstanding something the Ontongard said during a long-distance phone call, the cultists seemed to think they needed Kittanning to key Du-ae.

If they did, they could accidentally design a virus capable of killing all life on the planet except the Ontongard and their half-breeds.

Ukiah had to stop them; he didn't know how. Core's reasoning was twisted enough that it was possible that he *wanted* to kill all life on Earth. And saying the wrong thing could get Ukiah chopped up like Adam, and he really didn't want to live through that again.

"Maybe we should delay the Cleansing," Ice suggested as Io and others worked quickly unloading the truck.

"No, the time draws near. We must do it, or risk losing everything. The signs are clear."

Ice glanced upward at the night sky. "If I take someone with me who knows the back roads, I can get out of the state unseen. Should I steal a truck, or wait for morning and rent one?"

"Rent it with another fake ID. We need to be as invisible as possible."

Ice looked at Ukiah and his eyes were full of jealousy. "He's dangerous. Let me take him out and lose him with the truck."

"I said no," Core said.

"You're dosed up with Bliss and not thinking straight."

"My dear lieutenant, I'm thinking perfectly straight." Core kissed Ice lightly on the cheek, leaving the glitter of Blissfire. "We need another infusion of money. Even with Socket's allowance and the money we've gotten by selling Bliss, we've tapped ourselves dry. Bennett will pay to get his son back." He lowered his voice so that Ukiah could barely hear him over the chiming of the drug. "Or better yet, the boy might know account numbers and pin codes, or perhaps even inherit everything if Bennett is killed. If we can break his will, every-thing that is his will be ours."

Ice's whisper went husky as the Blissfire affected him. "Do we have the time to brainwash him? Will it even work on him? He's not the whining little discontented wimps we've molded before. I don't think a few days of exhaustion, star-vation, and hot sex is going to make him a willing tool."

"He's young and inexperienced," Core whispered. "It will work, given time."

"The puppy probably will not survive the ritual."

Ukiah controlled a growl; he could only save Kittanning if he was alive.

"He doesn't know what the puppy is." Core kissed Ice's other cheek and the Blissfire marked him like invisible war paint.

"Does he?" Ice whispered fiercely. "Why did he attack us on the turnpike? He came straight on like a stinger missile."

"Something must have led him to you."

"There was nothing."

"There was something." Core kissed Ice, a full silencing French kiss. Ice melted into Core's hold. "You just can't see it. If he found it, then others can. We have to move quickly."

"Yes, master," Ice whispered.

Core smiled at him. "Take the founts to the rendezvous, my dear, dear lieutenant, and come back as quickly as you can. I need you here beside me."

A shuffling of feet announced the arrival of the Lu-Ae. One could tell that the Ae was stolen technology; they had a sleek beauty that the Ontongard never grasped. It was as if the Ontongard, despite their host bodies, continued to see on too small a scale to understand visual beauty. Once stolen, of course, the Ontongard failed to see any reason to change the design.

In ways, *fount* was a good name for the Ae. On three of the sides were the upraised horns for raw materials, readily adapt-able for field use. In the front, an obvious spout poured out the biological poison in concentrated form.

The cultists had draped Lu-ae with a white altar cloth, trimmed with gold and embroidered with crucifixes. They brought it to the truck in a solemn procession and spread out sheets of silk to rest it on. Despite the ceremony of its arrival, it was quickly packed onto the truck and the gate once again lowered and padlocked.

The truck pulled away. Core dipped his hand into his pocket and drew it out glittering. "Come." Core drew a line down Ukiah's forehead, nose, and then traced Ukiah's lips. "There's much to do."

The Temple's refuge was an estate that made Max's mansion look modest. The cobblestone driveway circled a fountain, and beyond it sprawled an imposing limestone manor built on the lines and scale of a cathedral. Core led Ukiah through a facade gate, and into a deeply vaulted loggia facing a garden courtyard. Hash followed behind, apparently to guard against Ukiah trying to bolt.

The loggia was a kicked-beehive of activity. Cultists carried packed moving boxes out of various doors connected to the loggia. They glanced at Ukiah with interest but continued to work quickly, building a mountain of stacked boxes under the stone vaults.

"What is this place?"

"We call it Eden Court." Core turned them left and took them down a short flight of stone steps to a beautifully carved wooden door. "Parity's family owns it. The same architect that built the Westin William Penn Hotel and the old Mason Lodge in Oakland designed Eden. The man understood God."

Beyond the door, they stepped into a three-story great stair hall, the ceiling arched panels of carved wood, the walls dressed limestone, the tall windows all stained-glass, and the marble floors covered with oriental rugs. It felt more like a church than a home.

"And Parity's family doesn't mind you living here?" Ukiah asked.

"Parity is an only child, and his parents are in Europe. They think he's safely attending Harvard."

"So they don't know he's chopping up demons and burning them?"

Core tutted as he guided Ukiah down another flight of

steps and into a stunning living room with bay windows at either end, nearly twenty by sixty feet in area. "When I was growing up, I asked God to let me live here. I thought it would be the next best thing to living in a church. Then one day, I opened the newspaper and saw that God was sending Parity to Boston so I could initiate him."

Core paused in the living room. The original furniture had been pushed against the wall and the oriental rugs rolled up to reveal a random-plank oak floor. A nest of computers, thick with power cords and network cables, set up on a large round table dominated the room. While the floors and window gleamed from a recent cleaning, every surface was cluttered with belongings. Obscure electronics jostled with crucifixes and guns for space on a sofa table. A coffee table was littered with satellite photos, Bibles, and ammo.

The cultist Io was there, dissembling the computer equipment to be packed into waiting original boxes.

"Io," Core called him away from the computers. "Go tell Ping to finish with Parity and move to the master bedroom. We're initiating the Wolf Boy."

Io hurried away, and Core pushed Ukiah down onto a stool. "Sit. Stay."

Hash took up a position behind Ukiah, out of sight but not out of mind, making sure he stayed.

"So Socket talked." Core went to hunt through objects stacked on the mantel of a floor-to-ceiling stone fireplace carved like a mausoleum. "She's a worrisome child. So willing, one forgets she's never been fully broken, yet so strong that breaking her might kill her." Core found a pair of pruning shears and examined their blades. "I've let the issue ride because of her money, but maybe the time has come that the benefit outweighs the risk."

"I don't know what you plan to do with Du-ae, but you can't fight demons with it."

"Leave that to experts; I have been fighting demons for years. I've touched their stolen instruments of holy destruction, and tasted the angelic fruit of bliss. I've spied upon demons working their evil; I've captured them and killed them."

Ukiah eyed the shears in Core's hand as the cult leader walked toward him. "What are you going to do with those?"

"Afraid?" Core pressed them to Ukiah's cheek. "Fear is good." Core circled behind him. "I want to see how badly you're hurt." Core snipped through the wire binding Ukiah's wrist.

The sudden release shot agony through Ukiah, making him whimper.

"You were smart to wear leather." Core moved around Ukiah, snipping through the leather of Ukiah's jacket and peeling it back, exposing hypersensitive skin. "You abraded down to nearly skin. Ah, yes, it looks like you've cracked your clavicle, that's your collarbone, in the middle third. Looks to be nothing serious."

The Invisible Red was fracturing Ukiah's awareness. Some part of him stayed focused on Core and the monologue he carried on as he cut away the clothing. Most of him was only sentient of the cold metal pressing to his skin, the sharp snip as the blades came together, and the heat of Core's body as Core circled him.

Core's deep rich voice washed all around him, like warm dark water. "As a child, pure of sin, I walked in God's light and knew the comfort of his love. And then I left my home, and lost my way, until I was in prison, crouched on all fours, being raped like a mongrel bitch in heat. I thought God had abandoned me but Adam made me see that I had abandoned Him. God had shown me the path He wanted me to walk, and I had refused it."

Io came into the room quietly and whispered to Core that Ping was waiting. Core nodded, and sent him off for first-aid supplies. Only the tiniest part of Ukiah's awareness took note of Io and trembled; what initiation did Core and Ping have planned?

Core continued, drowning Ukiah with his voice. "I know as a child I believed so strongly that it seemed to weave into every fiber of my being. The sky was heaven. The thunder was angels bowling in the rain. And sunshine was His love, bright and warming. But there's always something chiseling away at your faith. A little here, a little there, until it's all gone. I had lost the last of it the year after I graduated from high school, and the world became cold, clinical, and sterile."

Core finished cutting off Ukiah's jacket and tossed the remains to one side, and paused a moment to examine Ukiah's hands and arms for damage. Blissfire still clung to Core's fingers, and each touch, skin to skin, spread more into Ukiah's system. Core's eyes widened with desire, and his voice went husky as he spilled out his heart.

"I felt so lost and alone, and then I saw this movie, and there was this one little thing in it, right at the end. If you look into the eyes of someone who is dying, it said, you'll see the face of God reflected in their eyes." Core held up a hand, fingers separated by a hair width of space. "Such a little thing, and yet it was as if all the heavens shouted to me. Yes, if I saw God's face, all that faith would return, and I would be the center of His love."

Couldn't Core see the flaw in his own logic? Nothing changed but Core's own belief. If God's love was controlled by Core's belief, then Core controlled God.

"So I became an EMT; what better way to see into the eyes of the dying?" Core pulled off Ukiah's boots and socks with calm detachment to his words. "I waited months for someone to die, and then I let God's will be done instead of checking his hand. I let nature run its course, instead of stepping in, other than praying for their souls. What is this mortal life compared to eternal salvation?"

In other words, he let them die. A tiny spark of horror was born in Ukiah. Adam might have been a monster, but someone made him that way; Core was a monster from the start. Sooner or later he probably would have been stopped, the death rate climbing too high to be ignored, but how many people had he killed?

Core picked up the pruning shears and started to cut off Ukiah's ruined leather riding pants. He continued his story, the deaths glossed over, deemed unimportant. "And then one day it happened. I saw my first fallen angel. After a bad ice storm, we were called to help with a multiple car accident on four twenty-two, around nine at night. A truck had lost its load of steel piping, and one of the pipes had been flung through a windshield and pierced a man through the heart. Amazingly, he was still alive, and struggling to remove the pipe from his chest. It was a huge risk, since I should have immobilized the pipe and let the emergency doctors remove it, but all I needed to say was that he pulled it free before I could stop him. It was dark, the police were directing traffic, and the rescue workers were busy with other drivers."

Io returned with the first-aid supplies: professional-looking gear boxes. Finding an arm sling in the boxes, Core slid it over Ukiah's head.

"So I leaned into the car, pulled the pipe free, eased him out onto the ground, and pretended to stanch his bleeding as I stared into his eyes, waiting for him to die. He spoke in the language of angels, which is beautiful and strange, as he bled to death. He closed his eyes at the very end, and I pried them back open. As with all the others, there was no sign of God. Heavyhearted, I moved on to the next car. That driver was pinned, all her ribs broken and her teeth smashed out by the steering wheel, and she was unconscious. She would live, though, and there was nothing I could do to change that short of cutting her throat, so I stood up and looked back at the first driver . . . and he was getting up. There was still a hole in his coat, front and back. He walked away, and just as he got to the edge of the light, he looked back, and his eyes gleamed with the unholy power."

Core shook two pills out of a medicine bottle and handed them to Ukiah. Ukiah stared at the pills in his hand, trying to focus on them. They were simple over-the-counter pain relievers, ibuprofen mixed with inactive material for bulk and stamped into a pill. His hand, though, barely seemed part of his body.

Realizing Ukiah's problem, Core laughed, and took back the pills. He produced a bottle of drinking water and opened it. Popping the pills into his own mouth, and taking a mouthful of water, he leaned forward, pressed his mouth to Ukiah's lips, and forced water and pills into Ukiah's mouth.

And the splintering of Ukiah's self became complete. His inner self howled in anger, fear, and helplessness, as his body responded, guided only by sexual desire.

Core leaned back, smiling. "Ah, we've got you. It's only a matter of time now until it's finished." He pulled Ukiah to his feet by his good hand. "Come, Ping is waiting."

They moved through the mansion, shadowed by Hash, ignored by the rest.

"Looking back," Core said, "I can see God's hand on me from the beginning, but it took Adam to open my eyes. I thought of myself as a man of peace, but I had been in the rifle club, the fencing club, and was one of the best war gamers in my school. I even formed my own Bible group and we called ourselves God's Warriors."

Where were they going?

Core opened a room and guided Ukiah into it.

Dozens of candles lit the room to a soft glow. A king-sized canopy took up the center of the room. An Asian woman waited, kneeling on the white satin sheets, dressed in a black robe so sheer it seemed to be just shadows. Core checked Ukiah just short of the bed, and she stretched with false casualness, the candles silhouetting her lithe form as she arched her back, lifting her breasts.

Ukiah wanted to flee.

His lips wanted to suckle at her breasts.

Ukiah wanted to be faithful to Indigo.

His body wanted to plunge himself into this whore.

As Ukiah stood there, fighting himself, Core sliced off Ukiah's boxer shorts. The cult leader pressed close, his own excitement obvious, and snaked an arm around Ukiah's hips to grasp him tight. "Mmmm, a natural man, as I hoped."

To Ukiah's disgust, his body responded. He wanted to say "no" but his mouth wouldn't shape the words. He started to growl instead.

Ping parted the gauze robe aside enough to reveal her sex, and it glittered in the candlelight. She stroked herself there, and lifted her damp, glittering fingers to him.

"Come to me."

Ukiah's legs started to move, carrying him to her, while Ukiah could only snarl in helpless anger. A moment later he felt Core's nude body beside him.

CHAPTER SIXTEEN

Eden Court, Butler, Pennsylvania
Friday, September 17, 2004

Only afterward, Ukiah realized that of his eons of racial memories, not one was from a breeder. Pack memory was from Get to Get to Get back to the beginning of the Ontongard venturing into space. The breeders were made, and after they served their purpose, destroyed. He had no memory of being under the influence of Invisible Red, and thus no warning at its intensity. The coating on Ping pushed him into a white haze of painful pleasure, and when his climax hit, he screamed as every nerve fired to white-hot intensity. It was like diving into the sun.

Through it all, he growled his anger at being used this way, but it didn't stop Ping from opening herself to him, or Core's rough hands and wanton mouth, or his own body betraying him. He had been saved from the worst of Core's attentions by Hash's arrival; the big man dragged Core off to deal with something causing a loud ruckus downstairs. Not that he noticed it at the time, his focus snared by Ping and pinned by the drug. Robbed of control, his unconscious leash on his inhuman strength vanished too, and bruises started to appear on Ping's pale skin. Dark handprints. Cruel kisses. His anger fled before dismay. Finally the drug's hold slipped, and he managed to wrench himself from Ping and throw himself onto the floor. Ping rolled over, eyed him sleepily, and drifted off to sleep. Momentarily safe, Ukiah crawled to the connected bathroom, and huddled in a cold shower, sick with himself.

Details ignored while he was under the drug's control now crowded in.

. . . pain flared jagged from his collarbone as he shoved Core from his groin and pushed into Ping. Outside the mansion came shouts and someone ran through the darkness below the windows. Ping's long hair fanned out, ink black poured onto pure white. Core sprawled unnoticed close by on the satin sheets, watching the frantic joining. As the candles suffocated them in hot vanilla scent and made a shadow play of his rape, the runner was captured in a hard collision of bodies . . .

Shivering now under the cold water, Ukiah swore as he realized that the cultists had captured someone while he'd been obsessed with Ping. Had it been Bear? Max? Sam? There was enough Blissfire in his system, though, to make the past fraught with sensory traps. As he tried to replay the cultists dragging the interloper into the mansion, the memory of Ping's slick wet warmth entangled his attention. He found himself standing up in the shower, and fought the desire to go back to the bedroom. Who had the cultists caught?

. . . the stone walls muffled the cultists' shouts, beyond his ability to pick out individual words, leaving only intonations of surprise and dismay. Core stirred to shift behind Ukiah and lick down his spine. Someone came running up the stairs.

"What the hell is going on down there?" Hash's voice came from just beyond the door. Apparently he'd been standing guard in the hall.

"We caught someone. Something. Can't tell which yet." Parity panted. "He had this."

"Fuck!" Hash snarled. "Core is going to want to deal with this."

"Really? Isn't he . . . ?"

"He'll want to deal with this." Hash repeated and walked into the bedroom without knocking or hesitation at the door. He physically pulled Core gently but firmly off the bed and out of the room . . .

Awareness of how close Core came to obtaining his desires

made Ukiah stumble out of the shower and throw up in the
toilet.

Who had they caught? How long ago had this happened?
Ukiah wasn't sure—he lost all sense of time when Ping first
touched him—but the candles had burned down to guttering
pools of wax. He guessed that it was well past midnight.

His memory recorded a short period of silence and a faint,
muffled scream. A few minutes later the mansion resumed the
frantic activity of earlier. Hash returned to the hallway.

"What happened?" Parity asked. "Who is he?"

*"Ice will be back in a few hours." Hash opened the bed-
room door, letting in a wash of fresh air and the smell of fresh
blood. "Good. They're still going at it like rabbits. Tell Ice
that Dongle found the puppy and we're going ahead with the
Cleansing. Socket picked Dongle up and is meeting us. Guard
the wolf until Ice gets here; the lieutenant is to take everyone
here to the rendezvous and wait."*

"What wolf? Where?"

*"We're playing cross the river with the wolf, the chicken,
and the grain in a speedboat." Hash checked the load on a
Colt forty-five.*

"Huh?"

*"You haven't heard the riddle? How did you get into Har-
vard? You need to get across a river in a boat, but there's only
room for one other thing. The wolf will eat the chicken if you
leave the two together and the chicken will eat the grain."*

"Is that in the Bible?"

Hash smacked Parity in the back of the head. "No!"

*Parity rubbed the back of his head. "Okay, okay, Oregon's
the wolf. Who's the chicken?"*

"Socket."

"Huh? Why is she the chicken? And what's the grain?"

*"You know, sometimes things don't match up exactly in
analogies. We don't want to take Wolf Boy with us to the
Cleansing and we don't want Socket to see the mess in the
wine cellar. So you're going to stay here and guard this door."*

Hash closed the door on Parity's startled, "Me?"

*"By the time Ping's done with the Wolf Boy, he'll sleep for
hours, and then Ice will be here."*

"But . . ."

"You'll have the gun. Kill him if he tries anything."

"But . . ."

"Just do what you're told, Parity."

Ukiah rinsed the traces of vomit from his mouth, and drank his fill out of the sink. The water helped dilute the drug some; food would work wonders on clearing his system. He'd have to deal with Ping and Parity, and get out of the mansion before Ice arrived. Hopefully whomever the cultists caught was still alive in the wine cellar. But most important he had to find out where Core had gone with Kittanning and the Ae.

The draperies were held back with silk cords. He used them to tie up Ping, hands and feet, with knots that would make his scouting master and Max proud. He gagged her with the remains of her gauzy black robe. She stirred as he knotted the gag tight, eyed him through the veil of her long black hair, and then arched, presenting first her breasts and then her groin, moaning seductively. In that movement and siren-song of a groan, she nearly captured him. He lowered his mouth toward her offered breast, suddenly aware that even tied, she remained completely accessible to him, and now deceptively safe.

Deceptively. He caught himself just short of touching his lips to her, the perfume of her silky skin filling his senses. If she could delay him, then he could be caught. And sexually enslaved again.

He jerked back away from her. "You bitch!"

Her eyes narrowed, and she writhed erotically again, moaning softly, the parody of a woman being pleasured.

He backed away, trying not to look at her, anger barely able to compete with the desire aching inside of him. He made it to the door, managed to focus on the hallway beyond despite Ping's heady distraction.

Parity paced the hall, murmuring softly to himself. "Cross with the grain. No. Cross with the wolf. No. Cross with the chicken, drop it off, go back and get the—get the—wolf eat chicken. Chicken eat grain. Get the wolf."

". . . we don't want to take Wolf Boy with us to the Cleans-

ing," Hash had said smelling of fresh blood, *"and we don't want Socket to see the mess in the wine cellar . . ."*

Ukiah dove out the door and took Parity down. The boy yelped as Ukiah slammed him to the floor. Ukiah punched him to silence him, and then again and again. He managed to stop himself after the third punch. His anger surged through him like a large dark beast, wanting blood and pain, pressing against the confines of his skin until Ukiah was trembling with the effort to keep it in. He had Parity pinned—lover's close, the pistol hard between their hips—and one hand tight around Parity's throat, thumb pressed to the windpipe and the boy's face going an alarming shade of purple.

He was going to kill the boy if he wasn't careful.

And the angry drugged part of him, the wild thing black as a midnight storm, didn't care.

"No, no," he growled and fought his rage back down. Reluctantly his hand let go of the throat, like a beast not wanting to give up a prize bone.

Parity had been flailing at him. He gave the boy a hard shake, and leaned down to growl in his face.

"Be still or I'll kill you." Because he wasn't sure he could stop himself if the boy kept resisting.

Parity went still, panting hard, eyes wide and leaking fear.

"Where's Core?" Ukiah snarled, his lips peeling back to show teeth, fighting the urge to bite, to maul through skin and muscle to bone.

"I don't know. Honest to God. I don't know."

"Hash talked like you knew. Where has he gone?"

"To do the Cleansing, but I don't know where. I'm just an initiate. I just joined six months ago. Ping dialed a wrong number and called me by accident one day when she was lost in Cambridge. She was just down the street, and she was so cute that I went out to help her. She took me back to her place and made love to me with Blissfire to thank me. I joined a few days later, but I haven't worked my way up to the inner circle."

Ukiah doubted that the call had been an accident nor that Ping had been lost. "What is this Cleansing? What is he going to do?"

"I don't know," Parity wailed. "Only the inner circle knows."

Ukiah struck him. "Quiet. What do you know, you worthless shit?"

"They bought boats for the ritual, and a generator, and gas tanks, and yards of white silk. They probably took the babies. They needed two babies and the puppy. A girl, a boy, any one of them would do, but they had to have the puppy. I didn't know anything happened to the two other babies. Ping only told me tonight that they died during the testing, that the machine they found at the airport was more deadly than they expected."

"What machine? Where is it?"

"I think in the wine cellar, but I'm not allowed down there. I'm only an initiate."

"It's your fucking house!" Ukiah roared at him. "I'm sick of assholes who let people like Core and Adam use them to hurt others. You know better than this! Any child knows better than this. Core might be insane, but at least he has an excuse. You're a fucking bastard to let him—fuck no, help him—do this." Ukiah caught Parity's hand and pressed it hard against the boy's face. "This hand! This hand killed Adam. This hand killed the baby girl." He started to hit Parity with his own hand. "This hand killed the baby boy. This hand threw those naked little bodies into the garbage."

"I didn't kill them! I didn't even know until afterward!"

"You fucking knew you had a house full of kidnappers and murderers, and the minute you didn't call the police, it's the same as you doing it yourself."

"You don't know the truth! There are demons in the world. Even if you don't believe it, it doesn't make them less real. You have to be ruthless to deal with such evil. The ends justify the means, and if a handful die to save the world, then the cost is worth it."

He could only growl, feeling the resonance of the Pack in Parity's words. He rebelled against the comparison, heart and soul, but some remote lucid part of him recognized that the cult and the Pack were the same, but different, and it was the differences that separated them into good and evil.

"You didn't hurt Ping? Did you?" Parity fearfully broke Ukiah's silence. "Oh, dear God, tell me you didn't kill her. That wasn't her fault. Core says it's the way we were really meant to be: freely sexual beings. The serpent tempted Eve to eat the fruit of knowledge, knowing that she gained only flawed knowledge: shame of natural functions, limiting love with prejudice . . ."

"Did that bullshit help you after Core took you?"

Bleakness came to Parity's eyes, and then he blinked the look away. "The Blissfire makes it feel good, and later it's hard to remember the details, like a bad dream. If you don't think about it, it goes away."

"What else do you know about the Cleansing ritual?"

"It's to kill any demons nesting in the area."

"Are you sure?"

"We found out what Dewey did when we intercepted a phone conversation between the nests of demons. When the FBI started to raid the nests, we recorded the demons talking about moving the founts. Orders were given to move them, but that nest was taken out before they could do so. After that, the demons started to speak in their own tongue instead of English, so we had to translate everything, and it took time. Only recently we learned that they had captured the nephilim, and what Dewey did."

The Ontongard language didn't match one to one with English very well. Ukiah guessed that the Ontongard used a word such as "breeder/offspring" to mean Kittanning and the cult translated it to nephilim.

"What did the demons say?"

"Well, it's hard to piece together anything. Even in their own language they talk in shorthand, and often do this weird duet, like they're reading from the same script. We call it test patterning. Ice says that once they confirm they're on the same page, they then talk about differences in the way they're thinking."

He shook Parity to get him back to the point. "What did they say?"

"They talked about using a machine to force the nephilim to the correct form. One said that Huey had been keyed with the nephilim and was now a detriment to them." *Detriment*? *Useless* was probably a truer translation. "The second one said if the nephilim could be corrupted, then the founts should be fetched, and the first said that so far the nephilim proved to be malleable but unassailable. They agreed in duet that if the nephilim couldn't be corrupted, they were far too dangerous to them and had to be destroyed. At first we thought they meant kill the nephilim, but then we realized that they were using plural verbs, whereas when they talked about the nephilim they used only singular."

The confusion lay in the fact that Ukiah kept changing in number. At the time of the conversation, he could have been in as many as four to a hundred different pieces. Hex had stolen three mice as Ukiah bled to death. Ukiah had awoken surrounded by a horde of mice that the Pack gathered up and moved with his dead body. He had been one but many. The Ontongard would use the singular to mean "the breeder" in a general sense, and "this piece of the breeder" but plural to mean "all parts of the breeder."

"No, no." Ukiah groaned. "You misunderstood. You got it all wrong. The br—the nephilim is one, but can be broken down, just like the demons, into lots of parts. It can be singular and plural. They were talking about destroying the nephilim because it's dangerous. The Ae—the founts can't hurt the demons."

"They can't?"

"Not without killing off everything on the planet, which is what Core might do by mistake. I need to find him. I need to stop him."

"I—I—I don't know anything. I don't know where Core is, and I don't know if you're telling the truth."

All the candles in the master bedroom had drowned out while he had questioned Parity in the hall. He dragged Parity now into the master bathroom and tied him up with a second set of silk drapery tiebacks. He told Parity before leaving about the dangers of Blissfire, but that seemed to do no more good than to salve Ukiah's conscious. He was gagging Parity when he thought to ask, "Where the hell are we anyhow?"

"Eden Court. Well, actually, it's Elm Court; Core renamed it. We're in Butler."

Butler? Butler was only ten miles northeast of his moms!

Ukiah searched Parity hoping for a cell phone. He found no phone on the boy, nor money and ID; a wallet-sized photo of Socket was the sole contents of Parity's pockets.

Ukiah considered waking Ping and asking her where Core planned to do the Cleansing ritual, but he found he couldn't even look at her sleeping form without his fragile control slipping. He went out into the clean air of the hall, returned for the gun he'd forgotten in the sink, and started off again. Reluctantly he headed downstairs to find out who was in the wine cellar and what Core had done to them.

Eden Court was a massive home, easily twice the size of Max's mansion. Off this second-floor hallway, there were six bedrooms alone. In his drug-fuddled condition, he made a wrong turn, and ended up in another corner of the house, with a set of five smaller bedrooms, apparently once belonging to servants. Finally he found steps leading to the first floor, and stalked through that maze of large, sprawling, interconnected rooms, occasionally silently backtracking to avoid a lone cult member focused on packing.

He found plenty of wall jacks, but no phones, as if Core had stripped them out of the house. Was it to keep his flock from calling out? Max said that cults kept their members isolated.

The house, he finally realized, was built around the center courtyard. A full wing of dining rooms of various sizes eventually led to a massive L-shaped kitchen with industrial appliances. He tried doors branching off the kitchen, looking for the wine cellar. The first opened into a walk-in pantry; he grabbed a jar of peanut butter to eat as he explored. Peeling off the protection foil released the heavenly aroma of roasted peanuts, making him drool. He scooped out half a cup with a finger and gobbled it down. It took half the jar before he could move on, licking clean his finger.

The second door led to a hallway with a laundry room and the empty garages off of it. Ukiah stole a clean pair of boxers and black sweatpants out of the laundry, and stalked back to the kitchen feeling more stable now that he was dressed, armed, and eating.

Across the kitchen, the last door led down into the basement. The smell of fresh blood and C4 wafted up on the cool air. He crept down the stairs into the low, vast space crowded with water heaters, furnaces, and a jumble of exposed pipes and ductwork. Apparently the great house required multiples of everything.

Worktables were tucked between the hulking furnaces, cluttered with electronic boards and wires, and wreathed with the odor of C4. Zip apparently had been working on more bombs before his death. Ukiah wondered what the cult planned to blow up.

One of the furnaces hissed with the sudden intake of natural gas, making Ukiah startle. With a slight cough of the gas igniting, it roared to life.

Keep focused, he told himself. Sooner or later, someone was going to notice Parity is missing from the hallway and find Ping tied up.

Ukiah followed the blood trail to a solid door with a prominent lock. An old-fashioned key was in the lock, dangling a new piece of string and a little white disk neatly labeled WINE CELLAR. The door was locked. Ukiah unlocked it and cracked open the door.

Blood scent flooded out, pouring over him.

From the door, Ukiah could see that the wine racks were empty. Core must have sold the bottles to raise money, or somehow drank it during the six months since he stole the house and child away from Parity's unsuspecting parents. If this cellar held a fraction of the wine that Max had put away, then the cult had carried off a fortune.

Just inside the door sat a clear plastic box studded with Taser-like probes. He recognized it from Kittanning's memories; it was the torture device Hex had used to transform the blood mouse into an infant. Ukiah controlled a snarl. Core must have used it to kill the two babies—but how? The machine had been designed to cause pain, not death.

A soft moan made him take the key out of the lock and slip

cautiously into the room. A lot of blood had been spilt in the room; the smell raising his hackles. He stalked through the empty wine racks, growling softly.

He caught another scent and stilled.

Ontongard.

The only sound was that of tiny claws against plastic, and something large, breathing heavily.

Alien thoughts touched his mind.

. . . Pack . . . Pack . . . hate . . . hate . . . death . . . Pack . . .

The minds were many, and small, and stupid, filled with frustrated anger and a sense of being trapped.

Trapped? He crept downward, gripping Parity's pistol tightly, wishing for a flamethrower and twenty Dog Warriors at his back.

Against the far wall was a set of shelves holding plastic cages designed for small rodents. Black rats with hate-filled eyes scratched frantically at the sides of the cages, trying to reach him, hating him, wanting him dead.

Ukiah focused on the source of the blood, the heavy breathing from something large. Did Core have a larger Get hidden down here, along with the memories? Sniffing, he found the scent, and recognized the source.

"Hutchinson!" He hurried to the federal agent.

Hutchinson curled on the floor, clasping something tight to him. It took a moment for Ukiah to realize how the man was hurt.

Core had hacked off Hutchinson's hand at the wrist.

Beside Hutchinson was a meat cleaver buried in a thick block of wood. On the table beyond, in one of the rodent cages, was Hutchinson's severed hand—just in case it changed form. Next to the cage sat Hutchinson's car keys, ID case and wallet, empty of money and credit cards. Wallet-sized photos of Socket littered the floor. Ukiah realized that the photograph he found on Parity had been what the boy had shown Hash, saying "he had this," which made Hash drag Core out of the bedroom. Hutchinson had saved Ukiah at a terrible cost to himself.

Hutchinson had made a tourniquet from his belt and clenched it tight. He was damp and chilled, breathing shallow and weak. He jerked when Ukiah touched him, his eyes flying open.

"Easy, I'm not going to hurt you. I'm here to help you."

"Wolf Boy?"

"I'm going to get you out of this."

"The bastard. He laughed at me and bragged about sleeping with Christa. He called her his whore. Bastard called my Christa a whore. He said that she was pregnant once already, and they didn't know which of the men had knocked her up, but she lost the baby."

Ukiah felt a stab of guilt; the Blissfire would have aborted any fetus that wasn't his. Suddenly he flashed to Ping writhing under him as he loosed his seed into her. He groaned in realization that the drug was busily engineering a pregnancy.

Hutchinson had gone unconscious again.

"Oh, shit. Oh, shit." He tore his mind away from Ping and forced himself to focus on the federal agent. He had to get the man to the hospital, and he should take the severed hand, just in case they could save it. How? He eyed the car keys sitting next to the cage; if the cultists hadn't taken the keys, then Hutchinson's car should be nearby. Ukiah pocketed the keys, made the belt as secure as he could around the bloody stump, and hefted Hutchinson up into a fireman's carry. The fragile knit of Ukiah's collarbone protested, threatening to break under the pressure. Trying to ignore the pain, Ukiah picked up the cage holding Hutchinson's hand.

He had to get them both out before the cultists realized he was escaping.

The mansion sat on a hilltop with several acres of heavily treed gardens. Two heavily armed cultists patrolled the grounds, dressed in black, with IR goggles. Ukiah spotted them before they saw him, and ducked behind a low stone wall. On his shoulder, Hutchinson's weight was growing monstrous. He eased the man onto the ground and lay beside him, panting from the effort of carrying him up the basement stairs and out of the house.

He tracked the cultists by sound and scent as a storm wind tossed the dark shaggy heads of the trees over him.

A tiny sharp voice came over their headsets, too muffled for Ukiah to understand, and the one answered with a gruff "What is it? Okay. Understood." After a moment of some silent communication between the two men, they purposely stalked off in opposite directions.

Had someone found Ping and Parity? Did the guards know where he was and were trying to circle him? He strained to keep track of them over the rushing wind. They seemed to move around the corner of the mansion and continue.

He had to risk moving. His chances weren't going to get any better. He heaved Hutchinson back onto this shoulder, and stumbled through the trees to the edge of the property. The street was empty of cars except those parked in driveways. Ukiah dropped to his knees, trembling with exhaustion.

Where was Hutchinson's car? Ukiah couldn't spot the white rental the agent was driving earlier. Had he swapped rental cars? Ukiah fumbled out the car keys, and hit the unlock button. Down the street, parked in a driveway, a red sedan flipped on its lights.

It was a relief to ease Hutchinson into the passenger seat and seat belt him in. The dashboard clock showed that it was one in the morning. Ukiah felt like he'd lived a lifetime in the last twenty-four hours.

He made four blind turns until he suddenly hit East Brady Street and recognized it. After that it was only a mile to Butler Memorial Hospital. He drove up to the ambulance-unloading zone and turned off the car. He sat there, shaking, trying to summon strength to get up and out of the car.

An orderly came out to investigate, opening the driver's door. "Hey, dude, are you okay? You're not allowed to park here if you're not hurt."

"My friend. They cut off his hand. I need a phone to call the police."

The orderly yelped and ran around the other side of the car, yelling, "I need help out here!"

Wearily, Ukiah undid his seat belt and climbed out. He heard a muffled explosion, and turned; thus he saw the fireball as it bloomed on the far hillside, roiling upward bright orange and bloodred. The sound hit him, and a second later the shock wave riding a hot buffet of winds followed; it shattered windows in bright clear twinkling of falling glass. In all directions came the howls of car alarms, and then the wail of the Butler Fire Department sirens.

CHAPTER SEVENTEEN

Butler Memorial Hospital, Butler, Pennsylvania
Friday, September 17, 2004

From the air, as the Lifeflight helicopter rose from the Butler Hospital helipad, it was clear that the stately mansion was indeed engulfed in flames. Ukiah stared at the destruction in sick bewilderment. Had Core left the bomb to kill everyone after maiming Hutchinson? Or had the cultists found Ping and Parity, freed them and fled, setting off the bomb to cover their tracks. Or had the cultists, finding Ukiah gone, simply chosen to die?

Despite everything, he hoped Ping and Parity had survived.

The level one trauma center at Mercy Hospital in Pittsburgh could do the delicate surgery needed in an attempt to reattach the agent's hand. After Ukiah explained that the same people that cut off Hutchinson's hand were also the ones that just fire-bombed their own house, the emergency doctors decided to send Ukiah with Hutchinson. Apparently the doctors felt that moving a possible target of madmen out of the area would be a good thing.

The Butler staff had put Ukiah on a glucose drip, and his body elected to sleep until the helicopter arrived.

The emergency-room staff had made good their promise to call Max; his partner waited at the end of the ramp leading to Mercy's raised helipad as the helicopter came in for a landing.

Hutchinson had been unloaded first, sucking most of the emergency staff with him. Max trailed behind Ukiah's stretcher as they brought it into the hospital and stayed back until they were satisfied that Ukiah was stable and his injuries light. Then another trauma claimed the staff's attention and Ukiah was able to sit up.

"Are you okay?" Max caught hold of him, and hugged him hard. Ukiah sagged against Max, relieved beyond words to have him there. "We've been worried sick since the police found your bike smashed on the turnpike. When they called to say they were flying you here, I was worried you'd show up in pieces."

"I'm a little shaky." Ukiah pulled out the long IV needle from his arm. "Did you get hold of Indigo?"

"Yes, she's on her way to Butler but she wants you to call with more details. What I had to pass on was fairly sketchy: the cult hacked a hand off of Hutchinson and blew up a mansion."

"That's the size of it." Ukiah slid off the stretcher. "Let's get out of here before they can connect monitors up to me and take blood samples."

Sam waited with the Hummer that was illegally parked out in front of the main entrance. Ukiah wearily climbed into the backseat, pleased to note that between the IV and sleep, the last of the Invisible Red had worn off. The only alluring thing about Sam was the fragrant Tupperware container she handed him, along with a fork. "Oh, kid, you look like hell. Here, we emptied the fridge for you."

"How the hell did you get in Butler?" Max slid in behind the wheel. "Were they the ones that kidnapped Kittanning?"

Ukiah peeled the lid off the Tupperware dish; inside was an odd assortment of take-out Chinese, fresh fruit, and expensive cheese. "I don't even know where to begin."

"When we talked to you a few hours ago, we figured out that William Harris was probably Billy Bob, and that the Temple probably had Kittanning, the Ae, and perhaps the two other babies, but not why."

Ukiah grunted around a mouthful of General Tso's Chicken. "You're going to hate why." He chewed, trying to think of a way to explain everything he'd learned. "Eleven or twelve years ago, Core—Harris—was on top of his world. He was a small-town preacher's kid, an all-around popular guy. Then he graduated from high school and had to deal with the real world. He didn't cope well, and while an EMT, started killing accident victims as part of an insane plan to see the face of God in the eyes of the dying."

Max swore vehemently and started up the Cherokee. "Well, that explains why he wasn't popular with the ambulance crews."

"Then one day," Ukiah continued, "Core saw a Get come back to life. He lost whatever hold he had on reality. He took off for California to get far away from the Ontongard and ended up in prison where he met Goodman."

"Who taught him violence and sexual deviancy," Sam said.

"Yeah. He did his time in prison, and then came back home a changed man. He gathered up his old Bible study group, and took them hunting Ontongard. Any reservations his friends had about killing were blown away when the Gets came back from the dead or splintered down into rats and so forth. He fed his friends lines about being holy warriors, and they ate it up. They put up a Web site to draw in other people looking for meaning in their life, and the Temple of New Reason was born."

"What a lure," Max said. "To be superheroes or at least Buffy the Vampire Slayer; kicking ass with no guilt involved."

"Two important things happened fairly quick afterward. The first was that they connected with Ice, who talks them into moving to Boston and going underground. That's when they dumped the public Web site and went covert. The second was something led them back to Iron Mountain. Either they came across information on Omega Pharmaceuticals being one of the Ontongard dummy companies, or Zlotnikov, alias Zip, finally connected Hex with the password he overheard, or maybe they learned something while wiretapping the Ontongard. Whatever. The Temple staged a raid on Iron Mountain using Zlotnikov's information and stole the Ae, leaving behind a bomb so they'd know when the Ontongard discovered that the Ae are missing. It takes the Temple a few years, but they get the first Ae working. Luckily, it's Hu-ae.

"By now they're short on money, so they use Hu-ae to create Invisible Red. Just like Goodman lured Eve out of the mall and into his car, Core starts seducing wealthy people like Socket. Once again he nails the deal by having true monsters to kill, but he adds in other brainwashing techniques, topped off with incredible sex. Even Hash falls under the combination."

"How does coming back to Pittsburgh to kidnap babies work in?" Max turned onto Bigelow Boulevard, and they swept along the hillside, looking down at the Strip District and the Allegheny River beyond.

"If you kill a Get and burn them before they can transform, then the residue left looks human. We saw that with Janet Haze in June. The Temple's burn site was found in Massachusetts, so they had to flee the area before they were connected to the killings. I'm guessing—from what we found on the Web site—they went to Buffalo because that's where the mother ship was going to land."

"In Buffalo?" Sam cried.

Max snapped his fingers. "The geological maps and the Niagara energy grid."

"Yeah. Remind me to send some of the Pack up to see if the Temple cleaned out all the dens in that area."

"Why would the Ontongard land their ship in upstate New York? Why not some place remote—like Africa?" Sam asked.

"Because Hex is in the United States, and doesn't like to travel." Ukiah finished the food and resealed the lid. "It puts him at mercy of the elements and human beings."

"And there's Niagara Falls for power," Max said. "I wouldn't be surprised if Hoover Dam was their backup landing site."

"Perhaps. But all hell lets loose in Pittsburgh. The Dog Warriors stumbled onto Hex's plan and killed Janet Haze's supervisor, who was a Get. Hex, in trying to salvage the plan, infected Janet Haze. She lost the remote key and got herself killed. Hex involved the FBI while trying to recover the key. Indigo raided several dens, and the Pack made sure those Gets stayed dead, leaving Hex shorthanded. All that means Hex probably pulled his Gets out of Buffalo, leaving the cult nothing to fight."

"And we blow up the mother ship," Max added. "And kill Hex, so everything goes quiet, as far as the cult is concerned."

Ukiah nodded. "I think Core was planning to move to Butler already and might have been just waiting for Parity's parents to clear out of their house. All things considered, I think Core sees Pittsburgh as the origin of the demons, not Oregon."

Max stopped for a red light. "If your prey goes suddenly silent, I imagine you get fairly paranoid."

It had the ring of profound truth. "Yes, I think you're right. They mistranslate something Hex says to mean that the Ae can kill the demons en masse and that becomes Core's top priority."

Max glanced in the rearview mirror at him, a look full of worry. "Can they?"

"No. Trying to will only make the Ae more deadly, but Core doesn't realize it."

"Shit."

"In the same conversation, the cult mistranslated 'breeder' to mean nephilim—the offspring of angels mating with humans." Ukiah sagged back in the seat, trying to piece together the events. "Most likely, Gunter had a photo in a local newspaper, so they raided his studio for everything he shot that day and then some. The pictures found on Zip clearly showed that a baby was recovered from the airport terminal, which confirmed the nephilim theory in Core's mind. He assumed that Kittanning was turned over to Child Youth Services."

"With their skills," Max said, "the cult could have hacked CYS for the list of infants in foster care without anyone being the wiser."

Ukiah hadn't thought of that, but it made sense. "But none of the CYS kids are listed as found abandoned at the airport. So Core decides to kidnap all kids under a certain age and test them using the machine Hex used to make Kittanning a baby.

Then I came home and made the evening news. Core recognized me from the photos, Socket did a search to get my 'home' address, and Goodman was ordered to kidnap Kittanning."

"Only Goodman decided to ransom Kittanning," Sam said. "Which gets him killed."

Ukiah nodded. "Goodman's view of religion had nothing to do with demons and everything to do with his sexual obsessions, but he was broke and dependent on Core. The ransom would have given him the money he needed to leave Core. Sensing the double cross, Core had his people tap into the spy satellite and follow Goodman back to the farm."

"That wouldn't have been too hard to do if Goodman was in communication with Core," Max said. "Once he called in to Core, they could have traced the call back to Goodman's location and lock on to him."

"After they got Kittanning," Ukiah continued, "they tried to test him and he proved to be the one they were looking for by turning into a puppy."

"A puppy!" Sam cried.

"A wolf dog puppy." Ukiah measured the size with his hands. "So big."

He told them about his failed attempt to rescue Kittanning and Hash's comments about Kittanning being recaptured. "Socket is taking Kittanning to Core, wherever he is, so he can key the Du-ae and do this Cleansing ritual. Parity told me that it had something to do with water."

"Well, the Allegheny River comes within twenty miles of Butler through the city of Kittanning," Max said. "Or he could be setting up at Lake Arthur, or Lake Erie."

Lake Arthur was a small man-made lake just west of Butler, and Lake Erie was just over an hour's drive.

"Eve might know something," Sam said.

"What?" Ukiah said.

"Think of it. Adam left everything he knew behind in California to join Core, and finds him fighting monsters. Pissed to hell, he breaks off with Core and tries to set up his own paradise. If he's like any other divorcee in the world, he's bitched like crazy to his new girlfriend about his ex."

"Maggoty ideas," Ukiah murmured, and then quoted back what Eve had said. *"In prison, Billy had crazy ideas, but they were small as fly eggs. It wasn't until these new friends of his filled him up with so much shit that the eggs became full maggots.* But Goodman had that backward. It was Core filling his friends up with crazy plans."

Ukiah replayed in his mind the conversation with Eve, the broken little sex toy in the blackberry bushes, bruises blackening to the color of ripe berries. Neither that discussion nor the one Ukiah had with Indigo after her questioning of Eve held any clues of where Core could be holding the ritual. At this time of night, there would be no accessing the girl either.

There had been so little evidence at the farm. The cult had carefully picked over everything and taken away anything damning. The only thing left behind had been the mural. As he considered, he started to see the biblical symbolism that he missed before: the tree of knowledge, the tempting snake, and the forbidden fruit. He considered the other images in the painting. The mysterious leaves had been wormwood. There had been information on the Temple's Web site about the falling star called Wormwood. Ukiah realized that the "sun" in the upper left-hand corner had been a star, dropping the leaves of the plant of the same name down to the treelike object.

Suddenly Ukiah realized that the drawing hadn't been of a tree, but of the three rivers, the Allegheny and the Monongahela Rivers joining to create the Ohio River. Only in the painting, the wormwood leaves turned the Allegheny black as death shortly before the confluence.

"They're going to poison the Allegheny, which will take out the Ohio and the Mississippi, the whole way down to the Gulf of Mexico," Ukiah said.

"What?" Max and Sam both cried.

Ukiah quoted back the Scripture related to the symbolism. "The third angel blew his trumpet, and a great star fell from heaven, blazing like a torch, and it fell on a third of the rivers and on the fountains of water. The name of the star is Wormwood. A third of the waters became wormwood, and many men died of the water, because it was made bitter."

Max made a face in the rearview mirror. "How do you figure any of that matches Pittsburgh and Du-ae?"

"I think," Ukiah said slowly, feeling his way, "this is what Goodman and Core might have parted on. Core planned to poison the water and Goodman saw it as a reference to the End Days. Goodman seemed to think the end of the world was coming—that was the whole point of having the farm with its own water source and no dependence on the outside world." Ukiah then explained the mural. "But Core didn't seem to act like that. He was planning to ransom me *after* the ritual."

"God save us from idiots," Max muttered and then frowned. "Oh, shit, the Allegheny Water Authority treatment plant is on the Allegheny, right next to the Waterworks Mall."

"Should we call the police?" Sam asked.

"We don't have enough to call nine-one-one." Max passed his phone back to Ukiah. "Call Indigo. She might be able to scramble someone to the treatment plant just on suspicions."

Indigo's phone rang and rang, frightening Ukiah, until she finally answered, shouting, "Special Agent Zheng." In the background was the ceaseless roar of a big fire and a siren growing nearer.

"Indigo, it's me, Ukiah. I'm with Max."

Apparently the siren drowned him out, because she shouted, "Where?"

Somewhere close to Indigo, a man was shouting, "Get behind the barrier. All nonemergency people get behind the barrier!"

Ukiah tried again, louder. "I'm with Max and Sam!"

"What happened here in Butler?"

"The Temple of New Reason knows about the Ontongard, but the cult thinks the Gets are demons." He struggled to keep the conversation short and precise. "Core has the water death, Kittanning, and the two babies. He thinks by sacrificing the children, he can create a poison that will affect only the Ontongard. He's doing the ritual tonight."

"Tonight?" she cried, and then waited as an emergency dispatcher blared a garbled report over a fire truck's radio. "Do you know where?"

"We think at the Pittsburgh Water Authority, on the Allegheny. If he gets the Ae to work, he could kill millions of people."

"Are you sure?" Indigo shouted over the din on her side.

"No. It's a wild hunch, that's all."

"Well, wild or not, we can't afford not to act on it," Indigo said. "I'll make it look a little less wild and ram it down throats on this end."

The fire dispatcher drowned the conversation again.

"Indigo, I left two people tied up in the master bedroom when I escaped: one on the bed and the other in the bathroom. I don't know if the cult freed them before the house went up."

"What about the two men in the driveway? Do you know who killed them?"

Two men? "No. I didn't go out the front."

"If I didn't know any better, I would say the Pack had been here."

He felt his hackles rise. If the Pack had been in Butler, they would have been searching for him and he would in turn sensed them. "Indigo, the cult had Ontongard cut up into rats in the basement. If there were any Gets in the area, they would have zeroed in on the mansion."

There was silence from Indigo. The sound from the fire changed, as she turned slowly in a circle. Was she studying the crowd watching the fire, wondering if they were Gets?

"Could they smell you on me?" she asked, cupping the phone now, speaking quietly.

"I don't think so. The Ontongard have the same senses, but they don't use them the same way as the Pack. They lack the wolf taint. They seem to hunt by sight alone."

"Oh, that's comforting," Sam murmured quietly from the front seat.

"I have to go after Kittanning," he told Indigo.

"I can take care of myself," Indigo said. "I'm not alone. Agent Fisher is here; I know she's human."

"Be careful."

"You too."

He hung up, torn. Agent Fisher thought the Ontongard was a run-of-the-mill terrorist group; she had no idea how exotic a threat she and Indigo faced. "Max, I left Rennie sleeping at my moms'. Did you call there after the police found my bike on the turnpike?"

"They said you went to get gas. I had them wake Rennie up to ask him where you were heading on the turnpike. He didn't know, but he was going to see."

Which meant he had no way of contacting the Pack quickly.

They were crossing over Highland Park Bridge when he hung up on Indigo. Below them, the Allegheny River was an absence of light. Downriver, barges waited for their turn in the locks to bypass the dam. Upriver, a train crawled across its own bridge. At the end of the bridge, they had swung onto Route 28; the same road Ukiah had rocketed up to save Indigo the night Kittanning was "born."

Route 28 took them behind the Waterworks Mall. They exited now onto Fox Chapel Road. At the red light, they stopped facing the mile-long water treatment plant.

"That's it?" Sam asked.

"Yes." Max scanned the other cars in sight. "The question is, where is the cult?"

Ukiah reached out to sense Kittanning's Pack presence. He found him on the edge of his awareness. He leaned forward to point upriver. "Kittanning's that way. He's moving. Hurry."

The light changed and Max turned left onto Freeport Road and gunned it. The Hummer leapt forward. They chased Kittanning's presence a mile down into the town of Blawnox.

"Wait." Ukiah pointed toward the river. "We passed him."

Max took the first right onto Center Street, drove down over the railroad tracks, and down another four blocks before coming to a dead end overlooking the river. Ukiah leapt out as Max stopped the Hummer.

"Ukiah!" Max yelled.

Sam threw open her door and caught hold of Ukiah on his way to the river. "Kid! No! Wait!"

"Kittanning's out there!" Ukiah checked less by the strength of her hold and more by the worry that he'd hurt her, if he wrenched himself free.

A set of stairs led down to a narrow beach with picnic tables. Ukiah, though, pointed out at the blackness of the river. As Ukiah watched, a boat eclipsed a beacon light on the far shore, proving that something was moving upriver.

"On the other side of the river?" Max came around the front of the Hummer. "Or on the boat?"

"The boat." Ukiah tried to gently wriggle himself free.

"You can't chase down a speedboat, kid," Sam said. "Use your head. We have to get ahead of them, not kill ourselves playing catch-up."

Max, though, was looking downriver, where the treatment plant lay hidden by the curve of the river. "If the water treatment plant is downriver, why are they going upriver?"

"Maybe they already poisoned the water," Sam said.

"Shit," Max cursed. "If it's in the water already, we're totally screwed."

Ukiah closed his eyes and pressed through his connection with Kittanning.

At the bow of the speedboat, Kittanning stood tense in a new plastic dog carrier. He "remembered" the machine riding in the stern of the boat; it was a bad, bad thing. None of the humans seemed to realize that death rode with them, merely waiting for power and instructions to start its killing. Socket stood at the wheel of the boat, watching the dark water ahead intently. The babies slept, unaware, unharmed. Kittanning sensed Ukiah then, becoming aware of the connection "Daddy? Daddy?"

"Hush. Quiet. I'm coming. Stay quiet."

Kittanning crouched, waiting, trusting.

"No, they haven't set up yet," Ukiah said.

"Where the hell are they going then?" Sam asked.

"There are islands upriver," Max said. "They're mostly uninhabited. Isolated. They could set the machine up and it could pour poison into the water unnoticed."

"How many islands?" Sam asked. "A dozen? Two dozen?"

Ukiah called up the river maps in his perfect memory. "There's five more in Allegheny County: Sycamore, Ninemile, Twelvemile, Fourteenmile, and Jacks Islands."

The boat passed a green channel light, rounding the bend to slip out of sight.

"There are marinas all along this shore," Max said. "Let's get a boat."

They scrambled back into the Hummer. Rather than trying to work their way through the narrow one-way streets, Max merely drove the Hummer down the railroad tracks until he hit a street running alongside the river.

The first marina they found was the Bell Harbor Yacht Club, with a hundred and thirty boat slips and a place to buy fuel. Luck held, and there was a light on in the small marina office, although the door was locked. A sign on the door stated the office manager was a Bobby Bradley, and that the office had closed at the sane hour of six p.m.

Ukiah pounded on the door, and got a man, presumably Bradley, to open the door.

"We're closed. I'm just trying to get the quarterly taxes done."

"We need a boat," Ukiah said. "Do you rent them?"

"Oh, no, we don't rent boats here," Bradley said. "You'd have to . . . gee, I don't know where you would go to rent a boat at this time of night."

"We'll buy a boat then." Max came up behind Ukiah, carrying his briefcase.

Bradley laughed. "All I have here is the *Endeavor,* a forty-foot cruiser for a hundred and fifty thousand."

"Okay. We'll take it. Does it have gas in its tank?"

"No, no, no." Bradley waved Max's questions aside. "I don't take personal checks for that amount—especially at this time of night. I'll need a certified check."

"How about cash?" Max held up his briefcase and lifted the lid. The ransom money still filled the briefcase.

Bradley's eyes widened at the bundles of twenties. "That will work," he said weakly. "Do you have any experience in river boating?"

"I do," Sam said. "My dad and I lived on a boat for a year in Portland."

"Let me get the keys."

There would be more haggling over the boat later, paper-work for the state with registration, licenses, and whatnot.

Bradley tested a random selection of the twenty dollar bills just to verify they were real, and then handed over the keys. He trailed behind them, listing out what they would have to do after their "test run." They each took two bags of gear from the Hummer, loaded down Bradley with two more, and carried them out onto the wooden deck of the marina.

Ukiah had expected one of the low, sleek speedboats that were common with water-skiers. The *Endeavor* was built on the same sleek lines, but expanded to contain an extremely compact house. Bradley scrambled ahead to turn on lights in the cabin to show off a kitchen, dinette, leather sofa, bathroom complete with shower, and two bedrooms.

"It sleeps four," Bradley called from inside the cabin, "but you fold this down, then you can squeeze in six."

Sam laughed at the boat's size, murmuring, "Bennett, I love your style." And then clambered up to the rooftop steering. "What's the draft on this baby?"

"I think its forty-four, or forty-six, something like that." Bradley came out of the cabin, leaving all the lights on. "I'd stay in at least ten feet of water, though you could probably squeak through as shallow as four and a half, but you'll be risking damaging your propellers. The shoreline has rocks and whatnot from old bridges and landings."

Max dropped his bags of gear on the seats of the dinette and started to dig through bags. "Get the lights, kid."

Ukiah found the various light switches and returned the boat back to darkness except the one over Max.

Up on the bridge, Sam asked, "What kind of engines?" as she switched them on.

"Twin inboards," Bradley said over the twin purr. "I don't know the exact specs. They're listed. And you've got nearly three hundred gallons of fuel; it's part of the purchase price."

Ukiah caught Bradley before he could climb up beside Sam. "Thanks. We've got to go. Help me cast off."

Minutes later, they left the bemused Bradley on the dock as Sam expertly backed out of the boat slip and into the river's current. Clouds thick with the promise of rain blanketed the night sky, cutting off the moonlight and star shine. With nearly a month of drought, the wind brought the smell of dust and dead leaves as it whipped down off the hills. The river flowed an ink black streaked with the elongated shimmer of shore lights.

Once clear of the docks, Ukiah scrambled up beside Sam. "They're still downriver. The river widens here as it goes around the bend. There are two islands: Sycamore and Nine-mile."

"Are the channels marked?" Sam asked nervously.

"Yes; there's still heavy barge traffic up here, so everything is well marked."

Max finished sorting through the gear, and came up to the bridge to hand Sam a pair of night-vision binoculars and laid a loaded shotgun along the windshield. "Kill the running lights."

They slipped down the river, running silent and dark. Sam guided the boat around the bend, navigating via the colored channel markers. The two low, heavily treed islands bracketed the channel, acting as a dark screen on the shore lights. Moving without lights, it was like gliding into a cave.

"Where did they go?" Sam whispered. She scanned the river in front of them with the night-vision binoculars. "Do you see anything?"

"No." Ukiah pointed in Kittanning's direction. "But they've just entered the cove between Sycamore Island and the Blawnox shoreline."

Max pointed out dots of light bobbing on the island like fireflies. "Someone's already on the island."

"Parity said they had more than one boat." Ukiah's eyes were adjusting to the darkness, his vision switching to the sharp grays he associated with night. "I'm going across; if they've got the machine set up already, it needs to be shut down quickly."

"I'm coming with you," Max said.

Ukiah looked at him sharply. "What? No! I'm the nearly indestructible one."

"If you haven't noticed, you're the one getting the shit beat out of you all the time," Max said. "You're not being careful enough, kid. I'm going in as your backup."

"I don't suppose I can come too?" Sam asked.

"No," Max and Ukiah snapped in unison.

"I thought so."

"Get us in close," Max said, "and then be ready to get us off fast."

"Okay," Sam said. She eased the boat around as Max and Ukiah geared up in vests, radio headsets, and guns. Then she pulled in as close as she dared without running the *Endeavor* aground.

"We're going to run on radio silence." Max duct-taped the laptop over the top of twin drink holders next to the steering wheel. "Unless something happens. If you hear us yelling"— Max tapped his headset—"come get us." He showed her the tracer marks on the tracking system. "This is Ukiah. This is me."

"I'll be waiting. Be careful."

The water was bitter cold with the early fall. It pulled like thousands of little hands on their legs as they waded through the hip-deep water, holding their guns above their chests. The riverbed was rocky and uneven as they worked their way to the low grassy bank. The wind thrashed the tops of the trees, and far downriver, a flicker of lightning heralded the oncoming storm.

They made their way through tall, parched grass, dying of drought at the center of a river. Ukiah pushed forward, into point position, and scanned carefully for traps. Crude spear traps were cunningly hidden in the grass except for the smell of sharpened wood and fresh-turned earth. He made sure Max saw them and moved on.

The island was over a quarter mile long, but only a few hundred feet wide. The Temple moved with stealth from two speedboats moored in the cove to the island's highest point. The weave of their flashlights, while minimal, was comforting; they weren't using night goggles. Kittanning was still in the crate on the bow of the nearest speedboat. The two babies and Du-ae, however, had already been moved ashore.

There had been houses on the island at some time in the past. Considering how low the island lay on the river, it seemed likely that a flood leveled the buildings. Footings and cement steps traced the outlines of the vanished houses. The cultist had Du-ae set up in one of these level areas beside the great rectangular pit of an ancient Olympic-sized swimming pool. Carefully shielded camp lights dimly lit the area so no one would trip over Du-ae or fall into the nearly empty pool.

The cultists had Du-ae covered with white silk. Two infant carriers sat at the foot of the Ae, the babies slept unbuckled. Seeing them there, and knowing that Core planned to sacrifice them, made Ukiah's blood run cold.

Ukiah counted ten cultists in all; Core, Hash, Socket, Io, and Dongle being the only ones he could name. Three men and two women made up the balance. He caught Max's eyes, and signaled his count. Max winced and indicated that he had only spotted eight. Ukiah pointed out two cultists standing guard, tucked between trees and standing still. Max nodded after a moment; he saw them now.

Hash and Io carried a generator up from the second speed-boat and set it down beside Du-ae. Evidence of earlier trips, a hundred-gallon fuel tank was already in place, reeking of gasoline; apparently only half full, the cultists had ten five-gallon cans that they were carefully filling the large tank with. As Hash connected the fuel to the generator, Core and Io un-coiled power cables to link the generator to Du-ae.

Lightning flickered on the distant horizon, and the cultists moved faster.

"It's going to storm," one of the women filling the fuel tank said.

"Do that later. Get the shelter out now," Core commanded without looking up. "Socket, light the sacrament candles."

Socket searched her pockets, quickly at first, and then more carefully. "I've lost the matches."

With a great sigh, Core paused to take his lighter from his pocket and fling it at her, striking her midchest. "There. Light them."

She flinched, catching the lighter before it hit the ground. It flashed gold in her hand as she turned it over and over, star-ing at it. "Where did you get this?"

"Who knows? Who cares?"

"This is Grant's." She held it out so Core saw it clearly. It was Hutchinson's diamond-studded gold lighter. Ukiah realized suddenly that the item was much too expensive for Hutchinson to buy. The lighter must have been a gift to Hutchinson—a present from wealthy Christa. "Where did you get it? What did you do to Grant?"

Core finally saw the crisis coming and stood up. "I told you to discourage him from trying to see you. The government ranks are full of Fallen; we can't let them know our true cause or the demons will use the gullible to close us down."

"What have you done to Grant?" she whispered.

"I tested him and left him at the mansion," Core said.

"Just say he's a little shorthanded at the moment," Io quipped.

Core turned and kicked Io hard. "Shut up!"

Socket went pale, clutching the lighter. "You only needed a little blood."

"He put everything into jeopardy," Core snapped. "And Hash had to drag me out of bed to deal with him."

"God forbid someone mess up your fucking some pretty boy," Socket spat. "So you just left Grant there? Left him to die?"

"I had Parity take him to the hospital and drop him off," Core lied.

"I don't believe you." Socket pointed to the babies. "You said that we were giving the babies back. Why do you have them here?"

"I said God willing, and God is not willing, so we're not taking them back."

"What do you mean?"

"Don't question God, Socket."

"I'm not questioning God, I'm questioning you! How can I trust you when you don't tell me the truth?"

"I am telling you the truth. This is God's work we do tonight."

"I mean about Isaiah and Kimmie." She named the two dead babies with a catch in her voice. "You could have told me that Adam killed them."

"I needed you focused on your work. Go get the puppy, bring it here, and then go back to the van."

Socket looked to the babies. "What are you going to do

with them, Core? You said we only needed the nephilim, and it's not even here."

"The puppy is the nephilim."

"Where's the Wolf Boy's son?"

"His 'son' is the puppy." Core used fingers to quote the word son, reminding Socket that the Temple didn't believe Kittanning was Ukiah's true son. "He transformed within minutes of being in the Persuader."

"You used that on him! Why? We knew he was the one because Adam cut off his finger and it grew back."

"Adam could have lied."

"You could have done a blood test like we did . . . " She fell silent, staring at him in horror. "You used that machine on the babies. My God, where is your soul? How could you?"

"We had to be sure! This will only work if we have the nephilim. The end justifies the means."

"They were babies."

"They died to protect the world," Core snapped. "Light the damn candles. Bring the puppy up from the boat, and then get your ass back to the van."

"You don't want me here because you're going to kill them all."

Core stormed to her and clouted her hard in the face, knocking her down. Reaching down, he tore the lighter from her hand, kicked her in the stomach, and stalked to the candles to light them himself.

Socket staggered to her feet, hand pressed to her bruised cheek, swaying. "I used to look at battered women and think 'never me.' I would tell them again and again, 'Look at what you're doing to your children.' And the good mothers would realize things had gone too far and"—her eyes went to the babies in the carriers, waiting for the ritual to be sacrificed, and her lips moved—*"take the kids and run."*

And she started to move, bullet-straight for the infants.

Core realized what she intended and turned, pulling out a twenty-two pistol. Both Ukiah and Max came out of the dark, shouting to draw Core's fire away from Socket. Only Max was closer. Core swung toward Max and fired. The bullet struck Max in the chest. Core shot again, and blood blossomed bright on Max's leg.

"Max!" Ukiah shouted and flung himself, snarling, at Core. The maddening scent of Max's blood filled his senses. He wanted to kill this murderer of babies, this child stealer, this madman. Hash tried to block him, and he went through the big man, smashing him aside, barely noticed. A gunshot close at hand as he caught hold of Core's throat, the bullet clipping the tree behind Core seconds before Ukiah slammed Core's head into the bark. There were more gunshots, people screaming, babies wailing, all from a distance as he locked his focus down on killing Core.

Max's whistle cut through Ukiah's awareness. "Move!"

He acted on blind trust, flinging Core away and ducking around the tree. Hash swung a machete down where he had been standing. The cultists who had held their fire in fear of hitting Core now raised their weapons. Ukiah dashed into the darkness, pulling out his gun. Knowledge that Max was still alive robbed him of the want to kill. While shooting over the cultists' heads might make them flinch, they were badly outnumbered and the rescue plan was shot to hell. He ran, crouched low. Whatever he did, he had to do it quick, before the cult turned their guns on Max, and he had to be sure that whatever happened, the cult couldn't use Du-ae.

Luckily, the Ae weren't indestructible.

Ukiah turned, aimed at the large tank beside Du-ae, and fired as fast as the semiautomatic would let him. The first two bullets merely punched their way through the sidewall, creating spouts of gas pouring out of the tank. The third though sparked the gas fumes inside the half-empty tank and they exploded in a deep cough of ignition and roar of flame. The dark suddenly became brilliant as a column of fire leapt skyward, blasting through the tree branches thick with dead leaves. It spread through the dry foliage, crackling and popping, growing until it became a sustained roar, like an oncoming train. Like giant torches, the burning trees lit the night a hellish red, a sudden assault on his light-sensitive eyes. He squinted against the sudden brilliance and emptied his gun into Du-ae itself.

What saved him was that the cultists fell into full panic. Some rushed toward Du-ae, trying to pluck it out of the heart of flame. Some searched in vain for buckets and pails. Some ran for safety. The empty five-gallon cans began to explode like little cannons.

Ukiah ran back around, searching now for Max. He found his partner tucked behind a fallen tree, shielded from the confusion, but not for long.

"Max!"

"Ukiah." Max lowered his pistol. "Do you have the kids?"

Ukiah looked to the altar and saw that it was empty. "They're gone." He searched back through his memory to see them move. "Socket took them. Core went after her."

"Ah, shit," Max groaned.

Ukiah pulled Max up into a firefighter's carry. "Sam?" He called into his headset's mike as he ran toward the far shore. Behind him, tree after tree was engulfed in flame. "Sam? We're going to need to be picked up."

"I'm coming!"

When he reached the shore, the river shimmered with reflected orange and reds. Here the island had been dredged so the river's bank dropped off straight to deep water. The *Endeavor* came heaving out of the darkness, turning at the last moment to bring the low stern sliding close to the bank. Sam fought the river current to hold the big boat steady, the water broiling into red pearls.

"What the hell did you two do?"

"Max is hurt!" Ukiah leapt the narrow space, landing lightly in the stern.

"Hurt? How hurt?" Sam cried. "How bad is he?"

"I'm fine!" Max snapped. "Get us out of here, Sam." As Sam pulled away from the shore, putting distance between them and the armed cultists still on the island, Max indicated that Ukiah was to put him down on one of the low benches built into the stern of the *Endeavor*. "I'm fine. Just get me the first-aid kit."

"Are you sure?" Ukiah lowered Max to the bench.

"Yes! We've got to get Kittanning back, or they'll just do this again, someplace else with the other Ae."

Assuming Du-ae was damaged beyond human repair, yes, there was Loo-ae yet. The air death. The most dangerous of the Ae.

Ukiah reached out for Kittanning and felt him speeding away, still on the bow of Socket's speedboat. "Sam, they're heading upriver fast."

"Okay." Sam wheeled the big boat in a tight circle. "How clear is the run? Is there anything I should know about?"

"The Oakmont Highway Bridge, Twelvemile Island, Fourteenmile, and another dam just after Fourteenmile!"

"Another dam? Where's the fucking first one?" Sam slammed the throttle to full open and the boat leapt up, throwing curtains of water out on either side that glittered in the firelight.

"Downriver, just above Sixmile."

He ducked into the cabin, leaving her to curse about high-speed powerboats in very small swimming pools.

Behind them, Sycamore Island burned, reflected in the black waters of the Allegheny River.

Ukiah found the first-aid kit and hurried back to Max. The rifle bullet had punched a neat hole through Max's thigh. The sight of it set him growling again.

"It's okay. It's okay," Max murmured, eyes closed, slumped in the chair.

"I should have killed him," Ukiah snapped, bandaging the wound.

"No. You shouldn't have." Max gripped his shoulder, gave it a weak shake. "You're better than him."

"He hit you twice."

Max nodded weakly, and gingerly touched a hole in his windbreaker. "Hit my vest."

Over their headsets, Sam said, "Ukiah, I can see them!"

"Go on. Kick butt." Max pushed him toward the ladder.

They were rounding the bend at Oakmont. Ahead, the Oakmont Highway Bridge spanned the river in an intricate weave of steel supported by five massive columns of stone, creating four water channels underneath. Warning lights blinked under the bridge decking, pinpointing the supports and marking the second channel from the right to be the sailing line.

Socket and Core were in high-performance speedboats, sleek and fast as bullets, visible as the shore lights turned their spray into waves of glittering pearls, their waves a slowly vanishing gleam. Socket, with Kittanning's presence in her boat, led. From Core's boat, flashes of muzzle flare spat out from the prow. Core had a gunman with him, by the size of the man's dark shape, Hash. The *Endeavor* was still several hundred feet behind the others.

"Can you catch them?"

Sam laughed. "There's a reason they call those speedboats and this a cruiser. The only way we'll catch them is by them running out of gas or river."

"There is the dam in less than three miles."

"There is that. How is Max, really?"

"He should be in a hospital," he told her truthfully as he reloaded his pistol. "But he's right. Kittanning is the key. We have to get him back."

"At this speed, we're going to be out of river fast." Sam nodded toward the weaving speedboats. "Socket is a much better pilot than Core. He probably doesn't have her experience in boats."

"So she can outrun him?"

"There's only so much outrunning you can do in a seven-mile stretch."

Socket suddenly veered hard to the left, and kept turning, aimed at the black stone column of the Oakmont Bridge.

"Shit, I think he hit her!" Sam cried.

"Come on! Pull out of it!" Ukiah shouted helplessly to Socket.

At the last minute, she did, flicking to the right to narrowly miss the column, and then cranked hard to the left again. Kittanning's dog crate fit snugly into the bow's wedge-shaped seating area of Socket's boat; the two babies, only resting in their infant carriers, went sliding across the wide stern of the speedboat and nearly upset.

Core started to follow in a wide arch, and suddenly he too veered hard to the left.

"Watch, watch, watch," Ukiah cried. "Twelvemile is right on the other side of the bridge! They're both coming back downriver!"

Sam swore and wretched at her wheel hard to the left, and dropped one of her motors to neutral, and a moment later into reverse. The *Endeavor* spun tight until they were pointing downriver.

Socket threaded through the bridge supports again, heading toward them. Core came flashing out from under the bridge moments later, Hash braced in his bow seating area.

"Hold on!" Sam slammed the throttle to full and leaned on the horn. Blaring out a warning, the *Endeavor* leapt in front of Core's oncoming speedboat.

Core frantically worked the steering wheel of the smaller boat, aiming for the *Endeavor*'s stern. Ukiah leaned over the side of *Endeavor*'s tall bridge and fired down at the bottom of the speedboat as it flashed by.

Sam heeled the *Endeavor* hard to the left. "Come on, baby, come on. I know that you're not built for this, but work with me."

Core floundered through the deep trough of chaotic water left by the big boat as Sam continued to turn, trying to bring around the *Endeavor*'s bow to ram the speedboat. She wasn't going to make it, the cruiser was moving too slowly to catch the more agile boat, and Core would quickly overtake the wounded Socket. Ukiah darted out of the *Endeavor*'s bridge, ran the length of the bow, and leapt to Core's boat just as it cleared their wake.

"Ukiah!" Sam shouted after him, but to her credit, kept the big boat locked on to the speedboat's midcenter.

Out of the turbulent water, the speedboat roared forward, surging out of the *Endeavor*'s path.

Hash emptied his gun at Ukiah as he leapt between the boats, the bullets cutting through the air around him, all missing. Ukiah stumbled as he landed, the speedboat rocking out from under him, and before he could recover, Hash was on him. The big man bowled the off-balanced Ukiah over, slamming him to the floor of the speedboat, and struck Ukiah in the temple with the butt of his empty pistol in an explosion of pain and momentary darkness. Ukiah caught Hash's arm before the cultist could hit him again, and they grappled for control of the pistol. They tumbled through the narrow cut in the instrument panel into the bow before Ukiah got the leverage he needed to suddenly heave the unsuspecting Hash over the side.

Ukiah rolled to his feet and turned to Core, who had a gun leveled at him while trying to keep the boat steady. They had traveled back down the dark river to the bend at Blawnox.

"Now, you disgusting sack of shit," Ukiah snarled, "where are Ice and the other two founts?"

"Don't move or I'll shoot!"

Ukiah checked for a moment and then realized there was no reason to play the meek boy anymore. He'd cleared the playing field of all innocents: Kittanning and the babies were safe with Socket, wounded Max was with Sam, and soon the river would be flooded with police.

Now, though, there was only him and Core—and Ukiah was nearly indestructible.

"You can barely see me," Ukiah growled, crouching in the darkness. "But I can see you clearly. You're an arrogant, power-hungry, lying perverted hypocrite. And you're going to tell me where the fuck the rendezvous is even if I have to beat the information out of you—and frankly I'm hoping that I have to."

"I can see you!" Core cried, but the gun wavered.

Ukiah laughed. "Can you? Do you have any clue what I am? Here's a hint—you bastard—I'm not human."

"You're not a demon." Core steered between the two islands; Sycamore still burned brightly. There were police cars on the cove's shore. "The Blissfire wouldn't have worked on you if you were a demon."

Ukiah decided it was useless to insist on the truth; aliens or demons, what was the real difference to an insane man? He'd face Core in his reality. "How do you get a nephilim without an angel, you stupid idiot? Have you so little faith that you can't believe Good walks the world as well as Evil? You've got it all screwed up. The founts don't kill demons; they only kill humans. You know that—you said it yourself!"

"What do you mean?"

"Blissfire doesn't affect demons. None of the founts affect demons."

"But Blissfire is a gift from God."

"It wasn't a gift—you stole it, and got what you deserved. Death. You've signed your own death warrant, and all those you've used Blissfire on, except me; that's one little trick of its that I'm immune to. Now, where is Ice with the other two founts?"

"You're lying!" Core started the boat into the nearly straight run to Highland Park Bridge. Ukiah could sense Kittanning ahead of them as Socket continued fleeing Core's speedboat, apparently unaware that Ukiah had intervened. "You're a demon! You're trying to stop me from doing God's holy work!"

"God's work?" Ukiah leapt, snarling at him. Core fired once, the bullet creasing Ukiah's side, before Ukiah batted the gun out over the river and caught hold of Core. A quick hard twist, and he had Core trapped, head craned back to lay bare Core's neck, and teeth inches from the flesh. Ukiah caught himself then, growling low. "God's work! Killing babies?"

"It was an accident! We didn't know that the Persuader was so deadly."

"Like hell!" Ukiah tightened his hold, feeling satisfaction from the whimper of pain from Core. "The machine was only to inflict pain, not kill! It would have been useless to Hex if it killed! You'd have to torture the babies for hours until the very stress killed them, not the machine. That's what you did, wasn't it? You had to have known that they couldn't have survived that much pain! You're a fucking EMT. Why did you do it when you had to have known it would kill—?" The truth hit Ukiah and he barely controlled the impulse to bite down hard and tear out Core's throat. He growled in anger, until he finally managed to force the words through clenched teeth. "You wanted them to die so you could look into their eyes and see God."

"I baptized them first," Core protested, as if this made things right.

"How much death do you need? Are not all the deaths of
the demons enough for you?"

"I'm beginning to think that demons are all part of one
great Evil, all its darkness spread out over many bodies. We
cut them up, and they only get smaller and smaller. We'll
never utterly kill Evil, so we'll never see God."

Was that the whole reason behind Core's war with the Ontongard, that the Gets were guiltless subjects to kill in his
quest to see the face of God?

"You're wrong," Ukiah growled. "You're wrong like
you're wrong about everything else."

"No I am not. You have to hold the baby's eyes open and
look carefully as they breathe out that last sweet breath, but
both times I saw Him—God's face—as He welcomed them
to heaven."

Ukiah flung Core away with revulsion; Core had killed the
second baby after "succeeding" with the first. He backed
away from the monster in human form, growling.

From Kittanning came a sudden flare of panic. Later they
would tell Ukiah that the tugboat was pushing four barges up
the night river, two barges abreast and two deep, loaded deep
with coal. Now it was just black, upon black, upon black.
Socket's speedboat was a crazed blur of running lights as it
tumbled away from the tugboat, spilling out Socket, dog
crate, and babies. Sam's horn blared. The tugboat's deep
voice joined, and under the chorus, Ukiah heard the deep
powerful throbbing of a tugboat engine and the shushing of
massive amounts of water being shoved aside.

And then Core's speedboat hit the front barge.

For a moment Ukiah was airborne, and then he hit cold wet
darkness. Instantly, he was yanked under the tugboat's powerful undertow. He sensed something thrashing in the water
near him. Instinctively, he reached out and caught one of the
babies, and together they were tumbled head over heels in the
tugboat's massive wake. Moments later he fought his way to
the surface, baby held tight against him.

"Sam!" he shouted, treading water as the current carried
him downriver. "Sam!"

The *Endeavor* surged out of the darkness and came up beside him. He caught hold of the swimmer's platform and scrambled up far enough into the boat to shove the baby toward Max. "Here! Take him! Sam, do you see anyone else?"

"There's Kittanning!" She pointed out the dog crate quickly sinking. "Hold on, I'll get you there quick."

Ukiah tucked his feet onto the swimmer's platform and Sam whipped the boat over to the cage as it vanished. Ukiah dove after it, following Kittanning's scent through the cold water until his fingers laced through the wire gate. It was like hauling a rock to the surface. When he reached the surface, he hefted the crate over his head, letting the water drain out. Kittanning licked at his fingers, whimpering. The puppy, though, growled at Max when Ukiah handed it up to his partner.

"Hey, big boy, it's Max! Don't you remember me?" Max crooned and risked his fingers through the wire.

"You might want to keep him in there." Ukiah clung to the side of the boat, panting, and scanned the water for Socket and the other baby.

"Ukiah!" Sam shouted from the bridge. "This thing has fishing radar!"

"So?"

"It's picking up a damn big fish, over there." She pointed out a featureless section of river. "About ten feet down and sinking."

Ukiah dove back into the water. The big engines of the tugboat still throbbed near at hand, pulsing through the river water, masking all other input. Ukiah bumped something, caught it, and knew he had hold of the child. By the time he brought it to the surface, he knew it was alive.

"Sam!"

Immediately, Sam had the boat beside him. As he climbed up to hand over the baby, Ukiah noticed that they were drifting toward the dam, slowly, inevitably. They were already past the warning signs anchored in the river and nearly to the Highland Park Bridge, which was deep in the restricted area deemed too dangerous to trouble.

He saw Socket then, floating like the dead in the water as the current took her downriver. "Sam, over there!"

Sam deftly maneuvered the big boat up beside Socket and

Ukiah pulled her out of the river. She had been shot in the back, high on her shoulder, and was unconscious from a blow to the head, but alive. Ukiah wrapped her in a blanket as Sam steered the boat away from the dam. Kittanning was still locked in the cage, whimpering for Ukiah.

"I have my hands full with the other two," Max explained guiltily. "But we need Kittanning as a baby, now. Before the police show up. We're not going to be able to produce him out of thin air later, without explanation."

"I'll work on it." Ukiah carried the cage into the cabin, shut the cabin door, and let Kittanning out of the cage. Kittanning tumbled into his arms, a squirming bundle of wet fur. "Come on, Kitt! You've got to go back to being human."

Kittanning resisted wordlessly, a flood of memories of being helpless, immobile, tied down even by the most loving of hands, dependent on those who didn't have time for him, left him behind for days and days. With spite disproportional to his body, Kittanning projected the weeks of utter loneliness, forever to an infant, while Ukiah was gone.

"I'm sorry. I'm sorry," Ukiah crooned. "But remember, we were together. We were happy." And he pulled from his own memory standing in Kittanning's bedroom while the aurora borealis danced in the window. "You can go back to this and only remember what you want to remember."

Kittanning countered with the knowledge that they were together now, on his terms.

Ukiah brought up the memory of his mothers' kitchen, all together as a family. But there was contention there. Mom Lara distracted by the return to work and a resentful Cally. Kittanning had picked up on the subtle tensions. Ukiah scrambled forward. "And there's Max."

Kittanning had inherited Ukiah's love of Max, and then built on it as Max showered his new godson with affection. Max, though, had gone away and left him, just like Ukiah had.

"Please, Kittanning," Ukiah whispered, searching forward and found the moment of pure contentment. "Give us a chance for this."

In that moment, Kittanning lay in Indigo's arms while

Ukiah held them both close. It had felt so right, a family, father, mother, and son.

Mommy! Kittanning wailed, the chord striking deep resonance, deep to a once shared pining for the mother lost and unknown, for Kicking Deer. Ukiah now had memories of a true mother, but Kittanning didn't. Indigo was the mother of his heart, despite all of Mom Lara's care, and it cried now for her. *Mommy!*

Go back to being a baby, and we'll be a family.

Mommy! And the canine whine slowly turned into a human baby cry.

CHAPTER EIGHTEEN

Mercy Hospital, Pittsburgh, Pennsylvania
Saturday, September 18, 2004

Mercy Hospital was built overlooking downtown Pittsburgh in 1847 by seven Sisters of Mercy nuns from Scotland. Ironically, Rennie had been six at the time, and still a human, and Magic Boy, living Ukiah's first childhood, was well into his fifties but stuck at the age of twelve. A hundred and fifty-three years later, Rennie looked like he was nearing his thirties, and Ukiah could finally call himself a man. The ancient nun sitting at the information desk, however, looked like she had been there since the hospital was built.

"I'm looking for Max Bennett." Ukiah spelled out "Bennett" for her. "He was admitted to emergency last night with a gunshot wound."

She eyed Rennie in his biking leathers carrying sleeping Kittanning in his car seat carrier. "I'm sorry, but . . ." She pointed a trembling, arthritic finger at Rennie. Ukiah flinched, knowing that they looked wrong together; he seemed too young to be a father, and Rennie too rough to own the well-cared-for child. Kittanning, though, had been refusing to let Ukiah out of his senses since last night, and Ukiah had complied, not wanting to give his son any reason to go back to being a puppy. Ukiah steeled himself for a series of difficult questions, perhaps even a demand to see some proof that Kittanning was his.

She finished, though, with, "Children under fourteen aren't allowed beyond the lobby. He'll have to stay here."

Ukiah blinked, and behind him Rennie snorted at his surprise.

"He's still sleeping. Go on up. I'll let you know when he wakes."

"That's okay, my dad will stay with my son."

She shook her head, and turned to the computer terminal murmuring, "God have patience with children of today." She tapped at the keyboard with infinite slowness, and it was a full two minutes later that she found Max's room number and told it to him.

Ukiah thanked her, nodded to Rennie, and went in search of Max.

The river rescue teams had chosen Max and Socket, as the most seriously wounded, to be flown via the Lifeflight helicopter to Mercy Hospital. Max groused about it since it meant that neither Ukiah nor Sam could come with him, nor follow directly behind in the Hummer. Between the lack of ambulances to go around, and Sam's prodding, Max had finally given in.

Ukiah had missed the full discussion and Max's departure because he'd been busy keeping custody of Kittanning. They had packed a complete supply of baby stuff in with the guns and rescue gear. While the other babies had been dried, diapered, and wrapped in blankets, they were still so traumatized that they were whisked off to Children's Hospital. Luckily, after guzzling down two cans of formula, Kittanning was extremely healthy-looking by the time the paramedics arrived. He proved that his lungs were none the worse for his dunking when the EMT tried to examine him, and quieted instantly for Indigo as she entered the fray.

In the end, they released Kittanning on Ukiah's promise to take his son to Mercy Hospital for a thorough examination. By then, Sam had returned the *Endeavor* to its regular boat slip and made arrangements for the final paperwork to be delivered to the offices, making sure that they had a receipt of the hundred and fifty thousand paid out in cash. Indigo sent them on their way before someone of higher authority could arrive to outvote her.

Max's room was on the fourth floor, with a view of the Monongahela River valley, the top of Mount Washington, and the hills rolling away for miles. Max had the bed levered up to a sitting position and was gazing out the window. An IV dripped fluid down a clear line into his arm.

Ukiah tapped on the door and walked in. "Hi."

"Hey, kid." Max lifted his hand in greeting, and Ukiah clasped it tight.

"You look horrible."

"Oh, thanks."

"What did they say about your leg?"

"The bullet didn't hit an artery, which we knew, or the femur. They called me damn stupid for getting shot and rolling around in the mud so much afterward. Considering how much pain I was in at the time, they're lucky you kept my Desert Eagle."

"And?"

"I'll be here a couple of days, and then they'll let me out with a cane, and orders to stay off my feet for six weeks."

"It should have been me that got shot."

Max made a raspberry at that. "Oh, you would have hurt for a shorter period of time, but you wouldn't have hurt less than me. Oh, stop with the puppy eyes, you're too old for that."

"How are Kittanning and the other two kids?"

"Children's Hospital released the others this morning. Jonah's mother is out on probation and has regained custody of him, and Shiralle's foster parents have decided to adopt her."

"Ah, good."

"Kittanning's downstairs with Rennie." Ukiah explained why, adding, "The hospital wouldn't let me bring him up, so I'll have to go when he wakes up. We had brunch with Indigo's family and they all fussed over him. We're doing dinner with Mom Jo's family at the farm tonight."

"Cally isn't going to take that well."

"Actually, she seems to have gotten over the worst of her

jealousy, although I suspect that she would have preferred the puppy."

Max laughed. "I'm sure she would have. He made a cute puppy, but I'm glad he's back to being a baby."

"I brought some stuff." Ukiah unloaded the computer bag onto the bedside table. "*Playboy,* for the articles, the new U.S. Cavalry catalog, the *Wall Street Journal,* and your laptop."

"Great. Thanks. All my vices." He waved a hand toward the window. "Isn't it a great view they've given me?"

"Very nice," Ukiah agreed.

They lapsed into awkward silence.

"Sam didn't come with you?" Max asked.

"She wanted to drive in on her own. She didn't want to depend on me."

"What's wrong?"

"Nothing."

"Come on, don't give that to me. We've been partners too long. Is it Sam? Is it not going to work out? I thought we worked well together as a team, the three of us."

"No, no, it's not Sam. Hell, it can wait. This isn't the time to talk about it."

"Kid!"

"I don't know where to start, and frankly I'm scared to even open my mouth, and maybe screw everything up."

"What about?"

"Us being partners."

Confusion warred with concern on Max's face.

"Nothing's wrong with you; it's all just me. I'm not who I was a few months ago. I'm not even who I was before we went to Oregon. I've changed a lot."

"Yes, and no. At the core, you're still the kid I took on six years ago."

"You really feel that way?"

"Yeah."

"I guess there was part of me that was afraid you wouldn't like the new me."

"Kid, you grew up. It was going to happen sooner or later, and it happens to everyone. Sure, you did it differently than most, but I expected it to happen. Hell, I would have been disappointed if it didn't happen."

"Considering my history with Magic Boy and all, you kind of lucked out, then."

Max gave a surprised laugh. "I hadn't thought of that. Is that it?"

"No," he chided himself for being scared. This was Max after all. "Things need to change because I changed. I'm not happy with the way things are in my life, and I'm trying to figure out how to get to where I want to be, and things can't work."

Max had nodded as he talked, and when he stopped, he raised an eyebrow. "I'm not following you."

"I need to move out of my moms'."

Max startled visibly. "You asked Indigo to marry you?"

"No, no, things are still . . . status quo with us. She loves me and Kittanning, but she's not sure if love is enough. Everything has been too frantic to take it beyond that. Moving out isn't about Indigo. It's just about me.

"I need a car. Not a new motorcycle, though I hate to give it up entirely, but with Kittanning I need a car. I need a place of my own, not a bedroom in someone else's home. I'm not fitting into the little boy's space anymore."

"Yeah. One gets that way."

"But that's where it gets tricky. I'm going to need help figuring out how to pay for everything, but I want a house somewhere close to my moms' and at least a part-time nanny for when Mom Lara is working and a car."

Max shrugged. "Between what you pull down as a salary and your savings, that's all doable. You don't have any expensive habits. We could even work in a bike, since insurance is probably going to total your old one. The car will probably be used, and the house a starter. If you're talking houses, kid, maybe you should just rent until you and Indigo come to some decision. Together, you'll get a different house than what you would get separately."

There remained one big hurdle, and he wasn't sure how Max would take it. Everything so far didn't affect Max personally, so it was easy for him to nod and agree.

"But the big thing is, none of this works with the offices in Shadyside."

Max didn't say anything, though his mouth pressed into a tight line.

"I'll go insane trying to juggle Kittanning if there's thirty miles between me and work, through rush-hour traffic. It's nearly an hour, one way, which is two hours out of my life, my life with Kittanning, just driving. I can't put him in a day care here in town; next to other kids, his leaps in development would stick out. God forbid he decided to change shapes again. Cally is in kindergarten, and next year will be going full time, and my moms really need Mom Lara to go back to work. I could pay her to baby-sit, but that doesn't come with health care on the level Pitt offers, not to mention self-esteem and doing what she loves."

Max's mouth relaxed as Ukiah talked, which was encouraging.

"You've said before that the mansion intimidates people; they don't want to intrude on a private residence. After all this, I'm not crazy about the fact that we mix home and work so closely, so that any trouble we stir up knows where we sleep. And if things go well with you and Sam, I would think you might want some privacy."

Max laughed. "Oh, that's low." Ukiah waited and Max eventually nodded. "You have valid points."

"The closer we move to Evans City, the better for me, but probably not for the agency. A compromise of the North Side, or the North Hills."

"Cranberry is booming lately, and they just finished up the connector last year."

"Well, I'm not sure I want to get too far north," Ukiah said. "There's Indigo's commute to consider, if things work out there."

Max laughed. "So you're okay with Sam?"

"We actually work very well together."

"Funny"—Sam leaned against the door frame—"I was just thinking the same thing."

"We were just talking about making some changes to the offices."

"Because of me?" Sam frowned slightly.

"Because of me, and Kittanning," Ukiah said. "I want to move out of my moms' house, but to do so means changes, like moving the offices out of Shadyside."

She nodded. "If I'm staying, I want a place of my own, no offense, Max, but I want to feel like I'm not being rushed, and moving in with you, even to the guest bedroom, would feel too rushed."

"Actually, I might move too," Max said.

Ukiah and Sam looked at him in surprise.

"I grew up in this city and always loved the view from Mount Washington. I wanted one of those condos with the balconies that look out over the edge and see for miles. It was one of those unrealistic goals in life that you never thought you'd hit: a million dollars in the bank, a trip around the world, and a luxury condo on Mount Washington. After I sold my company and deposited several millions into the bank, my wife and I drove up, went to the park, ate lunch at Christopher's, and then toured some houses and a couple of condos. Aileen got quieter and quieter, and finally she started to cry; she'd never told me, all those years of talking about the condo, but she was afraid of heights. She hated it. We settled on the house in Shadyside as a compromise."

It was the most Ukiah had ever heard Max talk about his wife sober; but then, perhaps, there were drugs involved now.

Sam took Max's hand, and he held it tight.

"We're going to make some real estate agent happy."

Rennie called him then, telling him that Kittanning was waking. Ukiah excused himself, saying, "I want to keep close to Kittanning until I know that he wouldn't slip back to being a puppy."

He started down the hall, but was checked five doors down by a set of familiar voices.

"I know no words of apologies could ever set things right with us," Socket was saying inside the room with an armed guard at the door. Apparently she had also been brought to Mercy for her minor gunshot wound. "I've betrayed you at a level of infidelity that can't be humanly forgiven. I've taken too much from you to ask you to even pretend that forgiveness is possible. But I want you to know that I'm deeply, profoundly sorry."

"That's good," Hutchinson slurred his words slightly, thick with the New England accent he normally kept filtered to a minimum. "It's good that you're sorry." He gave a slight laugh. "Oh, Christa, talking about this while I'm full of drugs is probably not the best of times to do this."

Ukiah stepped back so he could see into the room, despite the hard look from the guard. Hutchinson lay in the bed, clustered with monitors and IV stands. Christa was in a wheelchair beside the bed, dressed in a matching hospital gown. Two battered souls, betrayed by those they loved and trusted.

"I had to see that you were okay." Christa gazed at his good hand as if she wanted to take it, but lacked the courage to.

"Why?"

"I never really stopped loving you," she whispered. "But I suppose that I didn't love you enough. There was this void that I thought the Temple's mission could fill, the sense I was important for me, not my money. I was so stupid. It was all lies. It was always about the money and not me."

"To me, it was never the money." Hutchinson shushed Christa as she started to sob. "I know there's no forgive and forget, but we two both really could use a friend to get us through tomorrow. I have to deal with losing my hand, and you're going to jail, but it would be good to know that when the chips are down, there's someone who will be there."

"You're willing to—?" She stopped short of asking him to define what relationship he meant.

And battered, Hutchinson protected his heart, but still reached out his good hand, saying, "I'm willing to."

She clasped his hand and kissed it. "Thank you."

"Cub?" Rennie called from downstairs. *"In a minute or two, I'm going to be holding a puppy."*

Wondering if Hutchinson and Christa's new alliance was truly a good thing for Hutchinson, Ukiah took the stairs down to the lobby instead of waiting for an elevator. Certainly, the agent had suffered immensely out of his love for Christa, but was winning her back really a reward? Perhaps.

Kittanning greeted him with a squeal of happiness and settled into his arms.

"How's your partner?"

"Healing."

"Did he go for it?"

Ukiah looked at Rennie in confusion and then realized that the Pack leader must have sensed his thoughts on the way into the hospital. "Yes, Max did. We're moving the agency."

"So you're going to be looking for a house with a white picket fence?"

"Eventually." Ukiah shouldered Kittanning.

"What first?"

Ukiah waited until they were out into the parking garage, with new sounds and smells to distract Kittanning, then said, "We've only destroyed two of the four Ae. Ice has the other two, and he's gone into hiding. We need to find him, before he tries for Kittanning or, worse, realizes that he doesn't need him to make Loo-ae work."

Bitter rage flared through Rennie at the mention of the cult, quickly controlled for Kittanning's sake. Last night when the Pack caught up with Ukiah and realized he'd been with a woman, they had been aggravated at him. After they made Ukiah share his memories—a la Pack mind meld style—the annoyance became a full parental outrage aimed at the cult. Core was lucky that he was already dead.

"Are you going to tell Indigo about this Ping?"

"I already have. All the cult members knew where Core was and what he was doing last night. It wouldn't have been fair to let her find out from one of them."

"And?"

"She says that it's frightening how often she finds herself in alignment with the Pack."

Rennie laughed. "She wanted to kill the bastard?"

"Something like that."

Rennie glanced back at the hospital. "Does Hutchinson's woman know where the rendezvous is?"

"She's turning state's evidence and willing to cooperate fully, but Core didn't trust her. Indigo hopes to piece together

an address from what Socket . . . Christa might have overheard and general observation."

"The men will start dying soon without the Blissfire."

"I know."

Core had died instantly in the crash. Hash had drowned,
not from Ukiah throwing him from the boat, but in an attempt
to evade capture by river patrol. Ironically, only the female
cultists had died on the island; one had tried to pull Du-ae out
of the fire, and the other had been shot resisting arrest. That
left five men—Dongle, Io, and three others—in custody but
they would start dying within days.

And so would Parity, if the Ontongard didn't turn him into
a Get first.

The Butler Fire Department found no trace of cult members at Eden Court beyond the two men in the driveway; one
dead of a snapped neck while the other had a butter knife sunk
through his windpipe. Bear and Hellena had scoured the
smoking rubble early in the morning, slipping in under the police's noses. They verified that all the Gets in the wine cellar
had been freed before the fire.

Depending on what those cultists knew and what the Ontongard could learn, it might be a race to find Ice first, with
the fate of all mankind in the balance.

See what's coming in June...

MESSIAH NODE by Lyda Morehouse
A potent mix of technology and salvation is the trademark of Lyda Morehouse's brilliant novels. Now, Messiah Node takes her uniquely-imagined world one step closer to its fate—as AIs and archangels, prophets and criminal masterminds face the final day of reckoning...
45929-6

THE GLASSWRIGHTS' TEST by Mindy L. Klasky
Glass artisan Rani's divided loyalty are tested when she is forced to choose between King and Guild...
45931-8

MECHWARRIOR: DARK AGE #4: *A SILENCE IN THE HEAVENS (A BATTLETECH NOVEL)* by Martin Delrio
From WizKids LLC, creators of the hit game Mage Knight...Duchess Tara Campbell and MechWarrior Paladin Ezekiel Crow struggle to save the planet of Northwind from the invading faction of Steel Wolves...
45932-6

Wen Spencer

The Legend of Ukiah Oregon